LUCY'S STORY

Book two of *The Book Club* novels

Lucy's Story

ALI FISCHER

HYPERBOLE PUBLISHING

Published by Hyperbole Publishing
Cover design by SpiffingCovers
Copy edit by Dark Bear Media
Developmental edit by Laura Davies

DEDICATION

I dedicate this book to those that have a wonky crown and to those that help you straighten it.

There are five women that deserve a special mention. These women have kept me going when it got tough. Kerri, Keira, Jaquie, Laura and Taysha. This book is for you.

Obviously, I must also mention my husband. Without him, we wouldn't have been fed. Thank you for always bringing me coffee and helping with vital research.

PLAYLIST

Here is a playlist for you to listen to while you read. I have picked each song to match the mood and emotions felt. It is available on Apple Music and Spotify; search for The Book Club Series – Lucy's Story.

Halfway – Mimi Webb

Lost & Found – Lianna La Havas

Overthinking – Zoe Wees

Lonely – Zoe Wees

Brand New Me – Alicia Keys

Scars to Your Beautiful – Alessia Cara

Free yourself – Jesse Ware

Honest – Kyndal Inskeep & Song House

Playground – Bru-C

Pon De Replay – Ed Marquis & Emie

Everything I wanted – Billie Eilish

For My Hand (feat. Ed Sheeran) – Burna Boy

The Avengers – Alan Silvestri

Promises – Calvin Harris ft Sam Smith

I feel It Coming (feat. Daft Punk) – The Weeknd

Run Through Walls – The Script

Bright (feat. Aubrey Toone) – AIRGLØW

Toxic – 2WEI

Ready for War - Joznez, 2WEI & Kataem

Dusk Till Dawn (feat. Sia) [Radio Edit] – ZAYN

Pillowtalk - ZAYN

When I get my hands on you – The New Basement Tapes

All Your Exes – Julia Michaels

Lost on You – Lewis Capaldi

Love Me More – Sam Smith

Love on the Brain - Rihanna

Save a Kiss – Jessie Ware

Do It To It (feat. Cherish) - Acraze

Boys Like You - Tanerélle

Wild Love – James Bay

River – BRKN LOVE

Stay with Me (feat. Mary J. Blige) [Radio Edit] – Sam Smith

Him & I – G-Eazy & Halsey

Bad Guy – Billie Eilish

Darkside - Neoni

Wild – John Legend & Gary Clark Jr.

Ghost Town – Benson Boone

I'm Ready – Sam Smith & Demi Lovato

Way down we go - KALEO

Go (feat. Sam Smith) – Cat Burns

What have I done – Dermot Kennedy

Tears in the club (feat. The Weeknd) – FKA twigs

Vigilante Shit – Taylor Swift

Lion – Saint Mesa

I Am – James Arthur

Yours – **Ella Henderson**

Dirtier Thoughts – **Nation Haven**

And one day, she discovered that she was fierce and strong and full of fire and that not even she could hold herself back because her passion burned brighter than her fears.

- Mark Anthony

DEAR READER

A bonus chapter has been added to the back of this book. This bonus chapter is a recap of a scene in Imogen's Story—Book 1 of the series—and is significant to Lucy's Story. This chapter is read from Lucy's point of view.

If you have already read Imogen's Story, feel free to read this chapter as a recap. If you haven't read Imogen's Story, and do not intend to read it, then you would benefit from reading this. Be warned, this chapter is a major spoiler to Imogen's Story, so please don't read it if you are reading The Book Club series out of order.

CONTENT WARNING

Please be aware that this book contains:
   Explicit sexual scenes
   Violence (towards the end)
   Impact play
   Heat play
   Anxiety and recovering from trauma
   This is not an exhaustive list. This book is intended for adult audiences only.

PROLOGUE

LUCY

Halfway – Mimi Webb

The nicotine stains on her bedroom ceiling were irritating Lucy. She knew her mind shouldn't wander while Andrew was attempting to 'work his magic,' as he called it, but she couldn't stop asking herself if sugar soap would do the trick or if she'd have to buy a tin of white paint. She regained focus on current events as the telltale groans emanated from her boyfriend.

'Ah god, that was amazing, wasn't it?' Said Andrew as he rolled out of bed.

Lucy had known Andrew since their first year at university. A messy, drunken evening in fresher's week ended with him back at her student flat. Before she knew it, they were graduating and hoping for gainful employment. It wasn't clear when they morphed into official relationship status; she didn't remember being involved in that conversation. She likened her situation to when you've spoken with someone for so long that it's rude to admit you don't know their name. You can't admit that you accidentally fell into a relationship after four years.

She stared up at Andrew while he pulled his tracksuit bottoms on. He was handsome enough, tall and well-built. He was an avid football player with a degree in sports science. She wasn't sure what that meant, but it wasn't a job or place of his own. He didn't enjoy moving back in with his parents after graduating, but it appeared this wasn't adequate motivation for him to find work.

'Did you hear me? You looked miles away. Was the sex so good that it's addled your brain?' He said as he pulled on a sweatshirt. Lucy blinked and said, 'Oh, sorry, yeah, that was great. What are your plans for today?' She sat up, hugging her knees to her chest.

'I'm off out tonight with my footy team for some celebratory drinks. It's a given we're going to win the match today, especially after my lucky shag this morning,' he said with a wink.

Eyes down, she said, 'You're so romantic.'

He didn't pick up on her sarcasm as he said, 'I know. You're lucky to have me. What are you doing today?'

'I need to get decorating. I've not finished a single room in three weeks. That's not living up to my credentials as an interior designer, is it? This ceiling needs sorting,' she said, looking up.

'Well, have fun doing that. I'd offer to help, but you know I have this important match to get to. Can I come back here later? I'll get into trouble if I go home in a state.' Andrew rolled his eyes and did air quotes to emphasise the last three words. His mother treated him like a child, unable to accept that he was now a grown man, although he rarely acted like one.

'Um, I guess so. Are you going to be very late? I wanted an early night after doing all the painting myself.'

'You could give me a key, couldn't you? He trailed off, tapping his finger to his lip.

Unsure of how to navigate this conversation again, Lucy decided a distraction was her only option. 'You'd better get going, hadn't you? Text me later when you're on your way back; we can talk about keys tomorrow. Score some goals for me,' she said with a half-hearted smile.

'All right, see you later.' Lucy didn't mind the lack of a kiss goodbye. She snuggled under the duvet and sighed as the front door clicked shut. Lacking enthusiasm, she got ready for a day of paint shopping and decorating.

Hours later, Lucy rubbed at her neck as she admired her newly painted, crisp white ceiling. Her landlord had done the minimal work required after the previous tenants had moved out, which Lucy hadn't minded, being an interior designer and receiving a discount on the first year's rent. The light had faded, and her body ached. It was time for a hot bath, takeaway, and a romantic movie on Netflix while she waited for her drunken boyfriend to stagger in. She hoped he'd forgotten his request for a key; that was a conversation she wasn't ready for. Their relationship felt like one of convenience; he had somewhere to stay after a night out, and she wasn't lonely.

She'd arrived at work, and, as usual, the office manager was at her desk in reception to greet her. 'Hey Lucy, how was your weekend?' asked Sarah, beaming a smile at Lucy.

'Morning, Sarah. It was okay, thanks.' Lucy rubbed at her neck while she spoke. 'I painted the ceilings.' Lucy felt jealous of the beautiful woman before her. Sarah had the most amazing copper-coloured hair that fell to her shoulders in bouncy curls. In Lucy's opinion, she oozed self-confidence. Lucy felt inferior to most of the women she worked with. She was the youngest designer and lacked life experience.

'I suppose Andrew didn't help?' Sarah quips.

'Correct. He had an important football match and then a night of celebrating. I don't mind. I had a nice evening with Mark Darcy on the TV and a bottle of Pinot Grigio. What more can a girl ask for?'

'Mm, I need to take you under my wing, young padawan. I'm meeting my pal, Jess, for lunch, and you need to join us.' Sarah put her finger up as Lucy went to speak and said, 'No excuses, I'm staging an intervention.'

'All right, I'll join you for lunch, but I don't think an intervention will be necessary. I'd better get upstairs before James starts the team meeting,' Lucy says as she moves away from reception.

'Cool, see you at twelve o'clock on the dot,' Sarah called out to Lucy's back as she hotfooted it out of there.

Lucy stopped at the bottom of the staircase that led up to her office. She often took a moment to gather herself and soak in the glorious rays of sunshine flooding in through the glass roof. Once fully charged, she made her way up the stairs, ready to start another week at her dream job.

Lucy sat herself in the conference room just before James started the meeting. 'Good morning, everyone. It's lovely to see you all on this fine Monday morning. Some of you even look awake.' James turned to Lucy and hit her with a broad smile she couldn't help but return. James Spencer had a way of making her feel at ease. Fresh out of university, Lucy had been nervous attending her interview with the company's co-owner, especially when she saw how attractive he was. In his early thirties, James had mastered smart-casual. His signature look comprised chinos, tailored shirts, and hair that looked effortlessly styled and always finished with a polished pair of Jeffrey West shoes; Lucy was sure he must own half the store. He was fun and down to earth. He'd taken Lucy on as an assistant designer, and while he looked for someone to fill the senior designer position, he took on her mentor role. Lucy often felt like she was faking it and didn't deserve her place on the team. She didn't know how she'd landed the job, but so far James hadn't discovered she wasn't worthy, so she remained employed. She snapped out of her thoughts as James continued to address the team that sat around the glass-walled meeting room.

'Right then, folks, you all know what needs doing, so I suggest you get caffeinated and crack on.' Everyone chattered as they headed out to grab a coffee and pastry.

The kitchen was on a mezzanine area that separated the interior design team office from the architecture and building department. When she got there, she found a queue for the coffee machine. She joined the back of the line and chewed on a nail while waiting. She knew she shouldn't compare herself to others, but it was something she'd always done and couldn't stop now. Everyone seemed so glamorous, discussing their weekends, which were far more eventful than hers. James' laughter caught her attention, and then she saw who he was talking to.

'Shit.' James was standing chatting with his best friend, Cameron Black. Cameron was the other half of Spencer & Black Associates and headed up the architects, builders, and other skilled labour teams. Cameron was the definition of tall, dark, and handsome.

Lucy tried to avoid him at all costs since meeting him on her first day when she'd blurted out 'Wow!' She'd never felt so embarrassed. Cameron took it well and pretended it hadn't happened; she assumed he was used to that reaction. She decided that to survive in the job, she was to avoid him altogether. Some might think this was impossible, but she will give it her best shot.

In her opinion, everyone here was beautiful. Even when covered in brick dust, the men were ten times more attractive to Lucy than her boyfriend. She wished Andrew would grow up and take more care of himself. She was starting to realise he was no longer enough for her. She had ambition and wanted someone that would grow with her. Having only ever slept with Andrew left her feeling like she was missing out. She wondered what sleeping with a real man was like. Sarah's sexploits at the weekends convinced her there was more to it. Maybe one day, she'd pluck up the courage to ask her. Lucy gave up on getting a coffee in favour of escaping Cameron. She headed back to her desk; she could get a drink later.

'I'm going to be blunt with you, Lucy. I think you need to ditch Andrew and experience a bit more life,' said Sarah matter-of-factly over their lunch.

Jess rolled her eyes and said, 'And by "more life", she means more sex. She's obsessed with other people's sex lives. Don't pay any attention.'

'Thanks, Jess,' she said as she looked at her new friend. Jess was stunning, with a neat blonde bob and golden skin. Her demeanour was calming, and she had an understated elegance about her. 'She has a point—I think I've stayed with Andrew because I don't want to be alone. We met at uni, so I've never been alone. The problem is, I've grown up since we met, and he hasn't. It's scary,' said Lucy as she rested her chin in her hand.

'What's scary?' Sarah said, looking blankly at her.

'Making such a big decision. If I end things with him, I'll be alone. I won't be "Lucy and Andrew"; I'll just be me. What if I end up sad and alone?'

Jess reached over, placed her hand on Lucy's. 'You won't end up sad and alone. My Aunt always tells me you have to kiss a few frogs to find your prince. Andrew is frog number one, that's all. How does he make you feel? Do you look forward to seeing him or look forward to him going?'

Lucy remained silent for a few moments while she collected her thoughts. A sinking feeling formed in the pit of her stomach before she lifted her head and whispered, 'I look forward to him leaving.'

Jess squeezed her hand. 'Well, there you go. I think you have your answer, Hun.'

'If you don't want to be alone, get a cat,' said Sarah with a shrug.

Lucy took a deep breath and exhaled with purpose. 'Thanks, ladies, your pep talk has helped. I think it's time I told him how I feel.'

Lucy was about to hang up the phone when Andrew answered. 'Andrew, where are you? I thought you were coming over for dinner?' She said, annoyance clear in her tone. She'd invited him over to officially break up with him, but true to form, he was late.

'Oh, shit. Sorry about that, babe. I joined my friends in the pub for a drink. I'll leave now,' he said, out of breath. She rolled her eyes heavenward as she hung up on him.

An hour later, when Andrew finally arrived slightly drunk, she sat opposite him at her small kitchen table. Her palms were clammy as she watched him shovel lasagne into his mouth. Of course, he hadn't said thank you or complimented her cooking, forgoing manners to fill his beer-lined stomach. She imagined where they'd be in ten years. He'd shovel food into his beer belly, his fitness long gone, while she tended to the house and looked after him. She shudders at the thought of becoming his mother. The time had come.

'Andrew, I'm going to get a cat.'

CHAPTER 1

LUCY

Lost & Found – Lianna La Havas

One year later.

As the policeman cuffed Lucy, he said, 'You do not have to say anything. But it may harm your defence if you do not mention when questioned something which you later rely on in court. Anything you do say may be given in evidence.' She bent her head to her shoulder, wiping away a tear as they marched her off to the police car, passing Mark's body.

His blood pooled on the concrete of the multi-storey carpark where she worked. A second pool of blood belonged to Cameron Black. He was in an ambulance en route to the hospital. The sound of Imogen's screaming was still ringing in her ears.

Lucy had to stab Mark. She had to save her friends. She had no choice.

Once at the station, she was taken to an interrogation room where a tall man with light-brown hair sat opposite her and said, 'I'm Detective Constable Miller. The other police officer present is Detective Sergeant Abbott. Please state your full name and date of birth.'

Lucy stammered as she spoke, the shock of what had happened now sinking in. DS Abbott—a kind woman with wild blonde curls—continued the questioning.

'Can you tell us what happened this afternoon, Miss Steele?'

Lucy's lawyer sat straighter as he said, 'I'd like to remind my client that she doesn't have to answer.' Lucy's boss, James Spencer, had arranged for his lawyer to represent Lucy, not wanting her to take the fall for Mark's death.

Lucy nodded at her lawyer and said, 'It's okay. I stabbed Mark out of self-defence.' She picked at her fingernails and stared at the table.

DC Miller said, 'You stabbed him in the back, Miss Steele. That doesn't sound like self-defence. What can you tell us about the events leading up to Mark's death?' He leaned back in his seat as he spoke, giving the impression that he was open and willing to listen.

DC Miller and DS Abbott knew of Mark already. They'd investigated him for threatening Imogen after she left him, and her life, behind in London. Moving to Peterborough, she got a job working at Spencer and Black Associates and was Lucy's manager.

'I think it's best I tell you everything from the start. Then you'll see that I had no choice,' said Lucy as she leaned onto the table with her forearms. 'I met Mark when I was out with my friends from work. We were celebrating Imogen being with us for a week—'

'Is this Miss Imogen Taylor?' asked DC Abbott as she flicked through her notes.

'Yes, that's right. Mark chatted me up while I waited in line to use the ladies. He introduced himself as Paul. We hit it off, and he came back to my place.' Lucy blushed as she carried on.

'He ended up staying the night. It was great. He was attentive and made me feel special. When we were together, I thought he was trying to get to know me but now I know it was all an act. He was using me to get close to Imogen.

'My friends and I planned a night out in London. I was supposed to meet Paul afterwards to stay at his place, but I changed my mind. He'd become distant with me.' She took a moment to gather her thoughts, furrowing her brow as she remembered. 'He still dictated what I could wear on my night out. He was good at getting you to bend to his will.' She shook her head and blinked away the flashbacks.

'I guess the tequila and champagne gave me the courage to text him to say it was over between us and that I wouldn't be coming over. That's when it all went wrong. It's all my fault.' A lone tear tracked a line down her cheek, dripping onto the table.

DS Abbott passed over a box of tissues. 'It's okay; please take your time.'

She took a shuddering breath before saying, 'I saw Paul walking towards me in the club. He looked wild. That's when we realised Paul was Mark. I tried to intervene, but he smacked me across the face, and I fell. He went for Imogen, but Cameron stopped him.'

This piqued DC Miller's interest. 'What happened between Cameron and Mark?'

Picking at the stitching on her sleeve, she said, 'I don't know. The club manager took us to his office to look at the damage on my cheek. Cameron and Imogen met us there a few minutes later.'

'And which club was this? We could request CCTV footage to help with our investigation.' DC Miller sat poised with their notebook and pen.

Lucy didn't want the club to be involved. Tom was a good guy, and as he was a good friend of Cameron's, she didn't feel it was necessary to bring him into this. 'Um, I can't remember the name. I don't know where it was.'

DC Miller didn't look convinced but continued. He said, 'Why was Mr Black with you on a girl's night out?'

'He wasn't technically with us, but he was in the club. He worried that the harassment order Imogen had taken against Mark would anger him and that he'd show up at the club. I guess he had a gut instinct, and it was right. He and James had been sitting in the manager's office, watching the cameras to ensure Mark didn't turn up. But Mark used a false identity, got past the door staff, and found us.' Lucy folded her arms across her chest, desperate to feel some comfort. 'It was so scary. I'm grateful that Cameron was there.'

'And you're sure you don't know what happened between Mark, Cameron and Imogen while you waited in the office?' DC Miller was not letting this one go, and Lucy felt nervous. She didn't want to get her friends into trouble over this.

'I'm sorry, I don't. Mark left the club, and we all went home. We hoped that was the end and Mark would leave Imogen alone. Now we know he had other plans.'

DS Abbott paused her notetaking. 'Why didn't you file a complaint against Mark for his assault on you in the club? We could have arrested him with the harassment order already in place.'

'I didn't want to make things worse for Imogen. It's all my fault that this has happened. I led him right to her. He stole my access pass to leave a threatening note on her desk and found out all her movements from me. He knew she'd be in that club and came for her. I didn't want to anger him more.'

'That's understandable, but if anyone hits you in the future, you have a right to report it and press charges. Now, can you explain everything that happened today?'

Lucy took a shaky breath while shredding the tissue in her hands. 'We were at a meeting at a client's office this morning.'

'By we, do you mean you and Miss Taylor?'

Lucy nodded before carrying on. 'The client was Walter and Holmes. It went well until Imogen recognised the company logo as a subsidiary company of where Marked worked. We left in a hurry because she panicked. She said she thought Mark was involved in the meeting, as Walter and Holmes had requested her by name.' Lucy shifted in her seat.

'We were unloading the car back at the office, and Mark appeared.' Lucy took a moment to breathe. Panic was rising as she retold events. 'Once again, he knocked me to the floor, and I blacked out. As I came round, he was holding Imogen with a knife pressed to her neck and Cameron was there, too. Mark shouted that he would kill Cameron and take Imogen to his place to teach her a lesson.'

DC Miller interrupted again. 'He had plans to take her back to his house? DS Abbott, can you ask the local PD to search his house? There may be evidence of his intentions there.'

'Yes, sir.'

Miller spoke towards the recorder, 'For the record, DS Abbott has left the room. Carry on, please, Miss Steele.'

'I tried to stop Mark with a can of pepper spray, but I missed. Cameron was desperate to help Imogen, so I talked to Mark while Cameron crept closer to him. They fought, and as you know, Mark stabbed Cameron. I'd untied the rope around Imogen's wrists, so she ran to help Cameron. There was so much blood.' She stopped speaking, the tissue a shredded mess on the table.

'For the record, DS Abbott has entered the room,' Miller spoke again.

'The local PD is en route to his house and will update us as soon as they get there.' She took her seat opposite Lucy.

'Thank you. Now, if you're okay, please carry on.'

'He tried to grab Imogen again, but James threw him to the floor. There was so much blood. Cameron wasn't moving; I thought he was dead.' Lucy cradled herself as she looked at the officers, her eyes wide with horror. 'James and Imogen's attention was on Cameron, so they didn't see Mark get up. I couldn't let my friends get hurt because of my stupidity. I panicked. I wasn't strong enough to fight him off, so I grabbed the knife and stabbed him. He fell to his knees, but that still didn't stop him. James kicked him, and Mark fell backwards. Then he stopped moving.' She looked at her shaking hands and realised she'd killed a man.

'Okay, Miss Steele. I think we have everything we need for now. I'm afraid we're going to hold you here while we wait for information to come in.'

DC Miller concluded the interview and escorted Lucy to a cell. She sat on the cold, hard bed and hugged her knees to her chest. Despair overcame her.

'What do I do?' She looked up at the ceiling. 'If anyone is listening to me up there, please help me out of this. Maybe I shouldn't have wanted more. Maybe if I'd stayed with Andrew, none of this would have happened. I promise I won't take what I have for granted again.' Lucy sat on her knees and begged for help. Her muscles ached as the adrenaline that had kept her going left her body.

There was a tapping at the door before DS Abbott opened it. 'We're heading back to the interview room again. Follow me.'

Lucy took her seat at the same interview table as DC Miller entered the room, carrying a document wallet.

'Miss Steele, Mark Edwards had horrendous plans for Miss Taylor. I won't show you the photos; you've been through enough. His intentions included kidnapping, torture and murder, and he's been planning this for quite some time. He went to great lengths to set it up. Miss Taylor is fortunate to have you all as friends.' DC Miller leant closer, leaning on the table. 'Miss Steele, what you have done today is save your friend's life; of that, I know. You have shown great strength and courage. We have retrieved footage from Mr Black's car—what a stroke of luck that Miss Taylor took his car to the meeting. The onboard camera felt an impact when Mr Edwards threw Miss Taylor onto the bonnet and sent a recording to Mr Black's phone. That is how Cameron knew to come running, and Mr Spencer alerted us. We have spoken to Mr Spencer, and his recollection of events matches yours. We're in no doubt you were acting to protect yourself and your friends' lives. You are free to go, Miss Steele. My colleague will take you home. We're sorry for what you've been through.'

Lucy couldn't hold back any longer; she broke down and sobbed into her hands.

CHAPTER 2

LUCY

Overthinking – Zoe Wees

As she got out of the police car, she turned to the officer and said, 'Thank you. 'Lucy waited for them to drive off before walking down the cobbled path to her ground-floor maisonette. After seeing what a great job she'd done decorating her previous flat, her landlord sold it, forcing her to move out. He made more money selling it than renting it to her at the agreed discount. She chalked him up to being another man she couldn't trust.

Luckily, Imogen was renting out her place after recently moving in with Cameron. They'd hit it off straight away when he made her a coffee at work—textbook love at first sight. Cameron had asked her to move in with him to keep her safe from Mark. Lucy sighed. She wished someone would be her knight in shining armour. Instead, she'd been tricked by a wolf in sheep's clothing.

She was happy in her new home; it was the fresh start she desperately needed, and with Imogen being the senior designer, she knew that the decorating would be done to her liking. She'd happily never repaint another ceiling.

Closing and locking the door, she discarded her bag and coat in the hallway before calling out to her cat. 'Doris. Where are you, Doris?' She smiled as she heard the tip-tapping of Doris's claws on the wooden floor. A tabby cat was soon wrapping herself around her legs, purring.

She bent down to tickle the cat's ears. 'I can always count on you to be happy to see me. Shall we get you fed?' She walked through to the kitchen and topped up Doris's food bowl before pouring herself a glass of water.

Lucy didn't know how long she'd been staring out the window, but the phone ringing snapped her out of her thoughts. She let it ring out. She wasn't ready to speak to anyone yet. What would she say? She hadn't processed what had happened in the last twenty-four hours, and she wasn't sure she was ready to. She could still hear Imogen's screams as Mark pressed the knife into her neck. Images of Cameron's blood flashed before her eyes, followed by the sound of the defibrillator pulsing life back into his heart.

Busy. She must keep busy.

Knowing how to keep her mind busy, Lucy reached for the baking tins and ingredients. Baking cupcakes would keep her busy, and everyone at work will need comfort food. Plus, they all love her cupcakes.

As one batch went into the oven, she'd start on the next. Two hours and forty-eight cupcakes later, exhaustion seeped into her bones, but knew that sleep would not come quickly tonight.

She stood surveying her kitchen, tapping her finger to her bottom lip, deep in thought.

She looked down at her purring cat. 'Doris, I'm going to start some bread dough.' The doorbell interrupted their conversation.

Wiping her hands on her apron, she slid the chain on before opening the door. Mark wouldn't be coming for her, but she felt safer with it on.

'Hey, Lucy. How are you doing? I tried calling you but when you didn't answer, I got worried,' said James, through the gap in the doorway.

Lucy opened the door after taking the chain off. 'Hi, James. I'm okay. Do you want to come in?' She moved aside to let him in. He was wearing the same clothes he'd been in all day; his shirt was now untucked and creased. He grazed his fingertips over his stubble as he walked past her.

James inhaled deeply. 'Wow, it smells amazing in here. Have you been baking?'

'Yep, come in and help yourself. I'm trying out new flavours, and you look in need of an energy burst,' she said, ushering him into the kitchen.

He ran his fingers through his hair. 'Lead the way, Miss Steele. I'm well and truly exhausted. It's been a long day,' he said, wearily.

James halted as he entered the kitchen, scanning his eyes across every surface. 'Are you sure you're okay? That's a lot of cupcakes.'

'Don't worry; they're not all for me. They're to help cheer up everyone at work,' she said, wiping her hands on her apron, suddenly conscious of her state.

He leaned against the counter and said, 'That's why I've been trying to get a hold of you. The office is closed tomorrow. We need time to process what happened. Plus, I need to get contractors in to clean the car park before anyone sees it.'

Not wanting to hear about the blood, she busied herself with choosing a cake. 'Here, try this one. It's banana salted caramel.' Lucy thrust a cupcake into James' hand before he could reply.

He devoured the cake in three bites, nodding and smiling at Lucy as he swallowed. 'Mm, it's delicious. These will cheer everyone up but take all the time you need. You've been through so much,' he said, wiping buttercream from his lips.

'Thanks, I'll be okay. I want to keep busy. Have you had any news on Cameron? Is he—'

James nodded. 'He's alive. He's in surgery,' he said with a sigh of relief.

Relief flooded Lucy's emotions. It hadn't all been for nothing; Cameron was alive. For the second time that day, she broke down in tears. James crossed the kitchen and wrapped her in his arms, holding her tight.

'Let it all out. You're safe now, and Cameron will be okay. Everyone is going to be okay. It's over. Let it all out.' He stroked her back and kept comforting her. Once he had calmed her down, her legs gave way with exhaustion and they both slumped to the floor. James sat holding her until the tears dried up.

His voice turned serious as he said, 'If you need to speak to someone, I'll happily provide you with the best; you only need to ask. We're all here for you, Lucy. You're amazing and we're all so grateful for what you did for Imogen.' He looked Lucy directly in the eyes and repeated, 'You saved Imogen's life.'

She wiped at her eyes as her tears left track marks in the flour dusted on her cheeks. 'You helped. It could have been worse if you weren't there. How is Imogen?'

'I spoke to Sarah before I got here. She's okay. She's stitched up and has some sedatives to help her sleep. She's at the hospital waiting for Cameron to come out of surgery. I spoke to Julian too; he's gone over to wait with them.'

'Julian. I've heard the name. Who is he again?'

'He's Cameron's cousin. They're basically like brothers. He's a good guy. He'll make sure Imogen is okay, and Sarah will stay with her tonight.'

'Oh, is Sarah not staying with you tonight?'

James shook his head. 'No, we thought it best she kept Imogen company tonight.'

Lucy nodded and said, 'I'm glad everybody has somebody.' Her shoulders slumped as the realisation hit her.

James shuffled around on the floor so that he was facing her. 'Hey. There is someone you have. You have me, and Imogen, and Sarah, and Cameron, and Jess. You're not alone in this. Do you hear me?' James gently holds her upper arms, 'You're not alone.'

'Thanks. And thanks for coming over.' She knew he meant well, but she would still be alone tonight once he left. He dusted his hands off on his trousers as he stood and said, 'No worries. Are you going to be okay tonight? Do you want me to stay for longer? I can help you clean up all this.' He gestured around the kitchen while he helped Lucy up.

'No, it's okay. I'm quite looking forward to getting this cleaned up. Then I think I'll try to get some sleep.'

'Well, take it easy. I think it'll surprise you how exhausted you'll feel when all the adrenaline has worn off. Tell me if you need more time off; Karen or Chris can cover your workload.'

After seeing James out, Lucy cleaned the kitchen from top to bottom and boxed up the many cupcakes. She planned to ice them tomorrow now that she had a whole day to fill with keeping busy.

Covered in flour and dried tears, she soaked in the bath with lavender oil. As the water level slowly rose, she looked at her reflection in the bathroom mirror. The bruise on her cheek was the only sign of what had happened. The pain was much more than just a painful bruise on the outside. She pressed her finger to it, the throbbing pain reassuring her that she wasn't totally numb.

Checking her phone as she climbed into bed, she noticed a missed call from her mum. To say her parents had been calling her non-stop would be an understatement. Knowing that if she didn't call back, they'd hound her, she hit redial.

'Hey, Mum. Sorry I missed your call. James came round to check in on me,' she said, trying to keep her voice level.

'Hello, sweetheart. That's nice of him. He's such a good boss, isn't he? I hope he talked you into not going to work tomorrow.'

'He's closed the office, so we all have the day off.' She didn't want to tell her mother that they needed to wash the blood off the concrete.

Her mum hummed softly and said, 'Very sensible. I always did like the sound of Mr Spencer. Lucy, I know you think I'm biased, but I want you to know that you're a beautiful, strong woman. You're loyal and brave, and I know you have a fantastic future ahead of you. Please don't let anyone make you feel otherwise. Okay? What's happened is a blip. This too shall pass.'

This made Lucy smile as she sat back on her bed, letting the plump pillows cocoon her. Her mum's favourite saying always brought her feelings of comfort. 'Thanks, Mum, I'll keep that in mind.'

Her mum guffawed and said, 'Ah, not at all, my love, that's what mums are for. Okay, well, it's getting late, and you need some sleep. Take care, love you lots.'

'Love you too,' she said, ending the call.

Lucy plugged her phone in to charge on her bedside table. Her hand hovered over the drawer for a moment before pulling it open. Reaching inside, she took hold of her diary.

She stroked her hand over the familiar moleskin-soft cover as she considered if she should start writing in it again.

For years, Lucy wrote in her diary every night. It was her comfort blanket where she could write everything that was worrying her. She only stopped writing in it recently, as she was no longer in an unhappy relationship and had a new boyfriend (ignoring the fact he was a psycho killer), a great job, and amazing friends. But now she sought the comfort of her old friend, one she could talk to without fear of judgement.

With the diary open on her lap, her pen tapping at her bottom lip while she thought, she considered the myriad of emotions swirling around her brain.

Dear Diary,

Sorry I haven't written to you for a while. I've been neglecting you while I was busy getting on with my new life.

She paused as she looked at the previous page.

The last time I wrote was after I met Paul. That didn't work out well. Turns out his name was actually Mark, and he was Imogen's ex-boyfriend who stalked her and wanted to kidnap her. I say he was Mark, as he's no longer in the land of the living. It's all gone wrong.

I stabbed a man, and now he's dead. He has no future and no chance to pay for his crimes. He'll never get to say sorry to me for the hurt he caused. I'll never get to tell him what a wanker he was.

A man is dead because of me. I shouldn't be sitting here calling him a wanker; that feels wrong somehow.

Everyone has tried to make me feel better about it, telling me I'm not the one that killed him. James kicked him, causing him to fall on the knife, and that last stab did it, but that's nonsense. I'm the one with blood on my hands.

She shifted in her bed. Her diary always made her own up to how she was feeling, but she was fighting to keep her deepest thoughts and emotions hidden.

Growing up, Lucy was a nervous child. The smallest things stressed her out, which is why she stayed close to home. It was convenient to latch on to Andrew when she was at university. He was the constant she needed in her life when her parents couldn't be there. Her diary helped her see what the cause of her anxiety was, and it soon became something she needed to do.

She took a deep breath and put pen to paper.

How should I feel about that? I can try to convince myself that they're right. It wasn't my fault he was dead; the knife wound wasn't deep enough to kill him. I should be relieved, right?

I'm weak. I've been weak all my life. My parents wrapped me up in cotton wool because they knew it. Andrew treated me like he wanted me there for his convenience. He saw my weakness. And it turns out that when my friends needed me, when it was a life-or-death situation, I'm still too weak to even do a proper job of stabbing someone.

I should be relieved, but I'm not.

I'm a loser, a little girl pretending to be a woman. Why would a handsome, successful man be interested in me? Idiot. He was too good to be true. What annoys me is that he was right. I am a pathetic little girl.

Is Mum right? Will this pass? Or will I always feel the need to hang my head in shame? Hide behind a bubbly personality and a tonne of cupcakes?

How can I move on from this?

She lay the ribbon down the page and closed her diary. It wouldn't give her any answers tonight, probably never. With a deep sigh, she put away the diary and settled in for a restless sleep.

CHAPTER 3

LUCY

Lonely – Zoe Wees

'Welcome back, everyone. I hope yesterday gave you all some time to reflect.' James had called a staff meeting and asked everyone to congregate in the large open area downstairs. He'd taken a position on the staircase so that everyone could see him. Lucy stood in the back, not wanting to draw attention to herself.

'I want to start by letting you know Cameron has pulled through. He's awake and on the road to recovery. He'll be out of action for six weeks. In the meantime, Scott will take care of everything. Go easy on him; he has some pretty big shoes to fill.' The sighs of relief were audible in the crowd.

'I would like to address the rumours. On Tuesday, a dangerous man known to the police attacked Imogen and Lucy in the car park and stabbed Cameron as he tried to help. I hope she doesn't mind me saying this, but if it weren't for Lucy, it would've been even worse. She did what anyone else here would have done and stopped a dangerous man from killing her friend. Please do not question her about what happened. If she wants to talk about it, she will. If anyone from the press asks you anything, you're to say, "no comment." This is a private matter between the people directly involved. Please keep it that way.'

Lucy tried not to notice the glances her co-workers were aiming her way.

'For now, Imogen will work from home. Drop her an email and she'll get back to you as soon as she can.

'We're all shocked by what's happened, but this was an isolated incident, and you're all safe here. If anyone needs to talk, please come and speak to me or HR. Okay, everyone, back to work. Thank you.'

As the crowd dispersed, James found his way over to Lucy. 'Are you ready to return to work?'

'I'm so tired of everyone asking if I'm okay. Contrary to popular belief, I'm a big girl and I know my mind,' Lucy snapped before she stalked off to her desk, leaving James and Sarah standing, mouths agape.

Lucy could feel eyes on her as she made her way to her desk. Eyes to the floor, she picked up her pace. She wondered if perhaps her parents were right—she should've taken the rest of the week off. Sarah approached her desk, interrupting her thoughts; apprehension written all over her face.

'Hey, Lucy. These cupcakes are amazing. I'm on my second already.'

Without taking her eyes from her screen, she said, 'Thanks. Is that all you came here for?' She knew she was being mean to Sarah, but she couldn't help it. Sarah took a tentative step forward. 'No. I wanted to make sure you're okay. James and I are worried about you. Are you sure you won't take the rest of the week off?'

Lucy took a deep, calming breath before saying, 'Do you think I should hide away? Be ashamed of what happened?'

'No, not at all. That isn't what we mean.'

'I don't need to hide at home if I have done nothing wrong.' Her strong words didn't match her feelings. Her heart raced, and her face reddened. It was as if Sarah knew what she'd written in her diary and could see her deepest fears that she tried so hard to bury. Tears were threatening to break through. She wanted Sarah to leave so she could lock herself in a toilet cubicle.

'No one is suggesting you need to hide at home. You've been through a lot. This kind of trauma can affect you. No one will think less of you for taking time to collect your thoughts.'

Something inside her snapped. She'd spent so long being weak, because she'd allowed it. It was time to fight back. She would no longer allow people to treat her like she needed help, like she couldn't decide for herself what she needed. Suddenly, her mind cleared.

'I've collected my thoughts. Collected them up and threw them away. I'm done with being made to feel like a stupid little girl. Mark targeted me because I had "weak" written all over me. I'm tired of being seen as the weak one and it ends now.'

'Mark said some horrible things to you, but he was a crazy person. You're not a stupid little girl. He said that to hurt you because he knows that you're a strong woman. Men like that use words to hurt people because they're the weak ones,' Sarah said with absolute confidence.

'Yeah, okay,' Lucy mumbled back.

Sarah bent down to look her eye to eye. 'You are a beautiful, strong woman and we all love you dearly. It might seem like we're smothering you, but that's because we care about you, not because you're too young or too weak. Who else would bring in freshly baked cakes and keep us all going? You're our answer to a sexy Nigella Lawson.' Sarah had a sly smile on her lips.

Lucy couldn't help but smile back. A pang of guilt hit her; it wasn't like her to snap so fiercely at her friends.

'Now, repeat after me. "I am a strong woman,"' said Sarah in a firm tone.

Lucy looked down at her hands. 'I really don't want to.'

'Say it.'

Lucy rolled her eyes and said, 'I am a strong woman.'

'Right, now say, "I'm a sexy minx."'

'You've gone too far now. I'm not saying that.'

'You will be after our book club.' Sarah checked her watch and said, 'I need to get back to work. Give me a shout if you need another talking to.'

'Thanks, Sarah,' Lucy said with a small smile 'Oh, is there any news on Cameron? Is Imogen okay?'

'Imogen went to see him yesterday. He's doing okay, sore, as you'd expect, but considering what he went through, he's doing well. Imogen is good. She needed stitches and sedatives, but all things considered, she's all right. She's been looking over her shoulder for a long time. Did I tell you she met Cameron's parents at the hospital? What a way to meet the parents. They're lovely. They handled it all well. You can see where Cameron gets his good looks from. If I went for older men, his dad would be in trouble.' Sarah was rambling with all the news and laughed before composing herself. 'Sorry, probably not the time to be fancying Cameron's dad.'

'You're a wicked lady. I'll see you later.'

Lucy's day was not productive. She stayed at her desk, foregoing a lunch break, as she wanted to avoid people. It was nearly time to head home when James called her into his office. She prepared herself for another lecture about being strong.

'Take a seat, Lucy. I need to discuss something with you, and I'd appreciate your opinion.'

'What's up?'

'I'm going to get straight to it. Walter and Holmes have been in touch.'

Her skin prickled at the name. 'Why?'

'They wanted to apologise for Mark's behaviour.' Lucy's sudden laughter interrupted him.

'What?' Lucy looked incredulous. 'They said "sorry" for his behaviour? He blackmailed his boss into making him MD of Walter and Holmes so that he could set up an entirely new office in Peterborough, just to lure Imogen out of the office and attempt to rape, kidnap and murder her while stabbing Cameron and knocking me unconscious. And they're sorry?' Her voice cracked with rage as she spoke.

He sat back, resting his foot on his other knee. 'Yep, that just about covers it. You haven't heard the best bit.' James looked just as bemused as Lucy felt.

She flopped back into the chair, flicking her hand up in encouragement. 'Go on.'

'Walter and Holmes love the work you and Imogen have done, and they see the financial benefit of moving out of London. They're completing the project, and they still want you two on it.' Any trace of a smile on his face was gone. This was not a joke.

Blink.

Lost for words, she remained silent.

'How do you feel about that?' he asked, seeing many emotions roll across her face.

'This is a lot to absorb. I think I need to go home. Can I think about it?'

James held his hands up as he said, 'Of course. I need to speak to Imogen, too. If either of you isn't happy with it, the answer will be no. I'm not happy with it, but I don't think it's my decision to make. Don't rush to answer. Take your time. They can wait. In the meantime, go home and please don't bake tonight. I've had six cupcakes already.' He rubbed his belly, sighing.

'I can't make any promises.' Lucy gave James a weak smile before grabbing her things and heading out.

Lying on the sofa, Lucy absentmindedly spun her phone around in her fingers, bored with scrolling through social media, seeing all the fake smiles and perfect lives of her friends. She didn't feel like going out, and she'd already completed the housework. The thought of calling Andrew was tempting. He was like a comfort blanket to her—someone from a simpler time.

Before she could make the call, her phone vibrated in her hand. Imogen's face and name flashed up on her screen and she immediately answered it.

'Hey, Imogen. How are you? Is there any news on Cameron?' She stood and paced around the living room, eager to hear any news.

'Hi. I'm okay. My head's sore still, but other than that, I feel mostly numb, to be honest. Cameron is doing well. He's got some colour back in his cheeks, which is a relief. He'll be coming home soon. Are you doing okay?'

Lucy hesitated before answering, 'Yeah, all things considered. I left work early today. It all got a bit much. Hopefully, this will be old news next week.'

'I can understand that. Listen, I had a call from James. He said he'd already spoken to you, so I thought I'd call to talk to you. Do you want to carry on with the Walter and Holmes project?'

'It feels weird. I'm not sure.' Lucy was quiet a minute. 'What are your thoughts?'

'I immediately said no, but then I thought about it. Why shouldn't we? Mark is dead. He's not coming back to bother us. Are we really going to let him stop us? He's been controlling me for years, and I'd quite like to have the last word and finish what we started. I'd also like them to make a hefty donation to a women's charity. How does that sound to you?'

Lucy exhaled a deep breath she'd been holding. 'Okay. Let's do it.' She was confident in this. It felt right.

'If you change your mind, we'll pull out of the project.' Imogen paused, took a breath and said, 'There's another reason for my call. Please don't be mad at Sarah, but she called me this morning. She's worried about you. Do you want to talk to me about how you're feeling?'

She sat down and grabbed a cushion for comfort. Only Imogen could understand. She'd suffered at the hands of Mark too. For years Mark broke Imogen, took away her independence, confidence and isolated her from her friends and family.

'How'd you keep it together? You found the strength to leave Mark and start a new life. Mark stalked and threatened you and Cameron. He tried to hurt you and stabbed Cameron, and yet you keep going. You keep your head held high. How do you do it, Imogen? I feel like a fool. I feel humiliated, and I want a hole to swallow me up.' Her voice cracked, the tears threatening to flow.

'Oh, Hun. It took me four years to find the strength to leave Mark. I went back after leaving him once. That made me feel like a fool. I knew he was bad for me, but I wasn't strong enough to stay away. I believed his promises to be better, and I was wrong to do that. Mark was a narcissist with a knack for getting into your brain and getting you to bend to his wishes.'

'That's true. It's like he knew exactly what to say to get me agreeing to everything he wanted,' said Lucy, nodding to herself.

'Exactly. The problem with leaving someone like that is they stay in your head. Even after his death, I still hear him in my thoughts occasionally. You must learn to ignore the voices until they fade away.'

'I didn't know he got to you, even now.'

'Oh, all the time. Cameron is helping me re-learn what a normal relationship should be like. When we first got together, he would say something completely innocent and make me angry. I'm re-wiring my brain. It's a long process, but I'll get there.

'What has happened is still so raw. Give yourself a break; you need to process everything before you get back on the horse. Get out there and hold your head high. Find yourself someone you can trust and take it slowly with them. Rebuild your faith in men. They're not all losers and psychos. I promise.'

'Thanks, Imogen. I needed to hear that today. And you're right; I need to allow myself time and space. Everyone else should leave me alone. I'm not a child that needs looking after.'

'No, you're not, and no one thinks you are. They check in on me constantly. Don't worry; we all know you're a kick-arse, gorgeous woman. So don't stress it.'

'Maybe I'll treat myself to a day off tomorrow and go shopping. It's time I updated my wardrobe, and if all else fails, I can fake it 'til I make it,' Lucy stated with conviction.

'That's the spirit.'

'Thanks again, Jen.'

'No worries. You know where I am if you need me.'

Lucy hung up the phone, taking a deep breath. It was time to grow up. She had a lot to learn and plenty of life to live. This wouldn't hold her back; she wanted to explore everything that life offered. She wanted to be a confident person, and that meant acting like one, starting with dressing like one.

CHAPTER 4

LUCY

Brand New Me – Alicia Keys

Lucy stood in front of the full-length mirror that was propped against her bedroom wall, looking at her reflection. She hadn't gone to work on Friday, opting instead to get her hair done. Dark caramel highlights emphasised her shoulder-length, beachy waves. She'd had her eyebrows threaded to perfection and her nails French manicured as a treat.

A trip to a local department store had secured her a curated capsule wardrobe. Clothes from her university days were long gone, replaced with fitted dresses, stylish trousers and tops that showed off her assets.

Today was the first day of the rest of her life. The past was behind her, and she hoped everyone at work would stop treating her with kid gloves. She ran her hands down her tight, black, knitted roll-neck sweater and black cigarette trousers that hugged her rear and enhanced her slender legs. She twisted her hips to each side, feeling proud of her figure.

She'd spent so long coveting the womanly curves of her co-workers that she'd overlooked her own, hidden beneath baggy clothes.

Her credit card had taken a battering as she entered the shoe department, drawn to all the brightly coloured patent heels and unable to decide between them. A shop assistant helped her to the car with all the bags and boxes. She felt like Julia Roberts in Pretty Woman.

She wore her favourite shoes that she'd instantly fallen in love with and had to have them. They were ombre, black at the front, morphing into bright red towards the heel. A chunky red necklace finished her look perfectly.

Before leaving the house, she applied a red lip gloss—the rest of her makeup neutral apart from black winged eyeliner.

'Good morning, Miss Steele. I almost didn't recognise you there. Might I be so bold as to say you look fabulous today? What's changed?' Lucy didn't have time to answer. 'Don't tell me.' Sam Briggs, the security guard everyone knew and loved, tapped his finger on his lip while thinking. 'Ah-ha. Yes, that's it.' His kind green eyes twinkled and brought a smile to Lucy's face. 'You've had your hair done, and you look taller.'

'Yep, new highlights and shoes. Do you like them?' She twisted her ankle to show off her shoes.

'They're beautiful, my dear, just like you. Have a lovely day.'

'Thanks, Sam.' Lucy strolled into the office with her head held high. Her feet were already hurting, but she was determined to style it out.

Lucy bounced into the office and saw her friend already at her desk. 'Morning, Sarah.'

'Shit-a-brick. Who are you, and what have you done with Lucy?' Sarah had thrown her pen down in mock shock.

'I don't know what you mean.'

'You're a sexy little minx. It suits you. And who knew you hid that arse away all this time? I didn't realise you had a figure Marilyn Monroe would be jealous of.'

'Thanks. I feel a little self-conscious now.' She tugged her sleeves down over her wrists.

'Trust me. People will notice, but they'll notice how hot you are and not thinking about the shit that's gone down recently, which is a good thing, right?'

'That's true.'

'Give people a day to get over it. Then it'll be the norm. What's brought this on, anyway?'

Lucy shrugged. 'It was time for a fresh start.'

'Amen to that. It's nice to see that beautiful smile on your face again. Don't let anyone try to take it away from you again, you hear me?'

'Loud and clear. I need to sit down now; these heels are brutal.'

As expected, her co-workers made plenty of comments. Her confidence got a boost with each one, and she left the office that evening feeling like she was floating—well, apart from the pain in the balls of her feet, but Sarah reassured her she'd get used to high heels and the pain would go—she wasn't so sure.

As Lucy walked through her front door, she could feel her handbag vibrating against her hip. Kicking the door closed with her heel, she grabbed the phone, seeing Andrew's name on display. She furrowed her brow, tempted to let it ring out, but curiosity got the better of her.

'Hi, Andrew.' She didn't know why he was calling, but she knew she wouldn't like it.

'What the hell, Lucy.'

'Excuse me?' That stopped her in her tracks.

'I've just read in the paper that you were involved in a murder investigation. What the bloody hell have you been doing?'

'Not that it's any of your business anymore, but someone attacked me. They tried to kidnap my friend and stabbed her boyfriend. I'm okay, though, thanks for asking.'

His pause was too long before he said, 'Obviously, I was worried about you.'

Lucy pinched the bridge of her nose. This was the first time she'd heard from Andrew since she ended their relationship. He didn't try to talk her out of it, and he hadn't tried to win her back. He didn't care; she'd had enough of going along with his crap.

'No, you don't care, Andrew. This is the first time I've heard from you since we ended.'

'Since you ended it, Lucy, that was all on you.' She detected a hint of venom in his tone. 'We don't need to go over it again. Honestly, I wanted to make sure you're okay. Listen, do you want to meet so we can talk about it? You've been through a lot and probably need someone to talk to.'

'I'll pass, thanks. I have plenty of people to talk to. Imogen has been great; I couldn't have got through it without her.'

'Imogen? Isn't she the one he tried to kidnap? Lucy, if it weren't for her, you wouldn't have been there.'

'I think you'll find that if it weren't for her, I wouldn't be the person I am today. I've done a lot of growing up over the last year. You should try it.'

She heard his sharp intake of breath before he said, 'There's no need to be like that. I think we should meet up for a drink and talk about it.'

'You sound like you're trying to get an interview out of me.' The brief silence didn't escape her attention. 'Oh my god, Andrew, are you trying to sell a story to the press?'

'What? No. That would be crazy.' The squeaky voice was a giveaway.

'Don't bullshit me, Andrew. Tell me the truth.'

She heard a loud exhale down the phone. 'Okay, I admit the local paper has approached me. I need the money, Lucy, I'm in a bit of a situation.'

'Arsehole. I'm hanging up now.'

He rushed as he said, 'No, please hear me out.' The desperation in his voice had stopped her finger from hanging up.

She couldn't contain her rage any longer as she shouted, 'And why the hell should I?'

'Why? We were together for four years, Lucy. I'd have thought there's some part of you that still gives a shit about me, and there's no need to shout.'

A few breaths helped calm her before she said, 'You're right. I'm sorry for shouting. Please explain why you're trying to sell stories about me to the press. How can you justify this?' She felt like she was placating a child.

'I really need the money.'

'Oh god, what have you got yourself mixed up in?' Lucy was now sitting on her bed, removing her shoes and rubbing at her soles. As the tension left her feet, she could feel it increasing on her shoulders.

'It turns out I have a kid.'

Now it was her turn to remain silent. The shock left her momentarily speechless. 'Well, I guess now you need to grow up.' A thought occurred to her. 'So, when you say you've got a kid, you mean it's already born?'

'Um, yeah. Henry is eighteen months now.'

'Wait a minute. We were still together then.'

'Umm.' He'd run out of chat.

She didn't want to ask, but part of her was curious. Her words were a whisper as she said, 'Who's the mother?'

'Stacey.'

'Stacey?' She wracked her brain to work out why that name sounded familiar. 'From the pub? That's why you were always there. So, let me get this straight. You were sleeping with Stacey while you were with me? And now you're calling me to sell my story to the papers because you need the money?'

'When you say it like that, it sounds terrible.'

'Because it *is* terrible, Andrew. You utter, utter wanker.' The rage was back. 'You've just spouted a load of shit to me about how I should still care about you, yet you cheated on me.'

His voice rose to match hers as he said, 'Look, I'm sorry I cheated on you. I felt like you didn't want me, and Stacey gave me loads of attention. You pushed me to it, and you dumped me, remember?'

The rage consumed Lucy until a red mist descended over her. At the end of her tether, she would no longer take this shit from anyone.

'You're right; I didn't want you. I grew up and wanted more for my life. I realised I needed a man, not some overgrown boy. Good luck with Stacey, and I hope you grow up and be a good father to Henry. Now you can fuck off. Never call me again.' She hung up and threw the phone on the bed before covering her face with a pillow and screaming bloody murder into it.

Dear Diary,

You know how I told you I'd hold my head up high from now on? I updated my wardrobe to look the part, even if I didn't fully feel it, and it worked! I believed what people told me; that I was strong and brave. Why is it when things are on the up, someone comes along and ruins it for me?

Andrew told me today that he cheated on me. He was balls-deep in someone else just before I ended our relationship. Can you believe it? He's now a dad. I guess I should be happy that I finished it. I'm clearly better off without him.

Maybe I'm not so stupid. I should trust my gut instincts and only do what I feel happy doing. To hell with everyone else. It's just Doris and me now; I need to be okay with that.

It's time to put me first.

The days went quickly and soon turned into weeks. The whispers from co-workers stopped, and the office was almost back to normal.

Almost.

The office felt empty without Cameron and Imogen. Imogen had been with them for a short while, but they'd become close friends during that time. Lucy missed her desk neighbour and mentor; her absence reminded her of what they'd been through.

Imogen phoned her daily to check on her progress with their projects, but mostly it was to check how she was feeling. Imogen understood first-hand what she was going through and gave Lucy strength.

'I have a surprise for you,' said Imogen as she sat with Lucy in the breakout area on the mezzanine while Cameron had a doctor's appointment. 'But first, I want to enjoy this pastry. I've missed having these on tap while I've been at home.'

Lucy tapped her fingernail on the table while she watched Imogen have an intimate moment with the flaky pastry. 'Okay, I waited long enough. What's the surprise?'

Imogen licked the sticky sugar syrup off her fingers and said, 'Cameron has been sneakily planning a party. He wants to celebrate his recovery and allow everyone to let their hair down. Obviously, you're invited, but that's not the good bit.'

'Has he arranged for the cast of Magic Mike to be there? That would be a pleasant surprise,' said Lucy, her eyes wide with excitement.

'No, that would be good. I think you'll like this more.'

'I'm listening,' said Lucy, leaning forward.

Imogen sat back in her chair and steepled her hands together. 'Tom is going, and he asked if you'd be there.' Her face looked triumphant.

Her instant reaction was excitement before she remembered she didn't trust or need men.

'He's a nice guy; he was probably just being polite.'

'It's more than that; he always asks Cameron how you are when he calls. I think he really likes you.'

'He doesn't know me. He's just being polite because of what happened.' Her body didn't agree with her mind as her heart rate increased with excitement. She felt an instant attraction to Tom, and perhaps if things had worked out differently, she might have pursued something. But now she wasn't so sure.

Her track record with men was pathetic, and she wasn't ready to open herself up to more disappointment. Now wasn't the time to entertain the idea of meeting anyone else.

'Well, I think you'll change your mind once you see him at the party.'

'Mm, we'll see about that. I'll need a new outfit. I want to look good. Will you come shopping with me?'

'Of course, Hun. You'd look good wearing anything. Have you seen yourself lately?'

'You know the phrase, fake it 'til you make it? I hope by looking like a confident woman, I will one day be one.'

CHAPTER 5

LUCY

Scars to Your Beautiful – Alessia Cara

Lucy heard the taxi pull up outside as she nervously straightened out her dress and fussed with her hair. Imogen had picked out the perfect dress for her. It was the darkest blue, the tulip skirt showing off her shapely hips. The deep V-neck allowed her to still wear a bra while having the most amazing cleavage on show. Lucy had curves in all the right places and this dress showcased them. She wouldn't normally dare show so much flesh, but the new confident woman who stood before her would wear it with pride. She felt sick with nerves when she thought of seeing Tom again, despite the new outfit.

Tom Harper was the owner of the members-only club in London where she'd enjoyed a night out with Imogen, Sarah and Jess. In a moment fuelled by tequila, she'd sent a text to Paul, her boyfriend, telling him it was over. It was at that point they all learned Paul was Mark.

Tom had taken her phone number before they left the club, and he'd messaged a few times, but before anything could progress, things got a bit stabby, as Lucy called it. She'd sensed a connection between them as he held an icepack to her cheek in his office, but it was a case of the right guy, wrong time. Definitely the wrong time.

'Oi, Lucy, get a move on; we're going to be late.' Sarah's loud voice boomed through the front door, shortly followed by a car horn.

With a shake of her head at her friends' impatience, she headed out to meet Sarah and Jess in the taxi.

Sarah's eyes scanned Lucy from head to toe. 'Well, that'll do it all right.' She stood with one arm leaning on the open door to the taxi.

Lucy looked down at herself. 'What will do what?'

Sarah pointed as she said, 'You, in that dress. Tom won't be able to resist you. I hope you've sorted your bikini line.'

Jess popped her head out the door, visibly rolling her eyes. 'Crass as ever, Sarah. Will you leave the poor woman alone so we can get a move on?'

Sarah held her hands up before ushering Lucy into the middle and sliding herself next to her.

Lucy turned to her friends and said, 'Look, this dress isn't for Tom; it's for me. I've had enough of men to last me a lifetime. I'm not interested in pursuing anything with him, and he's probably not even interested in me. Can I just have a fun night out with my friends?'

They both replied quickly with an okay, before Sarah uttered under her breath, 'I think you'll change your mind when you see him.' Lucy glanced sideways but decided not to respond.

They pulled up outside the restaurant that Cameron co-owned with his cousin Julian. Julian managed it and was happy to host the celebrations this evening.

The tables lined the edge of the restaurant, leaving a large area in the middle for everyone to mingle.

'Good evening, ladies. Looking stunning as ever.' Julian greeted them at the door, kissing them each on the cheek as they entered. 'The champagne is over there; help yourselves.'

Lucy looked around as Sarah handed out the glasses of champagne. Imogen and Cameron's family had arrived and were happily chatting to each other; The air was filled with excitement. Everyone was glad of the excuse to put the past behind them and celebrate Cameron's recovery.

'I don't see Imogen or Cameron yet,' said Lucy, looking around while absentmindedly sipping at her champagne. The bubbles eased her nerves as they settled in her stomach.

Sarah bumped her shoulder into Lucy's. 'By that, do you mean you don't see Tom yet? Don't worry, he'll be here soon enough. He had to sort things out at the club before he left.'

Jess looked between Lucy and her glass and said, 'Either you're nervous or the evaporation rate is high in here.' Lucy's glass was already empty.

Lucy released a nervous laugh. 'I'm fine, just thirsty.'

Jess stepped closer and lowered her voice. 'You don't need to pretend around me. This is your first night out since you went through some serious shit. I'd be downing the fizz like there's no tomorrow if I were you.'

She was grateful for Jess's words of encouragement; she didn't feel the need to pretend to be okay around her.

'Everyone keeps telling me to get myself back out there and move on, but I just don't think I'm ready. I'm not as confident as I look. How can I ever learn to trust a man again? Andrew cheated on me. The night I dumped him, he was late getting to mine because he was shagging his bit on the side. And, well, we know all about what happened with Mark. I'm sure Tom is great, but why on earth would he like me? I've nothing to offer him. He's older than me, lives in London and owns his own club. What can I possibly offer him?' Her face fell. Thankfully, Sarah was deep in conversation with Imogen's sister. Lucy felt more comfortable sharing her anxiety with Jess.

'Oh, Hun. I didn't know Andrew cheated on you. What a total cock-womble. None of this reflects on you. You've had some shit luck with men, or should I say boys. You don't have to pretend to be anything with Tom. He's just a guy that met you in a club and liked what he saw. That's it. I don't think you have anything to worry about. Tom knows what you've been through, and he's still asking after you. I don't think he'll mind if you want to take it slow. Don't you think it's a good sign that he's given you space after everything that's happened but is now trying to reconnect?'

'Maybe,' said Lucy as she shrugged, unease settling in her stomach again.

'Just be open and honest with him. If it turns out he's not right for you, then we'll cross that bridge when we get to it.' She suddenly paused; her attention focused on the entrance. 'Don't look, but he just arrived.'

'Oh, god. What do I do?' Lucy looked for a hole to swallow her up, but she was shit out of luck.

'Just be yourself,' said Jess reassuringly.

'What's he doing?'

'He's chatting to Cameron's mum, Liz.'

'So, he's good with mums then. I'm going to get another drink. Do you want one?'

Lucy walked as calmly as possible over to the table of drinks. She felt eyes on her, boring into her and heating her to the core. Taking a chance, she looked over as Tom was tracking her movements while nodding along to whatever Liz was saying to him. She smiled at him but remained on her path back to Jess.

As soon as she reached her, Jess said, 'Have you noticed he can't take his eyes off you?'

'Don't. I don't want to get ahead of myself. He's probably wondering if I'm going to stab anyone tonight.' She tried to laugh off the joke, but it caught in her throat.

Excited clapping interrupted their conversation as Cameron and Imogen walked through the door.

Cameron's appearance didn't reflect the trauma he'd suffered only six weeks ago. He looked effortlessly stylish in his navy-blue chinos, crisp white shirt and tan leather shoes. With his olive-toned skin, dark hair, and stubble, you would think he was Italian. He and Imogen made a beautiful couple.

Lucy hung back as everyone crowded around them. Cameron didn't need her adding to the queue of people waiting to hug him.

'Where's Lucy?' Cameron's deep voice carried over the crowd. 'Ah, here she is. Come here.' His arms wrapped around her in a tight embrace as he spoke only to her. 'Thank you. I can never repay you for what you did for us, but if there's ever anything you need, let me know and I'll move heaven and earth to help you.'

'Thank you, but I did what anyone in that situation would have done,' said Lucy, tucking some hair nervously behind her ear.

Cameron furrowed his brow as he said, 'I'm not so sure about that. Regardless of whether you agree, I think you're one amazing woman. A force to be reckoned with, and don't you forget it.'

She could feel her cheeks glow at his kind words and was grateful when Julian announced the buffet was ready, as everyone turned their attention to the tables of delicious finger food.

Cameron patted his perfectly flat stomach. 'Excellent. I need to eat something. Not drinking for six weeks has seriously damaged my ability to cope with alcohol. I'll see you later.' Cameron stalked off to the buffet table, stopping to chat to well-wishers on his way.

She wasn't feeling hungry, thanks to the butterflies occupying her stomach, but she needed to eat something to soak up the champagne. As she turned, a broad chest promptly halted her in her tracks.

'Hello.' His deep voice was strong and sensual. With that one word, she could feel her body responding.

She slowly brought her eyes up to meet his. In this light, she wasn't sure if they were green or grey, but either way, her core fluttered in an unfamiliar way.

She swallowed her desire down. 'Hi, Tom.' She tried to remain calm, but her voice faltered.

His eyes didn't leave hers as he said, 'How have you been?'

Her gaze wandered to his mouth as she imagined biting down on his bottom lip. She blinked away her thoughts, shocked at where they'd come from. 'Not too bad, thank you. It was rough at first, but once the gossiping died down, I could move on.'

He took a swig of his drink and nodded. 'I'm sorry I've not been in touch. I figured you'd need some time to get over what happened. You certainly didn't need me pestering you.' He paused, still not looking away from her face. 'You look beautiful.'

Keeping her head down, she looked up at him through her lashes. 'Oh, I don't know about that, but thank you.' Her eyes roamed over his light blue shirt that was open at the collar and tucked into his dark blue jeans. The cut of it emphasised his broad shoulders, enticing her to stroke them. Her hands itched to touch him. She stuffed her free hand into her pocket, reminding herself to play it cool.

His eyes darkened, his voice more commanding. 'When I say you're beautiful, I mean it, Lucy.' His authoritative tone left no room for further argument, and her body flushed in response.

James slapped an arm around Tom's shoulder, saving her from responding. 'Tom, mate, how the fuck are you?'

Tom's smile was wide as he greeted his friend. 'James, good to see you. I'm good, thanks. The club is keeping me busy, but I can't complain. How're you?'

Lucy used the interruption to try to sneak away. Her reaction to seeing Tom in the flesh had shocked her. She wasn't ready to process her feelings, but the chink-chink of metal on glass stopped her in her tracks. Cameron was standing at the front of the room.

'Everyone, can I please have your attention for a few moments?'

The room fell silent as everyone's attention turned to him.

'I'd like to take this opportunity to thank you all for coming. As you know, Imogen and I have had a rough few weeks and we couldn't have got through it without you all, so thank you. And if it wasn't for Lucy and James, I might not have been here at all.' His voice was gravelly and laced with emotion.

Lucy's heart rate increased as a feeling of anxiety washed over her. She didn't want everyone looking at her, but they were. Her face reddened as she took a few steps backwards, trying to blend into the wall behind her.

Tom must have noticed a change in her as he side-stepped towards her, his shoulder pressing lightly into hers. She instantly felt safer and at ease, as if he was a protective wall around her.

'Please, raise your glass in a toast to the best of friends,' said Cameron as he raised his glass before placing it on the table.

Lucy was relieved when Cameron continued to speak, but this time to Imogen as he bent down on one knee.

'Imogen Taylor, will you do me the honour of allowing me to worship you, care for you and protect you for as long as we both shall live?' His features were full of longing for the woman in front of him.

Lucy's breath caught, her hand flying up to her chest. 'Oh, my goodness, that's so romantic,' she whispered. A tear of delight slipped from her eye.

'Hey, I hope that's a tear of happiness. I'd hate it if you were crying over Cameron being off the market.' Tom wiped the tear away with his thumb, his eyes burning into her soul. The intimate gesture left a trail of heat across her cheek. Her breath hitched as she regained her composure.

'I'm so happy for Imogen. She deserves to have someone worship her the way Cameron does. I can't imagine how that feels.'

Great way to sound like a loser, Lucy. So much for playing it cool, she chastised herself, looking at the floor.

'I can't believe you've never been worshipped.' His words washed over her, weakening her resolve to stay away from men. She lifted her gaze from the floor, her eyes meeting his, as flames danced across her skin.

He took a tentative step closer, reaching up as if to touch her, but something stopped him and he moved his hand away, opting to run his fingers through his hair.

Her skin had come alive at the prospect of his touch. She was drawn to him in a way she'd never experienced. She was north; he was south; their magnetism too strong to resist, but she was determined to try.

'Well, believe it. My experience so far is that men are arseholes.' She quickly brought her hand to her mouth before mumbling through her fingers. 'I'm sorry, I shouldn't have said that. I'm not saying you're an arsehole.'

Her wide eyes met his smile as he brought his glass to his mouth. He took a long, deliberate swig of his drink. 'I'd love the opportunity to show you we aren't all arseholes.'

Lucy didn't know how to respond. A thousand thoughts and feelings bombarded her, making her dizzy. Or was that the champagne? She wasn't sure. She released a deep breath while she contemplated how to tackle this.

'I'd like that, one day. Hopefully soon.' What was she going to do? Be single and alone forever? She didn't want that, but she couldn't see herself trusting someone again, especially so soon. She thought she could trust Andrew, and he proved her wrong. She needed time to rebuild herself and only then could she allow anyone else in.

'I'll be here. Waiting.' His eyes were so intense she wanted to fall into them. She needed to move away before all her plans went to shit.

With perfect timing, Sarah tugged on Lucy's arm. 'Come on sexy, I want to dance.' She was dragged onto the makeshift dance floor and engulfed by the crowd of women, all high on fizz and love. Imogen was in the centre flashing her engagement ring as Beyoncé's voice rang out with the words to Single Ladies from the speakers.

'I hope I wasn't interrupting anything?' Sarah was now whisper-shouting in her ear.

'You were, but I'm glad about the interruption. I'm not ready for anything now, but Tom's so bloody hot that my body was turning to mush around him.'

'You did look like a fish out of water. Let him work for it.' Jess promptly thrusted another glass of fizz into their hands as she made her way into the circle.

Lucy couldn't help but glance over to where Tom was standing, chatting with his friends. Her determination to stay away decreased as her blood/alcohol level increased. The music slowed, and people coupled off around her, which was her cue to grab a large glass of water and freshen up.

Her cheeks were flushed, and her brow glistened with sweat as she stood at the sink in the ladies' toilets.

She dabbed a damp paper towel across her face and around her neck, the air from the open window cooling her damp skin. She felt giddy from the champagne, steadying herself on the sink before straightening up and giving herself a pep talk.

Stay away from Tom. You're not ready to get involved with someone that can ooze that level of sex appeal. Stay away from Tom.

As she walked back into the restaurant, she opted to stand at the edge of the room, nursing her glass of water.

'You're too special to be hiding away in the corner.' Her breath caught in her throat as Tom stood before her, his piercing eyes on her again.

'Thank you; you're very kind.' She knew not to argue this time, and truthfully, she reacted well to the praise.

'No, I'm not. I just say it as I see it, and I see you.'

'Do you? Do you think you really see me?' She doubted he could really see what went on inside her mind. She hoped he couldn't.

He lowered himself, fixing her with a determined stare. 'I see a beautiful woman who's hurting and let down by the men in her past. I also see a strong woman who won't take anyone's shit. You've had to deal with things I wouldn't wish on anyone.'

She looked at the floor, unsure of herself. With his finger barely touching her chin, he gently encouraged her gaze upwards until their eyes met. As he caught his bottom lip between his teeth, it took all her willpower not to swoon. Everything about this man screamed pure sex. Part of her couldn't wait to discover what he offered, but a nagging voice in the depths of her brain was telling her she couldn't handle him. She could never satisfy someone like him. It wouldn't be long before he realised she was just a stupid little girl and ditch her.

Before she could step away, he closed his eyes and brought his lips down to meet hers. The kiss was gentle perfection, erasing the memory of those that came before.

He pulled away a fraction, his eyes seeking permission for more. Lucy tilted her chin up, giving him the answer he needed. His hand tenderly cupped the side of her face as he kissed her hungrily, his tongue slipping into her mouth.

His soft growl spurred her on, flicking a switch inside her. It was like she'd never been kissed before; she'd never felt so desired. Their tongues explored each other before he pulled away, breaking the kiss. His forehead resting against hers.

'I've thought about this moment since I first met you, and it didn't disappoint. You're perfect.'

'Really?'

'Yes. I watched you that night in my club, and I desperately wanted to dance with you, to feel your body pressed up against mine. Unfortunately, I had my hands full with some unsavoury visitors to the club—I believe Imogen and Sarah ran into one of them on the dance floor. Then, of course, Mark showed up. But let's not talk about that; I want to focus on you.'

'I had no idea.' She looked away, embarrassment overcoming her.

'What's wrong?' he said, resting a hand on her shoulder.

'I'd never think that someone like you would want me.' Her cheeks flushed with the admission, but she may as well be honest with him; she had nothing to lose.

'Perhaps that's why I'm drawn to you, because of your unassuming beauty. I'm surrounded by women every night who hide behind expensive dresses and a mask of makeup. They spend their evening parading around on display, there for the benefit of the men with more money than morals. I see it every night. Then you crossed my path, and I've been thinking about you ever since. It took all my strength not to come and see you, but you needed time to heal, and I would have complicated matters.'

'I don't know what to say.' She shook her head in disbelief.

'You don't need to say anything. I only want you to know how I feel about you. I don't play games, Lucy.'

Was this really happening? Or would she turn into a pumpkin at midnight?

Tom nodded his head over his shoulder. 'Without sounding like a teenager at the school disco, could we get some fresh air? There's a set of eyes burning a hole in me.'

Lucy looked around as Sarah raised her glass in a toast, her eyebrows wiggling suggestively. Lucy blushed, her hands quickly hiding her face. 'Yes, let's get away from prying eyes.'

It was a beautiful clear evening, with not a cloud in the starlit sky. Lucy shivered as the evening air cooled her flushed skin. Tom wrapped his arm around her, pulling her close.

They were in the restaurant's garden, an enchanting setting surrounded by weeping willow trees, their branches skimming the surface of the river. They walked arm in arm along the riverbank, coming to a stop under the branches of a tree. He wrapped her in his arms, and their lips met, instantly picking up where they'd left off. It felt so natural to be in his arms, and her body responded to his touch instantly. Her nipples strained against her bra, and her core burned for him. She squeezed her thighs together, seeking relief from her aching need. Just as she thought she'd reached the peak of sexual desire, he groaned, low and deep. The vibrations were almost enough to set her off like a firework.

His words broke the spell as he pulled away and said, 'I can't do this.'

Panic hit Lucy as her body shut down. 'What do you mean?' Had he already realised she wasn't enough?

'I'm trying so hard to take this slowly. I don't want to rush you, but—how do I put this politely?' He sighed, running his fingers through his hair.

She straightened her spine, ready for the disappointment. 'Don't. Just tell me straight.' She took a step back, distancing herself.

She watched as he tried to find the words, his jaw clenching. He sighed a breath of resignation and said, 'Not actively fucking you right now, right here, is causing me pain. I wish I wore looser jeans this evening.'

'Oh!' She wasn't expecting that.

'Yeah. I usually have more self-control, but I find it lacking around you.' Lucy could see his chest heaving and could hear the strain in his voice. How much should she tell him? Should she admit she'd never felt like this before? That her level of desire was off the charts, but she had no idea what she was doing or even if she was ready to be doing anything about it at all? Or that these unfamiliar feelings were so strong that they scared the shit out of her. Her resolve to avoid men was crumbling with every second that she was in his presence; her weakness was betraying her. No good could come from this. If she let him in now, she wouldn't survive the fallout when it inevitably ended.

Instead, she said, 'I don't really know what to say to that.'

'I'm sorry. I shouldn't have come on so strong. I can control myself around you. You have nothing to worry about.'

She took another step back, needing to get some distance between them. 'Absolutely. I'm not worried. I'm just not used to the attention.' She looked back up at the restaurant. 'I'd better get back inside before Sarah comes looking for me.'

He nodded in understanding. 'Of course. I'll walk you in.' He took hold of her hand and said, 'I'm not going anywhere. When you're ready to get to know me, I'll be a phone call away. No pressure, no time limits.'

Lucy swallowed down her emotions, smiled, and nodded. A weight lifting from her shoulders.

Dear Diary,

So, tonight was interesting. I saw Tom again. My body does a weird thing whenever he's near me. It did it when I first met him in the club all those months ago. It's what made me decide to end it with Paul/Mark. My body goes all warm. Not warm like someone's turned the heating up, but warm with a tingle. I talk like my body is separate from me, and I feel like it is. My mind is screaming at me to walk away from him. He's a man and therefore I can't trust him. My heart is asking me to protect it. But my body. My traitorous body tingles and glows like it's finally coming alive. I won't mention what was going on in my underwear; it's safe to say I don't need to worry about a drought.

He is unbelievably sexy, though. I'm like a teenager crushing on a member of a boy band. He isn't just divine to look at; he smells amazing. One sniff of him and I was ready to give him everything. How is that even possible? I wonder if it's his pheromones. I've heard about them but certainly never experienced them. Andrew had a smell, but it wasn't a pleasant one. Oh, and his eyes. I could gaze at them all night.

Bloody hell. I'm supposed to be mature and strong and yet I'm lusting after a man I barely know—who is way out of my league—like some sort of hormonal teenager. Maybe that's what it is, just my hormones being pesky.

I don't know what to do. Do I risk my heart again and go along with whatever this could be? Or do I add a few more layers to the stone wall?

CHAPTER 6

LUCY

Free yourself – Jesse Ware

'Are you going to fill us in on what happened with Thor or keep us in suspense?' Sarah was leaning on the sticky, dark wood table of their local pub, eyes boring into Lucy.

It was Tuesday night and Sarah, Lucy, Imogen, and Jess were meeting for their weekly book club. Lucy had avoided all talk of what had happened with Tom while they'd been at work—talk of Imogen and Cameron's engagement had provided enough of a distraction.

Jess looked confused as she said, 'Who's Thor?'

'Don't you think Tom looks like Chris Hemsworth when he plays Thor? Not the long-haired version, but after he gets his hair cut and looks sexy AF.'

Imogen piped up as she said, 'Oh, you're right. He does. I wonder if he has a massive hammer too?'

Lucy cringed into her hands. 'You're sounding like Sarah.'

Sarah looked shocked as she said, 'Hey, what's that supposed to mean?'

Jess laughed as she turned to face Sarah. 'I think what she means is that she's sounding like a cock-obsessed smut-whore.'

Sarah plastered her face with mock horror. 'Takes one to know one. In fact, that's given me an idea for what I'm going to get printed onto our T-shirts for the hen party.'

Imogen nearly spat out her gin and tonic as she said, 'You'd better not. Actually, we need to talk about the hen party. I know I asked you to be in charge, Sarah, but Cameron had an idea and I really like it.'

'Why do I feel like I won't like this?'

'You will, I promise. You'll still be in charge of entertainment.'

'Okay.' Sarah looked sceptical but remained silent, allowing Imogen to elaborate. Lucy sat in silence, glad that the conversation had gone elsewhere.

'Cameron's a little uneasy about us all going off and doing anything too crazy. I think it'll take him a while to shake the feeling that he should've stopped Mark before, well, you know.' She gave Lucy's hand a little squeeze before carrying on. 'So, he's found a country manor big enough for all of us.'

Sarah's face fell. 'Are you telling us he wants to have a combined hen and stag weekend? That sounds like a terrible idea. What do you two think? Lucy, how do you feel about it?'

She took a large gulp of her white wine before placing it back on the soggy cardboard beer mat, wondering why Sarah had singled her out. 'I'm not sure. I understand why Cameron feels that way. If I'm being honest, I'm a little nervous about getting back out there and partying, so it's nice to know they aren't far away if we need them. Not that we'll need them. We won't be doing stuff with them all the time, will we? I was looking forward to girly time.'

Jess then added, 'I'm okay with it if we do our own thing and you're not allowed to share a room with them. I'm not going away for a hen party and spending every evening listening to you and Sarah having crazy animal sex with your men.'

Sarah laughed as she said, 'I do not have crazy animal sex. And anyway, that isn't a problem, as James and I seem to have cooled off a bit. Sharing a room with Jess is my preference, and no, I don't want to talk about it.'

Lucy nodded her agreement. 'I agree. No bedroom sharing, as that won't be fair to Jess or me.'

Imogen looked torn as she agreed. 'Okay, Lucy and I will share a room. Sarah and Jess can share a room. We'll leave the boys to sort themselves out. Sarah, you can organise our entertainment for the weekend. We travel up on the Friday and come back Sunday night. I'll tell Cameron that we've agreed, and I'll give him our terms. Are we all okay with that?'

They all nodded.

Sarah turned to Lucy and said, 'We've not forgotten about you and the god that is Tom. So come on, spill the beans.'

'I thought I'd got away with that, damn you. There isn't anything to tell. He likes me, and he's going to wait for when I'm ready to get to know him more. Now, can we plan the next book, please? This is a book club, after all, and I haven't read a single piece of smut since I joined.'

After they'd all agreed on the next book, talk turned back to the hen party.

Imogen picked at her drinks mat as she said, 'Are you sure you guys are okay with sharing accommodation with the boys?'

Sarah's tone was a lot more positive as she said, 'Yep, don't worry, I think we can make it work. On the plus side, we get to eat more of Cameron's cooking. I bet his cooked breakfasts are to die for, and we're going to need those. It means I'll have to cancel my plans for a naked butler, though.'

'Oh, that's a shame. Maybe we could convince the boys to take the role?' Jess wiggled her eyebrows while trying to keep a straight face.

'Yeah, I'm sure they'd love that.' Imogen didn't look convinced.

The next two weeks were uneventful. Lucy kept busy on the Walter and Holmes project. She got the impression James had picked up on her need to stay busy, as he'd given her a few smaller projects and dragged her to every meeting he had with clients, using training as an excuse. Not that she wasn't complaining; keeping her mind busy kept away the nagging doubts and shadows.

Sarah closed down her computer and joined the others at the entrance to the office. 'Ladies, are you ready for a fantastic weekend?' They'd all booked the afternoon off work, and Jess had met them at their office. Imogen had Cameron's car, as it was large enough for all of them and their bags. They'd meet the men there later.

Imogen bounced up and down as she said, 'I'm so excited! I can't believe we're about to go to *my* hen party. It all feels so surreal.'

They loaded their bags into the car and Imogen programmed the address of the country manor into the sat-nav. Sarah plugged her phone into the car and turned up the volume as music blared from the speakers.

'I've put a party playlist together, and don't worry, there is something for everyone.'

'You're so thoughtful. Do you mind if I turn it down a bit, though? I need to hear the instructions from the sat-nav.' Imogen pressed a button on the steering wheel and the volume lowered to a more bearable level.

'Okay, have you all packed your gym gear as instructed?' Sarah twisted round to face Lucy and Jess in the back.

They both nodded as Jess said, 'Yes, but I hope your idea of entertainment isn't going to the gym.'

'Nope. I put a lot of thought into what we'd all need to make sure we enjoy this weekend. It's been quite a stressful time as of late.' They nodded as Sarah carried on speaking. 'And so, I have arranged for us to have a private yoga session. I had a good chat with Georgina—that's our yogi—and she has put together a session for us that will help relax us and move on spiritually, she's coming to us, so we don't even have to leave the manor.'

Sarah turned to Imogen as she said, 'Imogen, the next chapter of your life should be free from the demons of your past.' She then turned to Lucy. 'And Lucy, I want you to find some inner peace and strength so that you can write yourself a happier and sexy next chapter, hopefully with Thor. And Jess, we need a couple of hours working on hip flexes as we're not getting any younger and we need to keep ourselves primed and ready to go.'

They all looked stunned as they stared at Sarah, Imogen being careful to keep her eyes on the road.

Lucy swallowed the lump in her throat as she said, 'I don't know what to say, Sarah. That is so thoughtful.'

'Yeah, thanks, Hun. I don't know what to say. I was expecting a lot of inflatable cocks, but this is what we need,' added Imogen.

Sarah had a glint in her eye as she said, 'Don't worry, the inflatables come later.'

They all laughed before the excited chatter of wedding plans took over. Two hours later, they pulled up to a magnificent country manor in the heart of the Oxfordshire countryside.

Sarah let out a low whistle, her nose pressed against the car window. 'Holy crap. The photos did not do it justice. It's stunning.'

The tyres crunched on the gravel as Imogen parked the car up outside the front of the sprawling manor.

Lucy climbed out, stretching her limbs and gazing up at the impressive frontage of their home for the weekend. 'This must have cost a fortune. Is Cameron sure he doesn't want us to pay anything towards it?'

Imogen shook her head as she said, 'He wanted to treat. It's his way of thanking us for humouring him and compromising. Plus, he got mates rates on it as he knows the owner.'

Jess was unloading the bags as she shouted from the back of the car. 'Ladies, stop gawking at the house and come and help me with the bags. Are you guys planning to stay here for two weeks?' She let out an exaggerated huff as she dropped a bag on the ground. 'Bloody hell, Sarah, what on earth have you packed?'

'Wouldn't you like to know?' said Sarah, tapping the side of her nose.

Lucy was standing at the front door 'Do you have a key, Jen?'

Imogen joined Lucy at the front door. 'There's a key safe somewhere near here.' She was holding a piece of paper with the code to the safe written on it. 'Here we go. I'll leave the spare in here so Tom can let himself in when he gets here.'

'Oh, is Tom not coming up with the boys?' Lucy's heart began racing at the mention of his name. She'd tried to block out the thought of staying with him for the entire weekend—if she thought about it too much, the butterflies in her stomach made her feel queasy.

'He's going to drive up when he can, but that won't be until the early hours of the morning,' said Imogen as she opened the front door.

The familiar butterflies formed in her stomach, so she took some steadying breaths as Imogen opened up the large wooden doors.

'Oh wow, this place is amazing.' Lucy couldn't believe she'd be staying here for the weekend. The dark wood floor was glossy with layers of polish, and the air smelt of lavender and roses. She felt like she'd walked into the set of a historical romance movie.

'Cam said there are eight bedrooms, so we get one each. Take your pick, ladies.'

Jess dropped her bags down as she took in her surroundings. 'We'll still end up sharing. Knowing Sarah, she'll fall asleep in my bed when she gets too drunk.'

'That would be offensive if it wasn't true,' laughed Sarah.

They made their way up the sweeping curved staircase and inspected the rooms along what felt like never-ending corridors. They settled on rooms that were at the far end of the house as they connected to a large living area filled with comfortable sofas and an enormous fireplace.

Sarah looked at her watch and announced it was time to get ready for their yoga session.

Lucy met the others in the large kitchen where Sarah had poured them all glasses of champagne.

'Here you go, Lucy, get this down you before we start. Georgina will be here soon, and I reckon we need a head start on our way to relaxation.' Sarah raised her glass as she said, 'Imogen, we raise our glasses to you. You're an inspiration to us, as you've taught us a valuable lesson. You realised you deserved better, and you did everything you could to find it. If you fight for a better future, you'll find one.'

There wasn't a dry eye in the house.

'I believe there's a soul mate for everyone, and you've found yours. Let's hope the rest of us can find ours, and that they're as hot as Cameron, 'cause girl, you have landed on your feet with that one.'

In true Sarah style, she ended with some humour. The others laughed as they wiped their eyes and downed their drinks just as the doorbell rang out across the house.

CHAPTER 7

LUCY

Honest – Kyndal Inskeep & Song House

'Everyone, this is Georgina.' Sarah answered the door and showed the yoga instructor through to the kitchen. They all welcomed her and introduced themselves. Large bags of rolled-up yoga mats, blocks and straps were hooked over both of her arms.

'Good afternoon, ladies. Thank you so much for welcoming me into your celebrations.' Georgina was naturally beautiful. Her face glowed without the aid of layers of makeup. Her blond hair sat just below her chin with a simple clip holding it away from her face.

Sarah said, 'We're all looking forward to your class. Where should we set up?'

Georgina looked through the large French doors that led from the kitchen onto a spacious patio area and a perfectly manicured lawn. 'I'd like to start with grounding, where we'll walk barefoot outside, and then we need a room big enough for us to form a circle with our mats.' She glanced around at her surroundings before saying, 'I suspect we'll have plenty of places to choose from in this magnificent home. Do you mind if I take a moment to walk around and find the perfect location?'

'Please, go right ahead. Can I get you anything to drink?' Sarah offered.

'No, thank you. I'll go off hunting while you ladies prepare for some grounding.' She strolled out of the kitchen, taking in her surroundings.

Lucy looked at Sarah. 'She's like some sort of graceful goddess. Where on earth did you find her?'

Sarah shrugged. 'Google.'

They all giggled as they removed their trainers and socks and waited for Georgina to return.

'Okay ladies, I've found the perfect room down the hall, and I'm set up and ready to go. Good, I see you're all ready for your grounding. First, let me talk you through what we're going to do today. Sarah explained that this is your hen party, Imogen. Many congratulations on your upcoming nuptials. May your future together be full of love and peace.' Georgina bowed her head.

'Thank you,' said Imogen, mirroring Georgina's movements.

'Sarah also explained that the path to true love was not smooth, and that, Lucy, you were also involved in some rather traumatic events. I've designed a yoga session that will work through all the chakras, starting at the root and ending at the crown. We'll then move on to targeted breath work and meditation.'

She took a deep breath. 'The goal will be to start you on the path to unblocking chakras and allowing your kundalini energy to flow from your root to your crown. Please remember a kundalini awakening isn't the goal, but you can achieve it if you take this practice into your lives.'

Sarah released a snort. 'A kundalini awakening sounds like something I've experienced a few times before in the bedroom.'

The others rolled their eyes as Georgina smiled kindly. 'It sounds like something sexual, doesn't it? And you're not far wrong. It's your everything. Everything you think, everything you remember, visualise and everything that you are. When you awaken your kundalini, you might experience pleasurable sensations such as full-body orgasms, but that's not the only benefit.'

All their eyes widened at the thought of a full-body orgasm, but they remained silent, waiting to hear the other benefits.

'There are many signs you can spot when you awaken your kundalini, and I feel that some may be more relevant to you than others. You'll become able to feel love and compassion towards yourself as well as all that is.' She turned her attention to Lucy as she spoke, her eyes warm, giving the impression she could see into Lucy's inner thoughts and feelings.

'Old problems and traumas will no longer have the same effect on you. You'll remember them, but they'll no longer bother you.'

Lucy and Imogen shifted on their feet and exchanged glances. A feeling of unease crept over Lucy. She got the impression this session wouldn't be a few downward-facing dogs and chanting, and she wasn't sure this was the time or place to face her demons.

As if sensing her feeling of unease, Georgina said, 'This is a safe place. What we do today may bring out powerful emotions in you all. Old wounds may open, and feelings long forgotten may resurface. Let it all out, you'll feel better. I won't bore you with all the information, but one other benefit is newfound strength and clarity. This allows you to change your life without fear. I am so happy that I can start you on your way to enlightenment.'

Jess was wide-eyed as she said, 'Wow, this sounds like it's going to be the start of an amazing journey.'

Georgina's introduction hadn't convinced Lucy, but she nodded along anyway.

Georgina clapped her hands together and said, 'Okay, we're going to start with the root chakra. Let's get outside and do some grounding. The root chakra extends from the base of your spine and continues down your legs to your feet. Connecting to the earth with bare feet is essential to help you feel calm, in control, and present. It's a great way to start your yoga practice, so try to continue this at home.'

They all grabbed jackets and made their way outside into the crisp winter air.

'We'll start by standing still, close your eyes and feel your feet grounding into the earth beneath you. Try to avoid any fox poo though, that won't make you feel calm. Stand tall, shoulders back and down. Lucy, your shoulders are around your ears.' Georgina walked up behind her and gently pressed her hands onto her shoulders. 'There we go. That's where they should be.'

Lucy instantly felt better and quietly said, 'Thank you.'

'Now, drop your hands to your sides and turn your palms to face forwards. Take a moment here to breathe deeply. Deep, full breath in and a slow exhale. Repeat this until I say otherwise. No peaking, Sarah,' said Georgina as she gave Sarah a wink.

Sarah giggled as she said, 'Busted.'

After what felt like ages, but was only a minute, they heard music coming from the centre of the circle they'd formed.

'Feel the music. Let it wash over you and loosen your limbs. Let's dance, ladies, in whatever way your body chooses.'

Georgina stepped from side to side, swinging her hips and swaying her arms. The others looked at each other like she'd gone mad, but Jess shrugged her shoulders, closed her eyes, and copied the movements. The others followed suit and soon, they were all prancing around the garden to instrumental music.

When the song ended, Georgina announced it was time to take the session indoors and down onto the mats.

They made their way to a gloriously bright room where the outer walls and ceiling were glass. The bright sunshine had warmed the room, and it felt like being outside without the chilly breeze. Georgina had moved the furniture to the side, and four yoga mats formed a semi-circle, pointing inwards to what they assumed was Georgina's mat so they could all see her clearly.

'Choose a mat, ladies, and take a seat.'

They all took their places.

'We're going to carry on our work on each of your chakras with specific postures that will, in time, unblock them and allow your energy to flow. I'll talk you through them as we go, okay? Is everyone happy to start?'

Lucy desperately wanted to say no. Breaking down walls she'd spent the last few weeks building didn't sound like something she wanted to do. Perhaps it was time to trust her friends with her vulnerability.

'We're going to start in a standing position, so please stand and face me. Come to the front of your mats.'

A quiet calmness came over the room as they waited for the next instruction. Georgina tapped on her phone and gentle spa-like music played quietly from the corner of the room.

'We're going to finish the root chakra with the tree pose, watch me and then follow suit.'

Georgina talked them through the pose and explained how it would enhance their feeling of grounding. While they were all standing on one leg, trying their best not to fall over, Georgina said, 'Imogen, I believe your root is open as you found the strength and confidence to stand on your own two feet and have withstood a good many challenges as of late. Would you agree?'

'Oh, I suppose that's right, yes. I do feel more confident,' said Imogen, with a pleased look on her face.

Lucy wished she did. Her heart sank. Imogen had survived so much more than her, and yet here she was, happy and with an open root, whatever that really meant.

'Let's move on.' Georgina talked them through a downward-facing dog before they came to a seated position. They learned that the next chakra was the sacral chakra.

'We link the sacral chakra to our emotions, creativity, and sexual energy. I'm assuming you're all interested in removing any blockages here.' Her smile reached her eyes as she guided them into the butterfly pose that opened their hips. 'If you feel you've lost control of your life, it could be because of a blockage in this chakra.'

'Or it could be parents that refuse to let you live your own life,' said Jess, harshly. Everyone looked over at her in surprise. 'Sorry. Control over my life is a sore spot. Carry on.'

Sarah gave her friend a concerned glance, but they carried on regardless.

They strained as they took up the plank position, Georgina reminding them to breathe. 'This posture will open your solar plexus chakra, which is linked to feelings of self-worth, self-esteem, and self-confidence. A blockage here will feel like you have an overwhelming feeling of shame and self-doubt.' Once again, she glanced over at Lucy.

What has Sarah told this woman? This is getting spooky. I'm sure she can see right through me. Lucy's inner voice was in overdrive while she kept her expression neutral.

'And ladies, when you feel butterflies in your stomach, that is your solar plexus chakra giving you a hint. Trust your gut ladies, it knows what it's doing.'

Before long, all four of them were panting, groaning, and shaking with the strain of staying in the plank position.

'Okay ladies, lower down into the child's pose and take a moment. Deep breath in and a slow exhale. We'll be moving onto the heart chakra next, and this chakra is the bridge between the lower chakras—that are more materialistic—and the upper chakras that are more spiritual.'

As Lucy crouched into a child's pose, she felt a wave of strong emotions wash over her. They'd been moving at a steady pace, and yet she had never felt so still. Her mind was used to being busy, planning the next day's outfit, thinking up the next flavour combination for the next batch of cupcakes or engrossed in work. Occasionally, she let herself fantasize about Tom when her world went quiet and dark, and she was alone.

The music reverberated through her soul, and the deep breathing was almost hypnotising. She could feel her defences crumbling, brick by fragile brick. The sound of Georgina's voice instructing them to move into the next posture interrupted her thoughts.

'The heart chakra usually develops between the ages of twenty-one and twenty-eight, so this is a time for you all to pay attention. I'm going to show you the camel pose, not to be confused with the camel toe.' Sarah released a snort as the others smiled.

They found themselves on their knees, leaning backwards, their hands on their heels. 'You must remember to breathe; if you're struggling to maintain a steady breathing pace, then please bring yourself upright and place your hands on your hips instead of on your heels.'

Of course, no-one wanted to admit defeat, so they stayed in their current position, forcing air in and out of their lungs.

'You can't truly love another until you can love yourself. An open heart chakra will allow you to cope with the fear of rejection and allow you to accept the love from others. Look after your hearts, ladies, they are precious.'

Lucy noticed all eyes turned to Sarah, expecting a rude joke about self-love, but she was strangely quiet on the subject.

Next up was the throat chakra. This involved them on all fours, flexing their back in a cat-cow posture.

'The throat gives your heart its voice. When you unblock these chakras, you'll be able to communicate with your loved ones, tell them your desires, and allow them to join you on your journey. To bring this chakra into your everyday life, sing along to your favourite song while you drive to work or cook your dinner. Use your voice, do not be afraid to express yourselves. No harm will come from telling your lover what brings you joy. Am I right?'

This time, Sarah didn't disappoint when she burst out laughing and in between snorts said, 'Too true, like harder, faster, and deeper, for example.'

They all had to contain their laughter as they moved back into a child's pose, their foreheads resting on the backs of their hands as Georgina spoke about the third-eye chakra and how it wouldn't finish developing until they were in their early forties.

Sarah looked incredulous as she said, 'Hang on, is that why women in their early forties get really horny? If all your chakras aren't fully developed until later in life, then surely your kundalini energy can't properly flow.' She came out of her child's pose, pointing her finger excitedly. 'So, you don't unlock your full potential until you're in your forties. Well, that's something to look forward to.'

'Yes, Sarah. If you enjoy sex now, just imagine how good it can be when you reach a higher level of spirituality. On that note, let us take a seat with crossed legs, and begin on the final chakra; the crown.'

They worked on breathing and curling their tongues into the backs of their mouths as Georgina explained that the best way to unblock the crown is to combine the root, throat and third-eye postures into one sequence.

They remained in their seated position as they seamlessly began a guided meditation. The music volume lowered as they closed their eyes and listened to the calming voice of their instructor.

As they worked their way up from root to crown, Lucy felt her body relax. As they reached the heart chakra, her defences crumbled at the mantra.

'May I feel safe. May I feel healthy. May I feel joyful. May I know love.' A single, silent tear fell from Lucy's eye and tracked down her cheek.

Georgina spoke again, 'I'd now like you to visualise someone in your life that you love or appreciate and wish they feel all of those things too.' She gave them a minute to repeat the mantra in their heads until she gave them their next instruction.

'Now, please, repeat that process, but with someone you've had conflict with. It will help you find closure and move on.'

Lucy couldn't decide. Could she direct her wishes to a man she'd killed? Or should she direct her words of forgiveness to Andrew, a cheating arsehole? Was she ready to move on from that, or was that bitterness keeping her safe from future heartbreak?

She peeked at Imogen, who was on the mat beside her, and discovered that Imogen was glancing over at her, her pained expression mirroring her own.

Imogen silently mouthed the words, 'Are you okay?' at Lucy, and the wall crumbled to dust as the tears streamed.

Georgina must have heard the muffled sob and opened her eyes. She spoke softly to not draw attention to Lucy. 'Ladies, this may be very hard for some of you. To confront your demons and send them on their way is difficult, and I do not expect you to manage it all today. Accept where you get to in your practice and move on. I'd like you all to chant the following words out loud, for all to hear.' She took a deep breath before saying, 'Sat Nam. Sat Nam. Truth is my identity. Say it with me, ladies.'

Repeating the mantra calmed Lucy's emotions and gave her something to focus on. The tears slowed and Lucy quickly wiped them away.

'We are not our fears, emotions, beliefs or our judgements. Please repeat after me; I speak my truth always.'

After they'd repeated the mantra a few times, Georgina chimed a small bell to ring out the end of their practice.

'Thank you for all taking part in today's practice. I wonder if you'd mind entertaining me for a little longer, as I have an idea for an exercise I think you'd all benefit from.'

They all nodded in agreement.

'Fantastic. I'd like you to share how you found the practice and what your life goals are. We are safe here. What you say is not to be discussed with anyone outside of this room. Do you all agree?'

They all spoke in unison. 'Yes.'

'Jess, let's start with you and we'll work our way around.'

Jess cleared her throat before saying, 'I've found this session enlightening. I knew nothing about chakras before today, but it all makes sense now, and I suspect I have a blockage or two. My life goals and dreams?' she tapped her lip with her finger. 'That's a tricky one. I want the freedom to make my own choices. You spoke earlier about feeling out of control, and that resonated with me. My parents control every aspect of my life and it's suffocating.'

'Ah, Hun. I knew they were heavily involved, but I didn't realise it was that bad.' Sarah looked crestfallen as she spoke.

'It's okay. I'll deal with it. I don't want to talk about it anymore.'

'Okay, Sarah. What about you?' Georgina asked.

'I've also enjoyed this session and I think I'll look for a yoga class when I get back home. I agree with the notion that you have to learn to love yourself before you can love others, so my life goal is to love myself a bit more.'

'Excellent. I can recommend some yogis in your area if you'd like me to email you? Imogen, are you happy to share?'

Imogen nodded and puffed out a deep breath. 'We know who I was forgiving in the meditation. It was difficult to come to terms with, but I've found peace with Mark. I have confidence I can stand on my own two feet, and I can overcome challenges that come my way.' Imogen shrugged. 'What is my goal in life? Without sounding like a knob, I feel like I've achieved everything. I'm so totally in love with a man that loves all of me. My friends are amazing, and I love my job. I hope to be the best mother I can be. My children will be strong and confident in who they are and don't fall victim to the weaknesses of others.' She sat back on her heels and gave herself a nod.

'That's fantastic to hear,' praised Georgina.

Lucy's heart was pounding in her chest so hard she could hear her blood pulsing. She rubbed her hands together as they grew clammy.

'Lucy. I know that was tough. If you feel safe enough to share, I'm sure your friends would love to hear you speak your truths, but we will only go at your pace. So if not, please decline this offer.'

Her lip trembled as she battled with what felt right and what felt necessary. She inhaled a shaky breath and said, 'I'd like to share. Today was hard for me as I usually keep my mind occupied; I don't like where it goes when I let it wander, and today forced my mind to slow down. I've forced myself to put on a brave face. New clothes make me look good, but they don't reflect how I feel. My mantra is *fake it 'til I make it*, and it's not working out so well for me. I don't love myself. Shame, fear, and self-loathing are what I carry. I'm every example of a blocked chakra you could think of. And really, do you blame me?' She took another shaky breath as she swiped her hands angrily under her eyes as more tears fell.

Imogen went to speak, but Georgina held her hand up to stop her. She knew Lucy needed to get this off her chest without interruption.

'My only proper boyfriend cheated on me. To him, I meant nothing but a place to stay. I regret spending my time at university with him because he stopped me from experiencing so much. Maybe if I'd partied more and slept with more men, I wouldn't have been so naïve with Mark?' She hugged her knees into her chest.

'And what can I say about Mark? He tricked me, lied to me. The hurt he caused me went much deeper than the bruises he left behind.' Her expression was full of anguish as she looked at her friends.

'I feel violated. I consented to sleep with Paul, not Mark.' She closed her eyes, resting her forehead on her knees as the tears betrayed her yet again. 'I feel like I'll never trust again, but I desperately want someone to erase the feel of Mark's touch on my skin.' She broke down in front of her friends, her sobs echoing around the room.

Imogen slid next to her, hugging her tightly. 'Shh, shh. It's okay, Lucy. It's going to be okay.' Lucy sobbed in her arms until her tears ran dry.

CHAPTER 8

TOM

Playground – Bru-C

'Alex, are you sure you're okay handling closing up here?' It was late afternoon, and Tom was getting his club ready to open.

'Of course. I can do it more often so you can have a life. If you want one. Go as early as you need to; I know you're itching to see Lucy again.'

'Ha-ha. You're so funny, just remember who pays you every month.' He laughed, but the prospect of seeing Lucy was causing a plethora of feelings in the pit of his stomach and no amount of antacid was getting rid of it.

He knew Alex was very capable, but he wasn't comfortable leaving him to deal with a particular set of customers that were taking liberties at any opportunity, and Alex wouldn't appreciate how important it was to keep them sweet. For now, anyway.

'Yeah, I know. Admit that you've caught feelings for this girl. You've not been to see Kat since the engagement party, and that's saying something.'

'She's not a girl, Alex. She's a woman. It doesn't matter if I see Kat or not, as nothing is going on with her. I run a busy nightclub and don't have time to invest in getting to know women, and I can't stand the thought of using my club to pick up women for one-night stands. That's just tacky. So, I used the services available to me at Kat's club. A man has needs, you know.'

'I get that, I do. If you don't have time for women now, what makes you think you've got time for Lucy?'

Tom didn't have an answer. He rested his elbows on the bar he was stocking, brought his head into his hands and sighed out loud. 'Fuck knows. I just can't stop thinking about her. I've had plenty of women, so many I've lost count—'

'All right, now you're just boasting,' Alex said with a laugh.

'You're quite the comedian today, aren't you?' Tom ran his fingers through his hair, frustration showing. 'When I'm with the women at K's kink club, I'm with them. They have my undivided attention. I get to know every curve, every sensitive spot. I worship their bodies. But the minute we're finished, I'm over it. I don't feel the need to get to know them. I tell myself it's because they deserve a man that can devote himself to them, not just for a few hours a night. But having met Lucy, I think it's because I haven't found the right woman. Until now.'

'Can we just go back to you lasting a few hours? Are you serious? My girlfriend is lucky if I last ten minutes. What's your secret?'

Tom shrugged his shoulders. 'No secret, mate. You've either got it or you haven't.' He straightened up and exhaled. 'Can you stop taking the piss for just one minute? I'm seriously fucked up right now.'

'Yeah, sorry. Look, you've had your fun. Fun for ten men from the sounds of things, and now you're at a point where you want to settle down. It happens to us all.'

'It isn't a good time to bring Lucy into my world. She's been through so much drama; I don't want to add to it.'

'What's so bad about your life? You work unsociable hours, but that doesn't mean you can't pursue something with her.'

'There's more to it than that.'

Alex's eyes narrowed at Tom as he said, 'What are you not telling me? And don't bullshit me; you've been tense for weeks, ever since the Russian's turned up. I know something's going on.'

Tom wasn't sure how much he should tell Alex. He'd worked with him since the club opened and he trusted him, but he didn't want to bring Alex into something that could harm him.

'I'm having to keep a close eye on them. I don't want to drag you into it. They're more than just customers.'

'Listen, I run a tight ship in my casino. If you're entertaining criminals, I deserve to know so I can beat the shit out of you, to beat some sense into you.'

Tom stood taller and puffed out his chest. 'Let's be clear here. This is my casino, and you work for me.'

'And if you want it to stay that way, then tell me what the fuck is going on.' Alex's tone was harsh, any playfulness now long gone.

Realisation hit Tom that he needed to bring his friend into this. Alex could keep his eyes on his target and an ear to the ground. With a deep sigh, he pushed off from the bar. 'Come with me,' he growled.

Alex followed as Tom took the stairs up to his office. Once they were inside, he closed the door and flicked the lock. Alex caught the motion and gave him a questioning stare. 'Just how fucked up is this situation?'

Tom scratched his nails through his stubble as he landed on the chair behind his desk; Alex taking the seat opposite him.

He lowered his voice as he said, 'This must stay between you and me. Is that clear? I'm not playing games here. If I don't handle this situation carefully, people I care about could die.'

CHAPTER 9

LUCY

Pon De Replay ~ Ed Marquis & Emie

Lucy wiped the damp face cloth under her eyes, removing all traces of the mascara that had run down her cheeks.

'Sorry, Lucy. I thought a yoga class would be a good way to relax before the weekend. I'd not considered how it might affect you, and to be honest, I didn't know how powerful yoga could be.' Sarah perched on the vanity unit, watching Lucy as she cleaned herself up.

'Please don't be sorry. It was so thoughtful of you. Have I ruined the weekend?'

'Of course not. There's still an entire weekend ahead of us. We'll have a great time. You're going to have a few drinks, and we can all work on our throat chakras in the club singing our hearts out.'

'I need to drink and boogie.'

'Let's focus on having a good time. When we get home, we'll book into a yoga class and work on unblocking some shit.'

'Please don't unblock any shit in front of me, Sarah; I've been through enough trauma.'

'Oh my god, you're so funny.' Sarah pulled a goofy face before slapping Lucy on the arm and hopping down from the vanity unit. 'It sounds like the men have finally arrived. I'm going to head down.' She placed her hand gently on Lucy's shoulder and looked her in the eye as she said, 'You sure you're okay?'

Lucy nodded. 'I'm good. I feel like a weight has lifted, and I can build myself up instead of walls around myself.'

Laughter filled the air as everyone congregated in the large kitchen and talked excitedly about the weekend to come. Chinese takeaway boxes scattered the table as they tucked into the banquet James had ordered.

Sarah gave Lucy a sly glance before directing her question to Cameron. 'When's Tom getting here?'

Cameron raised a finger while he quickly chewed the spring roll he'd just stuffed into his mouth. 'He's just messaged. He's sorting some stuff out but hopes to get here before the early hours.'

'Why doesn't he just travel up in the morning?' Jess asked.

'We've got an early start tomorrow on the golf course. He wanted to be here for that. I think he also wants to take the piss out of our hangovers in the morning,' replied Cameron.

James reached across the table, grabbing the tub of Singapore noodles. 'Does anyone want any more of this? If not, I'm having them as I need to carb load. I'm going to be smug as hell when I don't have a hangover.'

Julian laughed and pointed his chopsticks at James. 'You're kidding yourself if you think you're escaping a hangover.'

'Positive mental attitude, that's all I need, but I find sex cures a hangover. Sarah, will you be kind enough to oblige in the morning?' James wiggled his eyebrows at Sarah, who rolled her eyes in response.

'Sod off. I've already told you no shenanigans this weekend. We may share a house, but I'm sleeping with the ladies this weekend.'

'Fuck, that sounds sexy as hell. Can I watch?'

'James.' Sarah's face was deadpan.

'Yeah.'

'Fuck off.'

The table erupted in laughter as Sarah blew James a kiss across the table.

'Where are you guys going tonight?' Lucy wouldn't admit it, but she was nervous about tonight; she wouldn't have minded if the boys went out with them.

James leaned in and whispered, 'That's top secret, I'm afraid. I've arranged a night of debauchery and I cannot share the details with the ladies. It's against the stag code.'

'You'd better not be leading my future husband astray, Mr Spencer. You may be my boss, but if you get Cam into trouble, I will smack you.'

'And I'll look forward to it.'

Imogen rolled her eyes. 'It's a bloody good job we don't have anyone from HR here this weekend; you'd be bang in trouble, Boss.'

'That's the downside of working with your best friends. In any case, what happens on the stag weekend stays on the stag weekend. Stag code.'

Sarah huffed. 'Tell that to the STDs you catch in those sorts of places.'

'Hilarious.' James rolls his eyes.

Cameron raised his hand, making a boy scout promise. 'Just for the record, I have no intention of sticking my bits anywhere that is going to result in an STD. Imogen, you have nothing to worry about, I promise. And on that note, ladies, you need to get ready.'

Imogen blew a kiss to Cameron and said, 'Very true. Come on, ladies.'

They filed out of the kitchen, and moments later, loud music and laughter echoed around the manor.

'Are you ready? There's a surprise down here waiting for you.' Cameron shouted up the stairs.

'Have you organised a naked butler for us?' Came Sarah's response.

'No, I bloody haven't. I've organised something infinitely more useful.'

The men stood back as a parade of beautifully made-up women bounced down the stairs, excitement written all over their faces.

'Wow, you all look gorgeous.' James let out a whistle as he admired the view.

Sarah had asked that everyone wear multicoloured sequined outfits, except for Imogen. Sarah had given her a silver sequined jumpsuit. They all twinkled like fairy lights as the hallway lights reflected off the sequins. As planned, Imogen stood out from the crowd, clearly the bride of the party.

'What have you been up to, Cameron?' Imogen was standing, her arms draped around his shoulders.

'Open the front door.'

Imogen led the way, and they gasped with excitement as their eyes met the limousine parked up; the driver leaning on the bonnet, waiting patiently.

As the driver saw them approaching, he tipped his grey hat and opened the rear passenger door.

'Your chariot awaits.'

After grabbing their bags and shoes, they thanked Cameron and said their goodbyes before piling into the back of the limo.

'Who wants a drink to get this party started?' Sarah was already taking the foil off the bottle of champagne that was waiting on ice. Lucy passed the filled glasses around as Sarah poured each one.

'How are you feeling, Lucy?' Jess was next to Lucy on the back seat, concern etched on her face.

'I'm okay, thanks. Nervous, but I need to get back out there. I can't hold on to this fear any longer. Today helped. I feel like I got it off my chest and that's the first step, I guess.'

'You did well today. We didn't realise how much you were struggling. Now we know we can help you. If you get stressed out tonight, just let me know and I can bring you home.'

'Thanks, Hun. I'll be fine after a few more of these.' Lucy wiggled her half empty glass.

'Raise your glasses, ladies. Here's to Jen marrying her sexy hero.' Sarah raised her glass as they all whooped, downing the rest of their drinks before topping up.

They pulled up outside the club, ready to party and already feeling the effects of the alcohol.

'I'll park up just over there.' On the other side of the road was a layby. 'Head out whenever you want to leave.'

Sarah had arranged for a VIP entrance and a table in the club. The table came stocked with bottles of spirits and mixers, so they didn't need to queue up at the bar.

The club hostess showed them to their table, and once again, Sarah started pouring them all drinks.

'Are you trying to get us drunk, Sarah?' Lucy was already swaying to the music as she watched Sarah giving everyone double vodkas with cranberry juice.

'Yep. I think we all need to loosen up tonight, especially when Jen sees what I have in store for her.'

Lucy giggled, knowing full well what Sarah had stuffed in her bag.

'Why do I feel scared?'

'Don't be scared, you just need to wear this.' Sarah whipped out a white lace veil, *bride to be* sash and cheap tiara.

'I hoped you were classier than this, ladies.'

'Nope.' Jess was laughing as she took in the expression on Imogen's face. 'You can't have a hen party without the classic cheap shit. You're going to love this.' Jess then pulled a necklace from her bag.

'Oh my god. Are you serious?' Imogen's eyes had grown wider.

'Very. Now put it on.' Jess placed the necklace over Imogen's head. 'You'll be glad to know, each penis is edible, so you can suck on cock all night long and not get in trouble with your husband-to-be.'

Jess turned to Sarah and Lucy, reaching into her bag once more. 'Don't worry, I haven't forgotten us. We can all suck on cock tonight.' They fell about laughing as they placed their own penis necklaces around their necks.

'I'm surprised to say, these are nice,' said Sarah as she bit a tip off, crunching down on the sugary treat.

'Just the tip though, eh, Sarah? It doesn't count then.' Jess winked.

Lucy laughed as she said, 'This is the best cock I've had for,' she screwed up her face while licking the sweet, deep in thought, 'since forever. If this is the best I've had, I need better cock.'

'Let's drink to that.' Sarah raised her glass as they all drained their drinks. 'And now to the dance floor.'

Lucy swayed in her seat, a smile on her face. The few drinks she'd consumed had put out the flames of anxiety that threatened to burn away her confidence, and even though their antics and outfits were attracting attention, the men that sidled over weren't sleazy; merely offering Imogen their congratulations and moving on.

'What do you reckon, ladies? Shall we make the night a bit more interesting?'

The other three looked at Sarah in fear. This didn't sound good.

With trepidation, Imogen asked, 'What did you have in mind?'

'Let's play a game of drink or dare?'

'I thought the game was truth or dare?' Lucy said.

'I reckon we had our fill of truths earlier, so I want to play drink or dare. We have a bottle of tequila and shot glasses, so we may as well.'

'Okay, let's do this.' Jess surprised everyone by lining up the shots along the edge of the glass table that sat in between the two velvet sofas in their private area at the back of the club. Lucy sat next to Jess on one sofa, Sarah and Imogen on the other.

'As I'm in charge this weekend, I'll go first. Imogen, I dare you to go up to,' she tapped her lip with her fingernail while studying the unknowing victims on the dance floor, 'him. The one in the white shirt.' He was dancing with his friends on the edge of the dance floor, his buttons strained as his robotic movements flexed his muscles. 'And I want you to use your charm to get him to suck one of your penises and bite it right off.'

'You're joking, right?' Imogen's face flushed.

'Nope. You can always take a drink instead. The choice is yours.'

Imogen tapped her foot, then rolled her shoulders as she flexed her neck. 'Fuck it. I'm doing it.'

She smoothed down her sequined outfit as she stood, winked at her open-mouthed friends, and sauntered over to the dancing hulk. They turned in their seats to watch the action.

Imogen was now on her tiptoes and tapping the guy on his shoulder. He turned with a smile. They couldn't hear what he said to her, but they were sure he used the word sexy.

Pulling him down with his shoulders, she spoke into his ear. He smiled and looked over at Sarah. He gave them a wink before bending at the knee so he could reach her neck.

'Oh, I think he's going to do it.' Jess was gripping onto Lucy's wrist, excited at how this game was turning out.

They all held their breath as Hulk angled his face and licked out at Imogen's throat, pulling one of the sugary penises into his mouth. He sucked on the tip and snapped it off at the base.

Imogen hugged him before dancing back to the table.

'How the fuck did you get him to do that?' Sarah looked incredulous.

'I shall never tell you my secrets of persuasion.' Laughing, Imogen grabbed the shot and knocked it back in one. 'Fuck it; I deserve a shot anyway. And now it's my turn, right?'

'Yep. Pick a victim.' Sarah was rubbing her hands with glee.

'I choose you, Sarah. Go up to Hulk and twerk.'

A blank look fell across her face until she realised what Imogen had done. 'That's how you convinced him to suck your penis—'

'Will you stop saying it like that? Anyone overhearing this will think I have an actual penis.'

Sarah carried on, ignoring her friend's pleas. 'I can't help being impressed, so I will honour your cunning by taking you up on the dare.'

She jumped up and marched over to the man as he stood waiting for his reward.

Sarah's arms encircled his thick neck as she gyrated, running her hands down his impressive chest and abs. He took his time running his hands down her back, but before they could reach her arse, she twisted around and ground it into his crotch.

She twerked like her life depended on it. He stroked up and down her back while he gripped her hip. It was obvious he imagined them hard at it, doggy style, and from the look on her face, so was Sarah.

One of his friends wanted to join the action. The three women gave each other concerned glances.

'Do you think we need to rescue her?' Lucy asked, putting her drink down, ready to head over, but before anyone could answer, Sarah lifted and grabbed the other guy's hips. She looked like she was in the middle of a spit roast, right there on the dance floor. Her mouth aligned to his crotch. Guy number two ran his fingers through her hair while the Hulk dug his fingers into her hips.

'Okay, we need to go in.' Jess stood, and the others followed.

'Sorry boys, we need our friend back. Off you toddle.' Jess grabbed onto Sarah and straightened her up. The two guys held their hands up in surrender as Hulk said, 'No worries, but if you fancy continuing this party, we'll be over there.' He pointed to the bar.

'Thanks, boys, that was fun.' Sarah gave them a little wave before sauntering back to the table and downing a shot of tequila.

'You're only supposed to take the shot if you don't want to do the dare. You both seem to have forgotten the fundamental rules of this game.' Lucy sat down and topped up the empty shot glasses. 'That was crazy, Sarah. What were you thinking?'

'I wasn't thinking. I got carried away. I got turned on when his mate wanted to join in.'

'Shit, Sarah, you are one kinky minx.' Jess giggled.

They soon forgot the game of drink or dare as they all downed their shots and headed back to the dance floor. The strobe lighting and booming music made Lucy's head swim. Between the flashes, she could see men moving closer around them, closing in on them as they danced. Anxiety crept over her as her alcohol-addled brain kept seeing Mark everywhere she turned.

The last time she drank shots of tequila, her world fell down around her. Flashbacks of that night in Tom's club got mixed into the events of the evening until she was dizzy with confusion.

She rested her hand on Jess's shoulder and spoke in her ear. 'I'm just heading to the toilet to freshen up, back in a minute.'

'Do you want me to come?'

'No, it's cool.'

Lucy made her way through the crowd to the ladies' toilet. She smiled at the woman in front of her and rolled her eyes to say, *always a queue for the ladies.*

'Hello, sexy.' A deep male voice was in her ear as she jumped out of her skin. She turned to find guy number two stood behind her. 'You're here with that saucy lady that was enjoying our three-way, aren't you? Do you all want to come back to our place tonight?'

Bile rose in Lucy's throat as flashbacks played in her mind. She fell for Mark's charms while he kept her company in the queue for the toilet, and she didn't need the reminder.

She swallowed and shook her head. 'No, thank you. I don't think my friend's fiancé would like that.'

He shrugged before saying, 'No worries. Thought I'd ask anyway, you don't get if you don't ask. Have a lovely evening.' As soon as he'd appeared, he was gone.

Lucy let out a breath. The encounter had done nothing to calm her nerves. Her breathing was shallow and her pulse racing. She knew a panic attack was imminent and needed to act quickly. When she made it into the toilets, she splashed cold water on her face and had hatched a plan to escape back to the safety of their weekend accommodation. As she left the toilets, instead of heading back to her friends, she turned right and headed for the way out.

Taking a refreshing, calming deep breath, she stepped outside into the cold winter evening and sighed with relief as she spotted the limousine parked up across the road. She dashed across the road and tapped on the driver's window.

The driver's face came into view as the window slid down.

'Oh, hello. You're here sooner than expected. Are the others on their way?'

'It's just me. I'm not feeling well. Would you mind taking me home and then coming back for the others?'

'Of course. I'll get the door for you.'

Lucy stepped back and waited for him to open the passenger door. As she settled at the back of the car, she took a few more breaths. She felt better, her pulse slowing to its normal rhythm.

Disappointment replaced panic. What happened with Mark was rare, and lightning doesn't strike twice in the same place. So why did she feel so anxious? Imogen had coped with him for years and she was out enjoying life to its fullest. She felt like such a loser.

CHAPTER 10

LUCY

Everything I wanted – Billie Eilish

When the limo was far from the club, Lucy pulled out her phone to message Jess. She felt guilty as she saw the countless missed calls and messages asking where she was.

> Lucy: Hi. I wasn't feeling well, so I went back with the limo. He's going to come back for you, so don't worry. Have a great night. Xxx

Almost instantly, Lucy saw the three little dots flashing on her screen.

> Jess: WTF, Lucy! We've been looking all over for you! Why

didn't you answer your phone?
Are you ok? We'll head home as
soon as the driver gets back
here. Xx

Lucy tapped out a response.

Lucy: I'm ok. Please don't head
straight home. Sorry, my phone
was on silent, and I didn't feel
it vibrate. Honestly, I'm good.
I think I had too many tequilas.
I'm safe and fine. If you come
home early, I'm going to be mad
and then I'll feel terrible,
and you don't want me to feel
bad, do you? Xxx

Jess: Well, we're all cross you
left without speaking to us
first. If you're sure you want
us to stay out, then we will,
but we're not happy about it.
Text me when you're home xxx

Lucy: I'm pulling into the
drive now. Sorry. Have a shot
for me! Xxx

The limo stopped outside the front door, and within
seconds, the driver opened her door.

'Here you go. I'll wait until I see you safely in, okay?'

'Thank you. And thank you for making a special trip for me. Sorry to be a nuisance.'

'Not at all. You did the right thing if you weren't feeling great. Take care now.'

Lucy made her way to the front door, her legs wobbly on the gravel driveway. Thankfully, she'd remembered the code to the key safe. After opening the door and safely putting the key back, she gave the driver a thumbs-up before stepping in and closing the door behind her. She heard the gravel crunching as the limo left.

She poured a glass of water and sat on the sofa in the living room. As the seconds ticked by, she could feel her heart rate decreasing to a normal level.

She leaned back on the plush red velvet sofa and noticed how silent the house was. All she could hear was the scratching of her sequins on the soft material of the antique furniture.

Shit. I'd better get changed before I damage the furniture.

She quickly changed out of her dress into her new pyjamas. Lucy had decided that oversized T-shirts with cartoon characters weren't quite in keeping with her new persona, so she'd ordered a pair of silk pyjamas with an elegant print of tropical leaves and birds. She loved how the silk skimmed over her skin as she returned downstairs, not quite ready to climb into bed.

She snuggled back on the sofa, allowing herself a moment to reflect on the progress she'd made. Opening up to her friends had taken a heavy weight off her shoulders, one she hadn't realised she'd been carrying since the attack.

I have to work on being in public. It's no good having this newfound confidence and wardrobe if I'm going to run home crying every time I go to a crowded club.

Dumbass.

Sighing, she reminded herself that progress was progress, no matter how small.

A wave of tiredness crashed over her as her eyelids grew heavy and closed without resistance. The comfort of the plump cushions enticed her into a deep sleep.

Lucy stirred as something soft caressed her body. Her eyes blinkered open, her vision blurry from sleep.

She wasn't alone.

Her body reacted before her brain caught up with events, throwing her up from her slumber.

'Ah, fuck.'

Her head hit something or someone hard as the stranger yelped out in pain.

'What the fuck.' Lucy rubbed at the sore spot on her forehead, her heart galloping like a stallion.

'Shit. Are you okay? I didn't mean to scare you.'

Lucy regained her composure as she saw Tom sitting on the floor, rubbing at his head with one hand while clutching a blanket with another.

'Oh, shit. Tom, I'm so sorry. You scared the crap out of me.' She rested her palms on her chest and took a few deep breaths.

'Yeah, I get that. I didn't want to wake you, so I grabbed a blanket in case you got cold. These old houses get chilly at night.' He handed the blanket to her but kept his distance.

She reached out and took the blanket before saying, 'Thank you. I thought I was alone, so it was a bit of a shock.'

'I was expecting to find the place empty. How come you're back on your own at two in the morning?'

She wasn't sure what to say. She didn't want to look weak in front of him. 'I wasn't feeling great, so I headed back.'

He took a seat next to her, a scowl on his face. 'What? And they were okay with you coming home on your own?'

101

She fiddled with the edge of the blanket. 'Um, not really. I didn't tell them I was leaving until I was on my way.'

He exhaled heavily as he said, 'Jesus, Lucy. How did you get home? Please tell me you did not take a taxi on your own?'

'Cameron hired a limo for us, so I got the driver to bring me home. He's gone back to the club to wait for the others.' She straightened as she said, 'I'm not a total idiot, you know.'

'I didn't mean it like that. I worry about you, that's all.'

This caught her attention, her eyes meeting his as she said, 'Really? You worry about me? You hardly know me. Why would you worry about me?'

He turned to face her, his voice gentle as he said, 'I've been worried about you since I met you at my club.'

She huffed. 'Oh, I'm that pathetic, am I?'

He shook his head. 'Pathetic? Did you think Imogen was pathetic for what happened to her?'

'No. Of course not. What's that got to do with anything?'

'Did you worry about her?'

'Obviously, she's my friend and went through some horrific shit.'

'So did you. It doesn't make you pathetic. We care about you, and you know it. That's why you snuck off tonight instead of telling the others you wanted to go home.'

There was no response to that. Instead, she sighed and leaned back into the sofa, pulling the blanket tighter around her shoulders.

'Do you want to tell me about it?'

'About what?'

'What made you want to come home? You can talk to me.' His voice was calming and coaxed Lucy out of her shell like a seasoned snake charmer.

'A guy propositioned me in the queue for the loo, and it scared the shit out of me. I had a panic attack and needed to leave. I didn't want to speak to the others about it. I couldn't stand the thought of them fussing over me like I was some helpless child. So, I took myself out of the situation.' Her voice was laced with resignation.

'I'm sorry, Lucy.'

'It's not your fault.'

'I know. I wish you didn't have to go through this. It pisses me off that you're suffering at the hands of another man.'

'Well, I reckon I had the last laugh, don't you?' She wasn't laughing. A single tear tracked down her cheek.

Tom's thumb gently wiped it away as he locked eyes with her. 'I want so badly to take away your pain.'

'I wish you could.'

They sat in comfortable silence. The surrounding air crackled with electricity as he rested his arm along the back of the sofa. She wanted so desperately for him to kiss her, and from the way his eyes kept darting to her lips, she guessed he felt the same.

Lucy inched herself closer, tucking herself under his arm. He brought his arm down to drape around her shoulder. The only sound she could hear was their breathing as her eyelids closed.

Lucy jumped out of her skin as the front door crashed open, and the rest of their friends burst through it.

'Whey-hey, what have we just walked in on?' James slurred his words as he stumbled towards them like a ping-pong ball, using the nearby furniture to steady himself.

Lucy quickly tucked a loose strand of hair behind her ear before standing. 'Nothing, Tom just got here.'

The other women stalked over to Lucy.

'We've got a bone to pick with you, young lady.' Sarah was waggling her finger in Lucy's face. 'We were worried sick about you.'

'Can you leave it, Sarah? I'm fine. I told you where I was, so let's drop it.'

Tom stood and put himself between them. 'Sarah, leave Lucy be, okay?' He looked at the drunken rabble and said, 'I'll get you some water, and then you can tell us all about your evening.'

'I'll come and give you a hand.' Lucy jumped at the excuse to leave the room.

She leaned on the edge of the counter, picking at the grain in the wood as she said, 'You don't need to fight my battles for me.'

Tom stopped pouring the water and looked at Lucy. 'I know that, but what you need and deserve are two different things.'

'Oh really? What do I deserve?'

He closed the space between them, her skin prickling at his proximity.

'You deserve respect.' Placing his hands on either side of her, he leaned down, his eyes level with hers. 'You deserve someone who will put you first, no matter what. Someone who can break through that stone wall you're hiding behind and use it to build a pedestal.'

Her heart beat out of her chest as his words washed over her. 'And can you give me that?'

She noticed something flash behind his eyes before he stepped back, cool air filling the void he'd left behind.

Another brick crashed down around her heart.

Of course he can't; he's Tom Harper. *You could never satisfy someone like him.*

Not wanting to give him a chance to respond, she grabbed a couple of glasses of water. 'I'd better get these to the others before they pass out.'

'James, drink this.' With one hand holding his head up, he took the glass.

'Cheers. I think I may need to—' *burp* '—go to bed.' As Lucy looked at him, he gulped the water down, her brow knitted with worry.

'You're not going to be sick, are you?'

James shook his head in response as Cameron said, 'No, you don't need to worry about James. Years of practice means he's never sick. He considers it a waste of alcohol.'

Tom walked in carrying a tray with glasses of water for everyone else. Setting it down on the coffee table, he glanced at Lucy before she averted her eyes.

Sarah stopped drinking. 'Can anyone explain how he got into this state?'

Cameron laughed. 'He tried taking on a group of uni students in a drinking competition and failed. We tried to stop him, but you know what he's like once he's got an idea in his head.'

They all mumbled their agreement as they quenched their thirst.

'How are we all feeling this morning?' As predicted, Tom was up early, cooking breakfast for everyone.

Imogen sat with her head in her hands. 'I'm glad we've got a spa day today. We need to chill out. What are you boys up to?'

Julian was the first to answer, his hangover not as brutal as the others. 'Golf today, although I'm not sure why. None of us play.'

'James likes driving the golf buggy and the drinks at the nineteenth hole back in the clubhouse.' Cameron looked over at James as he spoke. 'I don't want to be in his golf buggy. I think he might still be drunk.'

Jess turned to Lucy. 'How are you today, Hun? Ready for a nice, chilled-out day?'

Lucy noticed Tom watching her across the kitchen as he served bacon and eggs.

'I'm good. I'm looking forward to getting a pedicure. After wearing those heels last night, my feet are killing me.' She avoided the real question. Now wasn't the time for a heart-to-heart. That could wait.

'I'm with you on that one. Mine are fucked.' Sarah rubbed at her toes. 'Some drunken women trod on my feet with six-inch heels. I think I might have broken my little toe.'

'Want me to suck it better for you?' said James, hopefully.

'You still smell of vodka, so if you don't mind, I'll pass.'

'Okay, ladies, this way, please.' A lady dressed in a white spa uniform showed them through the large doors to the women's dressing room. The room was heavy with the scent of freshly laundered towels as they approached a wall of shelving stacked high with their complimentary towels and robes.

'This is the life.' Imogen lounged on the smooth wooden seating in the salt steam room.

Jess released a sigh of contentment. 'It certainly is. Let's do this more often. My mum is always at a spa retreat, and now I understand why.' She waited a beat before turning to Lucy. 'Are you okay? And I'm not talking about your feet. The guys aren't here, so come on, open up. And while you're at it, spill the beans on what happened when Tom arrived last night, you looked pretty cosy.' She wiggled her eyebrows.

'You saw me break down in the middle of yoga. There isn't more to it. Mark put Imogen and me through some shit.' She looked over at Imogen. 'Jen was lucky enough to find someone to get her through it. I'm not ready. Mark and Andrew have destroyed my trust in men.'

Imogen shuffled closer to Lucy. 'Oh, Lucy. I'm so sorry my past has right royally fucked you over. I should've seen the signs. Worked it out sooner.'

'I wasn't saying it to make you feel bad. You'd never guess what was going on, so stop blaming yourself. It won't help me get over it. I don't mean to sound harsh, but I need to work through this and build my confidence.'

'Can Tom help you with that?' asked Sarah.

'I think he wants to. He certainly hinted at that last night until I asked him outright, and he couldn't answer me. I don't want to rely on a man to build me up. What will I gain from that? We'll get together. It'll be great, and then he'll discover I'm not enough for him and he'll go off with someone else. Then where does that leave me?' She shook her head. Her mind was made up. 'No. I'm going to work things out in my own time. If it's meant to be, he'll be there when it's right for me.'

She decided she didn't need a man in her life. She needed to fall in love with herself before letting anyone else in.

CHAPTER 11

TOM

For My Hand (feat. Ed Sheeran) – Burna Boy

'How was the stag weekend?' Alex asked Tom as they sat in his office having their usual Monday afternoon meeting.

'It was good. Golf was interesting. None of us can play and we nearly got thrown off the course because James kept losing his grip on his clubs.'

'He sounds like a liability.' Alex said, before sipping on his coffee.

'He's a good guy. He's got some stuff going on in his personal life, so he needed to let off some steam.'

'Don't we all? Speaking of which, how was it with Lucy?'

Tom took a deep breath and slumped back in his seat. 'It was okay. I arrived early on the Saturday morning and scared the shit out of her as she was asleep on the sofa. She'd left the club early and, I don't know, I suppose she was waiting up for the others.'

'Cut to the chase. Did you get it on?'

'Bloody hell, Alex. No, we didn't get it on. She's not in a good place. Mark and her other ex-boyfriend have really done a number on her, that's for sure. I tried to tell her she deserved someone that would make her the priority.'

'And I assume you were referring to yourself?'

He shook his head and threw his pen down on the desk. 'That's the problem. She asked me if I was the one to do that and I couldn't answer her.'

'Why not?'

'How can I promise to make her the centre of my universe? We both know I can't.'

'I've already told you I can help with this place more. Christ, Tom, I've been asking for more responsibility for a while now.'

'I'm not just talking about the club. Kat needs to be my priority for the foreseeable future. How do you think Lucy will react to me spending my spare time in a sex club so I can be with the owner? It doesn't really sit well with a woman who's been cheated on and then used by a psycho in his evil plans. It's safe to say she has some serious trust issues and my inability to tell her what I'm doing and who I'm doing it with won't really bring out the best in our relationship.'

Alex rubbed his chin as he said, 'You make a fair point there. Do you trust her?'

'Based on the few encounters we've had, yes, I trust her. Why?'

'You could tell her what's happening.'

'No.' He shook his head. 'That's not an option. You know the saying what she doesn't know won't kill her? That's never been truer.'

'This is fucked up. You've given up everything for Katia, ever since school you've been there for her. It's your time, Tom. You deserve to have someone permanent in your life.'

'I've got you.' He gave his friend a weak smile.

'Listen, I know we're good friends, but I won't suck your cock and then cuddle you into the small hours. You need a woman in your life, other than the ones that just want a turn on the infamous Harper dick.'

'The way you've been talking about my dick, I think you might want to suck it.'

Alex flipped him the finger, making his feelings on that clear.

'Look, I appreciate what you're saying. I do. In a perfect world, I'd be sweeping Lucy off her feet. Katia wouldn't be in this situation and my club wouldn't be full of people I'm trying to avoid. But this isn't a perfect world. It's fucked up and I've got myself in the middle of it.'

'How have you got yourself into this mess?'

'I made a promise to a mafia boss when I was too young to know any better.' His vibrating phone interrupted their conversation. 'Speak of the devil. I need to take this call.'

'No worries. See you downstairs.'

As Alex closed the office door, Tom answered the phone. 'Gedeon, how are you?'

'Good afternoon, Tom. I'm doing okay. Thank you for asking. You know you're one of the few people in my life that ever asks me how I am. What does that tell you? You get to the top of a crime organisation like the Vory and suddenly people don't care about you.' After many years in the UK, his Russian accent was still thick.

'The important people care about you, Gedeon, you know that.'

'Speaking of important people, how is my daughter? I trust you are looking after her?'

'Katia is doing well. No one has paid her a visit, but I'm spending as much time in her club as I can, and I have someone on the ground here monitoring Ivan when I can't.'

'You know how I feel about strangers, Thomas. Who have you brought into this?' It grated when Gedeon called him by his full name, the vowels elongated and thick with his Russian accent, making him feel like a child being chastised by a parent.

'My casino manager, Alex. He's best placed to watch Ivan, as he's taken to spending all his time in my casino. So far, he's racking up gambling debts and drinking my brandy like it's water.'

'He's not paying his debts?'

'No, and it's causing problems. The cashiers are asking questions and I can only bullshit them for so long before they get suspicious. When people don't pay their way in my club, they're excluded, but I can't really do that with Ivan as we'll lose our advantage.'

'As a member of the Vory, he should live by our rules, and a Vory *always* pays his debts. It's enough for me to bring him in.'

'It's not enough to guarantee he'll be gone for good, though. We can't risk pissing him off before we've got something solid.'

Gedeon released a sigh. 'As always, you're right. I need to punish him in front of the others to remind them who's boss, and that you don't threaten my position and get away with it. I'll get someone to come down and settle his debt.'

'Thanks, I appreciate it.'

'Keep Katia safe, Tom. You need to focus on that— let this Alex man keep an eye on Ivan. I want you at her club as much as possible.'

'You're aware I have my club to run?' He took a breath, unsure why he was going to say what he was about to say. 'At some point, I'd quite like a life of my own.'

'I understand. You are a handsome man with needs. As soon as this is over, you can live your life however you want. You keep Katia alive, and I will be forever in your debt. For now, you have a promise to keep. Don't forget that, Thomas.' The threat was obvious. If anything happened to Kat, he'd pay with his own life.

'Good evening, Mr Harper. It's a pleasure to see you this evening.'

Tom leaned on the desk and smiled as he replied, 'Hey, Victoria. Is Kat in her office?'

The busty brunette fluttered her long lashes as she wrapped her severe ponytail around her hand. 'Yes, she is. I'll let her know you're on the way up. Will you be requiring a private room this evening?'

'Not tonight.'

Her eyes dropped as her bottom lip protruded. 'Shame, that'll disappoint the ladies.'

'I'm sure they'll cope. Thank you, Victoria. I'll see you later.'

Instead of heading through the main doors to the club, he walked behind the main desk, entered a code, and disappeared through a concealed door. He took the stairs two at a time before coming to a stop in front of another door.

'Hey, Sexy. I rarely have the pleasure of your company on a Monday. Is everything okay?'

Katia was leaning on the doorframe, dressed in her signature red silk waistcoat and tightly fitted pencil skirt. Her glossy black hair twisted into a bun at her nape, giving off the look of a sultry flamenco dancer. Tom wrapped his arm around her waist and gently pressed his lips to her cheek.

'Hey, you. I was feeling restless, so I came to check in on you.'

'Liar. What's really going on?' She took a step out of his hold and strolled into her office, taking a seat on her large red leather chair. Tom took the seat opposite.

'Can't I just pop in and visit my favourite person?'

Katia sat back and crossed her legs as she said, 'No. The club is open and therefore you'd normally watch over your baby, but you're here and you're still fully dressed. This leads me to believe that something is going on. Cut the bullshit, Tom, and tell me what's going on.'

'Ivan is up to something.'

She scoffed. 'Ivan is always up to something.'

'He's in my club all the time. He and his cronies are racking up debt in the casino and pushing my limits.' Tom paused, giving Katia a chance to process what that meant. Her face remained blank. 'He knows, Kat.'

Her shaky inhale told him she understood. 'Fuck.' Yep, she understood.

'I won't let anything happen to you. Your father won't allow it either. We're keeping a close eye on him and his men. As soon as Ivan steps out of line, Gedeon can end this.'

'You can't guarantee that. Ivan has been after the top spot for a long time, and he'll stop at nothing until he's knocked the mighty Gedeon off his throne.'

'You're safe here. He's being treated like a rockstar in my club, which is keeping him occupied.' Tom stood, leaning over the desk to look directly into Kat's eyes. 'Have I ever let you down?'

'No, you haven't. But has it not occurred to you he knows who you are to me? If he's set up in your club, it's because he's watching you. Who's protecting you?'

'I don't need protection. I can look after myself.'

'You always were cocksure.'

'If there's one thing I'm sure about, it's my c—'

'No! I do not want to hear about your cock.' She laughed as she visibly relaxed. 'Speaking of which, are you coming downstairs with me? The ladies have been asking after you. If I didn't know you better, I'd think you'd found yourself a special someone.'

'Am I that much of a loner that it's beyond the realm of possibility?'

Her eyebrows rose. 'Have you found someone?' Tom noticed something flash behind her eyes, only for a second, but it was there.

'You know I don't have the time to commit to anyone. But I would like to, once this is over.' She didn't need to know about Lucy—not until he was sure there was something there.

'It'll be a sad day when you're off the market. My memberships will drop for a start.' She smiled at him, but it didn't reach her eyes.

'Careful, I'm thinking I'm just a revenue stream to you.'

She uncrossed her legs and rested her elbows on her desk, her breasts protruding out of her waistcoat. 'You're more than a revenue stream, Tom.'

The atmosphere shifted into something unfamiliar, and an uncomfortable silence hung in the air.

Katia burst into laughter. 'You should see your face. I'm messing with you, Tom. You forget I'm immune to your charms. I know someone who isn't immune, though.'

He raised an eyebrow as he said, 'Oh really? Do tell.'

'Victoria.'

'From the front desk?'

Katia nodded. 'She's been asking after you, wondering where you are. Do you want me to set you two up?'

'We've established that isn't a good idea. I don't need the distraction.' The words hung heavy in his heart.

CHAPTER 12

THE WEDDING – LUCY

The Avengers – Alan Silvestri

'Okay, welcome everyone to the last book club with Imogen as a single lady.' Sarah and the rest of the book club were sitting at their usual table at the window of the local pub. Raindrops trickled down the glass, catching the light of the streetlight outside.

It was a typical English country pub with dark wooden furniture, sticky wooden floors, and a pool table in a back room; where the younger customers watched football, drank more than their livers could cope with, and tried to pot as many balls as they could—not all of them on the pool table.

Seth, their favourite barman, delivered a round of gin and tonics. 'On the house, ladies. My way of congratulating the lovely Jen on her upcoming wedding.' Seth's usual top knot was gone, and his dark, wavy hair fell to his shoulders.

'Thank you. That's so kind,' said Imogen, with a beaming smile. Lucy didn't think it would ever leave her face.

Sarah placed her hands on the table, her face serious as she said, 'For obvious reasons, we haven't read a book for a while and therefore can't discuss one, so tonight we'll sort out the final arrangements for the wedding. Imogen, what should we do this week?'

'There's nothing left to organise. I didn't believe for one second Cameron could pull off a wedding with so little time, but he's organised everything like some sort of army general. I'm impressed.'

'Is there anything that man can't do?' Sarah asked.

'I don't think so. If it didn't turn me on so much, I would find it sickening. I've booked us in for spray tans on Thursday; you'll need to head there straight from work.'

'You know, we could have worked on a real tan if we'd gone to Ibiza for your hen party.' Sarah's face was sulky, but her smile told her friends she wasn't being serious.

Jess laughed as she turned to her friend and said, 'Get over it, Sarah. We can go to Ibiza for *your* hen party.'

Sarah huffed. 'Fat chance of me ever having one.'

'Of course you will. You're amazing and gorgeous, but for now can we talk about my wedding as it's only a few days away?'

'Watch out, Bridezilla's about.' Sarah laughed.

As the drinks flowed, the conversation turned to subjects of a more carnal nature.

Jess put her empty wineglass down and said, 'You know what I think is weird about a wedding?' Everyone turned to face her. 'It's the one time when everyone, including parents and grandparents, knows that you're going to have sex. In the morning, you're having breakfast with everyone and they know you've been at it all night. Isn't that weird?'

Imogen put her face in her hands. 'Oh god, you're right. Everyone will know I'm not a virgin when they see me the next morning.'

Lucy looked earnest as she said, 'Don't worry, Jen. We all know you're not a virgin.'

Dear Diary,

I've had a great night at book club. Sarah has chosen a brilliant series for us to read after the wedding, so I'm looking forward to that. Imogen's wedding is this weekend, which means seeing Tom again. I don't know how to handle that. There's been radio silence since the hen and stag party. I guess he worked out I'm not right for him. I was pretty messed up at the time, so I don't blame him. We didn't get a chance to see much of each other over the weekend, not that I'm complaining; a spa day was what I needed, for sure.

My plan is to avoid eye contact this weekend. If I don't look directly into his eyes, I won't be tempted to kiss him. Mother Nature has ensured that I won't be hooking up with anyone this weekend as Aunt Flow arrived today. Bitch. Not that it matters. I'm done with men for now. This weekend is about my best friend getting married and I won't let my petty problems get in the way.

I know that's the right decision, but my body doesn't listen to my brain whenever Tom is near me. He puts something illegal in his aftershave, I'm sure of it, as I can't resist how he smells. I just want to nuzzle into his neck and stay there. Oh dear, I'm screwed, aren't I?

May the force be with me.

'You're beautiful.' Imogen's sister gasped as the makeup artist put the finishing touches on Imogen's makeup. Beams of mid-morning sunlight cast an ethereal glow across the room, catching on the diamante clips in her hair.

'So are you. Pregnancy suits you.'

'I don't know, I feel like a whale and I'm jealous of you all, dressed in a much sexier version of this dress.'

'Don't be silly. You look a lot sexier than we do. I think pregnant women are at the peak of sexiness,' said Lucy.

The others were ready to go to the quaint church on the grounds of the hotel. The hotel and private church were a popular wedding location; Cameron had lucked out, securing it at short notice.

There was a knock on the door. 'Are you decent?'

Sarah called back, 'Is Cameron with you?'

'Nope, just me.'

'Then yep, you can come in.'

Imogen's father, Paul, opened the door, coming to a halt as he saw them. 'Wow. You all look stunning. Imogen, Cameron is going to melt when he sees you. Claire, love, the chaps are heading down to the church. Are you ready to go with them?'

Claire nodded and turned to her daughter. 'I'm so proud of you, Jen. You've proved to be one hell of a strong woman. Your father and I are so happy that you've found someone as special as Cameron. Now, remember to speak clearly when you say your vows; I want that devil of a man who resides in hell to hear you loud and clear when you say, "I do".'

Lucy's heart thundered at the mention of Mark. She couldn't control how her body responded. Her fight-or-flight instincts always kicked in at the mention of his name. She took a few steadying breaths, plastered a smile on her face and busied herself handing out the bridesmaid's bouquets.

One by one, Izzy, Sarah, Lucy, and Jess hugged Imogen before taking their places, ready to walk down the aisle.

On cue, the organist played the opening song.

Sarah's brow creased as she turned to Lucy. 'Is she playing the theme tune from the Avengers movie?'

Lucy giggled 'Yep. Imogen was adamant she wasn't walking down the aisle to the traditional bridal chorus as it came from Richard Wagner's opera, Lohengrin, and I quote, "he was a well-known chauvinist and the couple in his opera were doomed as soon as they were married. That's not how I'm starting my marriage with Cam." She much preferred the Avengers theme tune, so she went with that. It was a secret, but I got it out of her when I overheard heard her on the phone.'

'This is why I love her.'

The excited chatter filling the pews died down as the bride took her first steps inside. They'd decorated the church with sprays of fresh flowers, the scent of roses heavy in the air, mixing with the myriad of perfumes and aftershaves the guests had doused themselves in.

Lucy glimpsed Cameron, who stood beside James at the altar, their backs to the congregation. Cameron rocked on his heels; his hands clasped behind his back. It wasn't until Imogen reached the altar that Cameron turned to face her, and his expression said it all, so full of wonder and pride.

Imogen passed her bouquet to Izzy, and they took their seats. The wedding party sat in the front few pews, and Lucy saw she was next to Tom. She'd avoided him so far as preparations the night before, and tradition, meant that the bride's party didn't mix with the grooms. As she took her seat, Tom's aftershave filled the air and, with every breath she took, her resolve to avoid him ebbed away.

He glanced her way, whispering a quick, 'Hello.'

She mouthed 'hi' in response and turned to watch the ceremony while concentrating on calming her ever-increasing heart rate.

It didn't go unnoticed that every time they took their seats after singing a hymn, his thigh inched closer to hers. His body heat seeped into her, chasing away the chill of the old stone church. She desperately wished he would wrap his arm around her shoulder, but he kept his hands in his lap, clutching onto his order of service. The ceremony was perfect, with barely a dry eye as they said their vows. Lucy was thankful for the tissue she'd stuffed into the pocket of her dress. Cameron couldn't keep his eyes off his bride throughout. She hated herself for it, but Lucy couldn't help the pang of jealously. As she followed the others out of the church, Tom walked alongside her, his palm resting on the small of her back. Her step faltered at his reassuring touch as he said, 'You okay?'

'Yes, thank you. Don't worry, these are tears of happiness.' He smiled and kept his hand where it was until they took their seats at the wedding reception.

Maybe a little flirting won't harm? I could always blame hormones and alcohol.

It had been easy for Lucy to ignore the crushing presence of Tom while the speeches were underway.

However, the rapturous applause that broke out gave an end to that welcomed relief. It was no coincidence she was sitting next to him, and while she appreciated the gesture, she wasn't convinced it was worthwhile.

He'd barely spoken to her throughout the meal; his body language and rate of wine consumption were screaming at how uncomfortable he was sitting next to her. As the staff removed the dessert plates and poured cups of coffee, her friends got up to mingle, leaving her alone with Tom. Again, Lucy doubted this was a coincidence, as Sarah had winked before encouraging the others to leave.

A moment of awkward silence fell between them. He cleared his throat. 'You look beautiful today, Lucy.'

The sound of her name on his lips sent shivers down her spine. She pulled herself together and said, 'Thank you. You look dapper in your suit.' That was no lie. He was hot as hell, dressed up in his traditional morning suit with the coattails.

He pulled at his cravat before saying, 'Why thank you. I feel like a gentleman from an episode of Bridgerton. It's not my usual style.'

'Well, I think it suits you.'

She caught a glint in his eye as he said, 'Oh. Can you see yourself being scandalous with me, young Lady Steele?'

Before Lucy could stop herself, she fell into comfortable banter with him, laughing at his jokes and playing along with the impromptu role play.

'You're beautiful when you smile. Your eyes light up with such joy.'

Unable to find the words to respond to his comment, she blurted out, 'Cocktails. Let's go to the bar and drink some crazy cocktails. I don't know about you, but I feel like letting my hair down and getting shit-faced.'

'That is a most excellent idea. To the bar we head, Lady Steele.'

Classical music played over the speakers at the bar. The older wedding guests were lounging in high-back chairs, sipping on whiskey and ginger ale or sherry, enjoying the peace in front of the large open fires.

They approached the grand, polished wooden bar. The barman was drying his cocktail shaker as he asked, 'What can I get you?'

Lucy tapped her finger to her lip as she perused the many bottles lined up along the glass shelf. 'I can't decide. Tom, you're the expert. What do you recommend?'

He stood behind her, resting his chin on her shoulder, his breath tickling her nape and sending shivers down her spine.

'We'll have two ginger French seventy-fives please.' The barman nodded at Tom and got to work making the gin cocktails.

Lucy pursed her lips. 'I was hoping for a screaming orgasm.'

'That'll come later, if you play your cards right.' He tapped his finger on the top of her nose.

She raised a single eyebrow. 'Are we still talking about cocktails?' Her pulse raced as their eyes met. She couldn't imagine what smouldering looked like until now. With every passing second caught in his gaze, she felt her resolve to avoid men, or rather this man, fall away.

'Here we go. Enjoy your cocktails,' said the barman, placing the martini glasses on the bar. She lifted the glass to her lips, careful not to spill any, and took a sip, humming in pleasure.

'Oh. That is so good.' She ran her tongue along her bottom lip, not wanting to waste any of the sweet drink. 'It's better than a screaming orgasm.'

'I assume you're still talking about the drink, as this is nowhere as good as an actual screaming orgasm.'

She waved a hand in dismissal. 'Oh, please. We all know that they're only found in romance novels and porn movies.'

He raised his eyebrows at her as he took a sip of his drink. 'Are you sure about that?' He traced a line across Lucy's hand as he spoke.

Was she sure about that? Lucy took a moment to consider her answer. It's not like her sexual history was anything to shout about.

She guffawed. 'I have no idea.' This conversation was getting out of hand, so she changed the subject. 'I know one thing for sure: when I said I wanted to let my hair down, I meant it. These pins are itching.' She ruffled her fingers through her up-do, trying to locate the many pins holding her hair in place. She let out a huff as her arms ached.

'Here, let me help you.' He gestured to the bar stool behind her. 'Sit.' He spun the stool round until he was standing at her back and removed each hair pin with care, placing them down on the bar. She closed her eyes as his soft caress calmed her racing mind. As he dropped the last of the pins, he ran his fingers through her hair, loosening the curls.

'Oh, that feels so good. I could sit here all night.'

'I'll gladly do this all night.' Lucy opened her eyes as her stool turned once again. He brought his hand up to cup her jaw, his thumb dusting over her cheek.

She wanted to say so many things. Explain that she wasn't ready for anything. That she wasn't his type and that he should walk away. But the words didn't come out. Tom had locked her in his gaze, and she was unwilling to break the spell.

Tom abruptly removed his hand, running it through his hair and stepped back. He looked over at the others dancing, and said, 'Shall we dance?'

The quick change in mood had her head spinning. 'Oh, okay. I'll take these pins up to my room and see you on the dance floor.' She scooped up the pins and awkwardly side-stepped Tom as she headed for the stairs that led to the rooms.

Fishing her room card out of her pocket, she mentally thanked Imogen again for buying dresses with pockets. A quick tap on the handle and she was safely back in her room. After freshening up, she ran a brush through her curled hair, remembering how it felt to have Tom run his fingers through it. It wasn't long before her inner monologue returned.

What was that all about? Just when I think he's going to kiss me, he wants to dance. I knew it. He's not interested in someone like me, and he came to his senses before he made a drunken mistake by kissing me. Well, that's fine. I want nothing to happen, anyway.

She applied some lip gloss, downed a bottle of water, realised she should have applied the lip gloss after the water, reapplied the lip gloss and took a long hard look at herself in the mirror.

'It's your best friend's wedding day. Enjoy yourself and stop overthinking everything.' After giving herself a stern talking to, she opened the door to head back to the party.

CHAPTER 13

THE WEDDING – TOM

Promises—Calvin Harris ft Sam Smith

'I'd like to take this opportunity to say thank you to you all. I believe that if it wasn't for you guys, Imogen and I wouldn't be here right now. I can't tell you how amazing it feels to find "the one".' Cameron had poured them all a glass of whiskey to hold a toast before they headed to the church.

'James, thank you for always being there for me. I couldn't have asked for a better Best Man. Cheers.' They all raised their glass in cheers before taking a sip. The alcohol burned Tom's throat on the way down but calmed the unease that had settled in his stomach.

'Tom and Julian, you're like brothers to me, and I'm so happy to have you here this weekend. Who'd have thought that a drunken night in London years ago, would result in Tom being one of my best friends? I'm thankful that I literally tripped over you. And Julian, you're my cousin, so you have no choice, you're stuck with me for life. I appreciate you putting your businesses on the back burner for us. Cheers.' They all took another sip before Cameron carried on with his pre-wedding pep talk.

'Please don't feel you have to follow stereotypes this weekend by sleeping with the bridesmaids. I would like to avoid any drama this weekend if possible. James, I'm looking at you dude.'

James' face was incredulous as he downed the last of his whiskey. 'What? Such a cheek. I have no intention of complicating matters any further by sleeping with a bridesmaid. It's Tom you should be worried about.'

'Me?' Tom pressed his finger to his chest.

'Yes, you.' James said with a serious look on his face.

'Hey, listen. I'm here this weekend to be with Cameron. Lucy needs time and space, which works well for me. I'm too busy with the club to give her what she needs and because I'm not a total dickhead, I won't start something with her I can't finish.'

'You're not supposed to finish it with her, mate. That's the whole point.' James laughed as he topped up his glass from a crystal decanter.

'You know what I mean.'

Cameron put his glass down. 'Tom, I think you need to give Lucy more credit. She's tougher than she looks, and I believe she has a right to be part of the decision-making process of what she needs. For all you know, she might want something casual. She's had one serious relationship and one murderous stalker, so she's probably not looking for anything heavy. Why don't you stop overthinking on her behalf and see what happens naturally? Don't force it and take her lead.'

Tom nodded in agreement. 'Since when did you get to be so insightful?'

'Since I found the love of a good woman. It changes everything. I thought I was happy being a bachelor with no responsibilities. Now I can't wait to start a family with the woman I'm going to spend the rest of my life with.'

Julian was topping up their glasses as he said, 'Hold up. You're already talking about babies?'

'Yep. I'm not waiting around on this one. If there is one thing I've learnt after nearly dying, it's that life's too short.' Cameron raised his glass once more and said, 'Carpe diem.'

They all repeated the motto before downing their drinks and getting ready to leave.

Tom wished he could tell them the real reason he wasn't ready to settle down. He'd fallen for Lucy in a way he'd never experienced before, and it scared the shit out of him. Katia had to be the only significant woman in his life, Gedeon had made that clear, and he couldn't in good conscious bring Lucy into this mess, no matter how much he wanted to. A small part of him clung to Cameron's words. Perhaps she had a right to a say in that? Maybe she wasn't looking for a boyfriend but someone to have fun with, and Tom could be whatever she needed right now.

Couldn't he?

Tom and Julian had finished performing their usher duties and were standing at the front of the church, waiting for the bride. As the organist played the Avengers theme tune, he felt his heart rate pick up at the prospect of seeing Lucy. The throngs of guests severely impeded his view, but he craned his neck, regardless.

As Imogen and her father walked down the aisle, the congregation whispered their praises and good wishes as she passed by. She was stunning. Tom couldn't help but feel deliriously happy for his friend. And then he saw her.

The bridesmaids wore beautiful peacock-blue chiffon gowns. The sweetheart neckline matched the wedding gown but had additional capped sleeves in the same chiffon as the dress. Sweeping floor-length fabric gave the illusion that they were floating down the aisle, and Tom couldn't take his eyes off Lucy. She'd pinned her hair up in curls and with every step she took, the sun glinting in through the windows caught on the diamond and pearl hair pins made to look like tiny flowers. Loose strands fell around her face and nape; his fingers itched to feel her hair wrapped around them. He knew he'd struggle to stay away. Cameron's words of advice replayed in his mind.

As Lucy sat next to him, he said, 'Hello.' He should have seen this coming. The bridesmaids and ushers were sitting on the same pew, so of course Lucy would end up next to him as the others paired off. She smelled like fresh roses and sunshine; such a contrast to the richer, muskier scents he was used to. She was literally a breath of fresh air.

His desire to get closer to her won out over his decision to stay away. Every time they took their seats after a hymn, he inched closer until their thighs touched.

He felt like such a child around her, unsure of what to do or say. He was used to his exploits being more like a business transaction. Women threw themselves at him, and the ones he liked, he caught, fucked, and said goodbye. Everyone knew the deal, and it suited them just fine. The occasional woman would want more, and Tom was quick to let them down gently. Now he was the one who'd caught feelings, and it wasn't sitting well.

As the ceremony ended and the congregation filed out of their pews one by one, Tom couldn't resist the urge to place his hand at the small of her back, guiding her out. It was a quick, gentle caress, but he hoped his message was clear. He was there for her.

Back at the hotel, Tom scanned the table plan to find his place and noticed he'd been seated next to Lucy. Of course he had.

It wasn't too difficult to get through the speeches and wedding breakfast. The conversation flowed easily at their table. The only people missing from their usual group was the bride and groom as they took centre stage at the top table. Onlookers would see a table of friends having a great time, enjoying the food, wine, and company. What they wouldn't see was how hard it was for Tom to keep his hands to himself. He watched as Lucy fiddled with her napkin; desperate to still her hands with his. The way she teased her fingers up and down the stem of her wineglass made his heart race and blood flow to all the wrong places, at least wrong for this setting. When not using his hands to hold the knife and fork, he opted to rest them on his thighs, like a customer in a strip club. He laughed under his breath at that thought, at what she'd reduced him to—a desperate punter in a club willing to pay the Earth for just one touch.

He finished another glass of red wine, courage filling his veins as he drank, his hands resting on the table.

After the wedding breakfast, people filed out of the room to head to the bar or the dance floor, and it wasn't long before he was sitting alone with Lucy. He couldn't avoid it any longer. He needed to speak to her.

'You look beautiful today, Lucy.'

After some polite conversation, they made their way to the bar. Tom watched as she licked a sweet gin cocktail off her lips, moaning in pleasure. He had to bite down on his bottom lip to stop himself from offering to lick it off for her. He could happily sit here all night with her laughing and getting drunk, but he'd much rather take her back to his room and worship her.

Instead, he made do with stripping away each hairpin, one by one, making the moment last as long as possible. He wanted to wrap her hair around his fist, tugging on it as he enters her. He wanted to be the one to make her moan, not some cocktail. And oh, how he wanted to make her moan.

He felt his blood coursing through his veins, travelling south as his cock swelled. He was getting too close and was too drunk to stop himself if things went any further.

'Shall we dance?' He needed to mingle with the others and give his cock time to deflate, but as he watched her face fall, he wondered if that was a mistake. Did she want him, after all?

'Oh, okay. I'll take these pins up to my room and see you on the dance floor.'

He watched her leave, or more accurately, he watched how her hips swayed, causing the dress to swish from side to side like a pendulum of a clock. She utterly transfixed him until a heavy arm wrapped across his shoulders.

'You really need to get with her before your balls explode, mate.' Alcohol infused breath hit Tom in the face, breaking him out of his trance.

'Thanks for the tip, James. My balls, however, are very aware of this.'

'Are you still overthinking things? Cam is right, mate. Life is too short for dicking around. She's an amazing woman, and you'd be an idiot to let her walk away.'

Tom clenched his jaw in frustration. 'I'm not letting her walk away. She's doing that all by herself.'

'Oh really? You don't think it's got anything to do with you giving her mixed signals?'

'What are you talking about? I'm not giving her mixed signals.'

James laughed as Julian and Cameron strolled over with another round of drinks in hand. As they passed them out, Cam asked, 'What's so funny?'

'Tom reckons he's not giving Lucy mixed signals.'

Cameron's eyes bugged out of his head as he looked at Tom. 'Are you serious? We just watched you massage her scalp and fuck her with your eyes and then you blurt out that you want to dance.'

'I didn't want to come on too strong. And why were you watching us?'

Julian cleared his throat before saying, 'We needed another drink, but didn't want to interrupt. It looked pretty intense from where we were standing. She's probably up in her room having to sort herself out as you left her hanging.'

Tom clenched his jaw again. 'Don't talk about her like that.' Three sets of eyes bored holes into him.

'What?'

Cameron said, 'You've got it bad for her. I've never seen you like this over a woman before. It's normally wham, bam, thank you Ma'am, and you're done. Drink this and go to her. Do it now or you'll regret it.'

Tom downed the brandy before he could think it through. Julian shoved a mint in his hand. 'Chew this on your way up.'

Their hands on his back pushed him out of the room. 'Hang on, I don't even know what room she's in.'

'Room 6.' Cameron called out as he headed towards the stairs.

He popped the mint in his mouth as he strode up the stairs.

'Come on Tom. It's time to live a little.'

CHAPTER 14

LUCY

I feel It Coming (feat. Daft Punk) – The Weeknd

Lucy quickly opened her door, a fist stopping mere millimetres away from her face.

'What the fu—'

'Oh my god, sorry. I nearly hit you in the face.' Tom looked as if he'd stepped straight out of Edvard Munch's *The Scream* painting, his hands rubbing at his pained face.

'Tom! What are you doing here?'

He ran his hands through his hair before saying, 'I don't want to dance with you.'

Oh, here we go again.

'Okay. And you felt that strongly about it, you had to come up here to tell me? You could have just gone back to ignoring me downstairs.'

He shook his head. 'No, that's not what I mean. I do want to dance with you.'

She shook her head in a mix of confusion and frustration. 'Do you know what? I'm sick of being messed around by men. How about you sod off and when you know what you want, you let me know?' She went to shut the door in his face, ready to scream bloody murder into her pillow before breaking down into drunken, hormonal tears.

'No,' he growled with determination. His foot wedged in the door, and before she knew it, his hands gripped her face as his lips crashed down on hers. His tongue lashed at hers like he wanted to devour her whole. He left her breathless as he pulled away, the taste of brandy and mint on her lips.

Tom stepped into her room, forcing her to step backwards as he kicked the door shut behind him. Standing there in silence, sucking in breaths and trying to calm her racing heart, she watched as Tom paced, his fists clenching at his sides, his behaviour now in contrast to the passionate kiss he'd just dished out.

'Why do I get the impression you're angry with me? I didn't ask you to come up here and force yourself on me.'

He came to a halt and ran his fingers through his tousled hair. 'I'm not angry at you. I'm angry at the situation.'

'What situation?'

He pulled at his cravat, leaving it to hang limply around his neck. 'You've been through so much; I don't want to wade in and add to your problems. My life is complicated. I can't always be around.'

'So, you think I'm weak?' She could feel the heat rising in her chest, but this wasn't lust. This was rage. 'Weak and needy?' She ground the words out through gritted teeth.

'No. I don't think you're weak.' He banged his fist against his chest. 'I'm the weak one. I told myself to stay away from you, but I can't. That alone scares me because I've never felt this way before.'

Scared to ask, she whispered, 'Felt like what?'

He released a sigh and took a step towards her. 'Like we could have something. Something special. I want you so badly that it makes my heart hurt. For weeks I've been itching to text you, call you, fucking drive to your house and bang on your door. But I didn't. You don't need me in your life. I've not had a girlfriend before, and you've had enough inexperienced pricks to last a lifetime.'

She couldn't believe what he was saying. He thought he was inexperienced. Was he mad?

'So, what changed your mind?'

'A good friend told me to stop dicking around because you only live once. I'm also a little drunk.' A rueful smile crossed his lips. 'I want you to come to London. Come and visit me for the weekend and I can show you a glimpse of my life. I want to stop overthinking and see where this goes. Are you up for that, or have I scared you off?'

This wasn't how she expected the weekend to go. Taking a seat on the edge of the bed, she inhaled, drinking in his scent as he sat beside her. The last of her resolve to stay away from him fell away.

She puffed out a breath of resignation. 'Okay.'

'Okay.' His shoulders visibly relaxed as his eyes turned to her. His words were hesitant as he said, 'Can I kiss you?'

'I think we're past the stage where you need to ask, don't you?' She'd barely finished her sentence before his lips were on her again, hungry to taste her. His fingers interlaced with the curls in her hair, pulling her into him. She'd never felt more desired than she did when he kissed her. Her heart raced, pumping blood and need to her core. She hesitated, pulling away from his embrace.

'What's wrong? Have I pushed you too far?' Tom's hand came to her face, his eyes searching hers.

Embarrassment washed over Lucy, her already flushed cheeks now positively glowing. 'I can't do anything with you tonight.'

His brows knitted together in confusion as he said, 'Do anything? What do you mean?'

'I can't have sex. Aunt Flow is staying with me.'

'That's okay, our first time won't be a frenzied quick fuck in a hotel. However much I want to sink into you now, I won't.' He kissed her forehead, tracing his fingers up and down her upper arm, sending sparks of desire skittering across her skin. 'How about we get that dance? The others will wonder where we've got to.'

'I'd like that. Can I have one more kiss before we go?' She didn't need to ask twice.

Tap. Tap. Tap.

Lucy rolled over and pressed the cool side of the pillow into her face.

Tap. Tap. Tap.

She let out a groan as her pulse thumped through her brain. She pulled her knees up as her period cramps roused her from her alcohol induced sleep.

Tap. Tap. Tap.

'Lucy, are you okay?' Lucy recognised the muffled deep voice coming through her door. She threw back the covers, rubbed at her eyes and croaked out, 'Yeah, I'm coming.'

'Oh really? I hope you're thinking of me while you do.'

'What?' She realised what he meant as she opened the door. 'You've got a dirty mind.' Tom was leaning on the doorframe, a takeaway coffee cup in hand and a grin plastered on his face.

'You have no idea just how dirty my mind is, but you're in no state for me to get into that. Here.' He handed the cup over. 'I've brought you a coffee, extra strong, as I figured you'd need it after the shots of tequila you did last night.'

'Thank you. Do you want to come in?'

Tom nodded as he walked into her room and closed the door. Lucy got back into bed and brought her knees up to her chest as she sipped at her coffee.

'Don't take this the wrong way, but you don't look so good. Do you need me to get you some painkillers?'

'If you don't mind? I have some by the sink.' She pointed towards the bathroom.

'Here you go.' He handed over two pills with a bottle of water from the minibar. 'What you need is a cooked breakfast. That'll sort out your hangover.'

'I don't think my hangover is that bad—unless I'm still drunk—it's my cramps. I know better than to drink when, well, you know.' She didn't feel comfortable discussing her periods with Tom.

He tapped his finger against his lip in contemplation. 'Mmm, I see. There are two things I know of that will help you.'

She swallowed the tablets and downed the bottle of water, the cool liquid quenching her thirst. 'Please tell.'

'It's scientifically proven that orgasms help with pain relief. That or gentle exercise. I'll happily help you out with either.'

She gulped her coffee. 'Um, perhaps we stick to gentle exercise this morning.'

'You can't blame a guy for trying.' He leaned over, kissing her on the crown of her head. 'Get ready, and I'll meet you downstairs for some breakfast, then we can take a stroll.'

Breakfast was more sedate than the last meal they'd all shared. Sarah's head remained firmly in her hands while groaning periodically. Imogen and Cameron didn't let go of each other, and their giddy smiles warmed Lucy's heart. The others were mostly silent as they chewed their breakfasts slowly.

Tom held the door open as she stepped out into the fresh morning air of the gardens surrounding the wedding venue. She wrapped her arms around herself, rubbing warmth into her arms.

'Come here.' Tom draped his arm around her shoulders and pulled her close. It felt so natural to be in his arms, her shoulder fitting under his arm perfectly.

'Do you feel better?'

'I do, thank you.'

'Good.'

The pebbled pathway led them around the perfectly manicured gardens until they reached a stone bench that faced a large pond, complete with a spectacular fountain.

'Can we sit? I want to talk to you.'

Her heartbeat faltered. She wondered if this was the part where he let her down gently.

'Now that you're sober, I wanted to make sure you're still happy to come and stay with me in London. I don't want you to feel you have to go through with it if you're not ready.'

'Oh.' She puffed out a breath. 'I thought you were going to tell me you didn't want me to come.'

He shook his head. 'Not at all. I'm a man of my word, Lucy. I hope I can prove that to you.'

'Me too.' They sat in comfortable silence, arm in arm, as the spray from the fountain created ripples across the pond's surface. After some time, they sauntered back to the hotel.

When it was time to check out, Tom helped Lucy load up her car.

'Do you want me to come and pick you up? Save you getting the train.'

'No, it's okay. I'll get the train down. You'll have to let me know what tubes I need to take to get to your place. I don't understand the underground maps.'

'I'll pick you up from the station. I don't want to risk you getting lost.'

Dear Diary,

It's been two weeks since I last saw Tom, and the weekend has finally arrived. I'm glad Jen and Cam got back from their honeymoon the other day. Jen gave me a pep talk and reassured me I could call her if I need to leave. She'd come and get me, no questions asked. I don't think I'll need to call her, though. I don't feel anxious when I'm with Tom. It's weird, but I feel like I can be myself around him. So that's a good start.

The girls took me shopping for clothes on our lunch break today. I may have purchased some new underwear too, not that I'm going to rush into anything, but it doesn't hurt to make sure you have matching underwear on.

I'm not bringing you with me tomorrow. I don't want Tom to know I write a diary, and I don't think I'll need you, anyway.

Wish me luck.

Why am I writing as if I'm talking to you? You're a notebook, not my therapist. Although, I guess you kind of are my therapist.

Anyway, I need to get my beauty sleep as I'm hoping for a late night tomorrow!

CHAPTER 15

LUCY

Run Through Walls – The Script

'The train is now entering Euston Station. The service terminates here.' Lucy fidgeted with some loose thread on her seat as she listened to the train announcer. There was no turning back now. She wiped her sweaty palms on the seat before gingerly standing to take her bags down from the overhead shelf and waited at the nearby door for it to open.

She took her time walking to the barriers. She couldn't explain why, but she always felt anxious when pushing her ticket into the little slot. What if it spat it back out? Being rejected by a ticket barrier felt like a low point. And what if it sucked in her ticket, and she doesn't get through the barrier quick enough before it aggressively slams the flaps shut again?

'Get a move on.' A gruff voice boomed behind her, only adding to her nerves. She fumbled with her ticket and thanked the Lord when the doors opened. She heaved her bags over and made it through.

Forgetting the queue of people behind her, she took a quick breath to steady her nerves before carrying on with her journey. The impatient man behind her had other ideas as he pushed past her, knocking her off balance. She braced herself to hit the floor, but instead of the cold, hard concrete floor, she was wrapped in two arms and a firm chest.

'Well, this is a first. I've not had a beautiful woman fall at my feet like this before.' The familiar voice was deep, gravelly and oozed sex. She looked up into enchanting green eyes and knew she was safe; a call to Imogen wouldn't be necessary.

'Sorry. That jerk was clearly in too much of a hurry to walk around me.' She was breathless, but that had little to do with the fall and more to do with the piercing gaze she was on the receiving end of.

'Are you okay? Here, let me carry your bags.' Tom took the bags from her before waiting for a reply. Lucy took a second to drink him in. He'd dressed casually in blue jeans and a black leather biker jacket, the neck of a white T-shirt visible underneath. His chunky, tan-leather boots finished his look off nicely. She shook herself out of her daydream when she noticed he had concern etched on his face.

'I'm good, thanks, no harm done. Thanks to you, my knight in shining armour once again.'

'Happy to help. Now, let's get out of here; I made lunch reservations.'

He swung her overnight bag onto his shoulder as he wrapped his free arm around her, pulling her closer, and guiding her out into the winter sunshine.

The sounds of horns blaring, people chatting, and a hum of white noise only found in big cities hit Lucy as she stepped outside. Ordinarily, she would feel anxious walking through the crowds, but being in Tom's arms calmed her.

'I'm parked just around the corner. I thought I'd best bring the car as I didn't think the motorbike would be practical.'

'Very sensible. I've never been on a motorbike.'

'I can take you out on it later if you like? We could go out this evening when the traffic dies down. It'll give you such a buzz.'

'Can I think about it? I'm scared I'd fall off.'

'Of course, no pressure.' He stopped and turned to face her. 'You don't have to do anything you don't want to.'

'Okay.' She nodded.

'Here we are, hop in.' Tom opened the passenger door.

'This is yours?' She said, rooted to the spot, staring at an Aston Martin in a sexy-as-hell racing green that matched his eyes.

'Nah, I stole it on the way here.' He laughed at her bug-eyed expression. 'Yes, it's mine. There are some perks to working every evening and weekend dealing with London's elite.'

'This is a seriously sexy car.' She resisted the urge to glide her hand along the sweeping curves.

'Fit for a seriously sexy woman. Get in.' As he put her bags in the boot, she slid into the passenger seat and swung her legs into the footwell, hoping the soles of her shoes were clean.

'It's sexy inside, too,' she said as Tom climbed into the driver's seat.

'Funny you say that. The interior is called Dark Knight. You have to have it with that name. Don't you agree?'

'I do. I love it. Can we just drive around all afternoon?'

'Maybe another day. We need to get to the restaurant.' He pulled out effortlessly into the traffic, turning heads as they drove.

Absentmindedly, she rubbed her hands together, interlaced her fingers, and rubbed them together again. Her anxiousness was obvious as Tom's hand captured hers.

'You look beautiful today. You always look beautiful.' He gave her a reassuring smile before looking back at the road ahead. 'I've been looking forward to this weekend. I've put fresh sheets on the spare bed, so don't feel you have to share a bed with me tonight. There's no pressure; this is the first date, after all.'

She released the breath she'd been holding. 'Thank you. I must admit, that has been playing on my mind.'

'I could tell; you haven't stopped fidgeting since you got in the car.' He didn't remove his hand until they'd parked up near the restaurant.

Tom dashed round the car to open the door, offering her his hand. As she stood, he caught the back of her head in his hand and pressed his lips to hers. He released a low groan as his hands roamed down her back, resting on her hips; her back pressed into the doorframe. The kiss left her breathless and panting as he pulled away.

'Sorry about that. I wouldn't have made it through lunch if I didn't get that out of my system.'

Words failed her, so she just smiled while thinking about what else he had to get out of his system.

'Let's eat.'

As Tom drove down into an underground car park, Lucy recognised where they were. As he opened the door for her, she asked, 'Are we coming straight to the club?' She'd hoped to have some chill time before getting changed into something more fitting for a date with a London club owner.

He smiled as he grabbed her things and took her by the hand. 'I live here too.'

'Oh. I didn't realise. I thought I'd seen every floor when we came here before. Where do you live then?'

'The very top. Cam did a great job of converting the loft space into a fully soundproofed apartment. You wouldn't know we were on the top of a club. It helps that the nightclub is in the basement. The other rooms aren't that loud in comparison.'

Lucy looked around as they crossed the car park. Flashbacks from the last time she was here came flooding back. Memories of the fight flooded her memory.

She shivered from the chill that ran down her spine. Something that Tom had clearly picked up on as he said, 'He's gone now, babe. He can't hurt anyone. My goal this weekend is to erase all the terrible memories of here and replace them with amazing ones. Do you trust me to do that?'

She wasn't so sure what she trusted in anymore, but the champagne from lunch gave her a dose of courage. 'I do.'

'Good.' He dropped her bags to the floor and wrapped his arms around her. The warmth from his body and the scent of his skin calmed her once again. If she wasn't careful, he'd become a comfort blanket she wouldn't be able to let go of.

As they stepped out of the private elevator, she took in her surroundings. She'd expected the place to be dark and like the club below them, but it wasn't. Massive windows looked out over the London skyline, making the open-plan living space bright.

'Do you like it?'

'I love it.'

'It's quite nerve-wracking bringing an interior designer home, although James was in charge, so it shouldn't be too bad.'

'It's gorgeous,' she said as she looked around.

The walls were light grey, and the window and door frames were satin white. A modern kitchen and furnishings blended in perfectly with dark oak flooring, adding warmth to the large space.

'I'll leave your bag in the guest room.' Tom held her hand and took her to the room at the far end. 'There is a guest bathroom through here. You can get ready in here if you want to.' He took her by the hand again and led her through the next door. 'This is my room. You can get ready in here if you prefer. It's entirely up to you.' The way he squeezed her hand as he spoke showed his preference.

Tom's room was more in line with what she was expecting. The walls were dark blue and contrasted strikingly with the white of the window frames. She nervously glanced at the bed, not wanting to draw attention to it. It was massive, bigger than a king-size, and the white bedding was obviously a high thread count by the sheen, the edges finished with dark blue silk.

'There's time before we need to head downstairs. Do you want to chill out on the sofa?'

'Sounds good.' Her feet ached already; she needed to get used to wearing heels, especially as the ones for the evening were an inch higher than what she had on.

Tom shrugged off his jacket and helped her out of hers before hanging them up.

'Can I get you something to drink?'

'A water would be good, thank you.' She didn't want to get drunk.

She took in the massive corner sofa, big enough for at least six people, and wasn't sure where to sit. The large footstool made the whole thing look like a giant bed.

'Get comfortable and put your feet up.' He sat down next to her, their thighs barely touching but close enough for her to feel his heat through their jeans.

He pressed a few buttons on the TV remote and as the opening scenes of Guardians of the Galaxy began; he put his arm around her shoulder and pulled her closer. She allowed herself to sink into him and close her eyes for a moment; wanting to revel in every moment. This already felt so natural, and it scared her.

She was determined not to get too invested this time, at least not until she was sure he wasn't using her to plot the death of one of her friends or was a loser with mummy issues. She sat herself up and turned to face him.

'Do you have any psycho tendencies I should know about?'

Tom laughed, the sound lightening the mood. 'No, not that I'm aware of. The only thing crazy is how much I want to kiss you. But I'm holding myself back so I don't scare you off.'

'Oh. Well, that's okay. I just wanted to make sure you won't try to kill me while I sleep.'

'You're safe with me. I can't promise I won't try to eat you at every given opportunity though.'

Her mind raced. Did he mean it in the way she thought he meant it? Was he flirting with her or trying to be funny? Before she could think of a witty reply, his lips gently pressed against hers, silencing her mind. Her traitorous body wasn't as invested as her mind in taking this slowly. Her reaction to his kiss and the feel of his hands roaming her face, her neck and her back was immediate and violent.

She ran her fingers through his hair, pulling him in. She wanted more of him—all of him. Her finger traced along the hard lines of his chest as she worked her way across his collarbone and down his biceps. They were hard beneath her hands; no wonder she felt safe in these arms.

Tom ran his hands down her back, squeezing her hips before pulling her onto him, knees straddling him. The contact of his groin on hers set fireworks off in her core. The pulsing need was now unbearable, but she desperately tried to keep it together. She pulled her lips away from his, breaking the contact.

'Are you okay? Is this too much?' His hands stilled on her hips.

'I've never wanted this so much. I feel like I'm on fire and I'm not sure how much I can cope with.'

He pressed his lips to her forehead before peppering her with kisses across her temple, her cheekbone and then her earlobe. He whispered, 'Let me take care of those flames, baby. I got you.' He stood—her legs still wrapped around his hips—with ease. 'Stand up. Tell me to stop if I go too far.'

She quickly nodded her head. Whatever he was going to do, he needed to do it now, before her mind took over.

Keeping eye contact, he lowered his hands to the waistband of her jeans and unbuttoned them. He paused, waiting for any sign of objection, but she didn't give him any.

He eased her zip down; the vibrations sending shock waves to her swollen clit. Lowering her down onto the sofa, he lifted the hem of her black, fine-knit sweater, peppering kisses across her midsection. Her abdomen contracted as his hot lips pressed against her fevered skin.

He hooked his fingers into the waistband of her jeans and pulled them down her legs. Lifting each foot, he stripped her of her trousers.

His hooded eyes raked over her as his hands glided over her thighs. He bent his head and kissed between her legs. She could feel the heat of his breath through her black lacy underwear. A low moan escaped her mouth.

Her heart thundered in her chest as a mix of anticipation, fear, and desperation mingled in her mind. His powerful hands gripped onto her rear, pulling her down to straddle his hips.

'Raise your arms, sexy.'

He pulled her top off and threw it to the floor. Leaning back, he sucked in a deep breath. She resisted the urge to cover herself up with her arms.

He bit into his bottom lip and said, 'You're fucking perfect.'

She ran her fingers down his T-shirt as she said, 'And you're fully clothed.'

He slid his hand into the waistband of her underwear and cupped her sex. The pressure from his palm almost sent her over the edge. 'This is for you. We need to take care of those flames, remember? You've got all night, and I fully intend to have you begging for it by the end of the evening.' As he finished speaking, he slid his middle finger into her folds. The sudden sensation of something inside her made her buck and gasp. In one quick movement, she was on her back, spread out across the large footstool, with Tom on his knees between her legs.

He folded himself over her, kissing her chest and sucking on her nipples through the delicate fabric of her bra. Her nipples rose to hardened peaks as he circled them with his tongue. His finger dipping in and out of her tender flesh.

'I can feel your need on my finger. Don't worry; I won't keep you waiting long.' He pulled her underwear off and spread her thighs wider. The anticipation of what he was going to do drove her crazy. For a few brief moments, he gently kissed the tops of her thighs, avoiding her throbbing clit, teasing her. Her hips writhed, desperate for his lips to make contact. He held onto her hips, stilling her as his mouth came down right where she wanted it.

She threw her head back with a gasp as he licked up her entrance with one long, firm swipe of his tongue. He closed his eyes, releasing a groan. 'Fuck. You taste so good.' He pushed the tip of his tongue inside her and sucked on her clit. She cried out with pleasure, her opening pulsing around his mouth, her hips rising to increase the pressure.

'Oh.' Her hands grasped at the velvet beneath her, desperate to keep control.

'I got you, baby. Don't hold back on me, just let go.'

He hooked her knees over his shoulders and leaned into her, opening her up to him. He drove two fingers inside while he lapped at her firm, swollen clit. Her breathing became ragged as she neared her climax. She could feel it coming and there was no stopping it.

'That's it, let go. You're so close, I can feel it, taste it.' His words vibrated against her and as he thrust in a third finger and sucked hard on her clit. She shattered. The anxiety, stress, self-doubts and tension exploded out of her body as she cried out.

Her back arched and her hands searched for something to anchor her, grasping onto the sides of the footstool.

Tom licked her clean of her arousal as she came back down, her back resting on the soft velvet beneath her.

'You're wound so tight. How long has it been since someone took care of you?'

As she sat up, he pulled her onto his lap, running his fingers through her hair, tucking it behind her ears.

Eyes cast downward, she said, 'No one has ever taken care of me like that.'

'Do you mean you've never had a man go down on you?'

'My ex, and only proper boyfriend, has gone down there,' she whispered, feeling almost ashamed of what she was about to say. 'But it never ended like that. I've never felt like I was going to explode, with or without a man's involvement.'

'Are you saying you've never had an orgasm?'

Too embarrassed to speak, she nodded. He lifted her chin until their eyes met. 'Then I've got some making up to do.'

As Lucy finished doing her makeup, she stared at her reflection in the guestroom mirror. As she came down from the high of her earth-shattering orgasm, doubts crept in. She picked up her phone and dialled Imogen.

'Hey Hun, how is your weekend going? This isn't a rescue call, is it?'

'No, I'm staying for the weekend. I need a pep talk.'

'Is it not going well?' She could hear the concern in Imogen's voice.

'I think it's going too well. Tom's amazing. He's so hot I can't control myself around him.'

'So, what are you worried about?'

'I'm worried he's going to think I'm easy.'

'Why would he think that?'

'We were kissing on his sofa earlier and things got heated. He went down on me, and it was amazing. I've experienced nothing like it before. I've not even seen him naked and there I am, spread out in front of him with his mouth down there.'

'Oh Hun, that doesn't make you easy. You two have chemistry, that's all. Every time Tom called Cam to check on him while he was recovering, he asked about you. Every single time. Don't tell him I said that, though.'

The thought of him asking after her warmed her through. 'I won't, don't worry.' She sighed. 'This is basically our first date. I wouldn't dream of having sex on a first date, but I really want to. He's given me the choice of where I sleep tonight. What should I do?'

'What do you want to do?'

'When I'm near him, I lose all self-control. My body goes into autopilot and my mind shuts down. I know that if he comes near me tonight, I'll be desperate to go all the way and stay in his room. I'm not a slut, though, and I don't want him thinking I am.'

'No, you're not a slut. You're a grown woman with needs. If it's what you want—and what he wants—then there's nothing stopping you. What you're experiencing is chemistry, and there isn't a lot you can do to stop it. Christ, on day three of meeting Cameron, we got so passionate in the woods behind the office I orgasmed, and we were both fully clothed. Honestly, Hun, you're not doing anything wrong. It would be wrong to deny yourself what your body craves. You deserve toe-curling sex for a change.'

'Thanks. Maybe I should stop overthinking this and go with the flow.'

'Exactly. Only do what you're comfortable doing. That he said you can choose where you sleep tells me he wants to make sure you hold the power. Take that power and use it for good, sexy lady.'

They said their goodbyes and Lucy finished getting ready. Imogen's words of encouragement made her feel better. Perhaps she deserved to have some fun, and toe-curling sex sounded like a great deal of fun.

CHAPTER 16

LUCY

Bright (feat. Aubrey Toone) – AIRGLØW

'You look beautiful.' Tom shook his head slightly and said, 'I need to come up with a better word; I've used it too many times already. Perhaps I should say you look fuckable?' Lucy had just stepped out of the guestroom to find Tom waiting patiently, his hands resting casually in his pockets.

She was wearing a simple black dress, off the shoulder and fitted down to her knees. It showed off her curves in an understated way. She didn't want to look like the other women in the club; Tom's words about how they hide behind the latest fashion and layers of makeup replayed in her mind as she chose it.

Her hair fell in thick, glossy waves around her shoulders, and kept her makeup simple.

She blushed. 'Thank you. You look good too.' That was an understatement. Casual Tom was sexy as hell. His jeans, chunky boots, leather jacket and stubble were hot, but this was something else. Dressed in a dark navy suit, fitted white shirt, dark tan leather shoes and belt and clean-shaven, he was simply stunning and very fuckable.

The heat was building in his eyes as he smiled. Stepping towards her, he trailed kisses from her cheek to her exposed collarbone.

'I don't want to smudge your lip gloss, so I guess I'm going to have to kiss you everywhere else.' The heat from his lips spread throughout her body, a need growing between her legs. He prowled around her, taking hold of her hair and moving it to the side as he trailed kisses across her shoulders. She closed her eyes as a moan escaped her lips.

'Do you like that?'

Her voice was breathy as she answered him. 'Yes.' Any resolve to resist her urges fell away as soon as his lips touched hers.

'Then I'll keep it up all night.' He interlaced his hand in hers, kissing the back of her hand. 'Unfortunately, it's time to head down. Do you have everything you need?'

They took the elevator down to the ground floor. It was early evening, and the club would open in less than an hour.

'It feels odd being back here and it being so quiet.' There were multiple levels to the club. The ground floor is where the casino and bar are; the basement contains the dance club, complete with flashing dance floor. Tom's office was on the first floor, along with another bar area that Lucy hadn't noticed before; too preoccupied by the fight the last time she was there.

'This is my favourite time. It's the calm before the storm. There's a buzz in the air as we all get ready; wondering what the night will hold. No two nights are ever the same.' He takes a two-way radio from its charging dock and clips it onto his belt, concealed by his jacket. 'Would you like a drink? You can take a seat if you like or wander around with me. I have a few things to check on before we open.'

'I'm good, thank you. I don't want to peak too soon.'

'Don't worry, delayed gratification is what I do best. You won't peak too soon.'

Lucy understood the innuendo. She blushed, wondering if she was out of her depth with him. He was treating her as if she was an experienced lover; someone who could handle this level of attention, but the knot in her stomach told her she wasn't.

They entered the bar, which was empty but for one man emptying the dishwasher and stacking glasses. The walls were highly polished wood; the furniture made from deep red velvet. This was where the male socialites of London would drink their brandy while their wives and mistresses danced and flirted in the club downstairs.

'Jack, meet Lucy. She's my guest for the weekend. Give her anything she wants, please. And don't leave her waiting.'

Jack puts the glasses down and offers Lucy his hand. 'Pleased to meet you, Lucy. Anything you need, just give me a shout. Be sure to order the expensive stuff.' He winks as he smiles over at Tom.

'Jack, I expect you to *only* give her the good stuff.' He absentmindedly trails a finger across her collarbone as he speaks. 'Are the fridges stocked with champagne? I don't want a repeat of last week.'

'Yes. I checked the stock myself earlier.'

'Good. Keep me updated on any potential issues with the guests tonight.'

He nodded his response. Lucy wondered what issues might arise; hopefully not another psycho ex-boyfriend coming to claim his property. 'Do you get a lot of trouble in here? I get the impression this place is too classy for pub brawls.'

'No, rarely. Most issues arise when a drunk husband becomes over-familiar with the bar staff in front of their wife. Then all bets are off.' He laughs, and the sound warms her. His eyes darken, and his smile falls as he says, 'Recently, we've had a few new guests that live by their own rules. One of them was here when you were here last. Do you remember the guy that gave Sarah and Imogen a load of hassle?'

Lucy nodded. 'Well, he unfortunately keeps coming back, and he brings his friends with him.'

'Why don't you just ban them?'

'It's not that simple—I wish it was.'

'I don't understand.'

'Don't worry about it. It's being dealt with. Sometimes, you pick your battles, that's all. They're harmless enough; they just need a reminder now and then on how to behave.' Tom carries on walking.

They go to the casino, where the same dark wood lines the walls, the only light coming from the chandeliers that hang over each table. The croupiers were standing at their tables, preparing the chips and loading the cards into the shuffling machines.

'Wait here for just a sec. I need to speak to my casino manager.' He walks over to a muscly, tall man dressed all in black. They confer with each other quietly before Tom shakes his hand and walks away. 'Right, let's head downstairs.'

They take the familiar stairs to the basement. The last time Lucy was here, she could hear the bass beat pounding through the door, but this time, it was quiet. As he holds the door open for her, she can hear the DJ testing his equipment. The room looked so different when the lights were on. The dance floor was milky white glass, with no hint of the flashing neon colours that come to life with the music.

She looked over at the table they'd all sat at when Imogen, Sarah and Jess came for a girl's night out. The hair on her arms stood on end as she remembered the moment she learned that Paul, a man she'd just dumped with a text message, was Mark. He'd played her for a fool and to add insult to injury, he nearly knocked her unconscious when he turned up to confront Imogen.

He must have sensed her change in mood, as Tom's arms wrapped around her shoulders. 'I'm going to erase all those memories. After this weekend, when you think of this club, you'll blush with heat, not shiver with fear.'

He kissed her nape as his hands roamed down her back and cupped her rear. The tip of his tongue caught the base of her earlobe as he sucked on it. She filled her lungs with his cologne—fresh citrus, vanilla and leather.

'The last time you were here, you were bent over my bar drinking tequila. This time, you'll be bent over my bar, but I'll be drinking you.' His whispered words and the intoxicating scent left her feeling dizzy as she remembered how it felt to have him between her legs.

A crash from behind brought Lucy down to Earth with a bang.

'What the fuck, Sophia?'

'Sorry, boss.'

'Lucy, this is Sophia.' He gestured to a woman standing near the bar.

'Ah yes, hello. I remember you; you served us when I was here with my friends.'

'That's right. You all enjoyed the tequila, if I remember rightly.'

'Yep, that was us. My head was pounding the next day.'

'Soph, can you watch Lucy tonight if I get called away?'

'No worries, I'd love to babysit your girlfriend.'

'Less of the attitude. Let's get this mess cleaned up, shall we?' Tom crouched down to help put away the case of mixers Sophia had dropped, giving her a warning look.

Lucy picked up on that he'd not corrected Sophia. She wondered what that meant. It was too early to be putting a label on whatever they were, but maybe that was his way of saying she was more than a weekend plaything. She didn't know and wasn't about to get her hopes up, that was for sure, but the word girlfriend sat nicely in her mind.

As they left the club and made their way up to the top floor, he turned and said, 'Don't pay any attention to Soph. Her bark is worse than her bite. She's been here since I opened and thinks that gives her the right to forget her place.'

'Her place? That sounds sexist, doesn't it?'

'That's not how I meant it. She has a habit of stepping out of line with me and the customers. Her mouth is going to get her into trouble if she's not careful. I just don't have the heart to sack her. At least if she's here, I can keep a check on her.'

A pang of jealously hit Lucy hard in the gut, taking her by surprise. 'Do you have a personal interest in all your staff or just the pretty ones?'

He stops and takes her in his arms. 'The only person I have a personal interest in is you. And for the record, I don't think she's pretty. She's a pain in my arse, but I trust her, so she stays.' He plants a kiss on her before continuing up the stairs.

They walk through another, more secluded bar area before reaching his office.

It felt like only yesterday when Lucy was sitting in the leather armchair in this office while Tom held an icepack to her cheek. The office hadn't changed; it was still every bit as masculine as it was before. His desk was solid oak, his chair and the two armchairs opposite were luxurious in dark brown leather.

While Tom worked, Lucy entertained herself by investigating the contents of the crystal decanters and studying the CCTV screens that covered most of one wall. It was strange to think that she was standing in the very spot where Cameron had stood that fateful evening when he spotted Mark making his way towards them on the dance floor below. She shuddered at the thought of what might have happened if Cameron wasn't paying such close attention to them that night. The sound of a laptop screen clicking shut interrupted her thoughts of Mark.

'Okay, I'm all yours. No more admin for me tonight.' He walked round to the other side of his desk and held his hand out, gesturing for her to stand. He wrapped his arms around her waist and pulled her in. The warmth from his body chased away the lingering shivers left by her thoughts. 'Thank you for waiting for me. I promise to make it up to you.'

'Oh really? And how do you intend to do that?'

'I can think of many ways, but first, I'll start with this.' His lips came down to meet hers, and he licked along her bottom lip, encouraging her to open up for him. His tongue dipped in as he groaned with appreciation.

Her hands spread across his broad shoulders, fantasizing about dragging her nails down his bare skin. She'd had a taste of what an orgasm felt like, and she wanted more, so much more.

She finally understood what all the fuss was about. Sarah would always revel in telling her about her conquests and how amazing they were; she assumed she was doing it wrong or just wasn't really into sex. Now she knew. If he could make her feel like that with just his fingers and mouth, she couldn't wait to find out what he could do with the rest of his body. Her skin tingled at the prospect.

His hands explored her body until his fingertips brushed the exposed skin of her inner thigh. Her legs felt weak as his finger brushed between her legs. She gasped into his mouth; the heat rising in her body radiating out from her core.

His voice was deep and husky as he said, 'Do you like that?'

'Yes,' she whispered.

He pressed kisses onto her nape as he asked, 'Do you want more?' She could feel his fingers skirting along the delicate lace seam of her underwear.

'Yes.' Her breathing was shallow as she gasped for air.

'I'm going to spend this weekend driving you crazy. Your body will scream for sweet release. You're going to come undone in my arms.'

'I already feel like I'm coming undone.'

He pressed his forehead to hers, closing his eyes and taking a deep breath. 'I haven't even begun to do all the things I want to do to you, Lucy.'

She knew that his words should have filled her with excitement, but she felt out of her depth. In the split-second that Tom's fingers paused in their caress, her mind interrupted her pleasure and reminded her she was pretending to be this confident woman. She pulled herself away, looking at the floor.

'Hey, I'm sorry. Am I coming on too strong?' Worry etched across Tom's face as he took a step back.

'No. No, you're perfect. The problem is me.' She didn't want to mess this up with him, but her mind was struggling to let go.

'What do you mean?' Tom encouraged her to sit back down as he perched on the edge of his desk in front of her. 'Talk to me.'

It was now or never. She owed it to him to be honest and lay her cards on the table.

'This is our first proper date. I'm not an experienced woman, and I have no idea what I'm doing. I changed my clothes and my hair to make others think I'd grown up and moved on, but it's all a lie. At the heart of it, I'm just a stupid little girl playing games. I don't want you to think I'm easy and then toss me aside, but I'm scared you'll realise just how inexperienced I am and toss me aside.'

Tom's gaze moved to the floor as he released a deep sigh.

'Maybe I should just go home.'

'What? No, you don't need to go home.' He took her hand in his, squeezing some reassurance into her. 'I had no idea you felt like that. If you want me to tone it down, I will. I didn't mean to come on too strong. I just can't help myself around you; it's like my body goes into autopilot and I can't control myself. I never normally date. In fact, I don't remember the last time I went on a date; and I've certainly never had a woman stay here with me. I'm making this all up as I go along.'

This catches her attention. 'Oh? I thought you were known for, how should I put this, your skills with the ladies? From what you did earlier, I figured you had women here all the time.'

'I've had a lot of sex, just not here, and not in the traditional sense.'

'What do you mean?'

'I think we should save that conversation for another time; I don't want to scare you off. And before you think it, no, I wasn't a hired dick.' His smile reaches his eyes, which have softened from the lustful look of only moments ago.

'When I saw you arrive at my club with the others, I couldn't keep my eyes off you, which was inconvenient,

160

as I was supposed to be watching the door and Imogen. Your very presence set something off in me, and when Mark hit you, I could have killed him. I knew you were more than just another attractive woman drinking in my club.'

A dark pink blush crept over her face and chest; no one had ever spoken to her, or about her, with such passion before.

'I don't care how many people you've slept with. I don't care that you think you're inexperienced. To be honest, it turns me on. The women that I used to sleep with were always chasing the next high, always wanting more and weren't afraid to cross lines. I think of you as a blank canvas. We're going to have the time of our lives breaking you in. The things I can do to you, teach you.'

He takes both of her hands in his. 'I wasn't joking when I said I wanted to worship you. If you'll let me, I'll worship you and take you to places you've never dreamed of. It angers me that your ex never put your needs first, and don't even get me started on what Mark did to you. It's my duty, and my pleasure, to erase all of that. Fuck convention, Lucy. Yes, it's our first proper date, but you've been waiting for long enough.'

Words failed her, but her eyes said it all. He wrapped his arms around her, their lips crashing together, their bodies taking over.

She forced space between them, panting as she said, 'Show me how to please you.'

His eyes were pure fire as his hands gripped her rear and hooked her legs onto his hips. Turning around, he placed her down on his desk as he deepened the kiss.

Cough. Cough.

They froze as they spotted Sophia standing in the doorway, a tray of sushi perched on one hand, the other holding the door open.

Tom rested his forehead on Lucy's and took a deep breath.

'Please knock in future, Sophia.'

'Sorry, boss. It won't happen again.' She walked in, eyeing Lucy up, before placing the tray down on the table across the office.

'Enjoy your meal. And again, sorry for interrupting.' She scurried out and quietly closed the door behind her.

'Oh my god, I'm so embarrassed.'

'Don't be. It takes a lot to shock her. She's never had to knock before, because like I said earlier, I've had no one in here.'

'I still can't believe that. Surely women throw themselves at you all the time. Have you seen yourself? You look like Thor.'

Tom laughs as he says, 'Why thank you, that is quite the compliment. I do have a big hammer.' He winks. 'You're right, women flirt with me. I'm the owner of an exclusive club in London. I'm a means to an end for them.'

Lucy looked at him, confused.

'I'm a good way to make their husbands jealous, or they want me for what I represent. They see wedding bells and a lifetime of partying with the rich and famous. With you, I know the attraction is genuine.' He spoke with such ease, as if what he was saying was normal. 'I hope you like sushi. I ordered it in earlier, figuring we'd have had a big lunch, but thought you might want something to line your stomach.'

'That's very thoughtful, and I love sushi. Thank you.'

They took a seat at the table and Lucy watched as Tom squeezed the wasabi paste into a little dish of soy sauce and mixed it with his chopstick. She picked up the chopsticks and tried to copy the way he was holding them.

'I'm shit with these. I apologise now if I flick a California roll in your face.'

'Use your fingers. I'm not sure I want wasabi in the eye. Or you can use this technique.' He stabbed a sushi roll with a single chopstick and lifted it like a marshmallow on a stick.

'Genius. I'll do that.'

They sat and ate in comfortable silence, exchanging heated glances now and then.

'Oh shit.' A trickle of soy sauce dribbled down her chin as she absentmindedly popped a whole avocado roll in her mouth.

'I'll get it.' Tom quickly leant over the table and licked the dark, salty liquid away. He closed his eyes as he licked his lips.

'Stop it, you minx.' Her laughter erupted as she swatted him away. It shocked her how comfortable they were with each other; her confessions had lifted a weight off her shoulders.

'Right then, sexy, time to mingle.'

CHAPTER 17

LUCY

Toxic – 2WEI

'Let's get a drink; then I can take you for a spin on the roulette wheel.'

They walked through to the bar on the ground floor. Tom ordered a coke for himself and a glass of champagne for Lucy. She knew the bubbles were going to go straight to her head, but that was okay; she needed the courage tonight.

Armed with some betting chips, he took her over to the roulette table.

'You'll have to tell me what to do; I've never played this before.'

'Don't worry; it's all about luck. The question is, are you feeling lucky tonight?'

Her eyes smoldered as they met his. 'Yes, I'm feeling very lucky this evening.'

She'd seen in movies that you place your chips down on the green felt, but as she looked at all the different sections and numbers before her, her brows knitted in confusion.

'Okay, where shall I place my chips?'

'That's up to you. What takes your fancy?'

'What does manqué mean?' She knew it must be French as she recognised the words noir and rouge, but this word escaped her.

'It means failed. The ball has failed to land on a number above eighteen. Passe means it has landed between nineteen and thirty-six. You can bet on red or black; below or above eighteen; odds or evens. There are lots of bets you can make, but for ease, maybe stick with the basics.'

She stared at the table for a minute, tapping her finger to her lip. 'Okay, I'm going to go all in on noir.' She slid the chips into the black box.

'Reckless. I like it.'

The spinning of the wheel and the buzz of placing a bet made her feel dizzy.

The croupier announced the result as the ball dropped. 'Noir.'

She jumped for joy and planted a kiss on Tom's cheek. 'Yes. Can I go again?'

'Of course.' Tom was smiling as he watched her bouncing around.

'Okay, this time I'm going all in again on rouge.' She clasped her hands together as she watched the ball spin one more time.

'Noir.'

Her face fell. 'That's pants.'

'That's gambling for you.'

'How much did I just lose? I don't even know what I was betting.'

'You've just lost a thousand pounds.'

'Oh shit.' Her hand flew up to her mouth in shock, her eyes wide. 'I'm so sorry. I didn't know I was playing with so much.'

'Don't worry, babe, it all comes back to me, anyway.'

'Oh yeah, that's true.' She giggled.

'Do you fancy a dance?' He looked at her empty glass. 'And another drink?'

'Yes, please.'

The club was back to how she remembered it, lit with disco lights and the dance floor. It was already full of people drinking, dancing and having a good time.

Tom led the way to the back of the room to a reserved table.

'Let's finish these drinks and then get on the dance floor; I can't wait to bump and grind with you.'

She blushed, the heat rising in her body. She could feel eyes on them, and as she looked out to the dance floor, she saw all the women dancing in Tom's direction, showing off their moves. They were all gorgeous and looked like they had stepped out of a copy of Vogue magazine. She glanced down at her own outfit and wondered if she'd made a mistake by dressing more conservatively.

Tom stood and held his hand out. 'Will you do me the honour of having this dance with me?'

She placed her hand in his and let him lead the way.

'Hi Tom.'

'Hi Tom.'

'Tom, would you like to join us for a drink?'

It was endless. Every woman they walked past wanted to speak to him. He smiled but kept on walking until they found a clearing in the dancing masses.

'Are you sure you don't want to dance with anyone else?'

'Positive. You're here, and I don't need anyone else.' Just to prove his point, he cupped the back of her head with both hands and pressed his lips to hers.

The onlookers had disappointment all over their faces, but they got the message and turned their backs just as his hands roamed her back and came to rest on her hips.

She could feel his hard chest pressed into hers, and she wondered what he looked like naked. She slid her hands under his jacket, stroking his back as they swayed in time to the music. He felt firm and powerful—nothing like Andrew; who was softer, more juvenile. But Tom was strong and chiselled. She could feel his muscles flexing as he moved and, once again, her thoughts turned to his naked body. She was shocked as thoughts of him having sex came into her mind. He wasn't making love to her; he was thrusting into someone else while she looked on. She wanted to know what he looked like; wanted to witness his power from afar.

His comments about sleeping with a lot of women—women who will cross lines—flooded her mind and she wondered what that meant, but also what that looked like.

She could only imagine how his arse looked as he drove into someone. How his muscles tensed with each thrust.

'Feeling horny by any chance, babe?'

His words snapped her out of her daydream as she realised her hands were squeezing his rear.

'Sorry.' She quickly brought them back up to his back.

He placed his mouth to her ear as he growled, 'Get those hands back on my arse now.' He finished with a quick suck on her earlobe that sent shockwaves down her spine and straight to her core.

His groin pressed into hers. 'Do you see what you do to me?'

She could feel his impressive erection pressing into her groin, the pressure driving her crazy.

'I could do with another drink. Do you mind if we sit down for a minute?'

'Not at all, but you're going to have to walk in front of me.'

She led the way back to their table, with Tom clinging to her from behind. They ignored the stolen glances as they walked through the throngs of his fans.

He gestured to Sophia to bring them some drinks as they took a seat next to each other. The table was in the far corner, away from the others; it felt secluded and intimate. Within minutes, Sophia delivered the drinks.

'Here you go, you two. I've added some tequila shots—I know how much you like those, eh Lucy?' Sophia winked as she walked off, not giving them a chance to object.

'Are you up for a shot with me?' Tom was staring at her; the double meaning in his question was loud and clear.

'Yes. Yes, I think I am.'

He smiled as he picked up the saltshaker and moved closer to her. Without warning, he licked across her collarbone before sprinkling the salt grains. She looked at him questioningly.

'Trust me, this is how we do shots.'

He nudged at her lips with his index finger until she opened them for him, instinctively sucking on it. He withdrew his finger and sprinkled that with salt too.

'And now we drink.' Lucy went to pick up a lemon wedge, but he stopped her. 'You won't be needing that.'

He licked the salt off her collarbone, getting every grain, as he pushed his finger into her mouth. She swirled her tongue around, lapping up the saltiness. When his finger was clean, he passed her the shot of tequila before taking his own.

'Bottoms up.' They downed the amber liquid. She could feel it warming her as it travelled down her throat. Tom sucked the lemon wedge and brought his lips to hers, sharing the juice in their mouths.

The intimacy of the act set light to the alcohol coursing through her veins. Her hips rocked, her thighs clenching with need.

'Tom. Come in, Tom.' A voice was coming from his hip, putting an end to the passion.

'Fuck. Sorry about this.' He unclipped his radio, pressing the button before saying, 'What is it?'

'Ivan. In the casino.'

He hung his head in frustration. 'Fuck.' He turned to Lucy, running his hand through her hair. 'Will you be okay waiting for me here while I sort something out?'

'Yeah, of course. Is everything okay?'

'It will be. I won't be long. Only a few minutes, I promise.' He presses his lips to hers before standing. 'I'm on my way.' He replaces his radio as he stalked off.

'Hey. I'm about to go on my break. Do you mind if I sit with you?' Sophia had walked over carrying a glass of coke and a large glass of wine.

'That would be nice, thank you.'

Sitting down in Tom's place, she says, 'Here, this is for you.' She hands over the glass of wine. 'I heard the radio conversation and figured you'd appreciate some company.'

'Thanks. And Thanks for the wine.' She lifted the glass in thanks before taking a large gulp. The coolness of the wine dampened out the residual flames.

'So, how long have you known Tom?'

'Oh, only since we were here last time. He looked after me after that dickhead hit me.'

'I'm sorry about all that. Tom told me what happened to you and the other girl. It must have been awful for you. At least he's gone now.'

'Yeah. It was the worst experience of my life, but I'd do it again if I had to.' She paused. 'Do you mind if I ask you a personal question?'

169

'If you're wondering if I've slept with him; the answer is no.' Sophia smiled.

'Ah, yes. I was wondering about that. Do you want to sleep with him?'

She took a long drink of her coke before answering. 'Yes, in all honestly, I would love to know what he's like in the sack. But I'll never know. He cares for me, even though I drive him mad. I guess he's become like a brother to me, watching my back and bailing me out when my motormouth gets me into trouble. I will say this: I've never seen him bring a woman here, especially not for the weekend. He normally goes elsewhere to get his kicks. You must be very special indeed.'

'What do you mean, he goes elsewhere?'

'It's not my place to discuss his private life, but he's never had a woman here. We'll leave it at that.'

Her mind races with what that could mean? What does he do for sex then? Prostitutes? Is that what he meant when he said his women will cross the line?

'He's not into something illegal, is he?'

She laughs as she says, 'No. Nothing illegal. Sorry, I didn't mean to give you that impression. He's just very private about his private life, that's all. You'll have to ask him.'

'Oh yeah, that sounds like a great conversation. "Oh, hey Tom, tell me, what do you do for sex then?"' She laughed at how cringy that conversation would be. 'What about you? Are you seeing anyone?' It would be nice to have a friend here, in case she became a regular visitor.

'I am actually.' She blushed as she spoke. 'It's a new thing, only a few weeks. I'm not getting my hopes up as I have a feeling he's a bit of a bad boy, and it never ends well with bad boys. Right, I'd better get back to work. Tom shouldn't be too much longer.'

'Thanks for the company,' she raised her glass, 'and the wine.'

'No worries. Enjoy your evening.'

Lucy sat back in the seat, sipping on her wine, waiting for him to return. It gave her time to address her earlier fantasies of her watching him in the act. She'd never fantasized about being a voyeur before, and it shocked her at how turned on she became. It was like her earlier orgasm had opened pandora's box, and all her darkest desires were flooding her mind.

And from the sounds of it, Tom had a darker side too.

CHAPTER 18

TOM

Ready for War – Joznez, 2WEI & Kataem

Tom strode up the stairs, taking them two at a time, anger coursing through his veins.

'Where is he?' He barked at Alex. Alex gestured to the back of the room with his head. 'Thanks.'

He smiled at his customers as he made his way to the back of the room while he inwardly cursed Ivan for coming tonight. He didn't want to risk him seeing Lucy; it would be all too easy for Ivan to use her as a pawn in the dangerous game he was playing.

Tom took in the dark-haired man who was currently chatting up a waitress. His black hair shone from the excess of product slicking it back, matching the shine of his shoes. Everything about this man screamed greasy arsehole. He sneered as he spotted Tom approaching.

'Ivan, to what do we owe the pleasure? I trust you're being looked after?' Tom placed his hands in his pockets, a sign he had no intention of shaking the man's hand.

'I'm visiting for pleasure, Thomas. You know how I love your brandy and hospitality.' His Russian accent was strong as he pronounced each syllable.

'Tom. Call me Tom.'

'I'll call you whatever the fuck I like, *Thomas.*' His smile didn't reach his eyes as he stood in confrontation.

Tom took a step closer and lowered his voice. 'I don't want to make a scene, so you would do well to leave now. You've had your fun and drank my brandy. Now it's time to leave.'

'Now, now, Thomas. There is no need for hostility. Be careful how you speak to me. It won't be long before Gedeon is no longer in charge. You'll no longer be under his protection, and I think you will be less cocky as a result.'

'Do you really dare call him by his first name? I think it's you who needs to be careful; his spies are everywhere, and you wouldn't want word of your behaviour getting back to him. Be sure to pay your gambling debt on your way out; it's racking up, again.'

Ivan sneered at Tom as he said, 'I wouldn't worry yourself over something as inconsequential as my gambling debt, Thomas.' He forced the T out through his teeth. 'I would be more concerned with my interest in you and what it is Gedeon is getting in return for this club being a no-go zone.'

Keeping his face impassive, he ignored Ivan's attempt to bait him in to giving something away.

'I wonder what, or who it is you are protecting.'

Tom drew himself up to his full height; a good few inches taller than this shmuck, and said calmly and quietly, 'My dealings with Mr Petrov are none of your concern. Now, if you'll excuse me, I have a club to run.'

He turned his back on the unwelcome guest, a sign that he was not afraid of him, and made his way out of the casino, stopping only to speak to Alex.

'If he doesn't leave soon, encourage him out. Let me know if he doesn't settle his account. Take over for me, will you? I have a very special guest to attend to.'

'Sure, boss. Consider it handled.'

He took his time descending the stairs to the club as he waited for his heartbeat to return to normal. He couldn't risk Ivan seeing Lucy here with him, especially not after he'd made it clear that Tom was being watched.

Running his fingers through his hair, he battled with the need to keep her close, and the need to ensure she wasn't dragged into this. He hoped his decision to give in to his heart wouldn't come back to haunt him.

He schooled his expression; a smile forming on his lips as he approached Lucy. She's tipping back the last of a glass of wine, her cheeks flushed from the alcohol. He can't help but remember how her cheeks flushed after he brought her to orgasm only hours ago. He groaned as his cock filled with blood. The thought of getting her off was turning him on. It took all his willpower not to get on his knees and bring her to orgasm right here. She'd gone so long without the pleasure she deserved, and he knew he could more than make up for it. But showing his true colours this early on could scare her off. He'd take his time, and he'd thoroughly enjoy every second.

The women he would normally pleasure were used to it, and went to Tom expecting it, but with Lucy it was different. His body buzzed with the anticipation of showing her so many new ways to experience euphoria. He could come just from the thought of it.

'Hey, gorgeous. Has Sophia looked after you?'

'Yes, thank you. We had a chat over a drink. I like her, she's honest.'

'How honest?' He sat down, a sense of trepidation creeping in.

'Don't worry. I don't know all your dirty little secrets. But I know that you're in her friend zone, or more like a brother zone, so I don't need to worry about her trying to shag you.'

'Well, I'm glad to hear it. I told you there wasn't anything to worry about.' Changing the subject, he continued. 'What would you like to do? I've clocked off for the evening, so I'm all yours.'

'Can we take the bike out for a spin? I'd love to know what it's like to ride a motorbike.'

He let out a breath of relief. Taking her out of the club while Alex removed Ivan was a perfect solution.

'I would love to take you for a ride. Come on, let's get changed.'

CHAPTER 19

LUCY

Dusk Till Dawn (feat. Sia) [Radio Edit] – ZAYN

'Here you go. You can wear my jacket. Sorry, I don't have a smaller one.' Tom handed Lucy a black leather biker jacket. Dressed in jeans, boots, and sweaters, they were ready for the ride around the city.

'This is perfect, thank you.' Lucy inhaled as she slipped the heavy leather jacket over her sweater. The leather smelt of him and made her feel safe, any nerves about going on a motorbike evaporated.

'Here she is.' He stood proudly in front of an impressive motorbike. It was more traditional than she was expecting. He clearly wasn't into showboating.

'This isn't what I was expecting. I thought you'd have one of those sleek modern ones, but this looks like there's more to it.'

'This is a beauty. It's a Triumph Thruxton RS. Born and raised in Leicester. I love British engineering, so it wasn't a tough decision to make when I traded in my old one.'

'I think she's gorgeous, and I can't wait to have a ride.'

'Bloody hell, Lucy. That's a sentence I never thought I'd hear you say.'

They both laughed at her unintended double meaning.

'Here's your helmet.' He kissed her before helping to put it on. He made sure it was secure before putting on his own.

Lucy watched as he swung his leg over the powerful bike. The strength visible in his thighs told her he could command this beast with ease, and it turned her on. She realised she was fast becoming a minx, and she liked this new version of herself.

'Okay, so hold on and swing yourself up behind me. You're going to have to squeeze yourself to me as this bike isn't great for riding two-up.' She could hear him clearly over the mic system that linked their helmets.

She didn't mind having to squeeze up to him, not at all. Shivers wracked her body as she mounted the bike, her nerves coming back at the thought of going through with this.

'I'm going to take it easy, so don't worry.' He ran his hand along her thigh as he spoke. 'You need to go with it and trust my movements. If you fight the turns, we're going to lose balance.'

'Okay, so I should just cling on for dear life and move where you move.'

'Exactly. Now get ready for the ride of your life.' A roar echoed around his underground car park, making her body vibrate and come alive.

He slowly inched up the ramp and out into the frosty night air. She dropped her visor as the air whipped around her face. She was glad of Tom's jacket, but she pressed herself to his back for more warmth.

'You okay, baby?' His dulcet tones calmed her as they picked up speed, now gliding along the streets of London. The traffic was light, with only a few taxis and delivery bikes interrupting their joyride. Their breathing and the all-consuming growl of the engine replaced the sounds of the bustling streets. She wrapped her arms tighter around his body as she settled in and enjoyed the ride.

'This is amazing. I feel so free.'

'Do you want me to go faster?'

She was on a high. The adrenaline coursing through her veins made her forget all her troubles. For months she'd been existing, but on the bike with Tom in her arms, she felt alive.

'Yes. I want to go faster with you, Tom. I don't want to go slow anymore.'

She could hear his intake of breath telling her he understood what she meant. 'Are you sure?'

'I've never been surer. I want it all. There's no point in wasting another minute of living on worrying about what might happen.' He brought his hand down to squeeze her thigh in reassurance.

She looked up between the tall buildings and soaked up the dark night sky, marvelling at how much had changed in her life over the last year. She'd left behind the certainty of being with Andrew, and once she'd shed that chain to her old self, she'd discovered that she was capable of so much more.

Of course, now she knew that being with Andrew wouldn't have given her any stability. He'd cheated on her and had become a father. She'd had a lucky escape and from that had taken the knowledge that it was time to trust her gut.

She was going to experience as much as possible from now on. Fear wouldn't get in the way. Standards and ideals imposed on her were going out of the window. She trusted Tom. He'd awakened something inside her she didn't know lay dormant.

Closing off her mind, she gave in to her body's desires and loosened her grip on his waist to trail a hand along his thigh.

'Is the bike having an effect on you, beautiful?' His gravelly voice warmed her body, stoking the flames.

'Yes.'

He squeezed her thigh in response. Message understood.

The bike slowed as Tom effortlessly took a tight turn before pulling over. Lucy hadn't been paying attention to where they were going—not that she would have known, anyway. Her knowledge of London was limited—but they'd stopped with the river Thames and London Bridge in view. It was beautiful and still so quiet.

'Hop off.'

She carefully swung her leg over the back of the bike and jumped down. Her thighs still hummed as if she was on the bike. It surprised her how shaky they felt; she must have been clinging on more than she realised.

Tom scooted to the back of the saddle, his helmet hanging off the handlebar. He offered Lucy his hand, pulling her to him. Removing her helmet for her, he hung it on the other handlebar. He kicked the bike stand out before saying, 'Get up front, beautiful, facing me.'

Tom took hold of her hips and lifted her so she straddled him on the motorbike. Their bodies now pressed together, face to face, her breath hitching.

He brought his lips to hers and gently kissed her before asking, 'Are you enjoying your weekend so far?'

'Let me see.' She tapped her finger to her lip, eyes heavenward. 'So far, a total hottie has picked me up from the station; I've been driven around in a sexy sports car.' She took a deep breath. The various glasses of champagne, wine and shots of tequila had broken down

179

her barriers and loosened her tongue. 'Experienced the best orgasm ever in the history of ever; danced with you while every woman watched on in jealously and have spent the night wondering what your arse cheeks look like when you fuck another woman.' She gasped and threw her hand up to her mouth, eyes wide in shock. 'Did I really say that last bit out loud?'

He raised an eyebrow. 'You did. And here was me thinking you were an innocent young lady.' He reached up to cup her face. 'Your dirty thoughts turn me on.' He leaned in, kissing her. The passion and hunger in their kiss increased as he pulled on her hips, lifting her onto his lap. She could feel his erection as it pressed into her sensitive nub, making her desperate for more.

Rocking her hips, she released a soft moan as their kissing became more frantic. She could feel his thighs working hard to keep the bike steady.

'I want you to grind on me until you come. Will you do that for me?'

'Out here? What if someone walks by?'

'Then they'll get a show.' He gripped her hips and encouraged her to rock onto him. 'Does that feel good?'

'Yes,' She panted as she gripped onto him with her thighs.

He slid his hand up her back, holding her tighter to increase the pressure on her core. His hard length and the zipper on his jeans created a delicious friction against her clit. The combination of his groans and the threat of being caught wound her tight like a spring. She could feel her climax building as she rocked her hips harder and faster, desperate for the release. As he raised his hips to meet her movements, her head fell back as her climax rocked through her body. A guttural moan left her lips as Tom whispered words of praise and encouragement. As the final ripples of her orgasm subsided, she kissed him with a fierce need for more contact.

Panting, he pulled away. 'Let's get back. I think it's time you saw me naked.'

'Hell yeah to that.'

The ride back gave them time to cool down, but an undercurrent of sexual tension vibrated between them. Once inside, Tom asked, 'Can I get you a drink? Another glass of wine, perhaps?'

'Yes, thank you.'

'Here, let me take this for you.' Tom reached his arms around her and removed the biker jacket. His hands grazed her shoulders as he dipped to kiss her neck before hanging up the jacket. 'Now, let's get that drink.'

Her heart raced as she watched him pour red wine into two stemless glasses. Her bottom lip caught between her teeth at the thought of what was coming.

'What are you thinking about, you little minx?' Caught red-handed, she blushes.

'Oh, um, nothing really.'

He took a swig of his wine as he narrowed his eyes at her, handing her glass over. 'Your face says otherwise.'

'Okay, so I may have been thinking about the things you did to me earlier, and...' She wasn't sure she was brave enough to finish her sentence.

'Go on. Talk to me, sexy. What's going on in that amazing mind of yours?'

'I was thinking about what you might do to me later.'

'What would you like me to do to you?'

'I have no idea. I have a feeling you may have some tricks up your sleeve that I've never seen before, and I'm curious.'

'Let's sit down. I'll light the fire and we can talk dirty.'

Lucy took a seat, her legs curled up next to her and the wine warming her from the inside. The sofa engulfed her as she sunk into it, watching, entranced, as Tom lit candles before starting the fire.

'I feel the need to apologise for the fact I have a gas fire. Clicking a button doesn't seem as romantic as spending all evening trying to light a log, but I have a fear of setting my building on fire, and therefore this is the next best thing.'

'You wouldn't know the difference. It's beautiful.' The room, even though it was large, felt cosy. The warm glow coming from the roaring fire cast light across the room and shadows from the candles danced up the walls. Tom joined her on the sofa, mirroring her position.

He leant across and dusted his thumb over her cheekbone. 'We need to talk.'

Her heartbeat skyrocketed. A conversation starting with 'we need to talk' has never ended well, in the history of ever. She leant away, breaking his contact. 'Oh, what about? Are you bored with me already?'

'Not at all. I want to talk about your past; about what turns you on; what you've tried; what you want to try but have never asked for. I know you're worried that you aren't enough for me. I want you to understand that you're wrong. You need to stop overthinking and trust me.'

'Oh. I wouldn't even know where to start.'

'I've noticed that when you have a few drinks inside you, you open up. You relax and have more confidence in yourself. I'm not the sort of man to get a woman drunk to make sure she has a good time; so, I want to talk to you about it, openly and honestly. Once you've opened up to me, you'll realise that you have nothing to be ashamed of, or worried about.'

'It's hard for me to talk about what I want because I don't know what the options are. My sex life with Andrew was run-of-the-mill, or at least I think it was.'

'Tell me the basics. What positions did you try? Were there any that felt better for you, or got you closer to reaching an orgasm?'

Lucy felt embarrassed talking so candidly about her past with Andrew. She'd grown up in a household where you didn't talk openly about sex. Magazines aimed at young adults were a no-no, and age ratings on movies were strictly adhered to. It wasn't until she left home for university that she realised just how much her parents had wrapped her up in cotton wool.

'I can see you're struggling with this, but I need you to be comfortable communicating with me. It's important to me you can tell me what's good and what isn't. How else will I know if you're in a good place?'

'No one has ever cared about what I want before.'

'And that's why no one has ever made you come. If I'm going to make up for that, I need to know what works for you, and I'm bloody well looking forward to experimenting with you. So come on, talk to me. You can't shock me; trust me on that.'

She knew he was right. If she wanted to be the strong woman she hoped she was, then talking openly about her needs was important. She took a large gulp of her wine and a deep breath. 'Okay. Here goes. Andrew and I were basic in the bedroom. We had a blueprint that we always stuck to. Every. Time. He would tell me he was horny while flashing his erection at me. Then kiss me as his finger would, and I quote, "get me ready," and then I'd lie back. He'd shove it in and out a few times until he finished.'

Tom's jaw ticked at her words before he said, 'And that was it?'

'Yep. He once complained to me because I didn't make any noise while we were having sex. He obviously watched porn and the women in that are always screaming, or so he says.'

'It's hardly surprising you weren't screaming; he didn't give you anything to scream about. Sex isn't just about getting you wet and shoving it in. Your body might show it's ready for sex by getting wet.' He adds air quotes around the last words. 'But that's just a physiological response to the environment you're in. Your body knows that it's about to have sex, but what about your mind? Did you feel your body tingling with anticipation? Did your core ache with desire? Did he kiss you? Stroke you? Talk to you about what he was going to do?'

'No. He just shoved it in.'

'Well, there you go. I think it's fair to say that no one has ever made love to you. Forget everything. Consider yourself a virgin. I'll pop your cherry tonight—if you want me to?'

With no hesitation, she nodded. 'Yes, please.'

CHAPTER 20

LUCY

Pillowtalk - ZAYN

'I'm going to take this slowly. I want you to tell me how you feel. We're going to work out what works for you, what you like—what you need. Okay?'

She swallowed, already feeling warm with desire. Her skin was tingling; the hairs on her arms were standing on end. She took another large swig of wine, the glass nearly empty.

Tom placed his wine on the table before unbuttoning his sleeves and rolling them up to his elbows. The light dusting of blond hairs on his honey-coloured skin caught her eye, and she craved the sight of more.

He turned back to face her, stroking her hair away from her face. 'I'm going to kiss you. I'm going to take my time getting to know every part of your mouth with my tongue. And then I'm going to get to know every part of your body with my mouth. I'm going to spend all night worshipping your body, giving you more pleasure than you've ever received.'

Just from his words alone, she could feel her body reacting, getting ready to take him. He reached over and took the glass from her hands, placing it on the table. With nothing to keep her hands still, they shook with anticipation. He took hold of them, steadying them as he looked into her eyes.

'Remember, I want you to talk to me. Tell me what's going through your mind. Your body will give me signals, but I need to know where your mind is at.'

She nodded as his lips came to hers. They were warm and soft, and for a moment, they didn't open. He peppered her lips with gentle kisses as he ran his fingers through her hair. He brought his mouth to her ear and whispered, 'I love the feel of your lips. They're so full and soft. I've spent the last few weeks imagining what they would look like wrapped around my cock.'

Her breathing became shallow as he drew her earlobe into his mouth, gently sucking. His lips trailed down her nape and her collarbone, stopping at the neckline of her sweater.

'Arms up.' He pulled her top over her head, discarding it onto the sofa behind her. 'That's better.' He traced along her collarbone with his finger until he met her bra strap. He slipped the strap down her shoulder and kissed along the indentation where her strap had been.

He repeated the process on the other side; her breasts sitting heavy in the cups.

'Your breasts are perfect. So full and round, begging for me to play with them.' He ran his fingers through her hair again, this time cupping the back of her head and bringing her lips to his. His other arm wrapped around her back. A second later her breasts felt heavier as he unhooked her bra with a quick flick of his fingers, discarding it along with her sweater.

He coaxed her lips open with his tongue, stroking it along her bottom lip before dipping it into her mouth. His free hand stroked its way from her back to cup her breast. His thumb flicked across her nipple as it pebbled under his delicate touch.

'Talk to me, baby. Tell me how you feel. Use your words.'

'I feel so good.'

'How does good feel? Tell me exactly.'

'My skin is tingling all over. I'm not cold, but my skin prickles, my hair's standing on end. My breasts feel full and heavy, and I'm aching between my legs.'

He bent his head, licking across her nipple and blowing cool air across her wet, fevered skin. Her nipple hardened further as she gasped at the sensation. A moan escaped from her mouth.

She could feel his smile against her sensitive tissue as he bit down. Electricity shot from her breast across her whole body as she arched her back in response.

'Your body likes that, doesn't it?'

'Yes.'

He did the same with her other nipple, her reaction just as violent.

She was breathless as she said, 'I want to touch you. I want to feel your skin against mine.'

'Take my shirt off and take your time.'

With shaky hands, she reached up, and one by one, unbuttoned his shirt.

Growing up, she always took her time unwrapping her Christmas presents. She revelled in the excitement and didn't want it to be over too soon. Unwrapping Tom felt like all her Christmases rolled into one. She didn't want to rush it. She'd been fantasizing about this moment all evening, but she remained true to herself and took her time.

Gasping, her patience was rewarded, as she peeled his shirt down his back and arms and dropped it to the floor.

She'd known he would be perfect under his clothes. His chest was the same beautiful honey colour as his arms, with a light dusting of dark-blond hair. His pecs were well-defined, and his abs sported an eight-pack. The magical V shape she'd heard Sarah talk about was visible at the waistband of his jeans, her finger itching to follow its path and see where it ended.

His arms were strong and corded with muscle and veins. But all of this wasn't what had taken her breath away.

'Your tattoos are beautiful. You're perfect.' She stroked her fingers across a raven; its wings covered his right upper arm. The raven's head wrapped around another tattoo that covered his right pec. It looked like a symbol or seal made of multiple spikes, all meeting at the centre and surrounded by a ring of ancient lettering.

On his left side, she could see one half of a wolf's face; it was large and covered the area from under his armpit down to his bottom rib. She noticed lettering running along the edge of the face; she traced them with her finger tenderly.

'X-M-R-I. What does that mean?'

'It's the wolf's name, Geri. And here,' he turned around to show her his back. 'The other half of his face represents the second wolf, Freki.'

'Oh, and another raven.' A second raven tattoo was back-to-back with the first.

'They're stunning. Do you have any more?' She was desperate to see what wonders awaited under his jeans.

The man before her was like a Norse god—the dirty-blonde hair, five o'clock shadow on his jaw and skin like honey made her want to drop to her knees before him. What the hell was happening to her?

188

'I don't. It's just these.'

She giggled as she said, 'Prove it.'

'Not yet. First, I'm going to worship you.'

She wrapped her arms around his muscular body, her hands splaying across his shoulder blades as their kissing continued.

He cupped both breasts and sucked hard on each nipple before encouraging her to lean back onto the sofa. He worked his kisses down her stomach; her abdomen fluttered with a thousand butterflies.

He unfastened the button of her jeans and lowered the zip. She lifted her hips to help him as he tugged her jeans down, taking her underwear with them.

'Tell me, Lucy, what do you do when you touch yourself?'

'I- I don't.'

'You haven't stroked yourself to orgasm before?'

'No.' Feeling ashamed, her eyes cast downward.

He closed his eyes as he growled, 'Fuck.'

'I told you I was inexperienced. I'm sorry, but I really don't know what I'm doing.'

'Don't apologise. The fact I gave you your first orgasm is amazing. It's special to me. You have nothing to be ashamed of. It just makes this weekend and what I'm going to do to you so much better. You've just turned up the heat telling me that. I want this to last all night.'

'Really. Are you sure?'

'We get to explore your body—which is uncharted territory—together. You were made for me, like a gift from the gods.'

She reached over for her wine and finished it in one mouthful. 'Teach me.'

He took hold of her hands and delicately placed them on her breasts. 'You don't need to go straight for the clit.

Take your time and get to know yourself. Tweak your nipples. Play with them.'

Her throat bobbed as she swallowed. Her voice was quiet and unsure as she murmured, 'I feel shy and a little uncomfortable with this.'

'Okay. I have a solution.' Standing abruptly, he whipped his belt out of the loops and threw it onto the sofa. He ripped his button fly open and pulled his jeans off. He stood in just his underwear, and the sight was magnificent.

His thighs were thick and powerful, and the bulge in his underwear was the biggest she'd ever seen.

'Take my boxers off.'

She shuffled to the edge of the sofa, his erection in her eye-line, and tentatively pulled his boxers down. He kicked them away, standing in all his glory in front of her, his erection bobbing in front of her face, enticing her to touch it. The light from the fire and the candles cast shadows under each of his muscles as they flexed. He reminded her of the man on the front cover of their latest book club book.

She licked her lips.

'Do you like what you see?'

She gave a brief nod. 'I do.'

He reached down and wrapped his hand around his firm length and pulled. His hand slid up and down his shaft as his eyes closed and he released a moan. His tip glistened and Lucy licked her lips, desperate to taste it.

Fuck it.

She leant in while his eyes were still closed and took his tip into her mouth.

'Oh, fuck,' he gasped. He gazed down at her with hooded eyes full of pleasure, giving her courage to carry on. She slid the tip of her tongue into his slit and licked out the pre-cum. It was delicious, and she craved more.

'I want you to reach your hand down and dip a finger inside yourself. Feel your desire on your finger.'

Feeling less on display in this position, she had the confidence to follow his instruction. He could hardly judge her while he fucked his own fist, and then she understood why he was doing this.

She reached down, slipping her middle finger into her entrance. She gasped against his penis, shocked by how ready she felt, and at how she clamped down onto her finger, pulling it in.

'Now, run your finger along your clit. It'll be sensitive, so be gentle at first.'

As she moved her finger to her clit, he tweaked her nipple with his free hand, the other still gliding up and down his length.

His breathing was heavy, his voice hoarse as he said, 'Circle it, increase the pressure until you get to a point where it feels so good you feel a pressure building up.'

She followed his instructions as she continued to lick and suck his tip. He pinched her nipples, and she let out another appreciative moan. With a mind of their own, her hips rocked in time to her circling finger.

He pulled his hips away from her mouth and sat next to her. Leaning over, he kissed her while whispering encouraging words in her ear.

Her body moved instinctively as her finger dipped inside, coating it in her arousal. As she pressed onto her clit, her back arched, and every muscle clenched in her body.

Tom brought his hand down and pushed two fingers inside her as she continued to circle her throbbing nub. The sensation took her over the edge as she released a strangled moan. Her body shuddering as his fingers thrust in and out, eking out every second of pleasure.

As he pulled his fingers out, she relaxed on the sofa, her eyes closed. She licked her lips. 'Oh my god. That was amazing. Thank you.'

'You did all the hard work.'

'No, really. Thank you for knowing what I needed in order to do that in front of you.' She laughs, saying, 'I don't think I'll be able to leave the house anymore, knowing what I know now.' She looked up to the ceiling as if looking to the gods, as she caught her breath.

'Just the thought of that makes me hard.'

She looked down at his length, still standing to attention.

'Do we need to do something about that?' She flicked her eyes down to his lap.

'There's plenty of time for that. Let's take this through to the bedroom for lesson two.' He took her by the hand, pressed his lips to her knuckles and walked them to his bedroom. They stood at the foot of the bed, his hands caressing her skin as they kissed. Her skin prickled with his touch, sending shivers down her spine.

She allowed her hands to roam his body and take in the soft curves of his hard muscles. She hadn't believed that men like this really existed, and they certainly weren't within her reach. But here she was, being worshipped by the most handsome man she'd ever seen. Feelings of not being worthy crept over her.

As if sensing her sudden change in mood, he tilted her chin up so that their eyes meet.

'Stop it. I can tell what you're thinking, and I don't like it.'

'How do you do that?'

'I pay attention.' He lowered himself so that he was eye to eye with her. 'You are beautiful and sexy and perfect. I'm the lucky one, do you hear me?'

She hesitantly nodded.

'Say it. Do you hear me?'

'Yes. I hear you.'

'Good girl. Now that's agreed, let's carry on.' He picked her up and effortlessly threw her onto the bed, prowling over her. She gasped with shock before bursting into giggles, any tension and worries now gone.

'Is this the bit where I just stick it in?' He wiggled his eyebrows at her.

'I hope not. Not after you've hyped yourself up all evening.'

'That's true. I believe I promised to kiss every part of your beautiful body, so I'd better get cracking.'

Normally she would feel self-conscious spread out on the bed, totally exposed, but she felt at ease around Tom. He'd carefully broken down her walls and filled her with self-confidence.

His bedroom was softly lit. The bedside lamp emitted a gentle glow that filled Lucy with self-confidence. She didn't feel the need to hide her curves under the covers, as her skin looked soft and inviting.

'How do you feel about being blindfolded? I'm assuming you've not tried it before. I don't want to push you, so if you're not entirely sure, then please say no.'

'You're right; I've never tried that before, but I trust you. I want to try everything, at least once.'

'Oh really? That's good to know.' Tom got off the bed and went over to a wardrobe, extracting a tie from a rail inside the door.

She bit the inside of her cheek to stifle a giggle before saying, 'This is very Fifty Shades. Or so I've heard.'

With a crooked grin, he replied, 'You could say that.'

He stalked back to the bed. 'Shuffle up, rest your head on the pillows.' She eagerly did as he instructed.

'Take a good look at me, baby. You won't be seeing me for a while, and then all you're going to be seeing is stars.'

'Promises, promises,' she giggled, more out of nervousness than his attempt at humour.

'On a serious note, are you sure?'

She nodded.

He lay the dark blue tie across her eyes and tied it loosely around her head.

'It's loose so you can take it off easily if you want to, but I recommend leaving it on.'

She was plunged into darkness, her other senses sharpening to compensate. For a few seconds, she was only aware of the sound of their breathing. She heard the sheets rustling and felt the bed dip as Tom adjusted his position. Her heart was racing at the anticipation.

The scent of his aftershave was stronger, and she was sure she could feel the heat of his body. He must be so close to her, and yet she couldn't be sure. She got her answer soon enough as she felt the warmth of this breath on her neck. His words tickled her ear as he said, 'Don't overthink this. Let your body take over.'

He peppered kisses along her collarbone, down across her chest, licking each nipple. She could feel her breasts swell and harden at his touch. And then there was nothing. The mattress sprang up, the energy in the room shifting. She was alone.

'Tom?' After a few seconds, she could hear him returning, his footsteps muffled by the thick, plush carpet.

'I'm back with a treat.' His voice was soft and calmed her.

'Do I get to know what it is?'

'You'll find out soon. This may take you by surprise, but trust me, you'll love it.'

'I can smell something familiar.' She breathed in the fragrant air. 'Is that the candle from earlier I can smell?'

He didn't answer. Instead, she could feel him sit astride her hips before she was aware of a unique sensation entirely. She gasped as something hot dropped onto the sensitive skin on her breast. The immediate sting soon ebbing away, leaving a warm tingle in its place.

'How does that feel? Talk to me.'

'It's strange. It's hot, but it doesn't burn. I like it. I want more.'

He rewarded her with another exquisite drip on the other breast, chased by a drip, drip, drip across her nipples.

She gasped and writhed beneath him. There was a new sensation as a pool of warmth formed between her breasts, moments before a trail of heat trickled down her abdomen.

Her back arched as her hips rolled, her body craving the heat between her legs.

'Is that good, baby?'

'Oh my god, it's like nothing I've felt before.'

His hands glided across her slick skin, his warmth mixing with the liquid until she couldn't tell where he was touching her. His hands were everywhere, reaching every part of her body and soul. She could hear his breathing, measured and controlled. A stark contrast to her rapid breaths, desperate for air.

True to his word, he massaged the oil across her entire body, right down to her feet. And when he finished working the oil deep into her skin, he kissed his way back up her legs.

His lips worked their way up her thighs, nudging them open with his nose. Tingles became full tremors as he got closer and closer to the apex of her thighs, her core clenching, readying itself for what it hoped was to come.

Her breathing hitched as she panted, waiting and hoping for his lips to reach her opening. The level of desire raging through her body was driving her wild. And then he swiped his tongue in one hard long lick along her opening.

He hummed in appreciation as she gasped.

'You're delicious, do you know that? I could eat you all night.'

'I need you. Please,' she pleaded for his touch, desperate for the release that he could give her.

'You're doing so well, Lucy. Don't worry, I won't leave you waiting for much longer.'

'I want you inside me. Please, Tom. I need you now.' She felt his breath against her clit as he said, 'Shhh. I've got you, baby.' He slid two fingers inside and stroked across what she could only assume was her G-spot. His movements were slow at first, but then his speed increased along with the pressure he applied to her sensitive flesh. He pulled out, spreading her desire over her clit, circling it until she felt another climax building. 'The next time you come will be around my cock. You're so close; I'm going to take it slow.'

She felt him move and seconds later, heard a packet being ripped open. She held her breath, waiting to feel him on her again.

Warm light from the room flooded her eyes as he removed the tie. She blinked as Tom came into focus. He knelt between her legs, the condom in place. She couldn't help but stare at his impressive length, wondering if she really was ready for this.

'Are you ready, beautiful?'

Breathlessly, she said, 'Yes.'

They kissed as he lowered his body over her, resting on his elbow. His other hand guiding his tip to her entrance.

'Are you sure?'

This simple question made her fall for him a little harder. Even with his crown resting at her opening, he wanted to make sure she was ready.

She answered by rocking her pelvis to draw him deeper. They gasped together as he drove into her a few more inches, before pulling out and driving back in until he was fully seated.

Their eyes remained locked together until the overriding feeling of pleasure that came from being so entirely full forced Lucy to close her eyes. Her body took over, thrusting her hips to meet his. Their movements were in perfect harmony as he whispered words of encouragement and pleasure into her ear. He repeatedly told her she was perfect, and a part of her believed him.

Tom reached over, grabbed a cushion and lifted her hips, placing it under her. He pulled out to the tip and then drove back in. The new position of her pelvis changed the angle as his hard length stimulated her sensitive flesh. He ground his pelvis against her swollen clit and the stimulation to both that and her insides sent shockwaves throughout her body.

Her head fell back as incoherent words fell from her mouth. Her hands stroked along his back as he sucked on her nipples. As he bit down on one, she lost control. She grabbed his arse and squeezed hard, forcing him to increase his pace.

'Do you want it harder?'

'Yes. Please. I need more.'

He braced his hands on either side of her, straightening his arms and ground his hips. He was so deep she could hardly catch her breath and the pressure on her pelvis drove her wild. She wrapped her legs around his hips as he increased his pace. Warmth spread in her body turning into an inferno as she gripped on to him, pushing him to go harder.

He slammed into her over and over until she couldn't hold back any longer. Her guttural moan as her orgasm hit was tribal as Tom kept up the pace. His release was just as violent as his moans blended with hers, their panting cooling each other's fevered skin.

Her breath caught with each of his measured thrusts as he slowed the pace until she fully came down from her high. As he stilled, he leant down to her and kissed her gently. 'Are you okay?'

Her hand covered her eyes as her emotions became too much to bear. The pain that wore heavily on her soul over the last few months had lifted. She felt reborn. Unable to control it any longer, a single tear fell from her eye and tracked down the side of her face to the pillow.

Tom's face soon turned to concern as he moved her hand and looked into her eyes, his thumb wiping away the tear.

'Hey, what's the matter? Was it that bad?'

She laughed. 'No. It was perfect. It was the most perfect thing that's ever happened to me. I would never have believed you could make me feel like that.'

'Well, get used to it as I intend to make you feel like that as often as I can. You did so well. You've had a lot of emotions and sensations to process tonight.'

Lucy went to speak but stopped herself.

'What do you want to say? Don't hold back, just come out with it.'

'You read me too well.'

'I think you'll agree that being able to read you has worked out well for you so far.'

'That's true.'

'So come on, out with it.'

She took a deep breath. 'I feel like a bit of a knob asking this, but was it okay for you?' She bit her bottom lip, trying not to cringe outwardly.

'It was amazing. Did you not get the hint when I was telling you repeatedly that you were perfect and that this was perfect?'

'To be honest, you could have been saying anything, and I wouldn't have had a clue.'

He pulled out, holding on to the condom, dropping a kiss on her lips before hopping off the bed.

'Let me take care of this, then I'll fix us a snack and we can snuggle.'

'Sounds good.' She eyed his perfect arse as he headed to the bathroom. Letting out a long sigh, she settled under the covers, feeling like she could sleep for a week.

Tom strolled back into the bedroom, fully naked, carrying a platter of vegetables, hummus, crisps, and sliced meats. 'You like to go all out with your snacks, don't you?' Lucy's eyes were wide as she took in the assortment. He'd even balanced two glasses of water on the board.

'Go big or go home, that's my motto. I also didn't know what you'd fancy, so I covered all bases. It's important to look after yourself, especially after a big night.'

'You're a thoughtful man. Thank you.'

He placed the platter in the middle of the bed before climbing in next to her.

'Open wide.' He smothered a carrot stick in copious amounts of hummus and brought it to Lucy's mouth. The look in his eyes was pure sex as she bit down on his offering.

Once fully satiated by the bounty of snacks, they brushed their teeth and settled back into bed. Lucy's head nestled in the crook of Tom's shoulder, her fingers tracing lines around the tattoo on his chest.

'They really are beautiful tattoos. Do they have a meaning, or did you just like them?'

'They have meanings, and to be honest, I didn't have a great deal of choice over them. You might say they were more of a necessity than anything else.'

'What do you mean?'

He was silent for a while, as if considering what to say.

'In my line of work, you encounter people that are not all that pleasant. Add to that the fact my club is also a casino and you double the number of criminals that want in on the action. Sometimes the lesser of two evils is making a deal with the devil.'

'I don't understand.'

'No, I don't imagine you do. Drug dealers want to use my club, and money launderers want to use my casino. I can't allow either, it's not in my nature. To keep me safe, I have these tattoos. I'm marked as a protected man. This here.' He pointed to the round tattoo her finger was still stroking. 'This is the Helm of Awe.'

'Wow, that sounds like something out of Thor.'

'You're not far wrong. It's a Nordic sign of protection. It was my first tattoo, which I chose for myself. The symbol is of a superpower that protected Vikings as they went to war.'

Lucy bent her head to kiss it. 'I like the thought of you being a Viking. Perhaps not the going to war part, though.'

'Oh really? Fancy a bit of Viking role play? I could come and plunder your village and take you away to be my slave.'

'Sounds hot.' A soft giggle escaped her lips. 'I think I'd enjoy some plundering. So, what about the other tattoos? Did you not choose those?'

'Not strictly speaking. I had to choose ones that portrayed a certain message. The Ravens, pronounced Hoo-gin and Moo-nin, represent Odin's messengers. Huginn is the raven of thought, and Muninn is the raven of memory.'

'This is fascinating. I think I need to brush up on my Norse reading.'

'The wolves are my favourite. They represent the good and bad, like two sides of a coin. One side for chaos and destruction, the other for protection, loyalty and wisdom. Odin had the wolves first, and he created the ravens to assist the wolves with collecting information.' He stretched as he took a deep breath. 'And there you have it. That's the story of my tattoos.'

Lucy wasn't so sure. She had a niggling feeling that there was more to this, but she didn't feel now was the time to push it. 'So, in summary, your tattoos represent protection for you and for a god, but they also represent that good old saying of knowledge is power.'

'Bang on. That's a quicker way of explaining them. And now this Viking needs to do some more plundering.'

He plunged them into darkness as Tom lifted the covers over their heads, his lips crashing down on hers.

CHAPTER 21

LUCY

*When I get my hands on you – The New Base-
ment Tapes*

'Do you have a train ticket booked for today?' Tom asked Lucy as they lay in his bed, his hand trailing up and down her arm as they snuggled.

'No. I'm going to play it by ear. Why?'

'I want to drive you home. We could spend the morning chilling out here, or I could show you the sights and then I can take you to lunch somewhere on the way back to yours. I'm not working today, so you can do with me as you please.'

'Can I do whatever I please with you?' Her eyebrows wiggled.

'Abso-fucking-lutely. But first, I'll make some breakfast. Throw something on and meet me in the kitchen.' Wearing boxers and a T-shirt, he went out to the kitchen, leaving Lucy to freshen up.

Without the distraction of his body or lips, Lucy's mind replayed the conversations she'd had with Tom over the previous day. Questions formed in her mind, and she knew she wouldn't be able to settle until she talked them through with him. Based on her record with men so far, she trusted too easily. Her first and only actual boyfriend had cheated on her and fathered a child under her nose, while the man she dated previously turned out to be a murderous psycho. She couldn't just blindly trust that Tom was a good man purely based on his friendship with Cameron, no matter how much she wanted to. He seemed too good to be true, and yet she wished he was all she thought he was. Perfection. Her Norse god.

She grabbed his shirt from last night, deciding it would look perfect on her. As she pulled it onto her shoulders, she could breathe in his scent and her body flushed with heat. She slipped on some underwear, brushed her teeth, and ran her fingers through her tousled hair before heading to the kitchen.

'So, what's on the menu this morning?' Tom's back was to her as he washed some tomatoes at the sink.

'As I didn't know what you'd fancy—' He'd turned to face her and stopped dead in his tracks. His eyes darkened as he cast them over her. He rapidly blinked as he shook his head and said, 'Sorry, I lost my train of thought. That shirt looks sexy as hell on you. We may just have to stay here all day. Come here.'

She padded over to him; cuffs pulled down over her hands as she fiddled with the hem of the shirt. Lacing his fingers into her hair, he pulled her in for a kiss. His magic worked on her once again as she surrendered to him; thoughts of uncovering his dark secrets forgotten.

'Before this goes any further, I need to feed you. Take a seat and I'll give you your options. All of which will come with a side of me.'

She perched on the edge of the barstool and watched as he resumed rinsing tomatoes.

'As I was saying, I didn't know what you'd want, so I got everything. I can offer you avocado, sourdough, eggs, bacon, sausage, smoked salmon, or yoghurt with granola. Oh, and tomatoes.'

'Too much choice. What are you having?'

'Avocado on sourdough; scrambled eggs; smoked salmon, and tomatoes—they're good for your prostate, apparently.'

'Good to know. I'll have the same.'

Coffee and orange juice sat ready on the counter, so she helped herself. Watching him get breakfast ready felt so natural. She could feel herself falling for him, and that scared her. It was too soon to expect this to be any more than a casual fling. He'd already said he wasn't used to having relationships, which left her wondering where she stood.

If she was going to be a strong woman, she'd have to act like it.

'Can I ask you a personal question?'

'Of course. You've seen me fisting my cock, after all.'

That threw her off what she was saying as her mind instantly went to the epic sex of last night, her cheeks turning crimson.

'I guess so. You said you've had a lot of sex, but not here and not in a relationship. Do you use prostitutes?'

Choking on his coffee, he spluttered saying, 'I wasn't expecting that.' He stopped what he was doing and turned her to face him. 'No. I don't use prostitutes. Just to clarify, I've never had to pay for sex.'

'Where do you,' Lucy gave a shy shrug, 'you know, do it, then?'

'Clubs. More specifically, K's.'

'K's?'

'My friend Katia owns a woman-led sex club. Only women can be members and they invite men in. It's a safe place for women, and people that identify as women, to explore their sexuality, knowing that the men there are a known entity.'

'Oh.' She wasn't expecting that and didn't know what to say.

'I'm sorry, that's probably not what you were expecting, although I hope it's better than me using prostitutes. One rule is that condoms are mandatory, so I'm as clean as a whistle. You don't need to worry about that. You also must have regular sexual health check-ups and prove you're clean. That's why I go there. I'd rather have no-strings sex with someone I know is clean and will be discreet, than pick up a woman from the dance floor.'

She realised there wasn't a conversation last night about protection. He'd automatically reached for a condom, unlike some men that assume you're on the pill.

'I don't have sex without protection. It's not just a woman's job to protect herself from pregnancy or STDs. It takes two to tango and both parties should play their part. I will never expect you to have unprotected sex with me.'

'You really are one of a kind.' He smiled as she ran her finger around the rim of her coffee cup, contemplating the next question. 'Your friend, Katia, is she the one you have sex with?'

'No. She's more like a sister to me. We've grown up together since she moved over from Russia and started attending the same school as me.'

'Who do you have sex with then, if you're her guest?'

The toaster interrupted their conversation as the sourdough toast popped up; its nutty, rich aroma filled the air, making her stomach growl with anticipation.

'Let me finish getting breakfast ready, and then I'll tell you all about it.'

A few minutes later, he set two plates down on the counter. Lucy took an appreciative deep breath before tucking in. 'This looks delicious, thank you. I'm starving.'

'Me too. Give me a sec to stuff some of this in my face and then ask me anything.'

They sat and ate in silence for a few minutes. As the first bites hit her stomach, it growled in appreciation. The grilling could wait until she'd finished.

Pushing her now empty plate away, she wiped her mouth before saying, 'I enjoyed that, thank you.'

She watched as he swallowed his last mouthful of toast before speaking. 'You're welcome. Now, ask me all the sex questions you have.' His smile put her at ease. She was worried that her invasion into his private life would annoy him, but he came across as an open book.

'Have you ever slept with Katia?'

He was clearly trying to suppress a smirk as the corner of his mouth turned up. 'Are you jealous of her, by any chance?' He'd turned their stools to face each other; his knees in between hers. He twisted a strand of her hair around his finger; the intimate gesture halting her reply.

'I think maybe I am.'

'Well, don't be. There is nothing to be jealous of, but you should know that she is special to me. I really am like the big, protective brother. That will never change.'

'Is the club basically an orgy then?'

'It's whatever you want it to be. If you went to only watch, you can. If you wanted to mingle, you can.'

'Mingle?'

'That's when you play with others outside of your couple. I don't strictly have a couple as I don't sleep with Katia, so I play with anyone where there is mutual interest.'

'So that's what you meant when you said the women you sleep with are used to crossing lines?'

'Yes. Sex with me was always a no-strings-attached affair. It's very liberating. There isn't a lot I haven't experienced, and the women there know what they like. You can learn a lot from these clubs.'

'Have you had threesomes?'

'Yep. I've had multiple women, women and men, more than three, and more than four. It can get intense if the right people are there.'

She pressed her hands to her cheeks, feeling the heat coming from them as she blushed. She shifted in her seat as her core throbbed. 'What's a threesome like?'

'Close your eyes.'

She furrowed her brow at the unexpected response. 'Why?'

His eyes locked onto hers, and his voice took on a commanding tone. 'Because I asked you to.'

She found she had no witty response. This didn't feel like a funny situation, instead she felt the need to do as she was told; to obey.

Closing her eyes, she felt him squeeze her thigh as he whispered, 'Thank you.'

She heard him lean in, his voice low as he said, 'Do you remember how you felt last night when I worshipped you?' He dropped a kiss on her neck. 'When I kissed your body?' Another kiss. 'Or when I dripped hot oil across your chest?' His thumb grazed across her erect nipples, straining against the cotton of his shirt. 'Do you remember how it felt to have my cock slide inside you?'

The rise and fall of her chest sped up as she remembered every sensation. Every nerve in her body came alive. Her skin hummed in anticipation of his next touch.

Her voice was breathy as she said, 'I remember.'

'Now imagine all of that happening at the same time.'

'Oh, god.' Her eyes met his as she blinked them open.

'That's what a threesome feels like. Every aspect of lovemaking all happening at the same time. Not everyone can cope with it.'

'Do you think I could cope with it?'

He takes a sip of his coffee, looking deep in thought. 'You may be able to, but I'm not sure I could.'

'Why? You've done them before.'

'Yes, but those women weren't mine.'

CHAPTER 22

LUCY

All Your Exes – Julia Michaels

The words he'd said played over in her mind as she stood under the powerful jets of his guest shower. She'd opted to shower by herself while Tom cleaned up from breakfast. He'd used every pot and pan he owned and refused to let her clean up.

Those women weren't mine.

He'd happily have a threesome if the woman wasn't his, but he wouldn't have one with her.

Did that mean she was his?

Lucy's head swam with thoughts, sending her dizzy. He'd answered every question she threw at him. No hesitation. No bullshit. As a result, she wanted to know where she stood with him. Something else was niggling in her mind, and she needed some time to mull it over.

She'd never been around someone so sexually experienced before, and she certainly hadn't been with anyone as adventurous. It left her curious about what she'd missed out on.

She quickly dressed and applied minimal makeup before heading out to find Tom.

The kitchen was spotless, and the sound of running water told her he was in the shower. She opted to wait for him on his bed.

She lay down, breathing in the scent left behind on the bedsheets and pillows. Closing her eyes, she remembered everything he'd done to her; her body came alive in expectation of a repeat performance.

She felt reincarnated, like a phoenix rising from the flames.

Was she his? She certainly hoped so but reminded herself not to get too excited. This wasn't like being a teenager; one night with someone doesn't mean you're going steady.

Lucy hadn't noticed the silence in the bathroom, the shower no longer running. It wasn't until she felt his hand graze her cheek that she knew she wasn't alone.

'I feel bad for disturbing you, but I couldn't resist touching you.'

Tom's skin was glistening from the shower, his tattoos looked freshly inked. He'd wrapped his towel low enough around his waist to show his magical V in all its glory. It took all of Lucy's willpower not to rip the towel off. Part of her wanted to be distracted from the world and her thoughts by what he did to her. The doubts and fears that gnawed away at her ebbed away as soon as his attention was on her. She didn't know how he managed it, but whenever she was with him, her mind was quiet.

As she lay there, she knew she couldn't use sex as a crutch to heal. Questions about Tom and the desires that surfaced deep within her needed answering, but that would be for another day. She wasn't comfortable enough to rip herself open to him entirely. They would spend the afternoon out in public getting to know each other.

She felt proud of her sensible decision while she watched Tom get dressed, even if her body temperature skyrocketed and her core screamed for attention.

'Are you sure you're okay to drive me home? I can easily grab a train ticket and save you the bother.'

'I won't hear of it. It would be my pleasure to take you home. Have you got everything?'

'Yes, all packed and ready to go.' They'd had a relaxed afternoon window shopping down Oxford Street and grabbed some lunch from a little French restaurant. The red wine Lucy had drunk warmed her veins and gave her a rosy glow.

As they drove out from the underground car park, Tom put a chill-out playlist on the car's sound system and gently tapped along to the music as he drove through the relatively quiet streets of London.

Lucy caught herself checking out their reflection as they drove past the large glass fronted shop windows. She didn't look out of place in the sleek car. In fact, it suited her. Only a few weeks ago, she fretted about wearing a pair of high-heeled shoes to the office and now she was comfortable driving through London in an Aston Martin with a Norse god behind the wheel.

Taking a deep breath, she relaxed into the luxury leather seat as a warm, firm hand squeezed her thigh.

'I hope you've had a good time this weekend?'

'It's been amazing. It's certainly been a weekend of firsts. My first,' she blushed, well, you know.'

'Orgasm. Your first of many, I might add.' His hand slid further up her thigh.

She smiled. 'I like the sound of that. My first time on a motorbike, betting in a casino.' She paused, debating if she should carry on. Sod it; she may as well. 'It was also my first time feeling truly desired. You made me feel like a woman and I'm a little scared about what you've released in me. I've spent the entire weekend fantasizing about things I've never thought about before, and I don't know if I should be excited or ashamed.' She chewed on her bottom lip, waiting for him to respond.

She looked over at him, his eyes fixed firmly on the motorway before them. One hand gripped the steering wheel as he clenched his jaw. She felt the car speed up, the engine roaring to life. The other hand still resting on her thigh, squeezed tightly as he said, 'The only people that should feel ashamed are the men in your past that haven't made you feel like the goddess you are. And as for your fantasies, I want to hear about them when you're ready to share them. I'll gladly take it upon myself to give you everything you want and desire.'

He turned to her, his eyes blazing with heat. Her thighs tensed; her body responding to his words.

They sat in comfortable silence for most of the journey home. Tom's hand remained on her thigh, only taking it off if he needed to change gear. The touch was simple but intimate and only added to her feeling of total bliss.

It was already turning dark, the sun low in the sky, as they parked up outside her house and turned the engine off.

'Can you come in for a bit or do you need to rush off?'

'No rush. I'd love to come in.'

Excitement flooded her veins at the thought of having Tom in her home; right before the panic set in as she couldn't remember if her knickers were still hanging on the radiator to dry.

As they entered the hallway, she did a quick dash around to make sure all the laundry was out of sight.

'Well, welcome to my humble abode. Can I get you a drink?'

They walked through to the kitchen. As Lucy busied herself with the kettle, two hands wrapped themselves around her waist and soft, warm lips pressed into her neck.

'I'm sorry I was quiet on the way here. I was contemplating.'

She swallowed nervously. 'Contemplating?'

He hummed against her neck, the vibrations sending shockwaves across her sensitive nerves. 'Do you think you're ready?'

Dread. It spread so quickly through her veins that she was certain her blood had thickened; her limbs turning to lead.

Her words were shakier than intended as she spoke. 'Ready for what?'

'For me. For my life. You say that you worry that I'm going to tire of you, when I'm wondering if I'll scare you away.' He turned her to face him. 'I know you're a strong woman. There is no debating that, but I can see the battles you're having in your mind. You say that I've awakened something in you, something you see as darker, I presume?'

Lucy nodded, not wanting to interrupt.

'I've been open with you about my past and I'm happy to leave it in the past to be with you, but if you want to explore your fantasies, then I'm happy to oblige where I can. I'm not the sort to sugar-coat anything. I don't play games and I sure as shit don't mess people around. This weekend was just as much a test for me as it was for you.'

'What do you mean?' Tea making now long forgotten.

'After I saw you in my club, I couldn't get you out of my mind. I went to K's more often than normal and fucked anyone that asked, but I still couldn't get you out of my mind.'

Jealously lashed out from her heart, but she forced it down. She had no right to be jealous. 'What are you saying?' His words were confusing her, muddling her mind. Had he been with other women recently, after they kissed at the party?

'After we met up again at the party, I knew it was you I needed. I've not been back to the club—in that capacity—since, just in case you're wondering.'

'How the bloody hell do you always know what I'm thinking? It's getting annoying.'

'Never play poker. You'd tell everyone your cards just from one look.' He held her tighter. 'Look, what I'm trying to say, poorly I suspect, is that I'm into you, and only you. Are you ready? Can I call you mine? Or is that moving too fast for you?'

Relief overwhelmed her. She didn't need long to think about it. Only a fool would say no to being with someone like Tom. 'I'm ready. In one weekend, you've erased the memory of Andrew's and Mark's touch and made me realise what I've been missing. I'm ready to try to put the past behind me and discover who I am, and I think you can help me with that.'

He released a deep breath as he rested his forehead on hers before kissing the crown of her head. 'I can't wait. We can start with you telling me what you were fantasizing about all weekend.'

Unable to look into his eyes, she busied herself with the tea making. 'It was the same fantasy repeatedly.'

'Watching me?'

'Yeah, but you already said you don't want to do that.'

'You're right, I don't, but there are other ways. Let me think about it, okay?'

'Okay.'

'Now, show me around. I'm particularly interested in where your bedroom is.' He was already peeling her clothes off her before they left the kitchen.

'Do you have to go now? You could stay until the morning if you wanted?'

'Unfortunately, I need to go. I have an important phone call to make and some bits to sort out.'

She didn't push it; she didn't want to come across as needy and so didn't question why he couldn't make the phone calls at her house. He had a right to go home to work if he wanted to. He'd just spent the last hour reminding her how good they were together and was now standing in her hallway, dressed and ready to leave.

'I'll call you. Lots. You'll be sick of me by the time we see each other again, I promise.'

'When will that be?'

'I'll have to sort something out so I can get away from the club more. I'll let you know, okay?'

She nodded.

'I mean it, Lucy. I'll get something sorted soon. This isn't me backing out. When I'm with you, you deserve one hundred percent of me.'

She stopped biting at her fingernail as she said, 'Okay. Thank you.'

'Stop thanking me for doing what I should.'

'Yes, Sir.'

Something flickered behind his eyes before he blinked it away. 'Goodbye, gorgeous.'

His goodbye kiss lingered for long minutes before he finally broke away and left. Lucy ran her fingers over her lips, missing his touch already.

She glimpsed her reflection in the hall mirror; her skin was glowing, and her smile was wide. She was genuinely happy to her very core. She just needed to work out how she was going to survive between visits.

CHAPTER 23

TOM

Lost on You – Lewis Capaldi

'Gedeon, you need to do something about Ivan. He was in the club again last night acting like he owned the place.' Tom ran his fingers through his hair as he paced around his office, his mobile phone held tightly in the other hand.

'Tom, you know I am doing all that I can to control him, but I fear he is up to no good. What can you tell me? Is Katia safe or do I need to move her?' Gedeon's Russian accent was thicker than normal, no doubt owing to the time he'd been back there.

'He hasn't mentioned her yet. Alex has been staying close, trying to pick up on anything he says. At the moment, there's just a lot of posturing and showing off. He knows we have a connection and is using that to intimidate me. He's drinking my brandy like it's water and refusing to settle the bill. His thugs are causing problems in the club too. I don't like it, Gedeon.'

'I know, I know.' He sighed heavily. 'I have business to attend to here, but I will be back in a few weeks to update my brigadier and keep up the act. I am grateful for you as you watch over my daughter and ensure her safety. If this all goes well, Ivan will no longer be a problem, but I suspect he knows of Katia, and you know that word of her cannot leak out. We will both come to a messy end if that happens.'

He released a sigh. 'I understand. You know I will always be here to keep her safe, but my circumstances have changed.'

'Oh? Have you finally found a woman that can tame the great Tom Harper?'

He smiled as he thought of Lucy. 'I don't think she intends to tame me.'

'Even better. You are lucky.'

'How'd you figure that? You branded my promise to spy for you and protect your daughter across my body for life. You know, it's been hard for me to ever truly belong to anyone else.'

'Now, now, Tom. Do not forget that your tattoos are also a promise from me. You do not have members of the Vory, or any mafia using your club as a place for their dealings, and you suffer from very little trouble. I told you I would protect you from my kind in return. Would you like me to remove your protection order and let you deal with the criminal scum who would destroy your fancy little club in a matter of weeks?'

'No, and I'm grateful for your side of the deal, but you need to know that I can't keep this up forever. The time will come when I can only have one priority in my life.'

'I understand. I will be back in a few weeks. Keep your eye on Ivan; find out what he's doing. And keep an eye on Katia. Tell her Papa lyubit tebya.'

'Daddy loves you. You really want me to say that to her in the middle of a sex club?'

'Yes. The people you associate with will think nothing of it. Do they not have daddy fetishes?'

'They do, but I'm not one of them. But I'll do it for her.'

'It seems I have found your hard limits, Tom Harper.' His deep laugh boomed down the phone.

He took a seat at his desk, leaning back in his chair. 'Okay. Be careful and try to remind Ivan of the rules. He's racking up debt in my club. I can't keep ignoring it.'

'Do not worry. The Vory takes rule-breaking seriously. This will benefit us when the time comes.'

The call ended abruptly; the Pakhan of the UK faction of the Russian Vory did not have time for pleasantries.

He strolled down to the casino to find Alex.

'Hey, how was last night? Did Ivan cause any more issues?' Tom leaned on the doorframe to Alex's small office.

'No more than usual. I caught one of his crew with Sophia, though.'

Tom stepped into the office and closed the door. This conversation didn't need to be broadcast to the other staff. 'What do you mean?'

'They were having a quickie in the drinks store. One of the camera's caught them.'

He gripped the back of the chair that sat opposite Alex's desk. 'What the fuck? Is that who she's been seeing lately?'

'It would appear so. I didn't confront her directly.'

'What's his name?'

'Andre. He and Sophia seemed pretty into each other from what I could tell.'

'Shit. Looks like I have another one to watch. Thanks for the update. Keep up the good work. Gedeon is sure Ivan knows more than he's letting on. Let me know everything you hear, okay? We can't dismiss the idea that Andre is using Sophia for information, so continue to be careful what gets said around her. I'll need to keep Lucy away from her until I can work out how best to play this.'

'Got it. Speaking of Lucy, did she have a good time?'

He couldn't help the smile that crept across his face. 'She did, thank you. And thanks for taking care of the club for me.'

'No worries. I've been telling you to take more time off. Hopefully, I've proved I can step up when you need me to.'

'That you have, my friend. Are you happy to do it more often? Lucy and I are going to give it a go, so I need to give her my time.'

'Sure thing.'

'Let me know if you need to bring anyone in to help you out. We can discuss your pay too. If you're going to be managing the whole club more often, we need to make it official and pay you accordingly.'

'I'm not about to say no to that offer. Thanks, Boss.'

That evening, Tom sprawled across his sofa with the fire blazing, contemplating when he should deliver the message to Katia from her father.

He didn't want to go to the club, knowing if he went there and didn't play it would look suspicious. How was he going to continue to protect Katia but keep Lucy out of it? Exhaling, he scrubbed his hands at his face in frustration. He needed a distraction.

Picking up his phone, he dialled Cameron.

'Cam, how's married life?'

'It's amazing. I can highly recommend it. Speaking of which, I hear you saw Lucy this weekend. How'd it go?'

He let out a long sigh. 'She's well and truly under my skin. Now I know what you went through when you met Jen.'

'Well, I've proved myself to be quite the wedding planner. Do you want me to get the ball rolling?'

He laughed. 'Piss off. No, I don't. I have far too much going on to consider marriage. We've had precisely one date.'

'Have you introduced her to Katia yet?'

And there was that feeling of lead in the pit of his stomach again. 'No, they've not met. Do you think I should take Lucy to the club and introduce her?'

'She's your best mate, well besides me, of course. I think it would hurt her if you didn't introduce Lucy to her. And before you use Lucy's sensibilities as an excuse, remember, she's a stronger woman than people give her credit for.'

'You don't need to worry about that. I'm not in the slightest bit worried if she can cope in the club. She'd be fine. It's me I'm worried about.'

'Really?'

'Mate, it's crazy. The thought of a three-way with Lucy makes my blood boil. Just thinking about someone else touching her makes me want to do violent things. I think she's interested in exploring that world, though.'

'You might just have to put your big-boy pants on and find a solution to that. It could be a nice little hobby for you both.'

'If you're just going to take the piss, you can fuck right off.'

'All right, calm down. Seriously though, if it's something she wants to explore, then you're the best man for the job. Just don't tell me about it. I'm technically her boss and there are some things I don't need to know about.'

'You don't need to worry about that; you know I don't kiss and tell.'

'Appreciated. Listen, I'm happy for you. I never thought I'd see the day that Tom Harper has a steady woman. We can finally go out on double dates.'

'Thanks, and I look forward to seeing you guys more. Well, I guess I'd better let you get back to your woman. Give her a big kiss from me.'

'Will do. See you soon.'

He threw his phone on the sofa with a groan. He wished Lucy was with him now. While he loved the freedom and excitement that came with his lifestyle, part of him was jealous of what Cameron had with Imogen. He wondered if he'd ever be able to have it with Lucy, and at what cost.

CHAPTER 24

LUCY

Love Me More – Sam Smith

'Before you all start nagging at me, yes, I had an awesome weekend with Tom and no, Sarah, I'm not giving you all the details.'

'You've kept us waiting all week and that's all you're going to say on the matter?' Sarah was incredulous as she placed the four gin and tonics on their usual table in the pub.

Imogen laughed as she said, 'Sarah, it's Tuesday night. It's hardly been *all* week, has it?'

Sarah pouted. 'It's been long enough.'

'Well, I don't want to talk about it in the office, and I wanted Jess to be here.' Lucy smiled over at her friend. Jess was one of her closest friends and she didn't want her feeling left out, as she didn't see her at work every day like the others.

'Ah cheers, Hun. I do want to hear more than "it was awesome," though.'

Imogen shuffled her chair in closer before saying, 'I may have overheard Cam talking to Tom on Sunday night, and I think Tom had a thoroughly good time.'

Lucy's eyes went wide. 'What did he say?'

'Oh, don't worry, he didn't give any details. I believe he also used the term awesome; you're clearly meant to be together.'

All eyes were on a blushing Lucy. Sarah broke the silence first.

'Can you give us some of the juicy details? You don't have to tell us everything.'

Lucy took a large swig of her drink before returning the glass to its soggy beer mat. 'Fine. He is simply perfect.' She buried her head in her hands to hide the blushing and the excitement.

'How perfect? We need specifics.'

Jess leaned over and said, 'I'm with Sarah on this one. You can't tell us he's perfect and not tell us why.'

Lucy wasn't comfortable telling them everything, but she figured it wouldn't hurt to give them something. 'He's the sexiest man I've ever been with.'

Sarah rolled her eyes and said, 'Uh, Lucy, I hate to point this out to you, but you've been with Andrew; the stereotypical man-child, and twat-features. That doesn't set the benchmark very high.'

Lucy fixed Sarah with a stern stare. 'That's below the belt, Sarah, but I see what you mean. Well, in a nutshell, he's Thor. He's even got Norse heritage and the sexiest tattoos.'

'I love tattoos. What are they?' said Jess, rubbing her hands together with glee.

Lucy described the tattoos and their meaning. The others sat enthralled as she spoke.

'Oh, and I finally know why you all rate screaming orgasms so highly. It turns out I'd never had one. Tom rectified that. Many times. Turns out he's not only a straight-up Odin-like god, but he's also a sex god.'

Their jaws dropped.

Jess asked, 'You just drop that in at the end? You didn't think that might have been more important than the origins of a raven tattoo?'

Lucy drew her shoulders up to her ears and gave them all an apologetic look. 'You know I need a bit more booze inside me before I can talk sex.'

'If you're now dating a straight-up sex god, then you're going to have to get over your fear of sex talk. We need another round of drinks. Who's round is it?'

'Mine. Same again?' said Imogen as she stood up.

'Have you seen much of Julian lately?' Lucy wondered if Jess might give her some welcomed relief from having to talk about her weekend.

'Not a great deal, no. With the unsociable hours he works and me working all the hours to make a name for myself, it's proving tricky to find the time to date. You may have to work around that with Tom, although at least you can join him at the club sometimes.'

'I didn't think that far ahead. He's going to get someone at work to cover for him, but it means we can't see each other whenever we want, which is already driving me crazy.'

'Girl's had a bite of the cherry, and she wants more.' Jess laughed. 'I don't blame you. I bet he's missing you too.'

'There is always phone sex; Cameron taught me how to do that. I've a feeling Tom would be good at that.'

'Okay, enough about my sex life, which I now have and think it's—'

They all said 'awesome' in unison. All four erupted into laughter until their cheeks hurt.

'I've been thinking.' The drinks had carried on flowing, and by the time Lucy had got home, she was feeling a little braver, so she phoned Tom.

'Okay, should I be worried?' She could hear music in the background and the clinking of glasses.

'Do you think you could take me to K's next time I come and visit you?'

He paused for a second before answering. 'If that's what you really want. Ask me again in the morning when you're sober.'

'Who's saying I'm not sober now?'

'Are you?' She could somehow sense his smile as he spoke.

'No. I'm three sheets to the wind, but I know what I want. You're a sex god and I need to learn how to be a sex goddess. Plus, I'm curious about what it's like in a club like that. How do I know if I'll like it or not if I don't try it? I want to try it, and if I don't like it, then we never have to go back. But, if I do like it, then you must take me there all the time.'

'You're rambling, but also,' he paused, 'you think I'm a sex god?'

'Yeah. I miss you.'

'I miss you too.'

'Do you wanna to try phone sex?' Her words were slurring as she spoke.

'Bloody hell. Who have you been talking to tonight?'

'Jen said Cam taught her how to do it and that she loves it. Maybe we could try it.'

'He always was a smooth talker. I'm currently in the club, hiding in the drink store so I can talk to you. Do you want me to call you later?'

'No, don't worry. I think I may be asleep soon.'

'Hang on a minute.' She could hear the music get louder as he stepped out of the drink store. She could hear the clinking of glasses, laughter and the occasional 'Hey, Tom' as he made his way across the club.

'Okay, I'm in my office.' He sounded breathless, obviously having rushed up the stairs. 'Time for phone sex one-oh-one. Am I on speaker?'

She nodded.

'I'm going to assume you just nodded. So, lesson number one is that phone sex is not a visual thing, Lucy. You need to use your words. Unless you want to switch to a video call?'

'No. I need to start out without seeing you. I'm shy.'

'Okay.' He let out a breath and said, 'What are you wearing?' His voice was husky.

'I've just got into bed, so I'm wearing knickers and an oversized T-shirt.'

'I bet you look cute. I wish I was there.'

'Me too.'

'Okay. Take your T-shirt off.'

She took it off, folded the T-shirt and placed it on the pillow next to her. 'Done.'

'Good girl. Now lie back and get comfortable. Keep the phone near your head, but make sure your hands are free.'

She snuggled down, pulling the covers over her shoulders to keep away the winter chill. Her words were slow and slurred as she said, 'In position, sexy sex god man.'

Tom's voice was low as he said, 'I want you to close your eyes. Take a deep breath in and slowly exhale.'

Unable to form words, Lucy responded with a mumble.

'I want you to dream of me while you sleep. Imagine everything you want me to do to you. I'm going to make

227

you feel so relaxed and satisfied, your muscles will melt into the mattress. Every part of your body will surrender to me. Can you do that, Lucy?'

'Mm-hmm.'

'Good. Now sleep tight, sexy.' The call ended, but Lucy was already asleep with a smile on her face.

She slept soundly. Right up until she had to throw up.

Sarah took one look at Lucy and said, 'Morning. Ah, you look like shit. I think that last drink did you in.' Sarah looked radiant and well put together. Lucy made a mental note to ask her what her secret was. She'd rolled out of bed and thrown on the closest pair of trousers and a sweater. She'd tied her hair in a ponytail, and only dabbed concealer under her eyes. Her pallor was still very much green.

'I feel awful. Three drinks are my limit, and I need to learn to stick to it. I know it's my limit and yet I let myself down every time. I'm going to get myself a green juice. Do you want me to grab you anything while I'm there?'

'I'm all right, cheers. Before you go, did you have phone sex last night with the boyf?'

Even though she could feel the bile rising again, she couldn't help but grin like a Cheshire cat at someone calling Tom her boyfriend. It had a nice ring to it. 'I don't think so.'

Sarah looked confused as she said, 'What do you mean? Surely, you'd know if you did or not.'

'I was very drunk, and I think he lulled me to sleep instead of getting me off. I'm glad he did, as it wasn't long before I was kneeling over the toilet.'

'Oh, so the night didn't end as planned. Oh well, you've got plenty of time to try it out.'

'True.' She waved, weakly, before heading upstairs to no doubt repeat the conversation with Imogen.

'James wants to see us in his office. Are you up to it or do I need to put him off?' Imogen looked genuinely concerned as she turned to face Lucy, hunched over her desk.

'Nope, I need to carry on, regardless. I can't skip a meeting because of a hangover.' She took a deep breath before standing. 'I'm good. Let's go.'

They took a seat opposite James at his desk. Lucy kept the door open to add some ventilation.

James looked dapper, as usual. He rocked his preppy chinos, shirt and zipped up sweater look. 'You look like shit, by the way. I'd say you've lasted long enough. Go home after this meeting and get some rest. Don't worry, I won't think any less of you. We've all been there.'

'Cheers, James. I will.' She sank into the chair as Imogen gave her a reassuring smile.

'Right, I'll keep this short, for obvious reasons. You've successfully finished the Walter and Holmes project. They emailed this morning to confirm they're happy with the plans. You two have done an amazing job getting this finished while getting over you-know-what. I'm proud of what you've accomplished, and you've raised the profile of the company. Well done.'

'That's good to hear. I'm sure Lucy will agree with me on this, but I'm glad that one is over.'

'Yeah, I agree. I feel like we have closure now. So, what's next?'

'We've got a few clients wanting full refurbs. I'll email over the details. You can take your pick. We can't fit them all in, so prioritise what you want to do first and let me know. You'll be pleased to know that Walter and Holmes wanted you both to have a bonus. Check your bank accounts tonight, ladies, and make sure you treat yourself.' He winked at them before gesturing to the door with his hand. 'Now, be gone. You can both have the afternoon off.'

As they shut down their laptops, Imogen suggested they went shopping. 'Trust me, a good shopping trip and a strong coffee are what you need to get over that hangover. Oh, and some greasy food. We'll grab you a sausage roll on the way.'

'Sounds good to me.'

'Are you okay driving? Cam drove me in this morning, so I don't have a car.'

'No worries, let's go.'

Lucy parked in the centre of town. They were now sat in a coffee shop fuelling up on grease and caffeine.

'Where do you want to look first?' Imogen asked.

'If I tell you, do you promise not to tell Sarah? I don't want her prying.'

'Of course. I know what you mean. She's very excitable when it comes to your private life, but it's only because she's so happy for you. We all are. It's about time you found your very own sex god.'

'I get it, I do. I'm just not ready to share this with everyone yet.' She paused while she took a deep breath and leaned in closer. The prim-and-proper older ladies at the table next to them didn't need to hear what she was about to say. 'It turns out that Tom goes to a club, you know, a special club where they do all sorts of sexy things.'

Imogen's jaw dropped before she regained her composure. 'Oh, I see. Has he asked you to go with him?'

'No. Quite the opposite. He hasn't been back since we kissed at your party, but I'm curious about it. I've asked if he'll take me. I'm intrigued; I quite like the sound of it. It's run by his best friend, Katia, and only women can be members. Women hold the power as they invite men in as guests. I like the idea of that.'

'Does Tom have sex with Katia? Is that not going to be awkward?'

'No, he hasn't slept with Katia. He's her guest, but he has no-strings-attached sex with the others there that want to mingle.'

'Mingle. No-strings-attached sex. Sex clubs. Who are you, and what've you done with Lucy?'

'Hilarious.'

'No, seriously, you're like a different woman. Or maybe that's the difference. You're a woman. You hold yourself differently, your head is higher and you seem, I don't know, calmer somehow. I was fond of the old you, but I am loving the new you.'

'Do you really mean all that?'

'Yeah, I do. It takes a strong woman to overcome what you went through and come out the other side a better person for it.'

Lucy swallowed down the lump that formed in her throat. It could be emotion, it could be vomit. She was ninety percent certain it was emotion. 'I've wasted so much energy telling myself I wasn't good enough and that what I had was all I deserved. I was wrong. I bought myself new clothes—inspired by you, Sarah, and Jess— and blagged the shit out of it. But in the end, I discovered I loved the way I looked, and it made me feel good.'

'Fake it 'til you make it.'

'Exactly that. I did the same with Tom this weekend. I was so nervous about being with him. As soon as he picked me up from the station, he made me feel at ease. We clicked, and something came alive inside me. I've never wanted to please someone before, you know, sexually, but with Tom I want to do it all for him and the thought of it turns me on. I want to dress up in sexy underwear and see what the club offers.'

'Good for you. It makes such a difference, doesn't it? Finding the right person. When the sexual chemistry is there, you feel alive inside, and you can't get enough. When I was with Mark, he took away my freedom of choice. Sex wasn't something I enjoyed because it was always about what he wanted. With Cameron, it's natural and as soon as my body realised that it was in control, well, wow, it went into overdrive. We were at it like rabbits. I couldn't get enough of the good stuff. It's like a drug, and let me tell you, it hasn't worn off either. The six weeks we had to wait for him to heal were torture.'

Lucy nodded her head and said, 'I can imagine. I'm already struggling, and it's only been a few days.' Resting her chin on her palm, she swilled the last dregs of her cappuccino around in the cup. 'I'm struggling not to fall too hard, too fast. I keep reminding myself that we've only had one weekend together. He makes me believe I can do anything.'

'I get that. And don't worry, this stays between us. Thank you for trusting me enough to tell me how you feel.' Imogen shrugged her coat onto her shoulders as she stood. 'I know just the place to take you.'

'Oh wow. This place is perfect.' Imogen had taken Lucy to a boutique down a little alleyway that was teaming with independent shops selling everything from pre-loved books to local farm-fresh produce.

The boutique was full of lingerie in every style and colour you could think of.

'Sarah told me about this place when I was looking for my wedding underwear.'

'Ah, Mrs Black, how lovely to see you again. Let me guess; the wedding underwear was such a hit; you're here for it in every colour?' A stunning woman came to greet them. Her skin was the colour of milk chocolate, and her hair sat in bouncy curls around her shoulders.

Her clothes stood out the most. She wore an exquisite corset made from blue silk so dark it was almost black and adorned with gold embroidered foliage that wrapped around her figure. It held her breasts as if on a shelf.

Lucy didn't know where to look. She'd paired the corset with trousers in the same dark blue. She looked elegant and wouldn't have looked out of place in a fine-dining restaurant or high-end event.

'Hi Roxy, we're not here for me today, although that's not a bad idea. This is my friend, Lucy. She needs kitting out with some special underwear.'

'Hi Lucy, pleased to meet you.' She placed her perfectly manicured hands onto Lucy's shoulders and air kissed both cheeks. 'Tell me, what is the occasion?'

'I have a new boyfriend—'

'This sounds excellent so far. Carry on.' Roxy was pressing her palms together as if in prayer.

'And I'd like some underwear suitable for a club, you know, a special sort of club. I don't want to wear any old underwear. I want to impress him.'

'You certainly won't find any old knickers and bra here. Which club, perhaps I know of it?'

'It's in London. It's called K's.'

'Ah, how fabulous. K's is perfect. I frequent it all the time. It's my favourite. Katia, the owner, is just simply fabulous. I'm biased, though, as we often play together.'

'Oh really? That's amazing. What a small world.' Lucy glanced over at Imogen, eyebrows raised, wondering if Imogen was thinking the same thing she was thinking.

'So, my love, how have you come to hear of K's?'

'My boyfriend is Katia's best friend and he, until recently, went there. A lot.'

'Please tell me you're talking about the delicious Tom?' Roxy was now rocking from foot to foot, the excitement clearly bursting out of her.

'Assuming there is only one Tom that is friends with Katia, then yes, I'm talking about Tom.' She was feeling slightly sick as she wondered if this goddess before her had experienced Tom for herself.

'Oh, this is marvellous! I can recommend so many outfits for you. Goodness, I've never met a woman who has tamed Tom.'

'Bloody hell, Lucy. When you said he was a sex god, we didn't think you meant an actual one.' Imogen's eyes were wide as she spoke.

'Oh, my darling, I can't speak for myself as I don't play with the boys often, but Tom rarely takes the same woman twice, and he leaves them all begging for more. I don't know why Katia hasn't given him a go, just once, but she never has.' She turned to face Lucy. 'I need to get you the finest items I have. You're going to look like a queen when you walk in on his arm, and I want to be there to see it.'

Roxy ushered them through to a back room decked out in ivory and gold furnishings with a soft ivory carpet underfoot. Lucy could understand why brides-to-be sought their wedding underwear from here.

Roxy handed them both a glass of champagne as she floated in and out, hanging more and more silk, lace and leather items on a rail.

'You're going to have to drink mine; I can't stomach more alcohol.' Lucy went to set her glass down. 'Bless you. I'll take one for the team. Hand it over.' As she did so, Imogen downed her glass and placed it on the ornate brass and glass table.

Roxy swept in, arms laden with more skimpy items, and hung them on the rack. She stepped back and surveyed the bounty hanging expectantly.

'Now, let the fun begin. Come, come.' She beckoned Lucy up. 'Look along this rack and point out anything that sings to you. If you're drawn to it, you're more likely to be comfortable in it. I assume this is your first time?'

'Yes, I've not done this before. I've never owned underwear like this either.' She knotted her fingers together as she spoke. This had morphed from a fantasy locked in the recesses of her mind to reality, and her body buzzed with excitement while her stomach churned with nerves; surely the aftereffects of too much gin. 'I love what you're wearing. It covers you up but still looks smoking hot.'

Roxy pressed her hand into her chest as she said, 'Why, thank you. This is a great place to start. I don't recommend you walk in there with minimal underwear on. It's much better to remain sexy while leaving something to the imagination. You'll be comfortable in your skin, and it'll give you a chance to scope it out, work out how much flesh you want on show. I suspect Tom won't want you showing much. I've never seen him with someone, in the romantic sense, and I can't imagine an alpha male such as he would be happy to share you.' The thought of having someone feel protective of her instead of using her left her with a warm glow.

'These are nice.' Lucy pointed to the row of overbust corsets.

'Nice? These are exquisite, darling. I've established you have very fine taste, young lady, but this confirms it. These are handmade in the finest silk. The beauty of a corset is that you can dress them up or down.'

'I had one in ivory for the wedding day. Cam's eyes popped out of his head when he saw what it did to my boobs.' Imogen brought her hands up to her chest. 'They look massive.'

'Sounds good to me.' Lucy was excited to see what her curvy figure looked like trussed up in a corset.

'Try this on. I think it's perfect.' Roxy handed over one of the silk corsets in the same dark, inky blue as hers, but the embroidery was gold, dark green, and deep purple metallic thread. Vines of delicate flowers circled the waist and around the bust.

Lucy traced a finger tentatively along the fine embroidery. 'I love it.'

'I knew you would. Pop behind the curtain and strip to your knickers. I'll come and help lace you up and show you how to do it yourself.'

'Wow.' Imogen froze, the champagne flute halfway up to her mouth. 'I have no words.'

Lucy was in the corset and matching pencil skirt. Her breasts looked like they could spill over the top at any moment. Her waist, cinched in, gave way to hips Marilyn Monroe would be envious of. The skirt swept down her curves and stopped at the knee. Her modesty was covered, and yet she oozed sex.

Roxy, looking impressed with herself, asked, 'Do you have some killer heels in this shade of blue?'

'I do, actually.'

'Good. I have the perfect pair of lace knickers to complement this outfit. Let's not go with a G-string. I think more demure French knickers would suit you, but I'll give you the matching G-string for later, my gift to you.' Roxy's wink had them all giggling like teenagers.

Twenty minutes later, they were at the counter watching as Roxy wrapped each item in tissue paper and boxed it all up. Lucy had blown most of her bonus on underwear. The rest would go on more new clothes; her transformation from chrysalis to butterfly was almost complete.

CHAPTER 25

TOM

Love on the Brain - Rihanna

'I need to see you. I'm going to swing by tonight.'

'Oh, the great and mighty Tom will grace us with his presence. The girls will be pleased. When you say swing, do you mean in the literal sense?'

'Katia, it's not that sort of visit.' Tom heard a small huff, 'I can hear you pouting.'

'Do you blame me? I'm bored with people asking me when you're coming back.'

'I need to talk to you about that. I'll see you tonight.'

He could spare an hour on a Wednesday night to see Katia. He hoped getting there early would help him avoid the regulars. As he walked into the club, his body came alive, going into autopilot and pumping adrenaline into his veins. He needed to calm it down, as tonight wouldn't be ending in the way it usually did. He strolled through to the bar and waited with a whiskey.

'Here he is. Give me a squeeze.' Katia joined him at the bar and motioned to the barman for a drink.

'Hey, you. How's it going?' Tom's smile was wide for his best friend.

'All right. Business is good. We've had some new members this week, and their guests have made up for losing you, in part.'

'Glad to hear it. Can we go through to your office?'

She raised an eyebrow as she spoke. 'That sort of visit, is it?'

'I'm afraid so.'

Once they arrived, she closed the door to her office and took a seat in a large, red leather chair. Tom sat on the opposite side, swirling his whiskey before taking a long drink.

'Your father wanted me to tell you, and I quote, "Daddy loves you." I think he hoped I'd say that in the club. He enjoys toying with me.'

'What do you expect? He's a brutal bastard and wishes you would join him officially, but you won't.'

'We've been over this. I'm not Russian; I'm not a thief, and I'm not willing to give my life over to the Vory.'

'Fair enough.'

'He's still in Russia dealing with business, but he's worried about you. He's certain Ivan has information on who you really are. If that's true, you know what that means.'

She stood up with a huff and paced around. 'I'm sick of this shit. Who does Ivan think he is? There is no evidence that I'm Gedeon's daughter. My mother was just a distant relative that he took pity on. That's the story and no one, apart from you and Dad, knows any differently. All birth records have been destroyed or amended.'

'I know. But if there's any chance of Ivan having proof, you know that means the end of your father's reign and his death. Ivan is his top brigadier, his second in command. He'll place a bounty on your head when he takes over. I can't let that happen. I promised your father years ago to be his eyes and ears, and you know I'm a man of my word. So just be careful. Watch who comes in here and keep me informed, okay?'

She held her hands up in surrender. 'Okay, okay. I get it; I really do. It's just shit. Anyway, what's going on with you?'

He couldn't help but smile. He felt a glow inside him when he thought of Lucy.

'Shit. You look like you've fallen. Am I witnessing the taming of Tom Harper?'

'I wish everyone would stop using that phrase when talking about me. I'm not a wild animal.'

'Yes, you fucking are. You're as wild as they come. So, who's the lucky lady?'

'Her name is Lucy, and she's perfect. She's the other reason I'm here.'

'Oh?'

'It would appear I've awakened something in her and she wants to explore it. I'd like her to be a member here so I can be her guest instead of yours. I can't come here as yours anymore.'

'Ouch. You've dumped me.' She slapped his arm playfully. 'Of course. I'll sort it now.' She sat behind her desk, swinging around to the computer monitor. 'Give me her details.'

Tom rattled off all the required information.

'Done. Lucy Steele is now officially a player at K's.'

'Thanks, gorgeous, I appreciate it.'

'We're having a party on Thursday night; it would be great to see you both there.'

'I'll speak to her. So, you've had new members? Anyone I should know about, like Russians, for example?'

'Not that I know off. I'd have to check all the new member details.'

He uncrossed his leg and sat up. 'I think you should, just to be on the safe side.' He really didn't need Ivan getting his crew inside K's. That would put everyone at risk.

'If I come across any Russian's, should I add them to the excluded list?'

He thought on that and shook his head. 'No. If they haven't broken the rules, you can't exclude him; Ivan would know we're onto him. Let me know if you spot any.'

She nodded in understanding.

'How has your week been?' It was Friday night and Tom was getting ready to open the club, but he needed to hear Lucy's voice. Not getting his fix at K's meant he was walking around fully loaded and the strain was showing.

'Long. I've been keeping busy with some new projects, but I feel like I'm on edge the whole time and my body won't stop tingling every time I think of you.'

'Have you not been practicing what I showed you?' The thought of not giving her what she needed was killing him. He craved her and wanted to take her to the edge every damned day.

'No. It doesn't feel right touching myself when you're not with me. It feels like I'm cheating on you.'

He let out a breath, trying to steady himself as he could feel the blood rushing to his cock at the thought of her touching herself. 'Soon. You'll see me soon and I promise to make up for it. Until then, don't touch yourself. You're not allowed to make yourself come. I won't either; trust me, it'll be worth the torture.'

'I trust you, and I can't wait.'

'I have a surprise for you. I hope you'll like it.'

'What is it?'

'I saw Katia at her club and while I was there, I arranged for you to be a member of K's. She can't wait to meet you. Welcome to the dark side, Lucy.' He wasn't entirely sure this was a good idea, but there was no way he was going to stop her from exploring her sexuality and finding out what turned her on. Everyone had a kink, and everyone had a right to work out what it was.

'Oh, wow. Thank you. I thought you'd arrange for me to go, but didn't consider you'd want me being a member.' Lucy paused before she said, 'You went to the club to see Katia?'

'Yeah. I had to pass on a message.'

'Could you not have just texted her?'

Shit. He needed to placate her until he could explain the situation without endangering her. 'No, I wanted to sort your membership out. There's a party on Thursday night, I'd love to take you. Do you think you can take Friday off? The parties don't get going until late, so you'll be in no fit state to work on Friday. It'll be perfect, you can catch the train down after work on Thursday. What do you think? Are you ready to see inside the club?'

She let out a shaky breath but steadied herself as she said, 'Yes. I'm ready and I can't wait. I'll drop James a text tonight.'

'Do you need my help to choose what to wear?'

'I have that covered.'

'Are you sure?'

'Yes. I met Roxy.'

'Oh.' Oh fuck. He knew he wouldn't be able to control himself for long if Roxy had dressed her. 'Now I really can't wait to see you.' He made a mental note to phone Roxy and have her send him a suitable mask for them both, which he would surprise Lucy with on the night. All his dreams had just come true.

'Don't forget, I don't want you touching yourself. Under no circumstances are you to imagine how it feels when I make you come with my mouth.' He could hear her gasp and a smile formed on his lips. 'I wonder, Lucy, how far you'll want to go on Thursday. Will you want me to fuck you with others watching, or will you want to play with the others too? Will you want me to bite your nipples, and if so, how hard can I bite before we find your limits?'

Her plea was quiet and breathless. 'Stop.'

'Is it proving too hard for you already? Because I can assure you it's hard for me too.' The double meaning was clear. Tom was torturing himself, his cock straining in his trousers, screaming for release.

'Is it hard, Tom? Is your cock straining against your perfectly tailored suit? Are you imagining how it feels when you first enter me? It's so tight, isn't it? It's hot and ready for you. I can feel myself pulsing, waiting for you to fill me. I could come just thinking about it.'

He took a second as he pressed his forehead to the cool glass of his office window. 'Touché. I've created a monster.'

'A sexy monster.'

'A *very* sexy monster. I need to talk to Alex; let's hope he doesn't notice the massive erection threatening to rip my trousers.'

The sound of her laughter warmed his heart. 'Goodbye, sex god.'

'Goodbye, sex goddess.'

He rearranged himself to hide the bulge before slipping his phone into his pocket and making his way downstairs.

CHAPTER 26

LUCY

Save a Kiss – Jessie Ware

'Speaking of perfect men; how's yours?' Imogen dropped her pen to her desk and swirled her chair around to face Lucy.

'He's torturing me, and it's not funny.'

'What on earth do you mean?'

Lucy gestured for Imogen to do the same as she ducked her head behind her monitor. They were both huddled behind their desks, with Imogen staring expectedly at her.

'I've got Friday off work.'

'Okay, and why is that torture?' They were both talking in hushed whispers.

'He's taking me to K's on Thursday night and he's been seducing me for days now. It's driving me mad.'

'Oh. Why don't you, you know,' she looked down into her lap suggestively, 'sort yourself out?'

'I'm not allowed to.'

'What?'

'Shh. I don't want the office to hear.'

'Sorry. What the hell do you mean you aren't allowed to?'

'It's all part of the game, apparently. Delayed gratification.'

'I see. Blimey, that must be hard. It was bad enough when Cam and I couldn't do it, but it was the best feeling when we finally could.' She ducked down further. 'What are you going to do at the club? Are you going to have S-E-X with other people?'

'No. And you realise that everyone here can spell?'

'Ha-ha. I'm aware of that, thank you, although I'm not so sure about James sometimes. But seriously, what are you going to do at the club? More importantly, will you tell me all about it? This is fascinating.'

'I don't know what to expect. I may get there and freeze up, think it's awful and leave.'

'Or you might think it's fun, meet new people and discover loads about yourself. It can't be bad if Tom went there all the time, and he'll look after you.'

'I can't wait to see what he says when I show him my outfit.'

'You'll be lucky if you make it to the club.'

Dear Diary,

Tomorrow is the day I finally get to see inside a sex club! I'm nervous, but not as nervous as I thought I'd be. Does that mean I'm weird and twisted? My parents would die if they knew what I was up to. They'd probably try to take me to church and cleanse me of my demons. I don't want them to do that. I currently like my demons. They make me feel good. Tom makes me feel good. When I'm with him, my mind shuts down and the voices in my head go quiet. I'm still. I can breathe. Even if he's just on the other end of the phone, there's something about his voice that makes my body listen to it and obey him.

That's probably because it knows what he can do with that mouth, amongst other things. I haven't thought about Mark much lately, and I don't give Andrew the time of day anymore. Tom has filled the gap they left behind. That scares me; that I can be so dependent on a man to make me whole. I couldn't help myself from being like that with him. We just fell into place.

There's something about Tom that I can't put my finger on. I don't question what he's saying. It's like he has power over me, and I feel safe doing whatever he asks me to. I assume it's because I've never been with a real man before, but I know one thing; I LOVE it.

He's been sending me suggestive text messages all week, and it's driving me crazy. I'm going to climb him like a tree when I see him. Sarah's been helping me increase my sexy vocabulary—annoyingly, they don't teach you all the synonyms for cock in school—so I can drive him just as crazy. I feel like such a minx.

Anyway, I'm going to get some beauty sleep and be ready for my exciting night tomorrow. Wish me luck.

'If you don't need me for anything else, I'll head to the station.' Lucy had her bags ready by her desk. Nerves fluttered in her stomach.

'I'm all good here. You can head off.' Imogen wiggled her eyebrows before quietly saying, 'Have a great time and only do what you're comfortable with. Remember, clubs like that are all about consent and staying within your limits, so don't worry.'

'Thanks, Hun. I'm so excited I could puke.'

'Do not puke on your corset; it'll cost too much to clean.'

'Good advice. See you on Saturday.'

Lucy grabbed her bags, said her goodbyes, and headed to London.

She spotted Tom straight away as she made her way through the train station, her small suitcase trailing along behind her. She remembered to be quick through the gates, so thankfully didn't end up on her arse.

Before they exchanged any words, two hands clutched onto her face, and his lips crashed against hers. Catcalls of 'get a room' erupted around them, but Tom didn't let go, not until the need for oxygen became too great.

He let out a long sigh. 'I've missed these lips.'

'What about the rest of me?'

'I've missed every part of you, but kissing you is the most I can get away with in the middle of a train station.'

It took longer to get to Tom's at this time of day, but she appreciated the chance to gather her thoughts. His hand on her thigh reassured her, while a nervous energy coming from them both filled the atmosphere.

As they stepped out of the elevator into his home, he dropped her bags and pressed himself against her, their lips desperate for each other. A low groan rumbled out from his mouth and the vibrations set her soul alight.

'I need to talk to you about tonight.' As he spoke, his fingers caressed her face and weaved through her hair.

'I'm okay with it. I want to go, really. You don't need to worry about me.'

'I know. I trust you to only do what you're comfortable with, but I wanted to talk about limits and boundaries.'

Lucy hadn't really thought about what her limits would be. She had no idea what happened in K's. 'Okay, I'm listening.'

Tom moved to the kitchen and poured them glasses of water before they took a seat on his sofa. She felt like she was about to be interviewed for a job, not go on a hot date.

'You're making me feel nervous.'

'I'm sorry, that's not my intention. It's just as important for you to know what I'm happy doing and what I'm not happy doing. We need to be open and honest with each other; it's the only way to make sure we both enjoy tonight.'

She drank her water and settled back, ready to listen.

'Before I met you, I was happy to go along with most things; I had very few limits. That's changed.'

She looked up at him and said, 'Because of me?'

His voice softened as he smiled and said, 'Entirely because of you. I know you've mentioned that you want to watch me fuck, but I'm not comfortable doing that to another woman, just like I wouldn't be comfortable watching another man fuck you.'

Her cheeks reddened at the openness of this conversation, but she figured if she was ready to go to a sex club, she should be ready to talk about it openly. 'Does that mean that we won't play with others?'

'Not entirely. I want you to experience as much as you want to, within *our* boundaries, and I know you mentioned a threesome. I'm happy to have a threesome with either another man or a woman, but I draw the line at penetration with anyone else.'

'I'm okay with that. Are we allowed to kiss other people, or do other things?'

'Define other things.'

'Oral sex. Can we give or receive it with others?'

'Is that what you want?'

'I'm not sure, but I feel a little horny thinking about it.'

'We can keep that on the table then.' He slid closer and ran his hand up her thigh. She clenched in response. 'My only limits are I don't share this,' he stroked his hand

248

up to the apex of her thighs, 'with anyone else. And I don't partake in anal play with other men.'

'There's not a lot of limits there.'

'Nope. What are yours?'

She grabbed his cock that was now straining against his trousers and said, 'I won't be sharing this either. I've been doing some research on different kinks and I don't want to be in pain or degraded.'

'That works for me as I get off from giving you pleasure, not pain.'

Lucy finished her water and placed the glass down on the table. 'Can I make one more request?'

'You can make as many requests as you want to, baby.'

'Mark called me a stupid little girl. That kind of stuck with me. Can you not call me things like that?'

He clenched his jaw, tempering his anger before he said, 'It's a good job he's no longer around or I would have to kill him. I'd never call you stupid, and you're certainly not a little girl. Is "good girl" okay with you? I've called you it before but didn't check first. I'm sorry if that offended you.'

Her cheeks went from rosy to crimson as she remembered the way he called her a good girl before. 'I liked that a lot, so yes please, call me that anytime.'

'I'll call you that when you please me.'

'Oh.' She bit her bottom lip, shocked by how his words sent her core into spasm. She exhaled and shook her hands out in front of her. 'I feel so many things right now. I feel excited and nervous and horny all at the same time.'

'Good. That's how you're supposed to feel. Let's grab a bite to eat and then we can get ready.'

Lucy had opted to get ready in the guest room, as she wanted to keep her outfit a surprise. She needed to stay away from Tom, and she knew that if she saw him naked, there was no chance she was keeping her hands off him. His teasing text messages and phone calls had driven her to distraction, and she was a volcano ready to erupt.

She wrapped herself in her long coat. All you could see of her outfit were her dark blue stilettos. Her stockings were nude and gave her legs a beautiful sheen. She tied the belt into a knot as she stepped out of the bedroom.

Tom was leaning on the back of the sofa, one ankle crossed over the other. He was holding a box in one hand, the other tucked into the pocket of his trousers.

Lucy steadied herself on the doorframe as she eyed him up and down. He was wearing trousers and a crisp shirt in the same deep, inky blue as her corset and skirt. She could barely resist him when he wore a suit, and she wanted to kiss his face off when he wore his jeans and a biker jacket, but this was something else.

His shirt had intricate gold stitching across his chest and down one arm. As she focussed on the details, she saw that the embroidery matched his tattoos. Clothing fit for a god, and my, how he looked every inch the god. The shirt was like a second skin and the trousers hinted at the power in his thighs. She couldn't take her eyes off him.

Tom closed the distance between them, snapping her out of her daydream.

'I would like to say that you look stunning, but you've wrapped yourself up already, like a present waiting to be opened.'

She chewed on her bottom lip as she breathed in his intoxicating scent. 'I want my outfit to be a surprise.' As she said the words, her resolve was crumbling, already questioning if they should go out at all.

'I have something for you.' He handed the box over. She passed it between her hands, trying to guess what it was. It was about the size of a necklace box, but much deeper.

'The intention is that you open it.' He smiled at her as he put both hands in his pockets and rocked on his heels.

She slowly opened the box and revealed a beautiful mask, cut from thin metal, but looked like lace.

'It's stunning. Thank you.'

'I forgot to mention that for the first half of the party, guests must wear a mask. It's my honour to give you your first one.'

Emotions washed over her. It was perfect. 'Thank you. I love it. I'm curious, though; how did you know to get me one in dark blue, flecked with gold accents?'

'Ah, well, I may have spoken to Roxy and asked for some guidance on what mask would work with the planned outfit.' He pulled his hands out of his pockets and held them up to her. 'But don't worry, she didn't tell me anything about the outfit. She just gave me a clue about the colour scheme. As luck would have it, my favourite party clothes match. We're the perfect couple.' He held her by the hips and gave her an encouraging squeeze.

'Promise not to leave me alone tonight.' Nerves hit her at the realisation that in a matter of minutes they would be on their way.

'I promise. I'm going to look after you in more ways than one. Let's go. I have a car waiting for us, and if I stay in here with you for a minute longer, I'm going to drop to my knees and bury my tongue in your pussy.'

She whispered to herself, 'Oh my god,' before taking Tom's outstretched hand and following him out the door.

They pulled up outside the club. To look at it, you wouldn't know that behind the large black doors was a den of iniquity. The building was unassuming, with black painted brickwork and a large black steel K sat above the doors. The only sign of life were the two doormen that stood outside, dressed from head to toe in black.

Tom helped her out of the car as the driver opened the door.

'Are you ready, beautiful?'

'Ready as I'll ever be.'

She took a deep breath as they stepped over the threshold into the club. The lighting was soft as it reflected off the dark green walls of the reception area.

'Good evening, Mr Harper. It's good to see you this evening.' The woman behind the desk was stunning in a black waistcoat and fitted black trousers. Her blond hair fell around her shoulders in soft waves. Her makeup was natural apart from the pillar box-red lipstick. She oozed class and sex.

'Hey Gwen, it's good to see you too. I'd like to introduce you to Lucy Steele; I'll be her guest for the evening.'

Gwen hit them with a megawatt smile. 'It's a pleasure to meet you, Miss Steele. I understand this is your first time here. We hope you enjoy yourself. I'm sure Mr Harper has filled you in, but I need to go over some house rules with you before you enter.'

Lucy shifted nervously on her heels. 'Okay.'

'Through the doors is where you can check your coat in and prepare yourself for the party room. You'll be required to keep clothes on and always wear your mask until the playrooms are open. They'll open at eleven.'

Lucy listened intently, even though Tom had talked her through everything on the drive over.

'Tom is your guest, and he must leave with you. You can't leave him here if you go.' She looked between them before carrying on. 'I don't imagine that's going to be a problem.' There was that megawatt smile again.

252

'You're in expert hands with Mr Harper.' She held her gaze at him for a little too long. 'Enjoy your evening.'

Lucy looked between them as she said, 'Thank you.'

Tom squeezed her hand in reassurance. 'Thanks, Gwen.'

She felt his strong hand press into her lower back as he encouraged her through the doors. She waited for the doors to fully close before turning to face him.

'Have you had sex with Gwen?' Her words came out harsher than she intended.

'I think it might be best if you don't think about that tonight. Or ever. I've been with a lot of women, but they were only what I needed at the time. You're the only one that's mine, inside and out of this building. Can you cope with that?'

That's a yes, then.

She pushed her thoughts to the side. 'I can't promise that I won't be jealous, but it's in your past, and I have to be okay with it. We all have a past, after all.'

He dished out orgasms like candy at Christmas, and I killed a man. Who am I to criticise?

He nodded his agreement. 'Let's get ready. I'm desperate to feast my eyes on what's beneath this coat.'

Tom had already shrugged out of his coat and the attendant had hung it up. She stood waiting; her arm outstretched for Lucy's.

She slowly untied the knot and slipped her arms out of the sleeves. The cool air hit her, sending shivers across her exposed skin. With the coat now hanging next to Toms, she turned to face him.

She couldn't tell what was going on in his mind. He stood stock still, his jaw clenching. She twisted her fingers together, unsure of what to do with her hands.

She saw his Adam's apple bob as he swallowed. His voice was husky as he said, 'I don't have the words to do you justice. You look stunning, beautiful. You're a goddess and you're mine. It was a mistake to bring you here.'

'Why? What's wrong?' She desperately hoped he didn't end the evening here and now.

'I've got to wait until eleven before I can fuck you.'

CHAPTER 27

LUCY

Do It To It (feat. Cherish) - Acraze

After helping Lucy with her mask and then putting on his own, Tom showed her through to the main bar area where everyone partied before the playrooms opened. She wasn't sure what she was expecting, but apart from the mask wearing, it looked like any other club she'd been in. A DJ played an eclectic mix of music while people milled about with drinks or danced with each other. This was a chance to check out the other guests.

'I'll get us a drink.' Lucy grabbed Tom's arm as he turned towards the bar.

'Wait. You can't leave me alone.' Her eyes were like a deer in headlights.

'It's literally just there.' He gestured towards the bar that was close by. 'Don't worry, it's just like any other nightclub at this stage, only safer.'

'My track record with nightclubs proves you wrong. We have one count of being picked up by a psycho-killer and another where I got punched in the face. I don't really have a good history with clubs.'

He smirked as he said, 'If I remember rightly, the last time you were in a club, I sucked salt off your collarbone and fucked you senseless. Your track record with clubs is on the up.' His facial expression morphed from playful to stern as his eyes locked on hers. 'Now, wait here while I get us a drink.'

Words abandoned her as she simply nodded. He rewarded her with a smile as he squeezed her hand once more. She felt like a puppy with a treat.

'That wasn't so bad, was it?' He handed her a glass of champagne before tapping his large glass of red wine against hers. 'Cheers. Here's to a night of self-discovery and perhaps a little debauchery.'

As she sipped on her glass of courage, she took in the sights and sounds around her. Everyone seemed happy and comfortable. Pockets of people had formed around the room; some had walked in together while others recognised friends and joined them. She felt at ease in her outfit, blending in with the others. The lacing on the corset was so tight she had no option but to stand tall, and she rather liked it.

Everyone's attention went to the double doors as a woman walked in. Her outfit was like Gwen's, but instead of head-to-toe black, it was dark red silk. The waistcoat barely containing ample breasts that bounced as she walked into the room. She reminded Lucy of a character out of Moulin Rouge.

People stepped in her path to greet her, but she stayed on course. Within seconds, she was standing in front of them. Her glossy black hair slicked back into a high ponytail.

'Tom, I've been waiting for you to get here.' She pulled him into a tight hug before he kissed her cheek. 'And you must be Lucy. It's great to meet you at last.'

She pointed at Tom with her thumb and said, 'Hurt him and I'll kick your arse.'

Tom rolled his eyes. 'Katia, go easy. She doesn't get your sense of humour yet.'

'Oh yeah, sorry, Lucy. Obviously, I won't kick your arse. I know people that'll do it for me.' She winked before grabbing Lucy into a tight hug. 'Seriously, it's great to meet you. I never thought I'd see the day.'

'It's nice to meet you too, Katia. Thanks for sorting out my membership,' said Lucy, taken aback by the embrace.

'No worries. It had to be done just to get this one back in the club. We've all missed our Dom.'

Lucy looked at Tom, wondering if she'd heard that right.

'All right K, don't you have a club to run?'

'I do, and you're spoiling my fun,' said Katia with a pout.

'Yes, I am, so sod off.' He grinned before waving her off.

'Sorry about Katia. She's crazy. Ignore most of what she says. I probably should've warned you.'

'I like her; she reminds me of Sarah. Did I hear her right? Did she say Dom or Tom?'

He put his free hand in his pocket and rocked on his heels. 'Ah, you picked up on that?'

'Yeah, I did. Are you a Dom? I don't want to be whipped and chained up.'

'There are different Dom and Sub relationships—'

'Sub? As in submissive? What is this? Are you expecting me to wait for you on my knees in the red room or something?'

'Lucy, listen. This isn't Fifty Shades. As I was saying, there are different Dom and Sub relationships. You're thinking of the stereotypical one, but I'm what's known as a Pleasure Dom.'

She put her hands on her hips and tapped her finger. 'Oh. That sounds all right.'

He took a sip of his wine and locked eyes with her over the rim of his glass as he said, 'Well, you've enjoyed what I've done to you so far.' That wasn't a question. She couldn't deny that, and she knew she wanted more of it.

'So, what does that mean, then?'

He gestured for her to sit down at a nearby table. He placed his drink down and said, 'I get off from giving pleasure and praise, not pain and punishment.'

'How is that different to normal sex? I'm sorry, Tom, I'm finding this confusing.'

'It's okay. I'll explain it to you. I'm the kind of person who likes to take control of a situation, whereas you're the kind of person who prefers to be told what to do—'

'Hey, that's not strictly true. I'm not a child.'

'I didn't say you were. There's nothing wrong with being the sub in this dynamic. In an equal relationship, the pressure to perform is on both of you. You want to please your partner, but you also feel pressure to orgasm because you know that pleases your partner.'

'That is so true. I'm anxious because I'm inexperienced and don't know what to do.'

'I know. That's why we make the perfect couple. You don't need to worry about that with me. I take the pressure away from you because I take away your control. I'm the one responsible for your pleasure, and that gives me pleasure. Do you understand?'

'I think I do. So, you won't whip me?'

'Not unless you want me to. A flogger can bring you an immense amount of sensory pleasure—not pain—just by slowing down my movements and picking the right one. I think it's best if I explain this as we go. I won't do anything to you without discussing it with you first, okay?'

She nods, taking a shaky breath. 'Yes, okay.'

'Do you want another drink? It's strictly no alcohol once the playrooms open.'

'I think I'm going to need one.'

They had another drink and danced. Her body tingled as Tom pressed his body to hers, grinding his hips in time with the music. Her body was impatient for the playrooms to open. She already knew what he was capable of in the confines of his home, but she was eager to experience the real Tom Harper in what appeared to be his natural habitat. Everyone talked of taming him; tonight, she wanted the animal.

People mostly kept to themselves. A few people stopped to say hello to Tom, mostly women, but each time he made it clear he was with Lucy.

It wasn't long before Katia took to a stage at the back of the room. She clinked her long red nails on the rim of her glass.

'Ladies and guests, it is with great pleasure I can announce the playrooms are open. Please remember the rules; break them and you're out. You can now remove your masks and your clothes. Let the games begin.'

As they walked through another set of doors, they found themselves in a room filled with luxurious oak changing rooms, their curtains made from heavy, bottle-green velvet. The lighting, once again, was low. The further they progressed into the building, the dimmer the lighting.

They walked into the first available cubicle and Lucy watched as Tom undressed.

'Do you go out in your boxers?'

'Yep. I don't think I could carry off lacey underwear. I wear some complimentary black flip-flops too. You'll be okay in your shoes, but it's not advisable to walk around barefoot; you never know what you might step in.'

'Bloody hell, I hadn't thought of that. Do I have to strip down to just my knickers?'

'No. Wear as much or as little as you're comfortable with. Do you have anything on under your corset?'

'I have a strapless bra on. Roxy told me it was best to layer up to keep my options open.'

'Good advice. If you're comfortable, you can take your corset off now, or we can come back in here later.'

She unzipped the skirt and shimmied it to the floor. 'I'm going to take it off.' Before she could start unhooking the front of the corset, he reached behind her and untied her mask. 'Seeing you dressed like this is testing my limits already. You really are the most beautiful woman here. I'm proud to be your guest, and I'm proud of you.'

He muffled her response as he kissed her, pressing her back into the cubicle wall. Her hands roamed across his broad shoulders as he grabbed onto the back of her thighs, lifting her legs around his hips. He rocked into her groin, sending shockwaves of desperation through her.

His mouth worked its way down to her neck, nipping and sucking on the sensitive skin under her ear. 'Are you ready to start?'

Breathlessly, she said, 'Yes. What are you going to do to me?'

'Have you heard of edging?'

She shook her head. 'No.'

'It's where I delay your orgasm. I'm going to get you close to climax and then stop. I'm going to see how long you can edge tonight before you beg me to let you come.'

'But I'm already close to begging you. I've been on edge all week.'

'I know. Imagine how good it will feel when I finally let you come tonight. Let's get this corset off and get you out there.'

Lucy wrapped her arms across her body, biting down on her bottom lip.

'Hey, are you okay?'

'It's just dawned on me that I'm about to walk around a club full of people in nothing but my underwear.' She sighed, looking down at the floor. 'What if people look at me and think I'm too fat, or what if we approach someone and they don't like me?'

He lifted her chin up, his eyes softening. 'Hey, every part of you is perfect. Did you look at the other people here and judge them?'

She shook her head. 'No, I'd never do that.'

'What makes you think that others will do that to you? I promise that when we walk through those doors, you'll see people of all shapes and sizes. People come here to escape the standards and norms dictated to us by society, and women with curves are celebrated in here.' He grabs her arse and squeezes. 'You need something to grab onto. Beauty isn't measured in inches, Lucy.'

She gives a slight nod of her head. 'Okay.'

'When I first laid eyes on you in my club, you took my breath away. I got a hard-on watching you dance, for fuck sake. I understand that this is a big deal for you, but please believe me when I say you're truly stunning, inside and out. Walk out there and be proud of your body. Are you ready to go out there?'

'Yes. I can do this. I want to do this.'

They placed their belongings in a locker and, hand-in-hand, made their way through to the playrooms. Lucy couldn't help but shiver, even though she was warm. Her nerves were getting the better of her as she tried taking some steadying breaths.

Tom stopped walking and turned to her. 'I want you to close your eyes. Tell me what you can hear, what you can smell and what you feel. To fully enjoy this experience, you need to step out of your mind, leave all the thoughts of the outside world behind. This will help calm you down.'

Without letting go of his hand, she closed her eyes and took a deep breath and shook out her shoulders. 'I can hear muted music and people talking in hushed voices. I can smell you. Your scent of citrus, vanilla, and leather is mixing with the air. The smell of leather is stronger, and I can smell an earthiness, like wood. Polished wood.'

'What can you feel?'

As he spoke, she was aware of his fingers loosening around hers and trailing up her arm. 'I can feel your hands on my body. They're warm, but all my hairs are on end like they're reaching for your next touch. I thought I'd feel cold in nothing but my underwear, but the air is warm.' She opened her eyes. 'How did I do?'

He wrapped his arms around her as he said, 'Perfect. I think you're ready to look around. Observe some scenes.'

She chewed on her bottom lip. 'Do you mean watch people do things?'

'Yep. I have a theory that your fantasies about watching me are because you like voyeurism.'

'Voyeurism. Isn't that, well, perving?'

His laugh was gentle and not at all mocking. 'It doesn't make you a pervert. Unless you start peeking through windows. Watching consenting adults have sex isn't that different from porn. It's more common than you realise. I think there's a closet voyeur in all of us. You'll see what I mean.'

'I trust you. Show me the way.'

As they walked into a large central area, Tom explained the layout. 'This is where we can sit with a drink and chill out.' The area was full of velvet and leather benches. A few people were sitting around with a drink, but most of the seating was empty.

He pointed out rooms as they headed down one of the corridors. They stopped outside some large chambers accessible by an open archway. 'These are popular with people looking for an orgy. You can walk in and join in, if accepted, or you can stand and watch. I'll show you some other rooms and then you can choose which you prefer.'

They carried on until they reached a few smaller rooms that had curtains instead of doors.

'These are smaller and contain more specialist equipment. You can choose to leave them open for others to join in or closed for privacy. If the curtain is closed, you leave them alone.'

They stopped outside an area surrounded by floor-to-ceiling glass.

'What's this one? Do people have glass box fetishes?'

'We affectionately call this the Fishbowl. It's invite only, but anyone can watch. Take a look; people are already in full swing.'

'Can they see us?'

'No. It's one-way glass. They know they're being watched, but they can't see who's watching.'

'Do you use this room?'

'I used to.'

'Would you like to use it with me?'

He didn't answer straight away. Instead, he stood behind her, walking her closer to the glass and wrapped his hands around her waist. 'Does that answer your question?'

She could feel his arousal pressed into her rear, and her body responded, her nipples tightening under the delicate lace of her bra.

She was hesitant as she said, 'I think I'd like that.'

They stood in silence as they watched the performance unfold.

Two men and women were sprawled across a large, black leather bench, easily twice the size of a king-sized bed. Their underwear was long forgotten, their skin glossy from perspiration.

One woman had brunette hair and was lying on the bench, her back propped up on cushions. To her left was a man on his knees, guiding his erection into her mouth. To her right was a blonde woman, also on her knees. The couple kneeling was kissing, their tongues lapping at each other's mouths as he reached down, his middle finger disappearing into her. They watched as she threw her head back, gasping with pleasure.

The fourth player, a well-built man, sat on his heels, knees spread wide as he drove into the brunette with punishing thrusts. They couldn't see his face as his back was to the viewing window, but Lucy imagined it was Tom. With every thrust, his arse clenched, and his muscles rippled with brute force. The view before her matched the fantasies she'd had since her first night with Tom.

She felt her core clench at the erotic scene unfolding. It was easier for her to watch knowing that they couldn't see her. She didn't feel comfortable watching the other room with the open archway, that felt too intrusive.

She could feel Tom's breath against her neck as he said, 'Are you enjoying this? If I was to reach down, what would my fingers discover?' His hand moved down from its resting place on her hip and slipped into her knickers. She glanced around nervously to see if anyone was watching them, but she saw that the few people still milling around weren't paying them any attention, too caught up in their own passionate endeavours.

She let out a whimper before he'd even reached her throbbing clit. His finger slipped inside as her knees buckled. He tightened his grip on her waist with his other hand, holding her up. 'I've got you, baby. Do I need to take you into a room?' He thrust his finger in and out of her core, painfully slowly, until she wanted to grind her hips to deepen the contact.

She knew she wouldn't last much longer, her arousal almost at its peak.

'Are you on the edge?' His whispered words sent shivers down her spine, her core clenched around his finger, desperate for more. And then his finger was gone.

'Come down from that ledge.'

She moaned as her body realised it wouldn't get the release it so desperately needed.

'Come on; I've arranged something for us.'

He led her back down the corridor towards the open area at the entrance.

'Hello, you.' As they entered the open plan area, a familiar face greeted them.

'Hello, Roxy.' Tom greeted her with a kiss on each cheek.

'Lucy, how are you, darling? You look stunning. I'm sad I missed the grand entrance in the corset, but I'm glad I get to see you now.'

'Hey, Roxy. The outfit went down well. And I believe I have you to thank for the beautiful mask that matches both of our outfits.'

'No thanks needed, but if you really want to thank me, you can join me in a room later. If he's lucky, I may even let Tom join in.'

'So generous of you, Roxy, as always. We're taking it slow tonight.'

Lucy couldn't believe how easily they spoke about the club. There was no shame or embarrassment here. It felt freeing.

Roxy fixed her eyes on Lucy as she said, 'Have you ever kissed a woman, Lucy?'

'No. I've never had the chance.'

'Let me know if you want to try it out. I can't stop looking at your lips. They're crying out for some Roxy love.'

Tom put his arm around Lucy. 'We'll be sure to let you know. See you later.'

As they walked away, he pulled her closer to his side.

'Do you think I should kiss Roxy? Would you mind if I kissed a woman?' She felt almost high from the endorphins coursing through her veins. Her drinks had removed her inhibitions, and she was eager to explore everything.

'If it's something you want to do, I won't stop you. I don't know how I feel about sharing you, but we can try. You've stepped out of your comfort zone for me, so it's the least I can do for you, but you don't want to overdo it on your first night. Ah, here we are.'

They'd made their way down another long corridor. This one was darker than all the others because all the rooms had solid doors, and all but one was closed. The only light came from small lamps over each of the doors, casting a beam of light over the dark green walls.

'What are these rooms?'

'These are the more specialised rooms. They're closed to onlookers unless you're invited in.' He walked her into the darkened room and closed the door.

He pressed Lucy's back onto the door and trailed his lips across her neck. The feel of his breath on her skin drove her crazy as he whispered into her ear, 'You're about to experience the real Tom Harper.'

CHAPTER 28

LUCY

Boys Like You - Tanerélle

Before she could adjust to the darkness in the room, he hoisted her onto his hips, her legs wrapped around his waist. He kissed up her nape and rocked his hips between her thighs.

'I'm going to drive you wild. I'm going to take you so close to the edge you'll feel like you're falling, but I won't let you fall, baby, not until I let you go. The question is, what can you take tonight? How far do you want to go?'

She trusted him. She trusted he knew how far to take her, and she wanted to experience everything.

'I want all of you,' she panted.

'If anything gets too intense or you're not happy, just tell me to stop. Okay?'

'Don't we need a safe word or something?'

'No, not tonight. Say stop, and I will.'

He laid her down gently on the bed. Unlike the other rooms, this was a large, dark wood, four-poster bed. Instead of a fabric canopy overhead, there was a lattice framework of the same dark wood.

She wasn't totally naïve; she knew this bed made it possible to restrain people, and her core tensed in response.

'I want to restrain you. Are you happy to try that or would it trigger you?'

He always considered her needs, and that made her feel safe in his arms. If anyone else had tried to tie her up, she knew she would freak out, but she had an overwhelming desire to please him.

'I think I'd be okay with that. I want to try it for you.'

He lay a kiss on her cheek, so gentle he barely made contact.

'Don't do this for me. I want to do this for you. I think you'll find a lot of freedom in being restrained. It'll take you out of your mind. You'll have no choice but to be here in the moment—just you and me.'

'I don't understand how being tied up will make me feel free. Doesn't it do the opposite?'

He shook his head. 'No. You second guess everything you do. Instead of enjoying the moment, you wonder if you're doing enough to please me, if you're making the right moves. You're never totally in the moment or taking all the enjoyment for yourself. When I restrain you, I close off that part of your brain. You have no control over your movements; you have no choice but to take what I give you. I give it to you because I choose to, because I want to, and because I fucking love it. You can lie back and relax.'

She thought about his words for a moment, chewing on her bottom lip. 'That makes sense.'

'I won't blindfold you this time. I want you to see how much I enjoy this.' He nestled himself between her legs, kissing her and guiding her until her back pressed into the mattress. She lost track of time as his tongue fucked her mouth, biting, sucking, exploring. He took hold of her wrists and encouraged her arms over her

268

head. She was stretched out and exposed, her back arching, trying to increase contact with Tom's hard muscles. She closed her eyes, committing every moment to memory. His hard body spread heat across her skin as she wrapped her legs around his waist, desperate to find some release from the pressure building between her legs. He ground his erection onto her in relentless thrusts as she felt her climax building and building.

And then. He stopped.

'Don't stop. Oh god, please don't stop.'

He nipped at her earlobe, sucked it into his mouth, and bit down. 'Get used to it, baby. I'm going all night,' he said before kissing down her nape.

And then his warmth disappeared. Goosebumps formed from the chill that coated her fevered skin. She propped herself up on her elbows and watched as he walked over to a cabinet and selected some dark red ropes.

He made his way to the end of the bed and pulled her slowly by the ankles until her body came to rest in the middle of the mattress.

Her breathing turned shallow as she watched Tom stalk along the side of the bed, stroking his hand up her arm. He bent to kiss her wrist before tying a rope around it and securing the other end to a metal ring on the bedpost.

'Does that feel okay? Not too tight? Wiggle your fingers and clench your fist for me.'

'It's good,' she whispered as she squeezed her hand into a fist.

He repeated the process with the other arm and returned to the foot of the bed. His kisses landed on her stomach, sending flutters across her belly. She could feel him smile as he pressed his lips lower. He looped his fingers into her underwear and pulled them down her legs and took his time folding her knickers and placing them on the table near the bed.

He removed her shoes and pressed his thumbs into her soles, massaging away the last of her tension before focussing on tying her ankles to the bedposts, all the while checking in on how she's feeling.

'I feel like I'm going to explode. This is torture at its most sublime.' Every light touch from his fingers sent shockwaves of pleasure through her body.

He released a low chuckle. 'We've not even started yet.' He crawled up her body, stretched out in the shape of a perfect cross, open and exposed to his every whim. He slid a hand under her back and released the clasp of her bra, also folded and placed on the table with her knickers.

With hooded eyes, he said, 'I wish you could see how beautiful you look, lying here ready for me. You're perfection.'

She wanted to move her legs, her thighs screaming to close, to increase the pressure between her legs. She dug her heels into the soft sheets, the only movement she was able to make.

Once again, she watched as he walked over to the rack in the corner, this time returning with a leather toy of some sort that reminded her of a horse's tail.

'What does that do?'

'You know I mentioned a flogger earlier? This is one. These leather strips will bring you intense pleasure. I need you to close your eyes. Can I trust you to keep them closed until I tell you to open them?'

'Yes.' She closed her eyes and waited. Her chest heaved with expectation.

As soon as her eyes closed, her other senses picked up the slack. Her body vibrated with anticipation as she felt the mattress dip between her legs.

She heard a swoosh, followed by a tickling sensation across her breasts. Her nipples hardened, asking for more.

Swoosh.

Gasp.

Swoosh.

Gasp.

The sensation grew stronger with every stroke of the flogger. Her back arched. Moisture pooled between her legs.

Swoosh.

Tom's husky voice broke through the haziness. 'Tell me if I reach your limit, Lucy. I'm taking you as far as you can go.'

Swoosh.

She gasped. 'Yes. Like that. I like it like that.'

With the next swing, the flogger stayed in contact. She felt it trail down her abdomen, desperately hoping it would graze against her clit.

Swoosh.

She groaned as the leather strips hit her sweet spot. It wasn't painful like she'd expected. Warmth spread from her core as shockwaves splintered outwards.

'Is that good?'

She squeezed her eyes closed. Fighting the urge to look at him. 'Too good. Please, I need more.'

'Shhh. Your patience will be rewarded.'

Swoosh.

This time, the sting emanated from her inner thigh. He worked his way down her leg and back up the other. By the time he reached the top of her thigh, she was gasping for air, lifting her hips, desperate for any contact she could get.

'Open your eyes.' Her eyes flew open as she watched him toss the flogger into a basket. As he reached the foot of the bed, he slid his boxers down, kicking them to the side.

She couldn't help but bite her bottom lip at the sight of him standing before her in all his glory. His muscles flexed as her eyes slid from his chest, stopping at his groin.

His arousal was solid, the tip purple with need. Reaching down, he wrapped his hand around the base and stroked.

'Ah, fuck.' His head rolled back as he continued to pleasure himself. Her body screamed for him.

She writhed against the restraints and moaned, 'Tom, please.'

He crawled up the bed until his knees were on either side of her chest. He placed a pillow under her head and nudged the tip of his cock to her lips. 'Lick it. I want you to taste what you do to me,' he commanded. His change in tone didn't scare her; it turned up the furnace burning in her core.

Obediently, her tongue flicked out and licked at his opening. The saltiness warmed her tongue as his cock jerked on her lips, more pre-cum dripping into her mouth.

'That's it, baby. Do you see what you do to me? Open those beautiful lips for me.'

She took his tip in her mouth, licking and dragging her teeth over the ridge as he thrust himself deeper, fucking her mouth with slow, measured movements. She strained at her neck to take him deeper, eager to take as much of him as she could.

He dragged a breath through clenched teeth. 'Ah, fuck. You're so eager for it. Do you like sucking my cock?'

She gazed up at him through her lashes and mumbled, 'Mm-hmm.'

'I'm going to come down your throat if you carry on like that, but tonight is about you.' He eased himself out of her mouth and slid his body down the bed, pressing his lips to hers.

'Now it's your turn.'

CHAPTER 29

TOM

Wild Love – James Bay

Kneeling between her legs, he caught his breath and admired the woman giving herself to him like a gift from the gods. He needed to slow the pace down. He wouldn't last all night at this rate.

He'd had many women in this position, yet none of them made his heart beat out of his chest with longing.

'It makes me angry to think no one has worshipped you before. I only hope I can give you everything you deserve and more.' He quelled the anger that rose as he clenched his fists at the side of his kneeling body.

Gripping onto her hips, he kissed her thighs. His lips barely touching her skin, but he could see the tiny hairs on her thighs spring to life. He brought his lips down onto her clit, giving her one long stroke of his tongue.

'Oh god.' Her words were a whisper, barely audible over the beating of his heart, but he heard them.

'I'll take you to the edge again, but I'm still not letting you fall. Not until I've buried my cock deep inside you.

I want to feel you milk every drop out of me as you come harder than you could possibly imagine.'

'Fuck. Tom, please. I can't take much more.'

He licked up her opening, her thighs straining against the restraints in her desperation to buck and writhe under him.

'What will happen if I slip a finger in?' Not giving her a chance to respond, he slid his middle finger in and gently nipped her clit with his teeth.

'Oh. Oh god. No, please, no more.'

'Unless you say the word stop, I'll continue with it. Do you want me to stop?'

She rocked her head from side to side.

'Say it. Use your words.' He barked.

She shouted, 'Don't stop. Fuck. Don't stop.'

A wicked smile formed as he muttered, 'Thought so.'

His tongue swiped across her opening as he inserted two fingers, twisting them to rub her underside. Bingo. The infamous G-spot.

He knew he needed to take it steady; a couple more licks would take her to the edge. He could see the tells all over her body. Her nipples were hard pebbles; her breathing was quick and shallow as she gasped for air. Arousal flowed from her as he lapped it up with his tongue.

Enough. She'd had enough. He if took it any further, he risked losing her orgasm. He pulled his fingers out to the sound of her whimpers and grabbed a condom from the table.

Untying the ropes, he released her arms and legs, rubbing and kissing where the ropes had held her body in place.

His voice was soft but commanding. 'On your knees, facing the headboard.' He moved the pillows out of the way as he supported her at the waist while she got into position.

'Put your wrists in the straps.'

She saw the two leather straps secured to the top of the headboard.

'Keep holding on. You'll want to let go, but it's best you don't.'

He nudged his knee between her thighs to spread them further for him. Kneeling between her legs, he guided his cock to her entrance.

She bucked and reared her hips into him, trying to take more than just the tip.

'Naughty.' He growled, spanking her ass playfully. 'Stay still and take what I give you.'

He dug his fingers into her hips, holding her still as he placed his tip at her entrance. Her heat made him weep. He couldn't hold back anymore.

In one hard thrust, he buried himself in her to the hilt. They gasped together as he bit down on her shoulder, thrusting into her with punishing blows until he felt his muscles tense. He reached around and circled her clit with his finger.

'I can't hold back. I'm going to come.' She gasped, and he knew it was only a matter of seconds.

'I'm with you. Fall off the edge, baby.'

He felt her pulse around him as she screamed his name. Her hips pushed back onto his cock as he slammed into her, his release no less violent than hers. His moans ripped from his lungs until he was milked dry.

She released her hands from the straps as they collapsed into each other's arms.

'Are you okay?' He cradled her in his arms, stroking her back while she caught her breath.

'I didn't think sex could get any better, but you proved me wrong. You're like a different man when you're here.'

His heart swelled as he said, 'Are you okay with that side of me?' His desire to please Lucy went above his natural instincts. This wasn't about giving her a moment of pleasure, he needed to please her to a deeper level.

'Yes. It's intense but amazing. It makes me feel like a different woman, too; I feel powerful.'

He held her a little tighter, not ready to let her go. 'That's because you are powerful.' He angled her head and pressed gentle kisses to her lips, her cheeks, and across her shoulders. His heart raced. The intensity of their connection shocked him. He hoped Lucy had the stamina to keep going. He didn't want tonight to end. As they got dressed, he ran his finger up her spine after helping her with her bra and rubbed at her shoulders. She groaned as he dug his thumbs into the knots of her muscles. Her body responded to his every touch as he ran his hands across her shoulders and down her arms, hugging her from behind. 'You need to drink something. Let's grab something at the bar and then you can decide what you want to try next.'

'Okay. I hope they have an energy drink; I'm flagging.' She turned and looked at him with hooded eyes, her body lax in his arms.

'If they don't, I'll send someone out to get you some. You're going to need the energy.'

Luckily, they had plenty of energy drinks to choose from. Tom opted for a bottle of water while Lucy guzzled a tropical flavoured drink.

Lucy patted him on the arm as she said, 'Isn't that Katia over there?'

He looked across the room to where Katia was standing, now in her play clothes, as she called them. She'd replaced her trousers and waistcoat with a scarlet red lace corset and matching thong. The outfit left nothing to the imagination.

'Yep, that's Katia. She allows herself to play at the parties. Everyone will be pleased.' He saw the look in Lucy's eyes and knew she needed further reassurance. It irked him that people didn't believe that they were nothing more than best friends. 'I've never played with Katia.'

'I don't understand why not. She's stunning.'

'She might be, but she's basically my sister, so that would be seriously fucked up. Her dad would also remove my bollocks if I ever touched her.'

'Are you two talking about me by any chance?' Katia stood with her hands on her hips, a smile plastered on her face.

'I was just explaining that we've never played with each other.'

She scrunched up her face as she said, 'Fuck, no. Not a chance. Although, full disclosure, there was that one time we kissed when we were fourteen, but we vowed never to talk about that.'

'That hardly counts, K. It was a drunken game of spin the bottle.'

'True. But it was still gross.'

Lucy visibly relaxed at her comments. He inwardly smiled at the thought of her being possessive of him.

'Anyway, I'm going to leave you two lovebirds alone. I'm off to the dungeon.' Her eyes were wide, like a kid seeing their first Christmas presents.

Lucy's eyes were wide but with shock. 'The Dungeon? What is that?'

'It doesn't surprise me he hasn't taken you down there. I have a dungeon in the basement. It's not for the fainthearted; let me put it that way. It's reserved for members that like to be pushed to their limits, myself included. I'm the polar opposite to Tom. He's all about pleasure, whereas I get off on pain—giving and receiving.'

'Katia's known as a Switch. She dishes out the punishment, but if a good Dom turns up, she'll take it.'

'You get the best of both worlds,' Lucy said to Katia.

'Mostly. A good Dom is hard to find. I've seen lots of men think they know what they're doing, but in truth, they don't know shit and that's dangerous. They don't understand that it's a power exchange not a power trip. They need educating on how to perform safely, but I don't reckon that will end up on the curriculum at schools.' She shook her head. 'Anyway, I'm off. Enjoy the rest of your evening.'

As she turned to leave, he noticed Lucy's eyes had caught on something. He followed her line of sight to Katia's retreating thigh.

'Do you two have matching wolf tattoos, or is that a coincidence?'

He could palm her off with a half-baked explanation, but she deserved more.

'There's a story behind that tattoo, but it's not for tonight. Can I tell you everything in the morning?'

He could tell that wasn't the answer she was expecting, but she agreed anyway.

'What would you like to try now?'

CHAPTER 30

LUCY

River – BRKN LOVE

Once they'd recharged, Lucy asked to revisit the Fishbowl. She couldn't resist the urge to watch. It fascinated her, and the more she watched others, the smaller her insecurities became. She found the people on show to be beautiful and awe-inspiring despite not being model-image perfect.

Tom pressed his chest into her back as he ran his hands up and down her arms. 'It's safe to say your kink is voyeurism. Do you want people to watch you?'

She thought about his question for a few seconds. 'No, not really.' Gaining more confidence, she nervously added, 'I'd like to watch someone more privately, and maybe do things while we watch. But not out here with all these people.'

'I can work with that. Come with me.' He took her by the hand and led her to one of the curtained rooms they'd seen earlier. The curtain was open but only one couple occupied it.

They entered the room, and Tom pulled the curtain closed. He looked over at the couple and they nodded; signalling they were happy for them to watch.

The room was almost pitch black except for a dim red light that hung directly over the bed.

It wasn't until Tom led her into a corner and pulled her onto his lap that she saw the large armchair in the room.

He whispered into her ear, 'Keep your eyes on them and follow my lead.'

As they sat and watched the couple kiss and stroke each other, she felt her arousal building again. Tom manoeuvred her hips so her back was leaning against his chest and her legs were straddling his. She was open and exposed to the couple on the bed, but she didn't feel vulnerable.

He pulled the cups of her bra down as he sucked on her neck and pulled on her nipples. She felt as though he was electrocuting her with each pinch and pull. She stifled her groan, not wanting to disturb the couple who were pleasuring each other orally in a sixty-nine position.

She could feel Tom's erection harden as she pressed her rear onto him. His moan was quiet, but she could feel the vibrations through her back.

One of his hands worked its way down to the waistband of her knickers. Her back arched into him, opening herself up further, allowing him access. His finger drew lazy circles over her clit, driving her crazy with desire.

She tilted her head back and whispered in his ear, 'Fuck me. I need to feel you fill me; I need it now. No edging, no games, just let me ride you.'

His hands left her body as he picked up a condom from the table next to them. She could hear the packet rip open.

'Shift forward while I get this on.' He didn't bother to take his underwear off; his erection had already broken free through the slit in his boxers. His hand moved her knickers to the side as he encouraged her down onto him.

Her legs shook with the sensation as he filled her. She lowered herself until she was back on his lap, fully seated. She remained still for a few moments, impaled, while she savoured the feeling of being entirely and deliciously full.

He continued to circle her clit with his finger as she rocked against his length.

His other hand stroked its way up and around her throat, gently pulling her head back to his, encouraging her to turn into his kiss.

'Fuck my cock, baby. Take your time; I won't come until you do. Rub yourself. Take what you need from me.' He removed his hand from her underwear, bringing both hands back to her breasts, kneading them and pinching her nipples.

The couple on the bed were in doggie style, enjoying each other without concern for the onlookers. The room was silent except for the slapping of flesh on flesh and the occasional grunt.

The man pulled on the woman's ponytail like the reins of a horse. As Lucy watched, she fantasized it was Tom grabbing her hair and riding her hard.

Her thighs were aching from her slow rise and fall, but she didn't care. The angle of his entry was rubbing perfectly on her sensitive flesh. The pleasure building with each grind of her hips. She knew she was going to come soon, the pressure reaching near unbearable levels.

'I can feel how close you are. Let yourself go. Give me what's mine. Come for me' He continued to whisper in her ear. His dirty words sent her over the edge as she reached down and rubbed at her aching clit.

'That's it. Fuck me hard, baby. You feel so fucking perfect riding my cock.' As he spoke, he pinched both of her nipples and she detonated. He grabbed onto her hips, lifting her and slamming her down as he came with a growl. She rode the waves with him and watched as the other couple reached their climax, collapsing into a messy pile of sweaty limbs.

Lucy rose to allow Tom to slip his still hard cock out. After Tom threw the condom in the bin, they straightened themselves out and made their way back to the bar, taking a seat on one of the large velvet sofas.

'How're you feeling after that? Do you want to go again, or do you think you're done?'

'Is it okay if we grab another drink and head back to yours? I'm not sure my legs can hold up to much more. They feel like jelly.'

'That's okay with me. You've done so well, and you'll soon build up your stamina. Sit here while I grab us some water.' He stroked his thumb across her cheek before walking over to the bar.

Every part of her body was spent as she flopped back, moulding to the shape of the sofa. Her eyes threatened to close, promising a deep sleep. She kicked her heels off, wishing she'd opted to wear the flip-flops. She'd remember that for next time.

The bathroom was heavy with the scent of lavender, and the steam whirled up from the surface of the water enticing her nearer. She was under strict instructions to relax in the bath while Tom prepared them some food.

With slightly shaky fingers, she removed her corset and other underwear and sank into the warm water. Her muscles eased as she leant against the back of the bath. A smile tripped across her lips as she closed her eyes, visions of the evening whirring around in her head.

'Can I join you?'

Her eyes fluttered open as she leaned forward, inviting him in.

He slipped in behind her, opening his legs wide enough for her to settle against his chest, her feet planted against the other end of the bath, wedging her in place.

His fingers lazily stroked up and down her arms.

'You were perfect tonight. I had to pinch myself to make sure I wasn't imagining it all.'

'I've never experienced anything like that before. I had no idea I could feel pleasure so intensely. You were right.'

He wrapped his arms around her and muttered. 'What about?'

'That I'd be able to focus my mind. I was present tonight; every part of me was there. Since Mark died, I've been carrying around a darkness, a black cloud. I do my best to ignore it, but there's always a trace of it. Tonight, it was gone. There was no room for it; the pleasure and desire filled me entirely.'

The bathroom was silent for a minute while he held her. She wondered if perhaps she shouldn't have revealed so much of herself to him.

'I'm sorry that you've had to carry such a weight around with you.' She knew he was clenching his jaw, fighting back the anger.

'It's inevitable. I killed a man and however much he deserved it—or rather, however unavoidable it was—it has marked my soul.'

He wrapped his arms around her tighter. 'Be careful, Lucy. You don't want to use your sexuality to find relief. You'll end up walking a very dangerous path. I know. I've seen it.'

She lifted and turned to face him; the water sloshing as she moved. 'What do you mean?'

'You'll become addicted to the feeling; it'll become a drug for you. I've seen women chase a new high, their current kinks no longer giving them that welcomed relief, so they take it further and further. Then they leave the safety of Ks in search of more intense adrenaline rushes. Sometimes it doesn't work out well for them.'

She shook her head. 'I don't think that will happen to me.'

'I'll make sure it won't. Whenever the need arises, I'll give you what you need.'

There was another long stretch of silence that felt as soothing as the warm bath they lay in. Her eyes closed, the rise and fall of her chest even.

'Did anything make you feel uncomfortable tonight? I need to make sure that you're okay.'

'I loved it all. I thought I'd be shocked or afraid to look at anyone, but I wasn't. Being able to choose what you're involved in, and not feeling forced to do anything, was amazing. I liked that aspect. Will you take me there again?'

'You'll have to take me, remember? Go there whenever you choose, with or without me. Although, I would rather I was there. The idea of men seeing you there, touching you or pleasuring themselves to you makes me all kinds of jealous.'

'What about women?'

'That just makes me hard.'

'Down boy.' She could feel his growing erection press against her back.

'Come on, let's get some food.'

He wrapped her in a large, fluffy towel, still warm from the radiator, before wrapping one around his waist. An extensive selection of food waited for them on the kitchen counter.

As they stuffed paté and baguette slices into their mouths, Lucy remembered the matching tattoo on Katia's thigh.

'I think there is more to your relationship with Katia than meets the eye. Are you going to tell me about it?'

Tom placed his food down on the counter while he slowly finished his mouthful, deliberating what he should say.

CHAPTER 31

TOM

*Stay with Me (feat. Mary J. Blige) [Radio Edit] –
Sam Smith*

He placed his food down on the counter; a ploy to buy him some time to work out what he should tell Lucy.

She'd opened up to him about the darkness that lived inside her since the stabbing, and he knew she deserved to know what she was getting involved with. He just wasn't ready to lose her yet. She didn't need more drama in her life, and he couldn't guarantee that the current situation with Gedeon, Ivan, and Katia wouldn't get messy.

He also knew he wouldn't be able to live with himself if he kept it from her any longer. It'd always been easier for him to avoid relationships. A permanent woman in his life would make it difficult for him to carry on protecting Katia, especially if he couldn't go to the club.

'Katia had to leave Russia when she was born. Her mother died during childbirth and her father couldn't care for her.'

'Okay, so where do you come in? And why couldn't her dad take care of her?'

'I'm going to tell you everything, but I need your word that you won't share this with anyone.'

'Will you kill me if I talk?' Her laughter stopped when she saw the look on his face. 'Bloody hell, Tom. What are you involved in?'

'Do you promise?'

'Yes. I promise I won't share this with anyone.'

'I need a whiskey.'

Tom fixed them both two fingers of whiskey and they took a seat on his sofa, the fire now roaring.

'I get the impression this is a long story,' she said as she settled down on the sofa.

'It is. There are only four people that know who Katia's father is. Me, Katia, her father, and Alex.'

'Your manager?'

'Yes. Katia moved to London as a baby. She never wanted for anything, money was no object, and she had a great education. We met at school, and I ended up becoming her adopted big brother. She had a hard time making friends and her only family were the people paid to raise her.'

'So, there has never been a romantic connection between you two?'

He sighed. 'No. I really am just her big brother. My parents died when I was a teenager, just finishing school, and my relationship with Katia became stronger. She felt like my only family.'

Lucy turned to face him, stroking his arm as she said, 'I'm so sorry. I had no idea your parents had died when you were so young. How did they die?'

'Car accident. A tired lorry driver fell asleep at the wheel on the motorway and that was the end of my family.'

He took a moment while he sipped on his whiskey. He could see the look in her eyes; it was the same look he got every time he had to explain his lack of parents.

'I'm so sorry, Tom. I can't imagine what that must be like.'

He leaned over and kissed her, a gentle kiss that calmed him.

'The inheritance funded this club. They made sure I was well provided for. For a while after their death, I didn't really know what I was doing. Katia kept me sane.'

'So where does her father come in, and why is it all so secretive?'

'I was at Katia's club when her dad arrived. I'd never actually met him before, as he lived in Russia for most of her life and hadn't been in the UK for long. He sat me down and asked something of me, in return for protection.'

'Protection? From what?'

'Criminals. Like I mentioned before, there are many people that want to use my club to their advantage. He knew I planned to open a club and casino and being the new kid on the block meant I was every criminal's wet dream.'

'I'm confused; who is Katia's father and how can he protect you from criminals?'

'Katia's father is a man called Gedeon Petrov. He's known as a Pakhan—the head of a mafia group called the Vory. The Vory are brutal and set in their ways. They live their lives by a code called the vorovsky zakon, or the thieves' code.' He took another swig of his drink, gauging Lucy's reaction. It didn't surprise him to see her taking it all in. She remained silent, waiting for him to continue.

'The code comprises eighteen rules, and if they get broken, it can mean death. They take them extremely seriously. The first rule is they must forsake their relatives. The second—and this is the most important one to this explanation—is that while they can have lovers, they must never have a family of their own.'

'Oh, I see. So, if anyone finds out that Gedeon is a father, they could kill him?'

'Correct. If Katia's mother had survived, she would have raised her with no involvement from Gedeon. He would have paid for her silence; they'd never need for anything. But she didn't survive, and he couldn't raise her himself. He sent her to the UK to have some control of her upbringing but had to keep her a secret. He fell in love with her instantly and couldn't bring himself to dump her at an orphanage.' Lucy shook her head but didn't interrupt.

'She kept a Russian first name, and her surname changed to Johnson. They registered her birth with no known father on the birth certificate. I'm sure Vory members have fathered children everywhere, but Gedeon was involved in raising Katia.'

'So where do you come in?'

'All was going well until Gedeon moved to the UK. A lot of the older, more traditional Vory members were fleeing Russia, and Gedeon used this as an excuse to set up in London. Now, one of Gedeon's brigadiers is getting above his station.'

'Brigadier?'

'They're like their second in command. One of Gedeon's brigadiers is called Ivan, and he became suspicious. He wants to become the Pakhan and is trying to pin something on Gedeon. To cut a long and complicated story short, Ivan saw enough to make him suspicious that Gedeon might have a daughter.'

'Can't Gedeon do something about it?' He nodded as he drained his glass. 'The head always has a few spies working for them. Their job is to spy on their brigadiers to make sure they're remaining loyal. That's where I come in.' He looked at her empty glass and said, 'Do you need a top up?'

Lucy looked down at her glass and nodded. He collected the crystal decanter from the table and poured them both another two fingers.

'Carry on,' she said, eager to learn more.

'Gedeon needed someone he could trust to look after Katia, and monitor Ivan. He needed me, and he knew I would need him to keep my club safe.'

'So, he asked you to spy on this Ivan person and continue to look out for Katia. In return, he makes sure the criminals know that you're not to be messed with.'

'Yes. He didn't need to worry about Katia. I'll always look out for her but spying on a member of the Vory is something different entirely. The Vory takes tattoos seriously. Each tattoo has a meaning; they're sacred. I refused to have their tattoos, but Gedeon was adamant he wanted to mark me; it was the only language they understood and respected.'

She ran her hands along his exposed tattoos, first the ravens, then the wolf. Her palm came to rest against the helm of awe symbol on his pec. 'Is that why your tattoos are all about protection and information gathering?'

'Yes. If I was going to be marked, it was going to be with tattoos from my heritage. I'm not Russian, and I'm certainly not a member of the Russian mafia. Gedeon made sure that my markings were known to people in his circle. I'm a marked man, Lucy. If anyone tries to harm me, they answer to Gedeon.'

She stroked her fingers along her exposed collarbone. 'That's quite sexy. I feel like I'm in a movie.'

He wrapped his arms around her and breathed in the lavender scent still on her skin. 'You continue to surprise me. I thought you'd run a mile when I told you I'm involved with the mafia.'

'Well, you're not really, are you? You're just someone who is looking out for someone you care for, and you're willing to do whatever is necessary to keep them safe.' She took another sip and lowered her eyes before saying, 'I can relate to that. So how do we stop Ivan from finding out the truth?'

'I love that you've just said, "we." Ivan frequents my club a lot more than I'd like. That's why I've brought Alex in. He can be my eyes and ears in the casino. He's overheard Ivan talking about how he plans to use Katia to bring Gedeon down and then take over. If that happens, he'll kill Gedeon, and I don't want to think about what will happen to Katia.'

'Shit. This is serious, isn't it?'

'Yes, it is. I get the impression it'll come to a head soon. Ivan needs to move on his suspicions before he gets caught. I need to get something on Ivan so that he has to answer to the thieves' code. He's running up debt with the casino and the bar, so he's breaking one rule already. But that's not enough to ensure Katia's safety.'

'How do we get proof, then?'

'I think I have an idea. Ivan has a man on his team called Andre. He's started seeing Sophia and I need to find out where his loyalty lies. I just don't know how to do that.'

She shrugs as she says, 'Sex.'

'I'm not fucking Andre, Lucy. That's just insane.'

'I don't mean that. What I mean is that you should speak to Sophia and ask her to get the gossip about if he's loyal to Ivan or Gedeon. Mark extracted everything he needed out of me after only a few nights together.'

Tom shuddered at the thought of what Mark had done to Lucy. He took a few seconds to steady his rising anger. 'That's not a bad plan. I'll give it some thought.'

'So why does Katia have the same wolf tattoo on her thigh?'

'She loved stories about Odin growing up, so when she saw my tattoos, she wanted one too. She often read stories of how Odin had fathered half-wolf children and she would joke that she felt she was half-wolf because of her parentage. Having the same wolf tattoo as me gives her a tangible link to someone, and it brings her comfort that she's not alone. She calls it our bond. I think she's bonkers.'

'I think she loves you and it scares her you also might leave her one day.'

'Then she really is bonkers.'

Silence fell over them as they sipped on their whiskey and watched the flames flicker in the fireplace.

'Thank you for being so understanding. I'm sorry I didn't tell you about it sooner, but I couldn't tell just anyone about this. I had to make sure.' He stopped himself, unsure if he should finish that sentence.

Lucy had nestled into the crook of his arm and draped herself over him, her towel barely clinging on. 'Sure of what?'

'Sure that it was worth the risk.'

'Oh.'

'You're worth it, Lucy. I don't want to lose you. I feel like I've hit the jackpot finding someone I can share my lifestyle with.'

'And by lifestyle, you mean an insatiable sex drive and a love of kinky clubs.'

He laughs quietly, kissing the top of her head before saying, 'Yep.'

It was the early hours of the morning and the sun had risen. He carried a sleeping Lucy into his room and tucked her under his duvet, drew the blackout curtains and put his phone on do not disturb. They both needed a good sleep. He gazed at the woman sleeping next to him and whispered, 'How did I get so lucky to find someone I want to call mine?'

He pressed his lips to her forehead as he tucked her back against his chest and he soon drifted off.

Bang. Bang. Bang.

'What the fuck?' Tom leapt out of the bed as the sound pounding on the front door ripped him from his sleep.

'What's going on?' mumbled Lucy, her eyes still closed as she snuggled deeper under the covers.

'Stay here.' He slung on jogging bottoms and a T-shirt as he made his way to the front door, gearing himself up for a fight. No one should be able to access his front door, not without him letting them in.

He let out a sigh as he saw Alex through the peephole and swung the door open. He quickly stepped out of the way as Alex barged in.

'What the fuck, Tom? I've been trying to get hold of you for hours.'

He raised his hands, palms outwards in surrender. 'What's the emergency? I've had my phone off; it was a heavy night.' Tom closed the front door, after giving the hallway a cursory glance, and followed Alex into the kitchen.

Alex looked around as he said, 'Are you alone?'

'No, Lucy's here, but you can speak freely around her.'

'Oh really?' He raised his eyebrows.

'Yes. Now get to the point.' Tom rubbed at his face, frustration at being woken so abruptly getting the better of him. He rested his elbows on the counter, waiting for his friend to get to the point.

'Ivan was in the club last night. He got wasted and boasted about how he's going to be taking over soon.'

Tom straightened. 'How soon?'

'He reckons within the next week or two. He's gathering evidence.'

'We know all this already. Did he say anything useful?'

'He plans to go to K's.'

'So, he's sure it's Katia then?' Tom rubbed at his chin, deep in thought. 'We need to know when he's going so we can warn her.'

'I can help with that.' Lucy stood, leaning on the bedroom doorframe, wearing Tom's bath robe.

Both men turned to face her. Alex said, 'Hi, Lucy. Nice to see you again.' He looked at Tom before turning his attention back to her. 'How can you help?'

Tom spoke before she could reply. 'I'll put some coffee on, and we can sit down. I'm too tired for this shit.' He turned to the beautiful, sleep-mussed woman strolling towards them. 'How're you doing, sexy?'

'Achy and tired, and I've never felt better.'

'Okay, I don't want to know what you two have been up to, so if we could get back to the issue at hand.'

Tom gave Alex a vulgar hand gesture before busying himself with coffee and toast.

Once sat down, they turned to Lucy. Tom's brows knitted together as he said, 'I'm scared to ask this, but what's your idea?'

'I have first-hand knowledge of how to charm information out of someone. Why don't I wait until he's drunk and then flirt with him? If he comes here tonight, I could see what I can get out of him.'

Tom shook his head. 'No. I don't want you anywhere near him. He's not just any run-of-the-mill dickhead, Lucy. He's a brigadier for the Russian-fucking-mafia.'

Lucy shrugged her shoulders, palms faced upwards, and said, 'Alex will be nearby if it goes wrong. It's perfectly safe. I'm only *talking* to him. I can chat to

Sophia and see how serious it is with Andre; see if she's willing to find out who he'd back when it comes to it.'

'Lucy, I said no. I'm not having you put yourself in danger. That's a hard limit.'

She straightened her spine as she said, 'If anyone in this room knows about being pushed to their limits, it's me, and I coped just fine.'

'You didn't though, did you? Cope, I mean.' His tone was calm as he looked at her with pain in his eyes.

Alex coughed. 'Do you guys want me to leave?'

They both turned to him and said, 'No.' Alex sat back down and tapped his fingers against his knees.

'Tom, please don't leave me out of this. I want to help. I can do this. Let me prove myself to you,' she pleaded.

'You don't need to prove yourself to me.'

'Then let me do this because I choose to. It's just talking. I promise to always stay where you or Alex can see me.'

Tom rubbed at his chin and said, 'I'm on board with you talking to Sophia; it'd be helpful if you spoke to her. I don't think she'd talk to me about her love life, somehow. Don't talk about Katia. We can't risk information getting back to Ivan.'

'I think you're on to something, Lucy.' Alex turned to Tom. 'I'll keep an eye on her; she'll be safe with me.'

'I don't like it. You've been through enough already. I told you about this to protect you, not bring you into it.'

'It's okay. I've survived worse. That's the plan and we're sticking to it. Now, I'm going to finish my toast and get dressed. If I were you, I'd see Alex out and join me in the shower. Bye, Alex.' Tom's jaw dropped as she stood, straightened the belt on the robe and sauntered back into the bedroom, munching on toast as she went.

Alex called out from where he remained on the sofa. 'Uh, bye Lucy, see you later.' He raised his eyebrows as he turned to Tom. 'You've got your hands full there.'

'She's going to be the death of me. I can't wait. You heard the lady. Sod off. I've got more pressing matters to deal with.'

He was already naked and heading into the bedroom as he heard the front door click shut.

CHAPTER 32

LUCY

Him & I – G-Eazy & Halsey

'Can I see if Sarah's free to come up tonight?' asked Lucy.

'Yeah, of course.' They'd gone back to bed after the hottest shower Lucy had ever had, and she wasn't talking about the temperature of the water.

'It would look less suspicious if I were with another woman. I don't know any women that go clubbing on their own, do you?'

'No, that's a good point. Good thinking.'

'I'll call her. She could get the train up and, if you don't mind, go back with us tomorrow.'

'The flaw with that plan is that my Aston is a two-seater, so unless you want to ride in my lap the entire way home, it won't work. I'm happy to hire a car for the weekend. Call her, let me know, and I can sort a car.'

'Are you sure?'

'It's my pleasure. Call her now while I get some food ordered in; it's getting late; I need to set up the club for tonight.'

He threw her phone onto the bed as he strolled out of the bedroom.

Sarah answered right away. 'Hey, Lucy. How is your sexy weekend going?'

'It's awesome. I have so much to tell you.'

'If it's so awesome, why are you calling me and not actively fucking Tom?'

She laughed as she said, 'We need to eat at some point. Also, I wondered if you fancied joining me tonight at the club? Tom is working, and I could do with the company.'

'I'd love to. I have nothing planned for tonight.'

'Fab. Can you get the next train up? You can stay here at Tom's, and then he's going to drive us all back tomorrow.'

'Perfect. I'll get a bag ready now and make my way to the station. See you soon, sexy bitch.'

Lucy found Tom ordering food over an app on his phone while pacing around the living room. 'She said yes. Can we pick her up from the station in a bit, or will that interfere with work? She's getting the next train in.'

'That's cool with me. I can pop out to pick her up while you hold the fort here—two-seater car, remember?'

'Oh, bloody hell. You need to consider upgrading to a bigger car.'

'You might be right. I'll look into it. I'll move the food delivery back and increase the order; no doubt she'll want to eat too.'

'Most likely. Thanks, you're the best.' Tom walked over and nestled in her outstretched arms.

'Now, get some clothes on, or I'll cancel all our plans.'

'Hey, Lucy. How's it going?' Sarah bounced into the hallway like an excited puppy; her glorious auburn curls bouncing before engulfing Lucy's face as she wrapped her in her arms.

'Hi, Sarah. Good journey?'

'It was great. I was stuck in a carriage filled with a drunken stag party. If the night gets a bit shit, I have an open invitation to join them later.'

'Good to know. Thank you so much for coming at such short notice.'

'Anytime. Especially if I get chauffeured around by this sex god in a posh car. I can totally see why you're hot for him.'

She pointed with her thumb at a retreating Tom, who called out, 'It's been brought to my attention that it's entirely impractical but thank you for the compliment.'

Lucy giggled as she said, 'Come on through, Tom ordered food.'

'Oh good. I didn't have time to eat, although that's probably a good thing, as my outfit for tonight is tight as fuck.'

Tom ate quickly so he could get ready and head straight down to the club. The girls were going to hang out for a bit and head down when ready.

As soon as he'd said his goodbyes and closed the door, Sarah pounced on Lucy. 'Tell me everything. Don't leave out any of the details. I mean it, leave nothing out.'

'I'm not telling you everything. I'll let your imagination fill in the blanks.'

'It's probably safer if you just tell me. You have no idea what my imagination will have you doing.'

'That's true, but it might be accurate this time.'

Sarah froze, her eyes bugging out. 'What. The. Fuck.'

Lucy told her about the club and its rules. She described the setup as Sarah looked on in awe, stuffing more prawn crackers into her mouth.

'This club sounds amazing. You must take me there one day.'

'I will, I promise.'

'So, what did you discover about yourself? Did you do a threesome?'

'We didn't get involved in one, but we watched a foursome. That's what I like to do, watch. It's amazing.'

'This is so awesome. You've changed so much. I feel like you've found yourself and have all this courage. I'm quite jealous, but mostly proud of you.'

'Really? You're proud of me?'

'Hell yeah. You've got over a shit time, picked yourself up and said "fuck it" to every fear you have. Look at you now; you're doing everything you want and you're not sorry for it. I love it. I love you, Hun. You're inspirational.'

'You realise that I've spent the last year being jealous of you? I look up to you and Imogen and Jess and wished I had what you had.'

'And what exactly do I have?'

'Confidence. A string of men queuing up for you. Style, friends, and a fun life.'

'Is that what you see when you look at me?'

'Yeah, it is.'

Sarah huffed out a breath as she shook her head. 'I feel like a fuck up most days. My parents pay for the flat I live in. And while I have flings often, there's no good having a string of men when you only really want one, and they're not interested. My life is fun, and I keep busy because I don't want to be alone with my thoughts—or just alone full stop.'

Lucy's face falls. 'I had no idea.' Lucy reached over and squeezed her arm. 'I don't know what to say, other than I think you're amazing.'

'Well, thank you, but you shouldn't use me as a role model. Come on, before I start to ugly cry, let's get ready and get our sexy little arses downstairs. I'm going to bag myself a rich city man tonight.'

Sarah wasn't kidding when she said her dress was tight. She looked phenomenal. Her lilac skin-tight dress hugged every curve, and its Bardot neckline showcased her collarbone. She wore a silver choker around her neck, a matching bracelet and patent silver heels. She meant business tonight. Lucy thought it was perfect for attracting a certain Russian man—not that she'd tell Sarah that.

'That dress leaves nothing to the imagination.'

'That's the idea.'

'Do you even have knickers on?'

'Nope. There's no room for anything in this dress, and I'm regretting the prawn crackers; they were a step too far.' She released an exaggerated breath as she rubbed her stomach.

Lucy wore a pair of tight black trousers and a black satin corset. She'd loved how the corset had made her feel and purchased a more demure one to wear out in public. In contrast to Sarah, she wore gold jewellery and her favourite ombre shoes.

'You're looking sexy too. You're like the classy, sexy one, and I'm the more rough-and-ready version. Come on, let's get your hunk of a man to buy us a drink.'

The barman greeted them as soon as they entered the bar. 'Good evening, ladies. Tom asked that I set up a bottle of Dom and two glasses over there.' He pointed to a table in the corner, the bench seating wrapped around the corner so they could sit next to each other and have a prime view of the surrounding people. 'But if you'd prefer something else, let me know.'

'I could get used to this.' Sarah was rubbing her hands together with glee. 'I'm Sarah. Nice to meet you.'

'Hi, Sarah, I'm Jack.' He held his hand over the bar. Sarah went to shake it, but he turned her hand and kissed her knuckles, his eyes remaining on hers. 'If you need anything, you know where I am.'

She lowered her gaze as she said, 'Thank you. I will come and find you if a need arises.'

Lucy looked between the two, rolled her eyes, and went to the table to pour two glasses of champagne.

'He's fit as fuck.' A flustered Sarah slid in next to Lucy and took a long drink of her champagne.

'Is there really nothing between you and James then?'

'Fuck knows. Nothing has progressed, even after he says all the right things, we just go back to being friends-with-benefits. It's okay; it serves a purpose. I don't feel ready to settle down, anyway.'

'You don't think it's uncomfortable being benefit-friends with your boss?'

'He's not technically my boss. Well, he's my half-boss. Cameron and he share me. Which sounds wrong on so many levels.'

'Don't worry, I know what you mean. If you're not getting hurt or making life difficult at work, then I'm happy for you.'

'Cheers, Hun. We are great together, and the sex is amazing, but there's something missing and I can't put my finger on it. I want more, but I don't know what I want more of. Does that make any sense?'

'It does. Before I met Tom, I thought I knew what I wanted, but after that first weekend with him I realised what I'd been missing. When you find the right person, it awakens something inside you and then you can't get enough of it.'

'That's what I want.' Sarah looked down at her fingernail as she picked at it.

Lucy reached out and gave her friend's arm a reassuring squeeze. 'Don't look so down. You're sexy and one hell of a woman. You'll find your fire starter soon enough.'

'Hey, you two. Nice to see you again.' Sophia had walked in and was getting ready to start her shift.

'Hey Sophia. How are you?'

'Good thanks, although I got little sleep last night, so I'm already knackered. Let's hope I get my second wind.'

'Oh yeah, any particular reason why you didn't get any sleep?' Lucy winked as she spoke. 'I heard things are going well with your new man.' This was probably the best opportunity she had to extract some information from Sophia before she was too busy serving drinks all night.

'Hilarious; the men here are worse than gossiping women, but yeah, it's great between us. We've barely been apart from each other. As soon as we're off work, we're hooking up. I can't get enough.'

'Bloody hell, it seems everyone is finding their fire starter apart from me.' Sarah downed her champagne, no doubt an attempt to drown her sorrows.

Sophia's gaze turned dreamy as she said, 'He's definitely a fire starter.'

Lucy was direct with her questions and asked, 'Is it serious between you two, then? What does he do for a living?'

'So many questions. Has Tom hired you to find out if I plan to run off and marry him soon?'

Lucy laughed that off, swallowing down a choke as she said, 'Of course not. We were just having a conversation about love. So come on, dish out the details.'

She took a seat next to Sarah. 'He's perfect. He has the most amazing body; I just want to lick it. That's what attracted me to him. I think he's a bit of a bad boy, but I just can't resist him. He works for a guy called Ivan, helping to run his business. I'm not entirely sure what that entails, but he seems to do well out of it.'

Lucy nodded along, careful not to interrupt.

'He's so caring and protective. He'd do anything for me. I think I may be catching feelings, but don't tell him that.'

Lucy smiled. 'That's awesome. Does he like the job?'

Sophia scrunched up her face. 'I don't think so. I know he thinks his boss is a dickhead. Sometimes he spends too much time moaning about him when he could be fucking me instead. I tend to whip his cock out at that stage and distract him.' She wiggles her eyebrows as she giggles.

'That is shit. Do you think he'd change jobs if he could?'

'I have no idea. Andre questions Ivan's morals, so maybe he'll leave him if a better opportunity came along. He'd like to start up his own business, but before you ask, I don't know what that would entail either.' She checked the time on her watch.

'Anyway, I've got to get downstairs before Tom sacks me for being shit. Lovely to see you both again. I'll get the tequila lined up and ready for later.' With a wink, she turned and left.

Sarah topped their glasses up. 'She seems nice. Do you think Andre has any friends I can investigate? I wouldn't mind a bad boy for a change.'

'I have no idea, but I think you're safer sticking to the gentlemen. Trust me on that one.'

They sat and caught up on the gossip and discussed the news that Cameron and Imogen were trying to start a family.

'I can't wait to see them with a baby. If anyone deserves true love and happiness, it's those two. They're going to produce the most gorgeous babies, don't you think?' Sarah propped her chin on her palm.

'Totally. I hope for Cameron's sake they have boys. Can you imagine how protective he would be with girls?'

Sarah laughed. 'He would be a nightmare. She'd never stand a chance of getting a boyfriend. Speaking of boyfriends, do you reckon Tom's *the one*? Are you guys going to get married and have gorgeous babies?'

'Shut up. We've only just got together, and while I think he's perfect, I don't think we are going to get married just yet. How would that work? I live miles away for a job I love, and he can't move out of London. This club means too much to him. Plus, what would I do with Doris if I spend all my time in London? It's not like I can bring her here. She needs the country air.'

'She's a cat. I'm sure she'd cope living anywhere as long as you fed her. What are you doing with her now?'

'My neighbour is looking after her for me. She's great. I think she must work from home as she's always there to take my parcels in for me.'

'That could be a solution, then. She could co-parent your cat with you. Nothing is insurmountable.' Sarah clinked her glass against Lucy's in cheers for her solution.

'All right, enough chat about marriage and my cat. Let's go downstairs for a boogie, and then we can have a go in the casino.'

'Oh, cool. I hope they can tell me what to do. I'm clueless.'

'In that dress? I'm sure the men will queue up to give you very detailed instructions on where to place your bets.'

After an hour of dancing and tequila shots that were now an established tradition, they went to try their luck in the casino.

'Hi Alex, did Tom get some chips put aside for us?'

'Good evening, ladies. He did indeed. Here you go.' He turned to Lucy and lowered his voice. 'There's plenty here, but if you need more to keep playing, come and find me and I'll sort more for you. Understand?'

Lucy lowered her voice. 'Yep. Is he here?'

Alex nodded over to the blackjack table where Ivan was sitting. His black hair slicked back with more gel than necessary.

'Wow, he really is a walking stereotype, isn't he?'

'Guys, who are you talking about?'

'Andre's boss is over there playing blackjack.' Lucy knew she needed to come up with a reason she was going to be flirting with him and grilling him all night. 'I'm going to grill him tonight and try to find out what he does. I've seen him here before, and I reckon he's dodgy AF.'

'This sounds like it could be fun. Our mission, should we choose to accept it, is to pump Ivan for information. Do you accept this mission, even though it could be dangerous?'

'I do.' They giggled. Lucy tried to school her features into a more serious look. 'Do you accept this mission?'

Sarah nodded and said, 'I do. I think I may have more success than you. I'm dressed to kill.'

'If you can find out what he's up to, then I'll take you to K's, all expenses paid.'

Sarah's eyes bugged out of her head in excitement. 'You're on.'

Alex raised his eyebrows at them before shaking his head. 'You ladies are crazy. Here are your chips. Please be careful with him.'

'Don't worry, we've got this. Let's see what Sophia is getting involved with.'

They didn't want to appear obvious, so went to play some roulette. Lucy explained the rules as a waitress brought over another bottle of Dom.

'Ladies, this bottle is on the house, compliments of Tom. He asks that you have a great evening.'

'Ah, Tom is the best. Tell him thank you.' Sarah was already tipsy, so this was going to tip her over the edge. Lucy felt the warm sensation of drunkenness take over her body. Her plan to extract information from Ivan felt easier with every sip.

After a few attempts at roulette, Sarah got the hang of it and didn't want to leave the table.

'YES.' Sarah exclaimed loudly. A few people nearby turned to see what the commotion was about.

Sarah clapped her hands and said, 'Sorry, I just won. I now have four of these black ones. It's my lucky night.' She waved a black poker chip in the air as she wiggled her hips.

'All right, Sarah, that's great, but maybe keep it down a little.' Lucy was whispering to Sarah louder than if she were speaking at normal volume. The two of them giggled together as the second bottle of champagne neared the end.

A heavily accented, deep voice interrupted their conversation. 'I think you should let your friend have some fun.' They turned to find Ivan standing next to them. 'I think your friend is having marvellous luck tonight. Perhaps she would like to join me at my table and blow on my dice.'

'Is that all you want me to blow?' Lucy nearly spat out her mouthful of drink as Sarah spoke.

'I think I'm going to like you.' Ivan wrapped his arm around Sarah's shoulder and guided her over to his table. 'Come, you must join us too.' He motioned to Lucy.

She tentatively followed Sarah over to a table. It was the biggest in the room and had attracted quite the crowd.

'Andre, move over and make room for these two lovely ladies.' Turning to them, he said, 'Please excuse my rudeness. I didn't introduce myself properly. I am Ivan, and this is my associate, Andre. Please, what are your names?'

Sarah pressed a hand to her chest before motioning to Lucy. 'I'm Sarah, and this is Lucy. Nice to meet you.'

'Beautiful names for such beautiful ladies. You appear to be without drinks. Let me rectify that for you.' He turned and clicked his fingers high in the air. Moments later, a waitress brought over another bottle of champagne and poured out four fresh glasses.

'Let us toast to beautiful ladies that will make me lucky tonight and blow well on my,' he winked at Sarah as he said, 'dice.'

Sarah leaned into him as she said, 'Cheers to that.'

In her periphery, Lucy noticed Tom had entered the room and was talking to Alex. She tried not to look too obvious as she glanced his way. The look in his eyes was fierce, clearly unhappy seeing her in Ivan's company. She tried to send him a message of reassurance with her gaze.

He worked his way around the room, chatting to customers, but his destination was clear to her. Not before long, he was at the table.

'Good evening, Ivan. I trust you're being well looked after?' He stole a glance at Lucy, his eyes then focussed on Ivan's grip around Sarah's shoulder.

'As always, Thomas. Your hospitality is second to none. And look what I have here, aren't these two beautiful? They will bring me lots of luck tonight, don't you think?'

'They are stunning, and sure to bring you luck. Have a great time, ladies. I'll come back later to join you for a drink.' He grazed his fingers across Lucy's back as he carried on greeting guests around the room. The light touch warmed Lucy, sending shockwaves to her core. There was entirely too much adrenaline coursing through her veins tonight. She knew she needed to switch to water soon before she got too drunk to remember what she was supposed to be doing.

Sarah let out a little squeal, bringing Lucy's attention back to the people she was sitting with.

'I told you, you are my lucky charm. I'm afraid I cannot let you go now.' Ivan's hand wrapped around Sarah's thigh as she stood next to him, as he perched on a stool at the edge of the large table. Lucy could no longer see where his hand rested. She raised her eyebrows at her friend. Sarah shrugged in response.

'I can detect an accent, but I can't place it. Where are you from, Ivan?' Lucy attempted small talk to distract Ivan from creeping his hand any higher on her friend's thigh.

'How very observant of you. I am originally from Russia, as is Andre, but we moved here many years ago. Our accent is more prominent when we have been drinking.'

Lucy tried to look nonchalant as she said, 'What brought you over to this country?'

'It was when many people were leaving Russia. A few of us thought we'd have a better chance of a successful life if we left. I think it worked out well for us. Look at us; we have everything we could want. Well, almost everything.'

'Why almost everything?'

'You ask a lot of questions. Here, have another drink and let's play. I see you both have quite a few chips to play with; I wonder how lucky you will get tonight.'

Lucy was wondering the same.

CHAPTER 33

LUCY

Bad Guy – Billie Eilish

'So, tell me, ladies, what are your plans for later tonight?' Ivan asked as he rolled a chip between his fingers.

They'd been gambling for a couple of hours; Sarah had been charming Ivan as if she knew what Lucy wanted to achieve tonight.

'We don't have any plans apart from having fun here. What are you guys up to?' Lucy tried to give Sarah a warning look. She didn't want to risk upsetting them but also wasn't sure if she wanted to leave the safety of Alex's watchful eye.

'We have a treat in store for us tonight. I have a friend who works in a more specialist club. She has added our names to the guest list tonight and is taking us. We are very excited, aren't we, Andre?'

Ivan turned to his associate, who'd remained relatively silent all night. 'That is correct. Ivan has been asking for a while now if he can go to the club, but unfortunately, men may not be members. He is lucky that he has friends in the right places.'

Lucy's heart was beating so hard she was sure they could see the anxiety that had taken hold of her.

'This club sounds amazing. Where are you going?' Sarah was leaning into Ivan, mostly because she was too drunk to stand up straight.

'It is called K's. Have you heard of it?'

Lucy was becoming desperate now; she didn't like where this was going. Andre caught her eye, his gaze burning into her, suspicion written all over his face. Sarah went to reply, but Andre cut her off.

'Ivan, I don't think these lovely ladies are interested in a club like K's. Am I right?' He made it clear he was talking to Lucy.

'I have heard of K's, but I'm not sure I'd want to go there. Isn't it a,' she lowered her voice as she said, 'sex club?'

Now it was Sarah's turn to look at Lucy suspiciously. To keep her friend's drunken mouth closed, she leaned in closer and pressed her hand against her leg, hoping this would give her the signal to run with it.

Ivan fixed an intense stare at Lucy. 'You seem so scandalised at the prospect of a sex club. It is a great place to act out all your darkest desires. I frequent them often, usually ones more tailored to my particular tastes.' His eyes darkened, sending a chill over Lucy's skin.

Lucy forced down the feeling of nausea that washed over her. 'What makes you want to go to K's? Are you bored with the other clubs?'

'There is something there that I am very interested in. Something I would like to see with my own eyes.'

'Ladies, shall we have a change of scenery? I would like to go downstairs and have a dance.' Andre's voice was higher than usual, and Lucy noticed his top lip glistening with sweat.

'Andre, it is rude to interrupt me when I am talking, but I think that is an excellent idea. I wonder, Sarah, would you do me the honour of dancing with me?'

'I'd love to. Let's go; I need to work off some of this alcohol.'

Alex stopped them before they could make it out of the room. 'Ladies, would you like me to look after your chips until the end of the evening?'

Lucy was grateful for the chance to let him know what was happening. 'Thank you, we're going downstairs for a dance, and then I'm not sure what the plan is as these gentlemen may head to another club.' She emphasised the last words of the sentence, hoping Alex would understand which club she was referring to.

'Sounds like you'll be having a great night. I'll keep your chips safe until you're ready to cash them in.'

As they went through the door into the club, Sarah grabbed Lucy's arm. 'Let's freshen up before we dance.'

'Great idea. We'll be right back.'

'Don't be long, ladies.' Ivan signalled they'd be over by the bar.

As soon as they were in the toilets, Sarah turned to Lucy. 'What the fuck is going on? Why did you act like you'd never been to K's, and who are these guys? No bullshit, Lucy. I know you, and I can tell there is more to this than meets the eye. Why am I here?'

Lucy twiddled her fingers before saying, 'I can't tell you.' She chewed her bottom lip, waiting for the backlash.

'Like fuck you can't tell me. What am I involved in? And where has Tom been all night? I know he has to work, but he's been suspiciously absent since we went into the casino. I'm not stupid, Lucy, and I'm also not as drunk as you think I am, so tell me, or I'm leaving.'

'Shit. I can't tell you all the details now. I need to speak to Tom first, but I'll tell you some of it. Please, you must keep this to yourself.'

'You can trust me. What's going on?'

Lucy shuffled them into a corner so no one could overhear. 'Ivan is not a nice man. He's involved in something that's putting a friend of Tom's in danger and I said I'd help by talking to him to get some information out of him. Andre is sleeping with Sophia and we need to know where his loyalties lie.'

'For fuck's sake, this sounds like some sort of mobster movie.'

Lucy stared back at her friend, unable to say the words in a public place.

Sarah's eyes widened. Her whispered words clipped with anger. 'Are they in the fucking mafia, Lucy?'

'Please, keep your voice down. We can't talk about it here. All I can say is that we can't let on that I'm with Tom. We don't know who they are, and we need to find out whose side Andre is on.'

'And how do we do that?'

'I'm not sure. He's been quiet all night and staring at me. I don't think he wants us hanging around. We can't let Ivan go to K's. Katia is Tom's best friend, and we can't bring her into this. We're doing all of this to protect her, and with good reason, but I can't tell you that bit.'

'But they said they're going tonight.'

'I know. I'm out of my depth and I don't know what to do.' Lucy flapped her arms in exasperation.

'Okay. It's going to be okay. I'm going to continue to charm Ivan, but if his hand grazes my pussy one more time, I might have to punch him in the dick. Now that I know he's an arsehole.'

Lucy narrowed her eyes at Sarah. 'Were you liking it before then?'

'Yeah, I was. It was hot. Not so much now, though.' She exaggerated a shiver.

'Sorry about that.'

'It doesn't matter; that's not the point. We know he said they plan to go to the club tonight, so we're going to have to give them a reason to stay. You stick with Andre and get to know him. I'll stick with Ivan and become the biggest cock tease known to man. We're going to have to see how this pans out, but if it gets too dangerous, you're going to have to get a message to Tom.'

'I'm hoping Alex has already told him we've moved down here. He'll no doubt be in his office watching us like a hawk on the monitors.'

Sarah released a deep breath and rotated her shoulders back. 'Okay, let's go do this.' Sarah stopped before she reached the door and turned on her heels. 'And one more thing. Next time you need some help with a hair-brained scheme, just do me the solid of letting me know what I'm getting myself involved in, you know, before I find myself right in the middle of it.'

'I'm so sorry. I didn't expect it to get this messy. I was hoping for a fun night tonight.'

'It's okay. You're lucky I love you. And you owe me, big time. You're taking me to that club and showing me the time of my life. Then we're even.'

Lucy nodded as she said, 'Deal.'

As they made their way across the heaving dance floor, they spotted Ivan and Andre sitting at a table.

Ivan stood and motioned to the table. 'Ah, here they are. Come, ladies, take a seat. We have some excellent cocktails, courtesy of the beautiful Sophia.'

'They look delicious, but Ivan, I would really like to dance first.' Sarah's pouting lips and puppy-dog eyes had him drooling, his cocktail long forgotten.

She took his hand and led him to the dance floor, pulling her to him so that his back was to the table.

Andre didn't waste any time before turning on Lucy. 'What are you doing?'

'I'm sorry, I don't know what you mean.' She tried to keep the stutter out of her voice.

'You're playing a very dangerous game. You don't want to be involved with this. I know you are Tom's girlfriend; I remember you from when you were here last time. You are lucky Ivan was too drunk to remember you, and I know about Katia. I also know you've been questioning Sophia.'

Lucy gulped. 'What are you going to do about it?' There was no point lying to him about it.

'Now I must keep you and your friend safe and try to protect Katia. I was trying to manage this situation myself.'

'I don't understand. You work for Ivan.'

'No, I do not. I work for Mr Petrov. Ivan is middle management and needs to be removed. I love Sophia and I do not want her involved in this. What is it with British women and their ability to interfere with the best laid plans?'

'Careful. I won't think twice about slapping you.'

'I don't doubt it. Ivan is a sick man. He loves to play games and inflict pain on people. I've seen him at these clubs, and he doesn't believe in safe words. Doesn't respect boundaries. I've seen what he does to women for fun. I cannot imagine what he will do to a woman for revenge.'

'He wants to hurt Katia as well as bring down Mr Petrov?'

'Yes. He feels our leader has betrayed him and wants him to suffer before he kills him. It will not surprise me if Ivan takes Katia as his own plaything after he replaces Mr Petrov at the top. We cannot let this happen.'

317

'No, we can't. Tom would never forgive himself.'

'I must be careful who I am seen talking to. Ivan doesn't trust easily. I have suspected Tom has been involved in this for some time now. Please get the message to him that I have done all I can to divert Ivan from Katia, so much so that he put others on the case. Tom can trust me; I will stand with Mr Petrov until the very end. I do not want Ivan in charge. He would bring shame to the Vory. I had hoped his blatant disregard for the code would get him in trouble, but he has so far avoided it.'

Lost for words, Lucy sat in shock.

Andre spoke quickly as he said, 'Will you help me get a message to Mr Petrov?'

'I can try.'

'When this is over, and it will be soon, I want out. I love Sophia and want to be with her. The Vory does not allow this. I need to leave and be a free man. I will do whatever I can to help with this situation, but in return, I want my freedom. And maybe Tom could offer me a job, as I suspect I will need a well-paying job to keep Sophia happy.' His smile warmed his face. She could see the love in his eyes.

'I'll pass on the message.'

'Thank you. Now, let's dance so he does not suspect us of collusion.'

Ivan clapped Andre on the back as they approached the dance floor. 'Ah, here they are. I was wondering what you were talking about.'

'Andre was telling me about Sophia.'

'As yes, the beautiful Sophia. It is a shame that will never come to anything, but I will allow him some fun while it lasts. And what about you? You are lonely tonight. Come here, I can happily satisfy both of you.'

Before Lucy could object, Ivan had pulled her into his arm; one draped over each of their shoulders.

'Look at me, Andre, two beautiful women in my arms. They are like night and day. Here I have the sultry Lucy, and here I have the fun Sarah. What more can I ask for?'

Andre's tone was casual. 'You are very lucky tonight, I agree. I am going to get another round of drinks in.'

'Ah poor Andre, what a sourpussy. Is that the right phrase?'

Sarah suppressed a giggle as she said, 'I think you mean sourpuss. But you were close.'

'I would like to get close to your pussy, Sarah. I bet it's as sweet as cherry pie.'

Sarah pressed her hand to his shoulder. 'Easy, stud. No one gets to taste my cherry pie on a first date.'

He pouted like a small child. 'That is a shame. I get hungry when I drink, and I like nothing better than eating cherry pie.'

Sarah pats his shoulder like a mother consoling a crying child. 'Maybe next time.'

'I will look forward to it.' Even from where Lucy was standing, she could see his eyes piercing Sarah's.

As Lucy wondered how she was going to navigate this evening, she saw Tom stalking over to them. He glanced at her as he reached them, giving her a quick once-over, no doubt checking she was okay.

'Evening, folks. Is everything going okay over here, or can I get something for you?'

'Thomas, my man.' He let go of Lucy's shoulder and slapped Tom across his back in greeting. 'Can you please dance with the lovely Lucy here? Andre is neglecting my guest, and I would like to spend some more time with the beautiful Sarah.'

Tom looked between Ivan and Lucy and said, 'It would be my pleasure if that's okay with you?' He directed the question to Lucy, acting like he hadn't spent the night balls deep in her.

'Thank you, I would like that. Don't let me keep you away from your work, though.'

'I can make time for you. I'm following a customer's request, after all.' She caught the glimmer in his eye and did her best to hide a smirk.

He took hold of her, keeping his hand placement respectful at the small of her back. It had to look like he was only meeting Lucy for the first time.

Ivan's attention was now fully on Sarah. His arms wrapped around her neck, tugging her closer. While his back was to Lucy, she mouthed to Sarah, 'Are you okay?' Sarah responded with a thumbs up. From the look on her face, Lucy suspected she was getting a thrill from this.

Tom brought his mouth closer to her ear. 'Is everything going okay? It's killing me not being here with you, but I'm watching you constantly from my office.' He brought a hand down her back and rested it at her hip, squeezing her gently.

The thought of him watching her all night set her skin on fire. She desperately wanted to kiss him, but that would have to wait.

'I have a lot to fill you in on. He might go to the club tonight, but we're all trying to stop that from happening.'

'Shit. Who's the "we" in this?'

She lowered her voice and checked Ivan wasn't close. 'Andre. He's on our side. You can trust him.' Tom nodded. 'Also, I had to tell Sarah some of what's going on, but I haven't told her everything.'

He swayed her in time to the music, trying to move away from Ivan and Sarah. 'That's okay. I figured you'd have to tell her something.' He held her closer, his fingers gripping her hip tightly. 'I wish I could kiss you. How much do you think we can get away with?'

'I don't know, but I'm willing to find out.'

CHAPTER 34

SARAH

Darkside - Neoni

Sarah knew Ivan was a dangerous man, but the feel of his hands on her bare shoulders was making her hot. The alcohol had lowered her defences and left her raw with need.

She was having fun with James but felt like there was something missing. Perhaps what she needed was to test her limits, as Lucy had done. Sarah had always considered herself adventurous in the bedroom, but when she thought about it, she was promiscuous, which wasn't the same thing.

Playing with Ivan could be fun, knowing that it wouldn't—couldn't—go anywhere. And as far as anyone else was concerned, she'd be doing it for the greater good.

Tonight was thrilling. She felt powerful and needed, and maybe just a little too drunk to be making these kinds of decisions, but she didn't care.

Lucy needed to speak to Tom, and that meant distracting Ivan. As a plan unfolded in her mind, her body came alive. She felt moisture pooling between her thighs. The lack of underwear made it even more sensitive.

She pressed her body against his.

'You are warming up to me, I see.' Ivan's voice carried a hint of his darkness; he released a low growl as he licked at the spot under her earlobe.

Sarah let out a moan in return. She couldn't help it; he'd gone straight for the jugular, literally.

She could feel his breath on the sensitive skin below her ear as he said, 'You can't hide how your body reacts to me. Your nipples are clearly hardening through that tight dress. I want to suck on them like a hungry baby. Bite down until you gasp with the pain. Then I will soothe them with my tongue.'

She gasped. 'Fucking hell.' She didn't need to pretend. His words were driving her crazy, and the knowledge that this was wrong turned her on even more.

'Do you feel what you are doing to me?' He ground his pelvis into hers, his hardness catching her sensitive nerve endings. 'I think I could make you come right here on the dance floor, in front of your friend. Would you like that? What is your darkest desire? Do you want me to finger fuck you right now, right here?'

Her brain was screaming at her to say no, but she couldn't form the words. Her leg lifted slightly, rubbing her thigh on his.

He brought his hand up to her neck and roughly pulled her closer until his lips smashed onto hers. His kiss was rough, devoid of romance and entirely full of animalistic need.

His tongue forced its way into her mouth and encouraged her to part her lips for him. The pressure of his hand on her neck increased, but it didn't scare her. She felt taken, owned.

His fingers dug into her rear, pressing into her flesh like red-hot pokers as his other hand increased the pressure on the back of her head. She felt a sharp pain in her bottom lip as he bit down. The tang of copper spreading across her tongue as she tried to pull away. A sense of dread overcame her—she was in deeper than she could cope with.

He kissed his way along her jawline, drawing her earlobe between his teeth and biting down. She flinched as he said, 'Are you being a cock tease, Sarah? Do you think you can finish what you start?' His voice was no longer flirtatious, but had taken on a darker edge.

Her body was reacting to his touch, but her mind was still screaming no. Visions of James formed in her mind, and guilt overcame her. How was she going to get out of this? Her heart rate increased as panic washed over her. She couldn't let Lucy and the others down, but this was going too far.

'I'm sorry to interrupt, but I need to speak with you, Ivan.'

'Andre, as always, your timing is impeccable. Can't it wait? As you can see, I have my hands full.'

Andre glanced at Sarah, concern in his eyes. 'No, it can't wait. We need to leave. There is trouble across town, and they are asking for you.'

Sarah released a breath she didn't realise she was holding when Ivan took his hands off her. The imprints from his touch burning her skin. 'Fucking hell, Andre. What is the point in me having you as my bitch if I still must fight with the dogs?'

'I think you'll want to handle this.'

'Fine. Change our plans for this evening. I want this one with me when we go to K's.' He grabbed her neck, drawing her face to his before sucking on her bottom lip. 'Next time I see you, I'm going to make you come. That is my promise to you.'

323

Bile rose in her throat at the thought, but instead of cringing away, she simply smiled.

'Andre, get her details.' He waved his hand in her general direction before stalking out.

Andre took a step closer to Sarah and lowered down to her level. 'Stay away from him. You've started something you will not want to finish. I can only protect you for so long before he takes matters into his own hands. Do you understand?'

She nodded. 'Yes. Thank you.' And then they were gone.

'Are you okay? What happened between you two?' Before Sarah could compose herself, Lucy was standing before her, concern etched on her face.

Sarah took some steadying breaths to compose herself while she straightened out her dress. 'I'm cool. Ivan got a little rough and kissed me. Thankfully, Andre interrupted.'

'Shit. I'm so sorry, Sarah. I shouldn't have let it get that far.'

'Can we talk about it later? I need a drink.' She needed time to organise her thoughts. Her mind was a scrambled mess.

Lucy didn't look convinced as she said, 'Sure. Let's get drunk on tequila like old times.' Sarah was grateful to her friend for dropping it for now.

Tom walked them over to a table. 'Thanks for helping me out tonight, ladies. I'll get Sophia to bring a bottle of tequila over for you. I'm sorry I brought you into this mess, Sarah, but I'll explain later. Are you both going to be okay if I handle business for a while?'

Sarah didn't need anyone fussing over her. She wanted to bury the nauseous feeling with alcohol—the coping mechanism of champions. 'No worries, it was quite exciting. Do what you need to do while Lucy and I become intimately acquainted with this bottle of amber sexiness.' She turned to Lucy and said, 'Now, let's get shitfaced.'

Tom looked torn. She could tell he didn't want to leave them, and who could blame him? He knew more about Ivan and what he's capable of, but she didn't want to think about that now. Sarah placed her hands on his shoulders. 'Honestly. Please go. I want some time with my girl here to ask her all about your skills in the sack.'

Tom laughed, and he shook his head. 'You girls are insatiable with your need to talk about cock.' He paused, looking between them. 'Okay. I need to talk to Alex, so I'll see you later. If you need anything, you come and find me.' He kissed Lucy before strolling off, stopping to speak to the ladies that stepped in his way.

Sarah looked at Lucy, who was now watching her boyfriend depart with a glazed expression. 'Don't you get jealous?'

'Of what?'

'The way all those women fawn over Tom.' Sarah pointed at the women on the dance floor.

'Maybe a little, but not really. I know he wouldn't do anything with them.'

'So, you trust him completely?'

'Yep.' Lucy smiled at her as Sophia interrupted their conversation, bringing the tequila along with two bottles of water.

She placed them down on the table and took a seat. 'Here you go. I'll join you for one, but don't tell Tom.' She giggled as she poured three shots of the amber liquid into glasses. 'Cheers. Here's to Andre not having to go to K's with that twat tonight.'

They downed their drinks and sucked air in through their teeth.

'Fuck. Let's do another.' Sarah was clearly up for a messy night.

'Laters, babes. I have to work.' Sophia dashed back to the bar with a spring in her step as Sarah set up another round of shots. They made their way through a large proportion of the bottle while Sarah tried to extract as much of the juicy details out of Lucy as she could.

Lucy slammed the empty shot glass down on the table. 'One more shot, a dance, and then I reckon we should get to bed. I hate to think how we're going to feel in the morning.'

'Don't remind me. I hope Tom has a hangover cure.'

Lucy blushed as she said, 'He does.'

'I do not want to hear you two shagging while I'm here.'

'I'll get him to cover my mouth, then.'

'Oh my god, who are you and what have you done with my innocent Lucy?' Sarah giggled as she surveyed her friend.

'Get your mind out of the gutter. I'm obviously talking about his amazing avocado on toast.'

Sarah side-eyed her as she said, 'Yeah, of course you were. Are avocado emojis replacing aubergines now?'

They downed one more shot and made their way to the dance floor. The events of the evening soon forgotten as they danced.

CHAPTER 35

LUCY

Wild – John Legend & Gary Clark Jr.

'You two have been suspiciously quiet about what happened at the weekend.' Imogen was eyeing up Lucy and Sarah from the rim of her coffee cup. The three of them were taking a coffee break on Monday afternoon, sat out on the mezzanine in their office.

Lucy side-eyed Sarah as she said, 'There's nothing to tell. Sarah came to London to keep me company, and we reached the bottom of a bottle of tequila. Something that I will never do again, I might add.'

'Oh, and the best bit was that Tom arranged for a driver to bring us home. I felt like royalty being driven home in a posh car and a chauffeur. I think I'm getting a taste for the highlife.' Sarah flicked her hair over her shoulder with a smile on her face.

'Could Tom not come back with you then?'

Lucy swallowed her coffee with a gulp. 'No. He had some business to deal with and he didn't want us getting a train, so we ended up back home sooner than planned.'

Sarah distracted Imogen by bringing up Lucy's visit to K's. 'Anyway, the weekend logistics is not what we need to focus on. What we need to do, Jen, is focus our energy on getting Lucy to crack and tell us everything that happened when she went to the club with Tom.'

'That's a waste of time. I've spent all morning grilling her and so far, her lips are sealed.' Imogen put on a whiny voice and said, 'Come on, give us something. Anything. I'm a married woman now; I need to live vicariously through you two.'

Lucy shook her head but figured they wouldn't give up on her until she gave them something. 'All right. I'll give you something, but you have to promise not to tell anyone else, well, apart from Jess. We'll have to update her at book club.'

In unison, they said, 'Deal.'

Lucy leaned in, the others copying her movements until they huddled around the table. 'Tom.' She paused dramatically, 'is a pleasure Dom.'

Sarah's eyes went wide. 'He's a Dom? That's pretty hardcore. Are you sure you're ready for something like that?'

'Yeah, Lucy, that's quite a lot to get to grips with. He must be a great one, based on what Roxy says about him.'

Lucy shook her head. 'No, you've got it all wrong. He doesn't whip me. Well, not in the way you think. He's all about pleasure, not pain.'

Sarah said, 'Yeah, but he's still a Dom. Which means he wants to dominate you. Are you sure you're ready for that?'

Lucy shook her head. 'Ladies, Tom is not the sort of Dom you're thinking of. It's a term used for someone that wants to give me intense pleasure. More pleasure than you can imagine. He takes control, so I don't have to think about it. There's no pressure on me to perform, and that's exactly what I need right now. Trust me. This is the best thing that could happen to me.' Imogen went to speak but Lucy cut her off. 'And yes, I am ready for this. I'm not the weak, naïve girl I was a few months ago. I'm a woman who's been through a lot. A hell of a lot more than most, and I've come out the other side stronger. So, to answer your question, yes, I am ready for this. I couldn't be more ready. In one night with Tom, he broke down my barriers, took me out of my mind and erased the stain on my soul left behind by the shitty men of my past.' She sat back and took a sip of her coffee while the others blinked, open-mouthed at her.

Imogen was the first to break the silence. 'I'm sorry, Lucy. I know you're a strong woman. Don't forget, I know exactly what you went through. What I'd forgotten is that I got through it because I found Cameron and you guys. I didn't mean to shame you for yours, or Tom's, sexual preferences.'

Sarah nodded. 'I second what she said. Also, I'm going to need some more information on the specifics of being pleasure dom'd. Exactly how many orgasms are we talking about here?' Laughing at Sarah broke the tension.

'A lot.' Lucy decided they weren't ready to hear about how much she enjoyed watching other people. That would blow their minds. She smiled to herself; she quite enjoyed having a secret sexy side.

'Hello, gorgeous. How is your week going? Has Sarah spoken much about what happened with Ivan?' Lucy was in bed having her regular phone call with Tom. He phoned every night to check in with her.

'No. She's not brought it up. It's like it never happened. We've not really spoken in private either, so that might be why. Has anything else happened with Ivan?'

'No. He's not been back to the club, but I fully expect him to turn up on Friday. I think it might be best if you stayed at home this week. I'll see you on Saturday when we meet up with everyone.' Lucy's heart sank at the prospect of not going to London on Friday. 'I want you to come here. You know that, don't you?'

She mentally batted away the niggling doubt that tried to work its way into her mind. Previously, she might have thought he said that because he didn't want to see her, but she understood he couldn't watch Ivan while she was there.

'I understand. And as you said, we'll see each other at Jen and Cam's for lunch.' The Blacks had invited everyone over for lunch for a post-honeymoon catch-up.

'I'll come and pick you up as early as I can; I don't want to miss out on your morning shower.' His husky voice made her hairs stand on end and her core clench with desire.

She panted as she said, 'God, I wish you were here now. I could do with some of your skills. My body knows what it's capable of, and it wants more.'

'I wish I was with you. If I was there, I'd bite down on one nipple while pinching the other with my fingers. Can you imagine that? Can you imagine how the blood would rush to your nipples in response? They'd become hard, needy bullets, desperate for more. You'd want me to stop as the pain would be almost unbearable, but as soon as I pull away, they'd be begging for more.'

'Tom.' She couldn't say much more than that, her breaths coming short and sharp.

'I want you to do something for me.'

'You're not going to turn me on all week and make me wait to come, are you?'

'No. I want you to focus on your breasts for the rest of the week.'

'What do you mean?' She furrowed her brow as she pressed the phone to her ear.

'I want you to stroke your breasts. Massage them every night and play with them. You can start tonight. Are you wearing a top?'

'Yes.'

'Take it off. No more clothes in bed.'

She put the phone on speaker and rested it on the pillow next to her, took her pyjamas off and dropped them to the floor.

'Okay, I'm naked.'

'Oh, Lucy. This is going to be just as hard for me as it is for you.' His husky voice was enough to turn her on. 'I want you to run your fingertips over your chest, collarbone, and stomach. Only your fingertips.'

Eyes closed, she did as instructed. Goosebumps broke out across her skin.

'Use your words. Are you doing as you're told?'

'Yes. It feels good.'

'Good girl. I want you to carry on doing this whenever you can until I instruct you otherwise. Do you understand? You're not to touch your clit, just gently massage around your breasts, working your way towards your nipple. You're going to want to touch your nipples, but you're not allowed to. To be clear, you're allowed to orgasm, but you mustn't touch anything other than your breasts.'

'I don't understand. Surely you can't come from playing with your boobs?'

'Don't question me, sweetheart. I've only just begun to teach you what you're capable of. That's all you're getting from me tonight. I'll reward you when I see you.'

'But that's ages away.'

'It's three days. Now, do as I say, no cheating. Understand?'

'Yes, Sir.'

'Good. Trust me; it'll be worth it. I'll see you in a few days. Also, let Sarah know we'll pick her up on the way to Cam's. I owe her an explanation, and I'd rather do it in the privacy of my car.'

'Two seats, remember?'

'I'll hire a car. Now get back to giving your breasts the attention they deserve.'

Throughout the rest of the week, Tom would call in the evening with further instructions. She was now at the stage of rolling her nipples between her forefinger and thumb with massage oil. Her nipples were permanent bullets, crying out for attention. With every touch, they sent shock waves straight to her core. By Friday, she was a frustrated, strung-out mess. Tom was right; she was on the cusp of pain but felt so much pleasure.

Lucy was under strict instructions to wait for Tom before having her morning shower, so when the doorbell rang, she ran for it dressed in nothing but a towelling robe; the fibres of which rubbed across her chest and drove her crazy.

As soon as she opened the door, hands were cupping her face as Tom pressed his lips to hers.

'I've missed you so much.' Tom shut the door and didn't waste a second opening her robe. 'Please tell me you've not showered yet.'

'I've not.' He swooped Lucy up into his arms and carried her through to her bathroom. He made quick work of turning on the shower, stripping and de-robing her.

Warm water cascaded over them as he pressed kisses all over her body. The sensation of his lips on her sensitised skin tore moans from her lungs.

'Close your eyes and take deep, slow breaths.' She did as instructed while he dripped body wash over her chest. Her breath hitched as the cool tiles pressed onto her back, out of the stream of warm water. The loss of warmth caused her nipples to tighten painfully.

Warm hands gently massaged the neroli-scented cream into her torso in circular motions. Her chest had never been so thoroughly worshipped, and she understood why he'd worked her up all week. As soon as he brought his fingers to her nipples and pinched, she arched her back and groaned with pleasure.

'Does that feel good, baby?'

'It feels so good. I want more. Please, more.'

Tom drew her nipple into his mouth, grasping it in his teeth and gently biting down while he continued to roll the other one between his finger and thumb. She forced air into her lungs through clenched teeth at the onslaught of sensations crashing through her.

'I can't take anymore, Tom, please.' She was begging, begging for any kind of release she could get.

'Not much longer now, baby.' He reached for the shower head and angled it towards one breast while he sucked and plucked on the other. The flowing water followed the contours of her body and trickled down her opening.

The tension from the week shattered, splintering across her chest as her orgasm rocked her whole body. She gripped onto his head, desperate for something solid to hold her up.

Wrapping his hands around her hips, he said, 'There you go, baby. You did so well.'

'I've never felt like that before. I didn't know that was possible.'

'Your body is beautiful and so receptive to whatever I tell it to do. I'm going to show you so much, but for now, we need to get ready.'

'I don't really want to leave the house. Can't we just stay here?'

He peppered kisses along her collarbone. 'Nope. We need to go, but just because we're out doesn't mean the fun stops.'

'Oh?'

'You'll be saying that later, but probably followed by god.'

'Is that a promise?'

'Always.'

Dressed and ready to go, they made their way to Tom's car.

Lucy's brow creased as she looked down the street. 'Where's your car?'

Tom grinned as he pressed a button on his key fob.

'Oh my god, what the fuck is that?' Lucy gasped.

She stood gawking at the sexiest SUV she'd ever seen. The winter sunshine gleaming off the rich black paintwork.

'That is the new Aston Martin DBX. Does it get your approval?'

'Tom, when you said you were going to hire a car, I expected to see a Ford Focus, not this.'

'No offence, but I'm more Tom Ford than Ford Focus. I spoke to my dealer and arranged a test drive for the weekend. If we like it, I may well keep it.'

'We?'

He stepped closer and wrapped his arms around her waist, dipping to be at eye level with her as he said, 'Yes, we. I have every intention of testing this car in every way possible, and you are very much a part of that. How convenient that it comes with privacy glass and acoustic isolation.'

'What's acoustic isolation?' Her big brown eyes were wide and drawing him to her.

He grazed his lips along her jawline. 'People won't be able to hear your moans of pleasure while you ride me.'

He loved to see her blush. It sent a rush of blood to his cock and a desire to make her skin flush all over. She formed an 'O' with her mouth as realisation set in. He brought his smiling lips down to meet hers, sucking on her bottom lip while squeezing her rear.

CHAPTER 36

TOM

Ghost Town – Benson Boone

'So, Tom, are you going to explain what the fuck Saturday night was all about? All Lucy would tell me is that I needed to help her with some douchebags and extracting some info out of them.'

They'd picked Sarah up on the way to their lunch date, and she got straight to the point as she got in the car. He made eye contact with her in the rear-view mirror, weighing up how much he should say. He only wanted to tell her as much as she needed to know, more for her safety than anything else.

'Yeah, sorry I didn't have time to talk to you before you left. Katia runs the club K's—'

'Which you guys are taking me to, soon, I hope.' Sarah had popped her head through the front seats and looked at them both expectantly.

Tom looked round to face her as he said, 'Oh, really? You fancy a bit of kink, do you?'

'Yeah, I do; Lucy's going to take me.'

He looked over at Lucy, raising his eyebrows. 'Were you planning on taking me with you?'

Lucy chewed on her bottom lip. 'I hadn't thought that far ahead, but I guess so. It would be weird going there without you, wouldn't it?'

'Yes, it would, but if you want to go without me, I won't stop you as long as you remember our agreed hard limits. You'd see a different side to me if they weren't observed.'

Sarah's head appeared between the seats again. 'I don't know about you two, but hearing you say the words hard limit turns me on, so get back to the explanation before I demand some avocado.'

Tom knitted his eyebrows together. 'What?'

'Avocado. Lucy's code for your cock,' said Sarah matter-of-factly.

Lucy looked shocked as she rushed to say, 'No, it's not. I was actually talking about a real avocado.'

Sarah mumbled, 'Whatever,' from the backseat.

Tom looked confused but carried on the conversation. 'Anyway, as I was saying, Katia is the closest thing I have to a sister. Her dad is a high-level criminal and must keep the fact that she's his, a secret. If anyone finds out he has a daughter, they could both end up at the bottom of the Thames with concrete shoes. That won't happen on my watch.'

'Your watch? What does that mean?'

'Her dad asked me to be his eyes and ears and keep her safe. The dickhead—who was sucking your face off—works for him and wants to take his place. He knows about Kat, and he needs to be stopped before he uses the info to take over. We thought we had more time to get something on him—let him hang himself—but he's too close to Kat now. We need to stop him sooner rather than later.'

'Fuck. This is some messed up shit.' She paused, looking deep in thought. 'I'm going to make a deal with you.'

Anxiety crept over Tom, his heart beating a little quicker, wondering if he'd said too much. He didn't know Sarah that well; had he incorrectly assumed he could trust her because of her relationship with Lucy? 'What kind of deal?'

'You keep my involvement in this a secret, and I'll keep yours. I'll do what I can to help you out. Ivan took a liking to me and wants me to go to the club. We can use that to our advantage.'

Tom's jaw clenched; he wasn't comfortable bringing anyone else into this. 'It's not my place to get involved in your relationship with James, whatever that might be, regardless of your involvement with this shit show. I'm grateful to you for your help that night, but I can't let you—either of you—stay involved in this. After seeing how he behaved with you, I can't risk him hurting you.'

'Just so that I know, exactly how grateful are you? Avocado grateful?' She said, whilst wiggling her eyebrows suggestively.

'I'm not giving you my avocado, Sarah. Lucy's the only one to get that from now on.' Then he muttered, 'Isn't there a bigger fruit or veg you could compare it to? Like a cucumber, maybe?'

'Don't worry, Tom, I don't want your cucumber, but I will help you out. If I've learned one thing from Lucy, it's that you help your friends out, no matter what the cost.'

Lucy twisted in her seat and reached her hand to Sarah's. 'You're the best, Sarah. I will reward you with many nights at K's. I promise.'

'Did either of you hear what I just said?' Tom almost roared, 'Neither of you is going to be dragged any further into this.'

'Yeah, whatever. You know Lucy is a kick-ass wonder woman, and I've never done as I'm told. Ever?'

'I'm serious. I can't protect all three of you. End of story.' His clipped tone made it clear he wasn't discussing it any further. Sarah settled back in her seat; the car grew silent.

Tom's hand settled on Lucy's thigh for the rest of the journey to Jen and Cam's house.

As they pulled onto the drive, the Godfather theme tune rang out in the car.

'I need to get this, ladies. Would you mind heading in and I'll follow?'

Lucy gave him a look that said she understood, and they got out of the car. Tom hit the answer button as soon as they were out of earshot.

'Gedeon, we need to step it up.'

'Have you forgotten your manners, Tom? No hello, or how are you?'

'Ivan was in the club on Saturday and took a liking to a friend; he's getting too close for comfort, and I have others to think about now. If it wasn't for Andre creating a distraction, he would've gone to K's that night. He plans to go soon, and fuck knows what he plans to do when he gets there.'

There was silence.

'Did you hear what I said? He knows it's Katia, and he has a way in.'

'You said Andre created a distraction?'

'Yes. Turns out he's on your side. He hates Ivan. He wants out and will go against him if you can guarantee he can walk away a free man.'

'That is a shame. He sounds like he'd make a suitable replacement for when I slit the throat of that cocksucker.'

'He's fallen in love.'

'Ah. Then he is a very brave man indeed.'

339

More silence.

Gedeon said, 'When this is resolved, he can go. He has my word.'

'How do we resolve this? I need this to end. He's taken a liking to a friend, and I can't allow that.'

'That may work to our advantage. She could lure him in, distract him.'

'No. Where she goes, my girlfriend goes, and I can't risk her getting hurt.'

'You swore to protect Katia, and that is what you will do. She is your priority, not your latest fuck.'

'Don't you dare talk about her like that.' Tom bellowed as anger borne by frustration exploded out of him.

'Don't forget whom you are talking to. You have benefitted greatly from our agreement, and I can end it as quickly as I started it. You are protected because I declare it. If anything happens to Katia, it will be you, and those you hold dear, that will pay the price.'

He slammed his hand on the steering wheel. He knew Gedeon well enough not to argue with him. It wouldn't get him anywhere.

'Stop pouting, Thomas. If you can come up with a way to resolve this without your girly friends, by all means, do it. If not, we do it my way.'

The call ended, plunging the car into silence.

'FUCK.' He roared as his hand slammed back down on the steering wheel. He ran his fingers through his hair. He needed to get his shit together. This situation had become impossible; how could he protect Lucy and Katia at the same time? He rested his forehead on the steering wheel, gripping it tightly with both hands as he calmed himself down.

Cameron greeted him as he walked through the open front door, clapping him on the shoulder.

'Hey, Tom. How're you doing?' The other guys came over to greet him.

'Cam, lads, nice to see you all.' Julian and James shook his hand.

'You look knackered. Hard night, or do I not want to know?'

'Cheers James, good to know I can always count on you to say it like it is. I've got a lot on, that's all.'

Cameron looked concerned as he said, 'Is it anything we can help with?'

'No, but thanks for the offer.'

They strolled through into the kitchen where the women were all chatting, Imogen handing out mimosas. Cameron kissed Imogen on the cheek before saying, 'Ladies, we're going to head up to the bar; leave you to have some girly talk time.' He turned his attention back to Imogen. 'I'll be down when the meat's ready to come out. The fires on in the lounge if you want to go through.'

'Thank you. You always look after us.'

James made a puking noise. 'All right, can we go to the bar now?'

Julian laughed as he said, 'Do you have a romantic bone in your body?'

'Nope. There's only one bone in my body worthy of note.'

Sarah piped up from across the kitchen. 'James, we do not want to talk about your cock. Piss off up to the bar and leave us alone.'

Holding his hand up to his head in a mock salute he, and the others, walked out of the kitchen and took the stairs up to Cameron's bar and game room.

Setting up the balls for a game of pool, James turned his attention to Julian. 'How's it going with Jess? Have you done the deed yet?'

Julian took a swig of his beer before saying, 'No, I haven't. I happen to be a gentleman.' He flicked the can's ring pull.

'While that is true, I suspect it has more to do with her parents being total cock blockers.' James said with a smirk.

'What have her parents got to do with this?' Tom barely knew Jess and had no idea what her story was.

They didn't give James a chance to respond as Julian cut them off. 'Can we please forget about it? It's no one else's business. I want to know how it's going with Lucy and why the fuck you have turned up in a family wagon.'

Tom looked out of the window overlooking the drive. 'I'd hardly call that a family wagon. I needed something with more than two seats; having a girlfriend means that I now transport her and her friends around, that's all.'

Cameron laughed as he said, 'I think you'll find that you're under the thumb, mate. She's already getting you to change your ways. Not that there's anything wrong with a sensible car. Plenty of space in the back has its upsides.'

'All right, before you compare car sex stories, let's get on with the game.' Julian stood chalking the tip of his cue.

'Says the man not getting any.' That earned James and punch on the arm.

They played pool until Cameron declared it time for lunch, but Tom's mind was elsewhere, replaying Gedeon's words in his head. A feeling of dread taking hold in his heart.

CHAPTER 37

LUCY

I'm Ready – Sam Smith & Demi Lovato

Lucy noticed Tom was quiet through lunch. Everyone was in high spirits discussing plans for Christmas, but when no one was talking to him directly, he looked deep in thought.

She leant into him and said, 'Is everything okay?' Her hand squeezed his thigh under the table.

'Yeah, I'm good. I just have a few things on my mind, you know?'

'I know. Please don't leave me out of this. We're a team, and I can help you. Don't shut me out, Tom.'

'Can we talk about this later?'

'You'd best make sure we do. Don't underestimate me, Tom. I'm involved in this now, whether you like it or not.'

He brushed his hand up her thigh, fire burning in his eyes as he looked at her, turning his back on Cameron, who was sitting next to him. He brought his lips to her ear and whispered, 'I'm desperate to sink into you. I can't stop thinking about it. We should have stayed at yours.'

He trailed his fingers up further, grazing her centre along the seam of her jeans. 'And I'd stop giggling if I were you, or I'll spend the rest of the afternoon torturing you.'

She closed her eyes, imagining how good that would feel. 'I think I'd like that.'

His lips brushed her ear. 'Be careful what you wish for, beautiful.' She bucked her hips forward to increase the pressure from his fingers.

He pulled his hand away. 'Careful. Your face is screaming sex right now.'

She lifted her glass to her lips, hoping the chilled white wine would cool her, but she knew the alcohol would only make her desire deepen. Tom carried on eating with his thigh pressed into hers for the rest of the meal.

As they finished their meal, James said, 'Why don't you two leave your cars here, stay over and drink? You're both being boring sods.' James was waving his pint under Julian's nose.

'I'd love to, but I have to work later, unfortunately.' Julian turned to Cameron as he said, 'Some of us have to keep the restaurant running, eh Cam?'

'I'm the silent partner, remember? Just hire someone in so you can take more time off. Stop being a control freak.'

'Yeah, I know. I'll think about it; I'm tiring of the unsociable hours.' His eyes met Jess's briefly.

'Can you stay, Tom? We could get a taxi back to mine?' Lucy gave him the full force of her puppy-dog eyes.

Tom squeezed her thigh. 'I wish I could, but I need to get back to the club tonight. There's too much going on there for Alex to handle on his own.'

Trying to talk in code, she said, 'Ah, okay. Your new partygoers are being a handful again?'

'You could say that.'

344

Imogen laughed and said, 'At least you know they're not trying to hurt Lucy and kidnap anyone. They were some crazy times, eh?'

'Don't worry, Jen. I don't think there are any more crazy people after us, are there folks?' Jess asked the rest of them sat around the table. Both Sarah and Lucy gave Tom a sideways glance, but his face remained passive.

'Nope, we're all good. You can relax, and even if there were any more weirdos coming for us, you can guarantee these chaps would go to great lengths to keep us safe.' Even though Sarah was talking to Jess, her eyes didn't leave Tom's.

Lucy felt his thigh tense under her hand. She whispered in his ear, 'I could do with some fresh air. This wine has gone to my head.'

Tom was quick to stand. 'I'll come with you.'

It was late afternoon, and the sun had sunk below the horizon, taking with it any residual warmth. They walked out onto the patio and headed for the wooden gazebo towards the back of the garden.

'Are you okay? And don't lie to me about being fine. You've been quiet all afternoon and I can see worry lines etched on your forehead.'

Tom sat down on the wooden bench, rested his elbows on the table, and put his head in his hands. 'I don't want to bring you into this. You're already in too deep and I can't stand the thought of Ivan getting close to you or Sarah.'

'We can handle him.'

He brought his hands down on the table with a bang, making Lucy jump. 'You can't handle him. He's a hell of a lot more dangerous than Mark. This guy is evil, he's hungry for power and he won't stop until he's taken Gedeon down—and everyone who gets in his way. I can't have you coming to London while this is going on.'

'Why does everyone underestimate me?' Lucy paced as she spoke, blowing warm air into her cupped hands. 'I'm not some dumb little girl. The last person who underestimated me ended up with a blade in his back and is now six feet under. I've been to Hell, and I came back stronger and unwilling to put up with any more shit. So, tell me, Tom, why can't I handle Ivan?'

He stood, taking her by the shoulders, and looked directly into her eyes. His breath rose in plumes around them as his chest heaved. 'I have no doubt that you can handle anything or anyone, but I can't handle the thought of putting you in harm's way. What kind of man would it make me if I willingly put you in danger?' He released her and ran his hands through his hair. 'I have an impossible task on my shoulders. Don't you understand that?'

She didn't respond straight away. Was there any point in her arguing with him over this?

'Fine. I'll do as you ask, but promise to keep me informed about what's going on. If anything happens to you, Ivan had better run.'

'You're very sexy when you're acting like a warrior princess.'

'Am I now?'

He nodded as he pulled her into his embrace. 'I just need some time where I can focus on the job at hand.'

'How long will that be?'

'I can't answer that for sure, but I don't think it'll be long. We can get through this.'

She wasn't so sure. Any time away from him was painful; her body cried out for his touch. 'You'd better make up for it later.'

'I'd quite like to make a start now.'

'It is way too cold out here for any funny business. Come on, we'd better get back inside before they send out a search party.'

'So let them watch. I'm not letting you go inside until I've removed the worry lines etched across your forehead.' He stroked his fingertips across her forehead before cupping her face and pressing a kiss to her lips. He turned his back to the house and walked her backwards, pressing her against the rough wooden wall of the gazebo.

'I want to take my time with you. I want to make you come so many times that your legs give out. But for now, I'll have to compromise and settle for one. Maybe two.'

'Oh god, Tom.'

'I said you'd be saying "oh god" today. I haven't even started yet.' As he spoke, one hand gripped on the back of her head while his free hand trailed down to the waistband of her jeans. 'Skinny jeans are a fucking nuisance. They give me no room to manoeuvre.' He popped open the button and dragged the zip down. 'Put your hands on my back, under my jacket. You're not allowed to move, do you understand?'

She slid her hands up his back, his body heat keeping her warm. 'Yes. I won't move.'

Without warning, his hand slid straight into the waistband of her underwear, his middle finger sliding into her already slick folds. The pressure of his palm causing a delicious friction on her clit.

'Fuck. You feel so good. I don't think this will take long.' He worked his finger slowly at first, before sliding in another. As he kissed her, his tongue mirrored the movements of his fingers as he swallowed her moans.

He withdrew his fingers and flicked them across her clit.

'Ah, please. Please.' She clawed at his back, desperate to rock her hips into his. Desperate to feel him fill her.

He took her mouth in a bruising kiss as he sank his fingers in so deep she was sure she'd lifted off the ground. His palm ground into her clit as his fingers stroked against her G-spot. She clenched onto his fingers, gripping on for dear life as the orgasm ripped through her. As the waves of pleasure ebbed away, she clung on to him. His soft kisses leaving her weak at the knees.

Tom pulled away just enough to remove his hand from her jeans. 'You can move your hands now.' As she zipped up her jeans, he brought his fingers up to his lips and sucked her arousal clean. 'You taste so good,' he said, his voice husky and his eyes hooded.

'Christ, Tom. That's so hot.' He returned her comment with a smirk and a glint in his eyes.

'Oi, there you are.' Sarah interrupted the moment, shouting from the back door. 'Julian's heading off. Do you want to come and say goodbye or are you too busy fucking about?'

Lucy shook her head and muttered, 'That woman has got a great sense of timing.'

'She's a pain in the arse.'

'But we love her.'

'Jury's out. Come on, let's head back in, make our excuses and get back to yours.'

As they pulled up outside her house, Lucy noticed a car pulling away that she didn't recognise. 'Oh, I wonder if my neighbour has a new boyfriend. I don't recognise him. Anyway, have you got time to come in?'

Tom watched the car drive away. 'Sorry, gorgeous. What did you say?'

'I asked if you were coming in. Are you okay? You look like you've seen a ghost.'

Tom shook his head, 'No, no. I'm fine, but I need to get back. Let me see you in, though.'

He didn't sound fine, but she figured he had a lot on his mind.

He walked her to the front door and waited while she unlocked it. She noticed he kept glancing around.

'I'll come in and use your toilet, if that's okay?'

'Of course it's okay.' She shook her head, thinking how strangely he was acting, as she dropped her bag in the hall and walked through to her lounge while Tom headed to the bathroom.

She could hear him wandering around and walked out into the hallway to see what he was doing. 'Tom, is everything okay?'

'Yeah, I just wanted to check the house was secure before I head off. I've gone a bit Cameron, I think.'

'By that, do you mean you've become the protective alpha male?'

'Exactly that.' He checked his watch, let out a sigh and said, 'I need to get going. I'll call you later.'

She walked him to the door; they shared a kiss, and he was gone; a feeling of dread left heavy in the air.

CHAPTER 38

TOM

Way down we go - KALEO

'Alex, can you check the membership database for anyone with a parking permit registered to this number plate?' Tom called Alex as soon as he was in the car and heading back to London. The car driving away from Lucy's house was worryingly familiar. He recited the registration plate to Alex.

'I'm doing it now. Do you want to tell me what's going on?'

'There was a black Mercedes pulling away from Lucy's house when I dropped her off. I couldn't get a good look at the driver, but he looked like one of Ivan's men.'

Alex's voice was low and calm as he said, 'You don't know that for sure. Stay calm. It could've been anyone; it's not like that's a rare car.'

He let out an exasperated sigh. 'I'm trying to stay fucking calm, but it's not very easy when the Russian-fucking-mafia are following you and could be after your girlfriend. Has the reg come up yet?'

'Shit.'

That one-word response told him everything he needed to know. 'Fuck. They must have followed me. This needs to end, and it needs to end now.' He slammed his palm against his steering wheel. 'I'll be back as soon as I can.' Tom gunned the engine, desperate to get back. He didn't know how to resolve this, but he knew he needed to come up with something, and he knew who he needed to call in. He selected Gedeon's name from the car's display screen and impatiently listened to the dialling tone.

'Come on. Answer the fucking phone.' He tapped on the steering wheel, anxiety stepping up a gear as he dropped a gear to overtake the cars in his way. 'Answer the phone, Gedeon.' The ringing stopped as the call cut off. He smacked the steering wheel again, pain radiating out across his hand. He tried calling again. It rang off again.

He tried again and again on the drive back, but Gedeon wasn't answering. The drive through London took too long, traffic getting in his way at every turn. By the time his tyres screeched into his underground parking, he was frantic. Alex came to meet him as soon as he opened his car door.

'Tom, you need to calm down.' Alex rested his hand on Tom's shoulder to stop him from pacing. 'What did Gedeon say?'

'That's the fucking problem.' He ran his hands through his messed-up hair. 'I can't get hold of him.'

'Maybe he's busy. He's the head of a massive criminal organisation. Sometimes he might be too busy to answer the phone.'

'He always answers my calls. I've been calling him non-stop. He'd know it was an emergency. Something's wrong.' Without thinking, he slammed his fist into the passenger window of the car. 'Fuck. Toughenedfucking-glass.' His frustration echoed across the carpark as he shook his hand, trying to wring out the pain.

Alex grabbed him by the shoulders. 'You need to calm down. Breaking your hand won't help. Take some deep breaths. You need to keep your head.'

He shrugged out of Alex's hold, breathing deeper and calming down. 'You're right. I need to get my shit together. I don't know what to do.' He looked at Alex with desperation in his eyes. 'They know about Lucy. They'll use her against me. If I can't get Gedeon to put this dog down, I'm going to have to get Lucy out of the picture.'

'Hey, it might not come to that. You need to get ready to go to the club and wait for Ivan to show his cards. Keep your cool. You don't want to start something you're not equipped to finish.'

His friend was right. There was nothing he could do now apart from waiting for word from Gedeon.

'I need to call Katia and fill her in. She needs to know that this is getting dangerous.' He dialled her number as he stalked up to his apartment to get ready. The problem was, he didn't know what he was getting ready for.

Tom heard his name being called on the radio attached to his belt. He grabbed it and said, 'Go ahead.'

'He's here.' That's all Alex needed to say. They knew Ivan would show his face tonight. It was only a matter of time. Tom straightened out his hair and tucked the collar of his crisp white shirt into his signature deep blue suit. His appearance didn't reflect the chaos playing out in his mind. To anyone looking at him, he looked every bit the rich London socialite.

He met eyes with Alex as he walked into the casino. A small nod thanked him for the heads up. It didn't take long to find Ivan and his crew. They were loud and brash, no doubt drunk already.

Ivan's accent, thick and loud, called out across the room. 'Thomas, my man. Come here and join in the celebrations.'

His heart rate increased as he made his way over. He rubbed his hands together as moisture collected in the folds of his palms. What could Ivan possibly be celebrating tonight?

'Ivan, what a pleasure to see you tonight.' He smiled through gritted teeth as he shook his hand, the smile anything but friendly.

Ivan handed Tom a glass of champagne. 'Here, take this and raise a glass with us.'

'Oh? What are we celebrating?'

'This evening, Thomas, we are celebrating the fall of the mighty. And oh, how they fell.' Ivan's eyes bored into Tom's, full of threat and malice, a sneer fixed across his face.

Tom knew he couldn't make a scene here. His club was full of customers, and he couldn't risk them getting hurt. 'Perhaps you'd like to take this celebration upstairs, to my office?' If he could get them upstairs and out of the way, he could at least do some damage control.

'I don't think so. I like it right here.' Ivan looked around at the casino. 'To be surrounded by all these happy gamblers.' Ivan knew exactly what he was doing. He put an arm around Tom's shoulder and pulled him in. Tom could feel his breath against his face and smell the liquor on his breath. His stomach roiled.

Ivan reached into his jacket pocket and pulled out a phone. As the display lit up, Tom could see the many missed calls from his number. Ivan brought his mouth to Tom's ear and said, 'You can stop calling Gedeon now. They don't have phones in hell.'

Ivan's grip on his shoulder became painful as he continued to say, 'You're no longer safe, Thomas. You're fair game, and anyone you hold dear is now mine to play with. Do you understand what I'm saying?'

Tom couldn't speak. The pounding of his heart drowned out the noise of the casino around him as the room spun.

'Times have changed, and I have a new deal for you. From now on, I'll do as I please when I come here, at your expense. This casino will become my personal laundrette for all my dealings. I will bring my girls into your club to earn a pretty penny from your wealthy, morally weak, prick men that come here. Deal?'

Tom swallowed the rage threatening to explode out of him. 'How is that a deal for me?'

'Ah, well. If you do what you're told like a good little lapdog, I won't get angry. Do you know what happens when I get angry?'

'I can imagine,' Tom growled.

'I'm sure you can. I like to take my frustration out on women. You see, I get a kick out of pain. If you were to have a certain special someone in your life, then I might be tempted to teach you a lesson by using them. I know you're a clever man, so I hope you understand what I'm saying.'

Tom didn't answer. He didn't want to face the reality of what Ivan was hinting at.

'But just in case you aren't catching my drift, you'd do well to make sure there is no one in your life that I can use at my pleasure. Just like you dedicated your life to Gedeon, you'll do the same for me.'

Tom gulped down the bile rising in his throat.

'Oh, and one more thing. I want you back at K's. I plan to take ownership of it, and I hear you were a popular attraction.'

'Fuck off. You don't get to pimp me out.'

Ivan pulled Tom in closer, smiling at the people milling around them as he said, 'If you don't do as you're told, Katia will die.'

'You can't get away with this.' As the words left his mouth, he knew they were pointless. Ivan had backed him into a corner with only one way out that he could see.

'The beauty of this is that I already have. I executed Gedeon today. It's his own fault. He broke the fundamental rule of the Vory and had a family of his own. That shows weakness, and I do not accept weakness. I will pin his murder on a rival gang.'

'Why don't you want to take the credit for it, Ivan? Scared of the repercussions of executing a Vory leader without a trial?'

'Ah, you ask a good question. I do not want word of Katia getting out. If the others find out, they will want to put an end to her. I would rather keep her as my pet, but also, I'd like to keep her as a bargaining tool. The others are not as business savvy as I am. They don't see the benefit of having you on your knees. This club,' he gestures at the surrounding walls, 'will be very lucrative for me. It will enable a lot of new business, but you would never willingly let me use it. It's a win-win situation for me. Now, I suggest you run along. You have a club to sort out, and affairs to deal with.' Ivan took hold of Tom's hand, shaking it with an unnecessarily firm grip before releasing him. Ivan took a step back as two of his henchmen took his place. The conversation was over.

In a dream-like state, Tom walked away. The room felt like it was getting smaller, closing in on him. He had to get out and speak to Alex.

His clenched fists remained at his side as he fought not to lose it on Ivan's face. He nodded over to Alex, signalling for him to follow.

He headed straight to the drinks cabinet as soon as he made it to his office. Pulling the crystal stopper out of the decanter, he poured two glasses of whiskey, setting them down on his desk. He didn't bother putting the stopper back; he was seeing the bottom of the bottle tonight.

Alex rushed in and closed the door. 'What the fuck is going on?'

Tom downed his glass, the amber liquid burning his throat, but he couldn't feel anything. He poured another as Alex sat down. 'You're going to want to drink that first.'

He repeated everything Ivan had said to him.

'Shit. Gedeon is dead.' Alex rubbed at his face, haunted eyes looking at Tom. 'We're fucked.'

'No, mate. I'm fucked, and everyone I love is now fair game to Ivan and his crew.' Before he knew what he was doing, his glass was flying out of his hand. He couldn't tell if it was the glass that had shattered into a thousand pieces, or his heart.

CHAPTER 39

LUCY

Go (feat. Sam Smith) – Cat Burns

'Hey. I'm glad you called. I got worried when I didn't hear from you last night. Is everything okay?' Lucy was sitting in her living room, snuggled on the sofa, reading the latest book club novel. Tom hadn't called her last night, and after the way he'd left it, she was worried he'd decided it would be easier to end their relationship.

'Yeah, sorry about that. Ivan was in the club and things took a turn for the worse. I ended up drinking myself unconscious on expensive whiskey and Alex had to put me to bed.'

That wasn't what she was expecting to hear. She straightened in her seat. 'Shit. Are you serious? What happened?'

She heard him exhale heavily down the phone. His next words chilled her to her spine. 'There's no easy way to say this.'

'Just say it.' Her voice cracked, her heart raced, and a hot flush of unease swept over her.

'I can't see you anymore, Lucy. I'm sorry. I don't know why I thought it would be a good idea to bring you into this, but I can't justify it anymore.'

'What do you mean, you can't justify it?' Her voice was icy, devoid of the emotions she felt.

'I can't tell you. It's safer that you don't know. I need you to trust me, Lucy. Do you trust me?' His usually warm voice was hollow.

She picked at her nails, trying to distract herself from the urge to beg and plead for him to stay with her. She decided she wouldn't give him the satisfaction. 'I did.'

'Please.' His voice was pleading and pained. Whatever was going on, it was serious, and she didn't appreciate being left in the dark, not trusted with the information.

'Tell me what's going on, Tom.'

'You need to stay away from London for a while.' He paused, taking in a deep breath. His next words came out quietly. 'I need you to stay away from me.'

'No. I told you I was in this with you, and I meant it.'

'I know, but you don't know what you'd be getting yourself into. This isn't a joke.' His voice lowered as he said, 'I'm no longer protected.'

She gasped. 'Oh my god. Is Gedeon gone?'

'Yes. So please understand that when I say you need to stay away from me, I mean it. It's over between us, Lucy.'

'I'm not accepting that.'

'I wish it was different, Lucy, I really do, but you don't have a choice. I need you to do something for me.'

Typical. This was so typical of the men in her life. Her pain and anguish made way to anger. The men in her life always wanted her to do something for them after they'd broken her heart.

'Tough shit. I'm not doing anything for anyone.'

'You can be pissed off with me all you like. I deserve it, and I don't know, maybe it will help you get over me. Right now, I need you to put that aside and listen to what I say.'

She refused to answer.

'Lucy, I need you to go somewhere else for a while. Just until after Christmas. I don't think you're safe. Can you stay with Imogen or something?'

'You dump me, tell me I'm in danger and then want me to stay with the newlyweds? How'd you think that'll make me feel?'

'Give me a fucking break, Lucy. I'm doing what's right.' She heard him take some deep breaths to calm down before he spoke again. 'Can you stay with your parents?'

'Fine. I'll tell them I want to come home for Christmas.'

'Thank you,' he whispered, full of sorrow.

'For what?'

He sighed. 'For everything. Goodbye, Lucy. I know this won't help, but this is the hardest thing I've ever had to do.'

'You're right. It doesn't help.' She pressed the end call button and threw the phone into the armchair.

She wanted the tears to come. The sweet, albeit temporary, release that would come from having a good cry. But her tears were dry. She'd cried too much over the men in her life already. The sound of her doorbell ringing interrupted her pity party.

She tentatively tiptoed to the front door. Tom's words of warning replaying in her mind. *She wasn't safe.* Surely the mafia doesn't ring the doorbell, though? She pressed her eye to the peephole and saw a worried Imogen staring back at her.

She straightened herself out and threw the door open. A fake smile plastered on her face. 'Hey, Jen. To what do I owe the pleasure?'

Imogen immediately wrapped her arms around her. 'Are you okay, Hun?'

Confused, she said, 'Yeah, of course I'm fine. What do you mean?'

'Tom called Cameron and asked that I come over to check on you. He wouldn't say why, though. What's happened?'

Confused, Lucy said, 'But I've only just got off the phone with Tom. How come you were here so quickly?'

'Tom phoned Cam earlier. He wouldn't say what was wrong, but he wanted to make sure I was here for you. Are you going to tell me what's going on?'

'You'd better come in.' Lucy wanted to tell her everything. Technically, she had no loyalty to Tom anymore, but she didn't want to bring her friends into this. She also didn't want or need their opinions on the situation.

Taking a seat in the living room, Lucy said, 'I've just got off the phone with him. In summary, he doesn't think this is the right time for him to be in a relationship, and he can't give me what I need. I guess he feels so guilty about it he had you sent over to pick up his pieces.' They were only white lies, but she wished she could come clean all the same.

She found herself wrapped in Imogen's arms once again, a comforting hand stroking her back. 'I don't know what's going on, and I'm sure Tom has a good reason, but I won't lie; I could punch him right now. Are you going to be okay? You can come and stay with us if you like?'

'No, it's okay. Thanks for the offer, but I'm going to stay with my parents for Christmas anyway, so I'll just see if I can go a bit earlier.'

'You can't beat having your mum at a time like this. She'll make you a cup of tea, just how you like it, and then everything won't seem so bad.'

'That's true. I'm going to throw some stuff in a bag and head over.'

'Do you want a hand?'

She wanted some time on her own to gather her thoughts before she's forced to act like everything's okay in front of her parents. 'No, it's okay. I've been through worse.' She half smiled as she said, 'At least this time, I'm not being chased by a psycho.'

'I suppose that's true. Well, if you're sure you don't need me, I'll head off. The offer stands. If you want to come to mine, you're more than welcome, day or night.'

She nodded. 'Thank you.'

After packing a bag, she spoke to her neighbour and asked if she could look after Doris. The poor cat was no doubt confused as to who owned her.

'Now, it's not that we don't enjoy having you stay with us, but what's the real reason you've flown home to the nest?' Lucy's mum was sitting in her chinos and maroon twinset, sipping tea from a China cup while catching up on Bargain Hunt on the TV. Lucy could never understand the fascination of watching people search around old flea markets, buying junk to sell on for a profit, but it kept her mother entertained, so she tolerated it.

Her dad was at his annual Christmas meal with his local bowls team. Lucy suspected her mum had waited for the opportunity to have an uninterrupted girly chat.

'I told you. I just thought that with everything I've been through recently, that it would be nice to come home for a bit.'

'Are you sure it's not man trouble?'

Yeah, it's totally man trouble. Did I neglect to mention that I started dating a man who's notorious in the local sex club for being a pleasure Dom, but he made a deal with the head of the Russian mafia and now my life is in danger? Again.

'I started seeing someone, but it didn't get very far. He owns a club in London and so he has to spend a lot of time there.'

Her mum looked at her with kind eyes. 'Oh dear. I imagine it is hard to find the time to court you when he's running a club. He doesn't sound like the sort of man to put your needs first.'

Oh Mum, if only you knew how much he put my needs first, and how many times.

'Yeah, it was never going to work out, but I don't want to talk about him.'

'No. What you need is a nice, dependable man. There is a lovely chap that goes to our church. Shall I see if he's interested?'

Mortified, she quickly replied, 'No. No, thank you. That won't be necessary. I'm staying away from men for the foreseeable.'

Dear Diary,

I wasn't ready to write to you last night, as so much happened. I'm staying with my parents for a few weeks, as Tom thinks I'm in danger. Yet another time I'm being underestimated. He acts like he cares about me, but at the first sign of things getting difficult, he dumps me. So, last night I found myself single again.

I'm determined not to mope about it. I've made too much progress to let a man break me. He made me feel so strong. He made me feel like I was beautiful. Do I need a man to make me feel those things? No. No, I don't.

I am strong.

I am powerful.

I am beautiful.

I'm a sex goddess!

When I walk into work tomorrow, I'll hold my head high. I'll finally be able to talk to Sarah and tell someone the truth about what's happening, and then I can move on with my life. Who knows, maybe I'll go to K's and meet someone new. Or maybe this mess with Tom will get resolved, and he'll come running with his tail between his legs. Or should that be cock between his legs? I might take him back. I might not. What if I'm not meant to be with him, and he was only given to me to teach me what I needed to know about life, love, and sex? He taught me so much about myself, and I'll always be grateful for that. If I ever decide to have another relationship, at least I'll know what I want.

It's time I stopped relying on other people, or things, to make myself feel better. I should probably stop writing in a diary like a school kid.

'Sarah, we need to talk.' Lucy had dressed in her favourite outfit; black trousers, killer heels, and black roll neck top. Her hair was longer and fell in soft waves down her front. She even wore her favourite red lip. Today was definitely a red lip kind of day.

'Yeah, we do. I saw Imogen this morning.' She gave Lucy a knowing look. 'What's the real story?'

'You know the mafia boss, Gedeon?'

Sarah nodded, her auburn curls bouncing.

'Ivan killed him.'

'What the fuck?'

363

'Yeah. It's pretty messed up. Tom's stressing out. He thinks I'm in danger, so he dumped me and made me stay at my parents' house. Apparently, it's not safe to be linked to him.'

'That doesn't make sense. You're already linked to him.'

'I think it's because we saw a car pulling away from my house on Saturday. He must think it's connected to Ivan. He doesn't want me near him.'

'Well, that sucks. I'm sorry, Hun. It sounds like he thinks he's doing the right thing, but it's still shit for you. I rarely stick up for the men in this situation, but this must be terrifying for him. His friend—who is his best friend's dad—has been murdered, he's no longer protected, and he's worried about keeping you safe. You certainly pick your men, don't you? Have you considered becoming a nun?'

'Based on the books we're currently reading, being a nun wouldn't protect me from men, either.' Lucy huffed a slight laugh.

Sarah tapped her lip. 'That's true,' she leaned onto her desk, resting on her elbows as she lowered her voice and said, 'Are you okay? You look smoking hot, and you're holding your head high, but how are you doing, truthfully?'

'I'm numb, but I'm done moping. If it's not meant to be with me and Tom, then it's not meant to be.'

'That's very philosophical, but I'm still going to get you drunk and feed you ice cream. Come and stay at mine after Christmas and we'll have a proper girly night in.'

'Deal. How are you anyway? I feel like everything has been about me lately.'

'I'm cool bananas. Actually, I did a thing.'

'A thing? What type of thing, and should I be worried?'

'I think it's a scary good thing, and it involves you.'

'I'm listening. And also scared.'

'You are looking at K's newest member.' Sarah puffed out her chest and flicked her hair over her shoulder.

Lucy's jaw dropped. 'I'm sorry, say what now?'

'I thought it would be a fun thing we could do together. You said you were going to take me, so I figured I'd join up and then I could bring a guest, too.'

Lucy looked at Sarah with trepidation. 'Sarah, were you thinking of bringing my boss to a sex club with us?'

Sarah blinked a few times. The cogs clearly turning in her head. 'You know what? Now that you say it like that, that is weird. Maybe I won't bring James with me when I go with you.'

'I would appreciate that. I won't be going now, though, will I. Thanks to Tom.'

Sarah swished her hand with a dismissive flick of her wrist. 'Nonsense. Just because you can't go to his club doesn't mean you can't go to K's. It's full of security and only men that are invited in can go in. You'd be safe in there.'

'Let's see how things go, okay? I need to get to work. I'll see you later.' Lucy knew it was a waste of time to talk Sarah out of it. Once she had an idea in her head, it was there to stay.

Thankfully, Sarah didn't bring up K's again, and everyone else left her alone throughout the day. Imogen brought her lots of cups of tea, which was her way of saying she was there to talk whenever Lucy needed it. She didn't need it. There was nothing more she could say, literally. She couldn't tell Imogen what happened, and felt bad for lying about it, so keeping it to herself was the only option.

On the plus side, she felt closer to Sarah. They'd bonded over their run-in with Ivan, and it was nice to have someone adventurous enough to understand why she enjoyed going to K's.

In the run up to Christmas, everyone at work was busy finishing projects to be ready for the Christmas break. James and Cameron closed the office for the week with everyone under strict instructions to switch off. Lucy had no problems following that order. She intended to sit with a box of chocolates in her pyjamas, reading books all day and night while her mum brought her turkey and stuffing sandwiches. After the year she'd had, she was looking forward to hiding away and seeing in the New Year with her family.

She didn't hear from Tom. Not once did he call or text. She knew he was still alive, otherwise the others would have told her, so she guessed he was busy running his club and keeping Ivan away. It wasn't her problem anymore.

CHAPTER 40

TOM

What have I done – Dermot Kennedy

'I'm not signing K's over to him, Tom. I'd rather die before I see my club go to a man like Ivan.' Tom was sitting in Katia's office while she worked at her desk. It was during the day, so she wore her favourite ripped black skinny jeans and a vintage band T-shirt. She'd tied her hair up in a messy bun and her face was devoid of her signature red lip. He was trying to talk some sense into her, but she'd always been stubborn. He couldn't blame her. She'd put her life and soul into creating K's.

'I don't want you ending up dead over this.'

Katia threw her pen onto the desk, letting out an exaggerated huff. 'My genetics won't allow me to bend to his will. Think about it. Sure, at first, he wanted me dead for no other reason than he's an evil son-of-a-bitch. Now, he's seen my club and wants a part of it, just like he wants a part of yours. I'm not signing over my club to him, but if he kills me, the club will automatically pass over to you, and he knows he has no chance of getting you to sign it over. He'll have nothing to force your hand with; I'll be gone. His best chance to get his hands on my club is to bully it out of me. I say, let the games begin.'

'Christ. How did we get into this mess? How the fuck did he find you?' He scratches at his two-day-old stubble with one hand while the other holds a now empty glass of whiskey.

Katia shrugged, closed her laptop and leant on the desk, looking Tom in the eyes. 'You look like shit, by the way. Don't tell me you're doing okay. I can see that you're not. What's going on?'

'What? You mean apart from Gedeon being murdered, Ivan trying to deal drugs and prostitutes out of my club, and laundering money through my casino?'

'Yeah. You know this is all temporary while we work out how to get rid of Ivan, right?'

He sighs, his body caving in on itself. 'I wish I had your positivity.'

'I've never seen you like this; it scares me. You've always been my rock and I feel like you're crumbling. This is because of Lucy, isn't it?'

'I put myself in an impossible position. I made a deal with the devil to protect his daughter and a promise to a goddess to protect her heart. I had to break Lucy's heart to keep her alive, but I did it knowing how strong she is and how she'll get over it. Now I have to get us out of this situation; I can't have lost Lucy for nothing.'

'Listen to me. My dad is dead. Your deal with him is over. You've given your whole life to me, and I won't ask you to give me any more. And you might not have lost Lucy. You can still try to win her back when this is all over.'

He slouched in his seat, shoulders dropping. 'I can't see a way out of this, Kat.' He felt utterly defeated.

Katia released a long sigh, rubbing at her temples. 'I'm not going to sugar-coat this. My dad has died. He wasn't present a great deal in my life, but he was still my dad. He'd be turning in his grave right now—wherever that might be—if he knew you'd given up. That fucker denied my father his right to a trial. He murdered him in cold blood and did god-knows-what to his body, which no one has found.' She jabbed her finger at him as she said, 'You can still fix this. For you. Not for me, but for you.'

He rolled the cut crystal glass between his palms, processing her words. He didn't know how to fix this. Ivan was a psychopath in the purest form. He could handle the everyday thug trying it on in his club, not that it happened often, but this was another level. Without the backing of Gedeon, he was just one man against the mafia. And not just any mafia, but the fucking Vory.

'I need to get back to the club. I think I have an idea.'

'Sophia, I need a word with you in my office. Now.' He didn't wait for a response before striding up the stairs to his office. Moments later, an out of breath Sophia rushed in.

'Shut the door.' He pointed at the chair, silently telling her to sit down.

She took a seat and nervously picked at her nails. 'What is it?'

He leant back in his chair, hands steepled. 'You're dating Andre.' It wasn't a question.

She shifted in her seat. 'Yeah. I don't see why that's any of your business, though.'

'It became my business when his boss threatened to kill Katia, has killed a close friend of mine and has threatened anyone that is close to me. I've had to end it with Lucy to keep her alive. He's now trying to launder money through my casino and sell drugs and prostitutes in my club. So, it *is* my business.'

'What the fuck are you talking about? I'm not involved in any of this, if that's what you're thinking.' She went to stand.

'Sit down. No, I don't think you're involved with it, but I need you to be. Andre can help us, and I need you to get a message to him. I'm sorry to bring you into this, but I really don't have a choice now. I can't talk directly to Andre, as Ivan will know something is going on.'

She chewed on her fingernail and said, 'Ivan might know already. Andre came over to see me the other night and was battered black and blue. He said he'd pissed Ivan off but didn't give me any more information than that.'

'Sounds like he's even more motivated to get rid of Ivan then. When you next see him, tell him there's a job for him here. I need a head of security with his level of insider knowledge. Tell him I'm willing to do whatever it takes to end Ivan. If he can get word to you of his movements and plans, I can work on the rest. This must end, Sophia. I can't take him down on my own. Will you help me?'

She put her head in her hands and took a deep breath. 'Of course I'll help you. It's the least I can do. Andre is a good man; I know he'll help too. I can call him now. He'll only answer if it's safe to.'

'Thank you.'

'Hey, I'm sorry about Lucy. I hope when this is all sorted, you can win her back.'

He didn't think his heart could sink any lower, but at the mention of her name, it dropped further into the pit of despair. 'Don't tell anyone about this conversation, okay? We're not playing games here. People have died and I don't want you coming to harm.'

She pretended to padlock her mouth shut before standing up, slapping her hands against her thighs. 'Right then, Boss, back to work I go.' As she got to the door, she turned back and said, 'Easier said than done; but don't worry about this. We'll work it out. Good always wins over evil.' She held her hand up in salute and closed the door on her way out.

Tom looked up at the ceiling, releasing a deep sigh. 'Let's hope you're right on that one, Sophia. Let's hope you're right,' he mumbled into the air.

'Shit, Tom, take it easy.' Tom's trainer was straining against the heavy impact that came with each of Tom's punches.

'I don't want to take it easy.' Sweat ran down his body, following the curves of every muscle as he took his frustrations out on the trainer's pads. 'I need to step my training up.'

His trainer put his hands down, signalling it was time to take a break. He grabbed a towel and wiped at his face and arms as he said, 'Are you gearing up for a fight or something?'

Tom looked him square in the eyes as he said, 'Or something.'

'Oh, shit. You got problems with someone at the club?'

'You could say that. When the time comes, I need to know I can take someone down. Your specialised skills are what I need. Can you train me in more than simple stop and restrain techniques, and fast?'

Tom's personal trainer was no stranger to hand-to-hand combat. They met in school, and after leaving, he entered the army and finished his career in special ops. He doesn't talk about what he had to do, but his face carries the haunted expression of someone that has seen some truly horrific things.

Scratching his bald head, he considered what to say. 'I won't ask for any details. I figure it's best I don't know. Do you need weapons training?'

'No. I need to take him down without weapons. I'll either be in my club or at K's.'

'Okay. So, you'll either be in a crowded room or naked. Got it. Definitely no weapons. Although, I have heard your cock described as a weapon of mass destruction.' He let out a booming laugh at his joke.

Tom threw his damp towel at his friend. 'I'm glad you can laugh at this.'

'Okay, come on. Let's get started.'

By the time his training session was over, sweat dripped from his body. He was out of breath and ready to take Ivan on.

The club was full of people cramming in the last of their Christmas parties and so far, there'd been no trouble. To avoid Ivan and his crew, he spent most of his time scanning the CCTV screens, trying to spot anyone dealing drugs or any women that looked to be selling themselves. He'd doubled his security team and had kept incidents down to a minimum.

His door burst open as an uninvited guest strolled in. Tom recognised the cloying scent of the liberal dose of aftershave; there was no need to look up to know who was standing before him.

'Ivan, do I need to remind you of basic manners? It's customary to knock.'

'And do I need to remind you to shut the fuck up?'

Tom clenched his jaw. There was no point in starting an argument with this scum. 'What do you want?'

'I'm so glad you asked.' Ivan pulled at his trouser legs before taking a seat, one leg crossed over the other. 'Are you not going to offer me a drink?'

'I'm working on the assumption that if you want one, you'll get one yourself. You're not known for waiting to be asked before trying to take something that doesn't belong to you.'

'This is true. However, on this occasion, I think you'll need a drink, so I suggest you pour us both a glass of your favourite whiskey.'

CHAPTER 41

LUCY

Tears in the club (feat. The Weeknd) – FKA twigs

'Thank you, everyone, for all that we've achieved this year. I think you'll agree that this year has been interesting.' James and Cameron were standing in the middle of the stairs that lead up to the mezzanine in the office. They'd congregated all the staff in the open space on the ground floor, each with a small glass of fizz in their hands.

Cameron cleared his throat and said, 'I agree. A lot has changed this year.' He raised his left hand and wiggled his ring finger. 'For one, I'm now happily married to the gorgeous Imogen.' He smiled over at her as she blushed. 'And some of us have gone through great personal tragedy. We've all come together and shown great strength and loyalty, so from the bottom of my heart, thank you for ensuring this year ends well. Spencer and Black Associates have gone from strength to strength this year and we hope to further expand our services and locations next year, so watch this space for some exciting times ahead.'

James raised his glass and said to the crowd, 'Merry Christmas, everyone. Cheers.' They all raised their glasses before taking generous sips. 'Now, sod off home and have a great time with your families. You've earned it. See you in the New Year.'

Lucy finished her drink as Sarah said, 'What are your plans for Christmas?'

'Same as every year. Mum and Dad will cook, and Uncle Frank will fall asleep in the armchair and fart, blaming it on too many sprouts. What about you?'

'Similar. I'll be at my parents' but it's usually me farting and falling asleep on the sofa. Do you fancy having a night at mine between Christmas and New Year? We can get drunk and watch movies.'

'That depends. Are you going to be eating sprouts beforehand?'

'I promise not to. Come on, you must get sick of staying with your parents.'

'Yep. I won't be staying there after Christmas. I've not heard from Tom, but I'm sick of hiding away.' She took a second to decide. 'Okay, I'd love to come over. I'll bring the wine and ice cream.'

'Deal.'

They said their goodbyes to everyone and packed up their desks, ready for a well-earned break.

Imogen gave Lucy a big hug, and while wrapped in her arms said, 'If you need anything while we're off, call me. I mean it. We're here for you, no matter if it's day or night.'

Lucy pulled away and said, 'Thank you. I'm going to be okay, though. I never expected it to last with me and Tom. What hurts the most is his complete lack of communication all together. I guess I'm just unlucky with men, but I won't waste any more time thinking about it.'

'This doesn't sound like Tom. I'm really shocked by how it's ended.'

Lucy shrugged as she said, 'In my experience, men as friends are a lot different to men as boyfriends. Anyway, I'm going to go home and stuff my face with mince pies. I'll see you next year. Have a great first Christmas with your husband.'

Lucy drove home feeling positive. She couldn't wait to see the end of this year.

'I'm going to open the bottle of Baileys.' Lucy and Sarah had made their way through two bottles of red wine over the course of the afternoon and evening and were now about to start on the Irish cream liquor.

Sarah stumbled back into her small living room with the brown bottle and two glasses. She sloshed some into the glasses and handed one to Lucy. She closed her eyes as the creamy liquid warmed her throat as she swallowed. 'This tastes like Christmas. I love it.'

'Me too,' said Sarah, smacking her lips together. Suddenly, she jumped up from the sofa and grabbed her phone from the table. She opened up her emails and started scrolling through.

'What are you up to?' Lucy dreaded to think what her friend was doing. She had that mischievous look in her eyes again.

'Have you been checking your emails?'

'Yeah, why?'

'Did you see the newsletter from K's?'

'I didn't get one.'

'Check your junk folder. I saw it come through on my notifications earlier but haven't read it yet. Let's look.'

Lucy grabbed her phone from the pocket of her hoodie and looked through the endless emails from people telling her she'd won a prize and all she had to do was give them her bank details. 'You'd think criminals would be clued up to the fact that people don't fall for this shit anymore.'

'I don't know. I reckon people still fall for it.'

Lucy mmm'd her agreement before saying, 'Ah, here it is.' She opened the email and read the update on what had been happening at K's.

Sarah sounded very excited as she exclaimed, 'Oh, there are photos of their Christmas party. This place looks awesome. I can't wait to use my membership. Oh my, Lucy, look at this one. He's fucking hot. Did you see him there?'

Lucy scrolled down on her phone until she got to the photos. You couldn't see anyone's faces. They were not in the shot or blurred out, but she knew which person Sarah was referring to. As she stared at the screen, bile mixed with Baileys rose in her throat. The man in the photo had his head between a woman's thighs, but the wolf and raven tattoo gave his identity away.

She swallowed down the hurt and anger as she calmly said, 'Yeah, I saw him there. Most of the time I was there, he had his cock or his fingers inside me.'

Sarah's mouth opened wide before she regained composure and said, 'You had sex with another man while you were there?'

Swallowing down the bile that threatened to rise, Lucy said, 'Sarah, that's Tom in the photos. He's clearly over me already and back to his old ways. I guess I can't blame him; he's free and single and very much in demand, judging by the amount of women in that pile.'

Sarah put her phone down and put her arm around Lucy. 'I'm so sorry, Hun. I can't believe you had to see that.'

She continued to stare at the photo, unable to take her eyes off the vision of Tom pleasuring another woman. It sickened her at how it was turning her on. Something in the newsletter caught her eye.

'Hey Sarah, they're having a New Year's Eve party. I think we should go.'

'Are you crazy? What if Tom is there?'

'I don't care if he's there. I have just as much right to be there. Actually, I have more of a right to be there, as I'm a member. I'm done hiding away and licking my wounds. Someone else will lick them for me. I'll go with or without you, but I'd rather you were there with me.'

'Okay, what if a psycho mafia dude is there?'

'It doesn't look like Tom is too concerned about the mafia situation, does it? Judging by the fun he's having between that woman's legs, I'd say the problem has been resolved.' The hurt in Lucy's voice was still tangible, but she told herself she was ready to move on.

Sarah chewed on her bottom lip. 'Fuck it. Tomorrow, you're taking me to see Roxy and we're going to go to that party in style.'

They chinked their glasses of Baileys together and Lucy told Sarah all about the rules of parties at K's while they searched for hotels with availability.

She hoped Tom was there to see her move on with her life. She was going to go into the new year screaming someone else's name.

'You look amazing.' Lucy and Sarah were getting ready in their hotel room. They'd had to pay a premium at one of London's nicest hotels, but it was worth it. Tonight was going to mark the start of the rest of her life.

Sarah adjusted a boob in her corset as she said, 'Thanks. I love the way these corsets make my boobs look massive. It's like they're sitting on a shelf.' Sarah had listened to Roxy's advice and gone with a dark green corset and matching pleated mini skirt. She looked stunning with her copper curls draping over her shoulders.

Lucy was wearing the same outfit as before. If Tom was there, she wanted an obvious reminder for him of what he was missing out on. On what he pushed away. They wrapped up in heavy winter coats as snow had fallen earlier in the day.

As they made their way into the club, they helped each other with their masks. Roxy had talked Lucy into buying a new navy-blue lace mask. Sarah had bought the green version. The lace felt soft and comforting against her skin.

After signing in and going through the formalities of the rules, they discarded their coats and entered the bar.

Music was blaring and everyone seemed in high spirits. The drinks were flowing, and everyone received a complimentary glass of champagne on arrival. Sarah opted to buy a bottle for them to share before they went through to the playrooms.

'I need to get a little tipsy before we go in. The limit on alcohol once we're in is stressing me out.'

'Don't worry about it. Once you're in there, you'll soon forget about needing a drink. You'll get drunk enough on the endorphins. I feel buzzed just thinking about it.' Lucy shivered at the thought of what was in store for them.

The buzz of being back here mixed with nerves. However much she tried to convince herself that she was over Tom, she knew that seeing him in person was going to bring all her feelings to the surface. His presence made her body react in ways she couldn't control. Doubts entered her mind. Perhaps this was a bad idea.

'If you're not sure that you want to go in, we can go home. It's up to you.' Lucy wasn't sure what she wanted Sarah to say to that.

Sarah shook her head. 'No way. We're going in there and having the night of our lives. Lucy, I'm not stupid. I know you're nervous about seeing Tom, but I'll be here for you. He might not even be here. Tonight is the busiest night for him. He probably won't have time to come here.'

Lucy hadn't considered that; now her heart sank at the thought of *not* seeing him. It made her wonder who she was here for. Was it for her to move on with her life, or was it to make Tom jealous and want her back? She supposed it didn't matter now; he won't be here.

People were dancing and getting to know each other, so Sarah suggested they did the same. 'So, what's the etiquette when turning up without any men? Can we borrow someone else's or are there spare men walking around?'

'Oh, I don't really know. I didn't have to think about that with Tom. I think we should mingle and play it by ear.'

'Sounds like a plan. Half-baked, but a plan nonetheless.'

Sarah scanned the room, licking her lips like she was admiring a buffet. They downed the last of their champagne and joined the others in the middle of the room.

The music was perfect for the mood of the evening, dark and dirty with a heavy bass beat. People were grinding up against each other, desperate to get to eleven so they could shed their clothes and play.

They soon found themselves swallowed up by the crowds. Bodies pressing into them from all directions and the shared body heat increasing the temperature in the room. They were getting hot in more ways than one. Lucy felt hands press around her hips, pulling her onto someone's chest. She noticed Sarah was in a similar situation. Catching her eye, Lucy mouthed *are you okay?* to her friend. Sarah winked in response.

It felt wrong to be in the arms of someone else, but there was only one way to get over Tom, and that was to get back on the horse and ride it. And she planned to ride one hard tonight. She pushed the feelings of doubt down into the depths of her soul and interlaced her fingers with the man who joined her. She heard a deep growl of appreciation come from him, a smile pulling at her lips.

It felt good to elicit such a reaction from someone. The power she felt from it coursed through her veins and gave her the courage to continue.

She glanced over at Sarah to discover her friend's tongue well and truly down the other guy's throat, so she figured Sarah was more than happy with the situation.

The room fell quiet as Katia's voice rang out, declaring the playrooms open. Her mystery man took her hand and led her into the changing rooms to get ready; Sarah and her man close behind.

They got ready together in one changing room, while the men got ready elsewhere. Sarah was full of confidence and opted to remove her corset and spend the evening in her underwear, whereas Lucy felt vulnerable without Tom at her side. She kept her corset on. They placed their masks and other belongings in the lockers before walking out to the communal area to meet the others.

Sarah released a low whistle as she laid eyes on the men they'd walked in with. They both clearly worked out. A lot. Their bodies were all hard edges and muscle. Sarah licked her lips in anticipation.

Lucy couldn't take her eyes off the men in front of her, but not for the same reason as Sarah. Both men were tall, dark and very handsome, and Lucy would have jumped at the chance to be here with either of them. What Lucy noticed, however, was that they were both covered in tattoos from the neck down. Barely any unmarked skin remained. What caught her eye was that both had the same tattoos of stars on their knees. She knew that meant something but couldn't remember what.

'Are you okay?' Sarah was leaning into Lucy so she could whisper.

Lucy shook her head, bringing herself out of her thoughts. 'Yeah. I'm good. Seeing their tattoos reminded me of Tom, I think.'

'Oh, Hun. That's understandable. You're bound to feel weird about all this at first. Don't worry, you'll soon warm up to them. My kiss was top-notch; you should try kissing your one and see how you feel.'

Lucy wasn't convinced, but maybe it was worth a go. 'You're right. I need to get back on that horse.'

'Are you ready, ladies?' Sarah's man stepped forward, offering his hand to Sarah, which she eagerly accepted.

'We don't know your names. Do you think we ought to introduce ourselves?'

'I'm Peter, this,' he indicated to man number two, who was now holding Lucy's hand, 'is Kane. It's a pleasure to meet you. Where would you ladies like to go first?'

'This is my first time, so I have no idea what I fancy doing. Lucy, what would you like to do?'

She blushed as she admitted, 'I like to watch. We could go have a look around, show you what's on offer and then maybe go to the Fishbowl.'

Sarah's eyes lit up. 'The Fishbowl sounds like fun. Let's get in there, sus it out and then head there. Is that okay with you two?'

Peter and Kane nodded as Kane said, 'Sounds like a perfect plan.'

The atmosphere in the central room was different this time. It was buzzing with excitement; everywhere you looked, people were kissing and caressing each other. The smell of sex hung heavy in the air.

Peter and Kane went to the bar to get them all a drink. Sarah opted for an alcohol-free gin and tonic, while Lucy opted for a virgin Moscow Mule. They figured they could at least pretend to be drinking something stronger. While they were at the bar, Sarah said, 'This place is amazing. I can see why you love it. I can't wait to see what else there is. I'm already horny as fuck.'

'Bloody hell, Sarah, you're going to explode when you see the rooms.'

'Are you okay hanging out with these guys? You look a little tense.'

Lucy shook her head. 'I'm fine. It's strange being here with someone else, but I think I just need to get used to it, that's all.'

'All right, but if you change your mind, tell me. Oh, we should have a safe word that we can use as a secret way to say, "party's over bitch."'

'That's a good idea. What shall we use?'

Sarah scrunched up her face while she was deep in thought. She lifted her finger in triumph. 'Let's use Spencer as the safe word.'

'Spencer? You want to use your bosses, and sort of benefit friends surname as your safe word out of a sex club?'

'Yep.'

'You're not normal, you're not. But I love it. Okay, Spencer it is.'

'But if we meet someone by that name, we'll have to change the safe word. I don't want to be in the middle of an orgasm, screaming out his name and you come running in to rescue me.'

Lucy giggled as she said, 'Oh, can you imagine? That would be too funny. Oh, but ew, I'm not sure I want to see you having sex. If we get to a point where we want to split off, we'll have to see how we're both feeling.'

'Good plan.'

Their conversation was interrupted by the arrival of their drinks.

Peter handed Sarah her drink. Lucy noticed how her eyes had locked onto his as she seductively took a sip. Sarah looked to be on a mission tonight.

Handing Lucy her drink, Kane said, 'Here you go, beautiful. One Russian cocktail.' He then mumbled, 'It's good to know you like something Russian down your throat.'

Lucy looked up at him. 'Sorry, I didn't catch that.'

'I said it's a nice drink.'

'Oh, yes. It's nice. 'Lucy didn't believe that's what he'd said. Her gut tried to give her another warning, but she'd stopped listening.

CHAPTER 42

LUCY

Vigilante Shit – Taylor Swift

'Come on, guys. I want to see the Fishbowl. It sounds awesome.' Sarah stood up, ready to get into the swing of things. 'I don't feel right sitting around in my undies.'

'Your friend is keen, isn't she? Let's get going. We don't want to disappoint her.' Kane said as Peter took Sarah by the hand.

Lucy quickly finished the rest of her drink and stood, walking to the other side of Sarah. She didn't feel right taking Kane's hand. It felt overfamiliar to walk hand-in-hand, which seemed silly considering what they may end up doing together.

Lucy explained the different rooms to Sarah as they passed by each one. 'It's a lot busier tonight than when I came here before, I guess because it's New Year. I don't think we'll be lucky enough to get ourselves private rooms. I think they were booked in advance.' She didn't feel disappointed. Coming here without Tom now felt wrong; the buzz she felt when she arrived had depleted.

Sarah's eyes lit up as they approached the Fishbowl. A sizeable crowd had gathered, but with some squeezing in, they got a spot where they could see in. The men stood behind them, their hands once again resting on their hips.

Lucy felt a warm breath on her neck as Kane whispered into her ear. 'I like to watch, too. I particularly like to watch with a beautiful woman in my arms.' He pressed his lips onto the sensitive skin below her ear. She closed her eyes as she let the sensation wash over her, waiting for her body to come alive.

He ran his tongue across the spot he'd kissed before sucking her earlobe into his mouth and biting down. The sudden pain made her jump. His hands gripped onto her hips, his fingers digging in to the point of pain. He pressed his erection into the small of her back.

'Can you feel how much I'm enjoying this already? I think we'll have a lot of fun together.'

She didn't know how to reply. This felt different to how it did before. When Tom whispered in her ear, shivers would flutter across her skin, but with Kane she only felt chills. His right hand trailed from her hip down to her thigh, before sliding towards her core. His index figure traced small circles around the lace edging of her knickers. Her breath hitched with panic.

'You like that, don't you? Me teasing you in front of all these people. You've barely looked at the people inside the room, have you?'

She altered her stance, pressing her thighs together, feeling the need to close herself off to Kane. She focused on the room in front of her. It was darker inside than she'd seen it before. They'd turned the soft lighting low, and she noticed the people in the room still wore their masks. She could see two women restrained by their wrists to loops hanging from the ceiling, their ankles shackled to the floor. Two men stood near them. The

386

taller of them stood at the edge, watching as the other flogged the women's backs, alternating between the two. Lucy figured this must be a special show put on for the party.

Kane's grip on Lucy tightened, the hand from her thigh now spread across her stomach, his other hand still gripping her hip.

'I have a surprise for you.' Kane's voice was low, but not in the raspy, sexy way Tom used to talk to her. His voice had a chill to it that made him sound threatening.

She swallowed. 'Oh? What's that?' A feeling of dread descended on her.

'We're going into the Fishbowl. All four of us. We're going to be part of the show.'

Lucy's eyes grew wide, her breath coming fast as she tried to pull away from him. 'No. No, we're not. I don't want to.' He tightened his grip on her, holding her in place.

He gripped his fingers into her hip until she sucked in a sharp breath of pain. 'You have no say in it. If you don't come with us, and convince your friend to do the same, she'll not see the sun rise again.' He brought his hand up to her jaw to keep her looking ahead. 'Ah-ah, don't look over now; keep your eyes on the room. We don't want to make a scene, do we?'

Lucy's chest was heaving with the effort of breathing. Her skin flushed as panic threatened to overcome her. Onlookers would assume her state was down to arousal.

'You need to tell your friend about our surprise and make sure she comes willingly. Any sign of trouble, Peter will take her to a private room, have fun with her and then dispose of her. Do you understand what I'm saying?'

She couldn't speak, but nodded her understanding.

'Good. Let the show begin.' He gripped onto her hips with both hands as he guided her towards the other two.

Lucy took the few seconds she had to calm her breathing.

'Hey, Sarah. Kane has organised a treat for us.'

'Oh really? Do tell.'

'We're going into the Fishbowl. To meet Spencer.'

Sarah froze, but Lucy's intense stare warned her to go along with it.

'G-great. Are we sure we want to do that, Lucy?'

'Apparently, it's a once-in-a-lifetime kind of offer.'

Lucy couldn't be sure that Sarah understood what she was getting at, but thankfully, she played along. 'Okay. Let's go.'

Sarah grabbed Lucy's hand and squeezed it as Peter and Kane pushed them along past the crowd to a curtain at the back of the viewing area. They pulled it aside to reveal a door.

As Kane pushed them through the door, Lucy noticed the masked men were covered in the same tattoos. And then it clicked.

She cursed herself for being such an idiot. These were Ivan's men.

'Kane. Peter. I see you have brought our VIPs. Well done.'

Scratch that.

This was Ivan. She'd recognise his accent anywhere.

'Andre, the masks can come off now. Please remove the masks for the ladies.' He turned to Lucy and Sarah. 'As you can see, they're a little tied up.' He chuckled maniacally at his own joke.

Lucy's attention turned to the women tied up, and to the wolf tattoo that adorned one of their thighs. 'Katia. Are you okay?' Kane grabbed Lucy as she went to go to her friend. Katia, whose back was to them, tried to see them, but couldn't turn her head enough. 'I'm okay. For now.'

Her heart sank as she recognised Sophia. She looked at Andre, shock and anger on her face. He shook his head in warning, keeping his eyes on the ground. The tattoos on his body did a good job of disguising the bruising across his arms and torso. His face was mottled with the same greens and purples as the markings across his body; clearly the focus of a brutal beating.

Ivan swished the flogger through the air, its tassels hitting its target across Katia's chest. Lucy saw her back muscles tense, but she didn't make a sound.

Sarah looked around the room. 'What the fuck is going on?'

Ivan stopped mid-swish and looked over at her. 'Ah, my beautiful auburn princess. I am so glad you came along tonight. We have unfinished business, you and I.'

'Like fuck we do. Let us go. Have you forgotten that there are loads of witnesses outside? You can't possibly get away with this, whatever this is.'

'Ah yes. Isn't it perfect? They think they're watching a special show, and I suppose they are. It's such a shame the infamous Thomas Harper isn't here. He can draw quite the crowd.'

Lucy's heart stopped at the mention of his name.

'What a shame he dumped you.'

'Lucy. Don't listen to him,' implored Katia.

Swish.

Her muscles tensed, but again she didn't make a sound.

'Keep your mouth shut, bitch.'

But she didn't keep her mouth shut. 'I told him he's not to come back here ever again. You think you can control us with your threats, but you can't. He won't come here to protect me. I won't allow it. He knows you need me alive to get your hands on this club.'

Swish.

'That's right. He won't come here to protect me,' Katia ground out through gritted teeth.

Swish.

'Ah, but you underestimate what he'll do to protect her.' He pointed to Lucy with his flogger.

Swish.

Katia's ribcage expanded rapidly as she tried to catch her breath. 'Keep it coming arsehole. I like it rough.' She spat at his feet.

'You are going to get yourself killed talking to me like that. I don't *need* you alive. I *want* you alive so I can have some fun. Aren't you having fun with me, Kitty-Kat?' He pronounced the Ks with such venom, spittle flew from his mouth. 'What do you think your daddy dearest would say if he could see you now?' He paced in front of her as he spoke. 'Ah, but we'll never know. Such a shame.'

Sarah pulled herself free from Peter's grip and walked further into the room. 'Can someone explain what the fuck is going on?'

'You are a feisty one, aren't you? Do we need to tie you up? Put a ball-gag in your mouth?'

'Fuck off.'

Lucy looked over at her friend, her eyes pleading with her to be quiet.

'Andre, be a good boy and help tie these girls up.' Andre's fists clenched at his sides as he stalked over to where Peter was pushing Sarah onto one of the St. Andrews crosses on the wall. Peter tightened the cuffs onto her ankles, stopping her from kicking out. Andre worked on the cuffs at her wrists.

'Get your hands off me, dickhead.' Sarah struggled in his arms, but he easily overpowered her.

Lucy was pushed up against the wall. Andre took his time strapping her wrists into rings attached to the wall.

As Peter walked away, Andre whispered close to her ear, 'They're loose, so you can get free.' She blinked and gave him the slightest nod in understanding before he walked back to Ivan's side.

Ivan prowled around the room as he said, 'Now you've taken care of the whores; we can have some fun. Andre, go over to the other cross. Kane, strap him in. The crowd is no doubt getting restless. It's time I gave them a show.'

Andre looked over at Kane and backed up, his hands clenching into fists, ready to defend himself. 'Back off, dickhead. You're not strapping me into anything.'

Ivan's hand gripped around Sophia's throat, making her gasp for air. 'Go willingly or your girlfriend will choke on a lot more than my hand.'

Lucy watched on, nausea hitting her in waves as Kane dragged Andre over to another wooden cross on the opposite side of the room. His body was rigid, unwilling to bend to the demands of the psycho in the room. He kept his eyes on Sophia as Kane strapped his limbs to the cross.

Ivan walked over to Lucy, the flogger swinging in his hand, the white leather strips gliding across the floor like an obedient pet. She winced as he dragged his finger along her jawline. 'I'm so glad that you came tonight. My revenge will be sweeter for it. Thomas thought he was being clever, distancing himself from you. But I was on to you long before then. I've been watching him closely; I have eyes everywhere. You two were quite the explosive couple, by all accounts. I only wish I could have seen it.'

Lucy spoke through gritted teeth. 'Why are you doing this?'

He dragged his nose up the side of her face, breathing her in. She squeezed her eyes closed, but his silhouette floated behind her eyelids, taunting her.

'You smell good enough to eat. I look forward to tasting you, Lucy.'

Her weakness betrayed her; a tear slipping from her eye. His tongue was on her, lapping it up. Her breath shuddered as she forced the sobs to stay hidden.

He closed his eyes, groaning in pleasure. 'I could drink your tears all night. I love the sight of a tear glistening on a woman's face, so beautiful, like a diamond.'

'Sick fuck.' Sarah mumbled from her cross. Ivan stepped in front of her and, without warning, flicked the flogger across her exposed stomach. Her skin immediately coloured as her head fell back. Lucy could see her gritting her teeth; her stubbornness not allowing a scream to escape her lips.

'Keep your mouth shut. You're interrupting my conversation with your friend.' He turned his attention back to Lucy as he said, 'I apologise for the interruption. You asked a good question; why am I doing this?'

'You two.' He pointed over at Kane and Peter. 'You can leave. Get yourself some playthings and go to our private room. You've earned a treat. Oh, and make sure the onlookers think they're watching a show.' They nodded a silent response and left the room. Now it was just the six of them. Lucy tried to look out to the crowd, but the one-way glass made it impossible to see who was out there.

'Gedeon betrayed us. We gave up our lives in Russia to follow him here and remain loyal. He told us it was because there were more opportunities for us in London. The new mafia, as he called it, had taken over many parts of Russia and the Vory was soon cast out.' He strolled over to Katia and began flogging her back, his wrist moving in a figure of eight in a continual motion. The cracking sound grew louder with every rotation, her back crimson. He sucked in a deep breath as his head rolled back in pleasure. He ran his hands across her tender skin.

'I need to keep your customers entertained, dear Katia, you understand?'

Katia was breathless as she said, 'Keep it coming, fucker. I like it.'

'What a shame we didn't meet in better circumstances. I like it rough, but rarely can I find someone who can take it.' He shook his head as he stepped back. 'I digress. I was sceptical of Gedeon's reasons for leaving, so I followed him, watching him closely for years. I didn't understand why Thomas was a protected man. Why his club was off limits. Who was this Thomas Harper, and why should I give a fuck about him?'

Lucy wriggled her wrists, testing the restraints. She could feel them slip out. She gripped onto them, knowing she could free herself quickly.

'My attention turned to Thomas, and of course, he led me straight to Katia. It didn't take a genius to see the resemblance.' He focussed his attention on Lucy and Sarah. 'You must understand, the Vory must obey the Vorovskoy Zakon—'

Sarah rolled her eyes as she said, 'What the fuck are you talking about?'

Lucy answered before Ivan could. 'It's the Thieves Code. Eighteen rules they live and die by.'

'Clever girl. Your pillow talk with Thomas is clearly educational. To be in the Vory, we must forsake our family and must not have a family of our own. Gedeon broke this rule in spectacular fashion by moving his entire crew to a new country so he could be in her life. We left our lives behind so he could have a daughter.'

'I'd hardly say he was my father. I barely saw him. Tom was more like a son to him than I was his daughter.'

'And yet he moved us here, anyway.'

Swish.

Katia was taking the full brunt of his anger, evidenced by the welts forming on her creamy skin.

'Rule three of the code is to live only on means gleamed from thievery. And yet here is Gedeon prohibiting us from using Thomas' goldmine of a club—'

Andre's voice boomed as he said, 'Rule twelve: don't gamble without being able to cover losses. Rule fifteen: don't lose your reasoning ability when drinking alcohol. And most importantly, rule 7,' his voice rose higher as he said, 'Demand a convocation of inquiry to resolve disputes. You failed to follow those rules. You jumped straight to carrying out the punishment. And for that, we should try you before Gedeon's crew. You are a disgrace.' The rise and fall of Andre's chest was rapid with anger. 'You are not fit to lead us, and you will suffer the consequences.'

Ivan stepped up to Andre, a deep booming laugh erupting from his chest before his fist swung round, the handle of the flogger landing on Andre's temple, his body giving out; only held up by the restraints on his wrists.

'You will pay dearly for that. Or should I say Sophia will?'

Sophia's eyes pleaded as she begged. 'No. Please, no.' She tugged and pulled at the ropes holding her open to him.

Ivan walked over to the rack of equipment, replacing the white leather flogger with a whip that screamed of violence and pain. He cracked it against his palm as he approached a flailing Sophia.

Lucy couldn't allow this. She pulled her hands free and ran at them, shoving into Ivan and shielding Sophia with her body. Ivan quickly regained his composure. 'I don't mind who I whip, you stupid girl. Are you volunteering?' His lips formed a sneer as he brought the whip up into the air. She tilted her head to the side and closed her eyes, waiting for the impact.

'Touch her and I'll fucking kill you.'

CHAPTER 43

TOM

Lion – Saint Mesa

'Tom, there's a woman called Roxy on line one. She says it's urgent.' Tom was sitting in his office staring at an empty glass of whiskey, wondering if he could get away with not joining the hundreds of customers enjoying their night in his club, when someone's voice came over the radio.

He lifted the receiver on the phone. 'This is Tom.'

'Tom, it's Roxy. You need to get to the club. I think Katia's in trouble,' she said breathlessly, rushing her words.

He sat bolt upright. 'What do you mean?'

'She's in the Fishbowl with a man that looks dodgy as fuck. I don't like it, this isn't her usual style, he's got her tied up.'

'But you know she's a switch. Maybe she's found a good Dom for the night.' He hoped that was the case, but his gut instinct told him otherwise.

'He's not a good Dom, trust me on that. He's got Lucy too, and her friend.'

He didn't need to ask who 'He' was; it was clear Ivan was at K's. 'Fuck, Roxy, why didn't you start with Lucy being there? I'm on my way.' He slammed the phone down and radioed Alex to let him know he was leaving as he went straight to the car park.

He ran straight to his motorbike, not willing to waste any time by putting on his helmet. He swung his leg over the bike, the engine roaring to life as he gunned it out of the carpark, the tyres screaming as they gained traction on the smooth concrete.

The streets were bustling with drunken partygoers heading to their next location. His bike weaved around the taxis, limos, and stumbling pedestrians; the engine roaring as he pushed it to its limits. The wind whipped his exposed face, making it difficult for him to keep his eyes open. All the while he cursed Lucy for going to the club when he'd given up everything to keep her safe.

As he rounded the corner, he cut the engine, throwing the bike to the floor, not stopping to flick down the stand. He crashed through the doors as two security guards stepped in his way.

'Sorry mate, you need to be accompanied by a member.'

He tried to push past them as he shouted, 'Get out of my way! I need to get in there. She's in danger.'

They crossed their arms as the larger security guard said, 'No can do, mate.'

Tom clenched his teeth. 'I'm not your fucking mate.' He turned and was thankful to see Victoria behind the desk tonight. 'Victoria, tell them to let me in. Katia's in danger.'

Victoria took her time looking up from the computer screen, her ruby red lips plastered into a fake smile. 'Tom, how lovely of you to join us this evening. It's okay boys, let him through. He is the guest of honour after all.'

'What are you talking about?' And then he realised. Ivan had someone on the inside all along. 'Are you working for him?'

She flicked her hair over her shoulder, a look of indignation on her face. 'Of course, silly. Now run along. I believe they're in the Fishbowl. How fitting, as it's your favourite place.'

Tom burst through the doors, pushing the guards aside and bolted for the Fishbowl. Roxy was waiting for him in the corridor leading up to it.

He grabbed onto her shoulders to keep her walking with him, desperate to get to Lucy and Katia. 'Roxy, what's going on?'

'He has the women tied up. Fuck, Tom, everyone thinks they're watching a show.'

He shook his head trying to think clearly, but panic was washing over him. 'How many men are in there that you don't recognise?' He reckoned he could comfortably take two with the element of surprise, but any more than that, and he was screwed.

'There are two men in there now. One of the guys— the one holding the flogger—sent two men away earlier. They've gone to play.'

'Roxy, this is serious. I can't go into details, but you need to get everyone out. Do whatever you can.'

She nodded and ran off as Tom pushed through the crowds, not stopping to look.

Bursting into the Fishbowl, he quickly took in the scene, his eyes zeroing in on who Ivan was about to whip.

'Touch her and I'll fucking kill you,' he roared.

Ivan dropped the whip to his side as he looked across to Tom. 'Look who's showed up in the end. I suggest you stop where you are.' Ivan grabbed at Lucy, her back pressing into his chest, his arm around her throat.

'Get your hands off her. You don't get to touch her.'
His face reflected the fury that burned through him.

'Oh, really? Because it looks like I have my hands all over her. She feels so—'

Crack

Tom threw himself at Ivan, his fist colliding with Ivan's nose, his head whipping back, releasing Lucy from his grip. He reached out for her but was grasping at air. Lucy was already going to Katia. 'Lucy—'

A fire alarm ringing and the sprinklers bursting to life drowned his words out, raining down on them.

Sarah's shouts were barely audible over the chaos and screaming that came from the people outside. 'Tom!'

He turned in time to see Kane and Peter barging through the door. The floor was sodden and slippery underfoot, giving Tom an advantage. He sprinted to the men running towards him and threw himself to the floor, kicking his leg out, taking them both out in one move. Turning, he punched one of them in the nose, knocking him out cold.

The other guy lunged at him as they crashed to the floor in a muddle of wet limbs. Tom struggled to grasp onto anything. The man on top of him was semi-naked and slipping out of his grip. He felt the man's hands tighten around his throat; the air leaving his lungs too quickly. He could hear Lucy screaming his name as a black mist formed in his vision. He clawed at his attacker's arms until his limbs went limp.

Suddenly, he could breathe again. Air flooded his burning lungs as a dead weight pressed down on his chest, the man now lax, unmoving. Andre was standing over them, a heavy wooden paddle in his hands, dripping with blood.

Andre locked hands with Tom and hoisted him up to standing. They gave each other a cursory nod of thanks before turning their attention back to the room.

A stunned and groggy Ivan was on his knees, trying to stand. Andre and Tom grabbed him and made light work of stringing him up where Sophia had been only moments ago.

'I'm going to take care of the fucking fire alarm and get these sprinklers turned off,' said Katia. She pointed at Ivan as she said, 'Don't kill him before I'm back. I want to teach that son-of-a-bitch a lesson.' She stalked out of the room, flicking her wet hair away from her face.

Ivan raised his head, water mixing with the blood from his nose as it ran down his body. 'You haven't won. What do you think will happen to you when my crew finds out that you helped Gedeon hide his bitch of a daughter? You'll never be safe, always looking over your shoulder. And you.' He looked at Andre through his swollen eyes. 'Tonight, you will die a traitor.'

Andre spat at his feet. 'You are the traitor, Ivan. I will tell my comrades that you killed Mr Petrov to take his place at the top. You will not survive the night.'

Tom stepped forward, holding his hand up to Andre to hold him back. 'No. Ivan isn't leaving this room unless it's in a body bag.' His fists clenched in time with his jaw. It took all his willpower to not beat him bloody, but Lucy didn't need to see any more bloodshed.

Ivan spat blood and laughed. 'Oh, Thomas.' He shook his head as he said, 'They are big words for someone like you. You're nothing but a pretty boy who knows how to fuck. Leave this to the real men.'

Andre slammed his fist into Ivan's face. Blood sprayed out from his already broken nose as his head dropped, his chin resting on his chest. Andre took a step back, gestured towards Ivan in a sweeping motion, and said, 'Be my guest. I need him alive, that is all I ask.'

Tom cracked his neck to the left and then to the right. Adrenaline flooded his system as he prepared for the fight. 'I can't promise to keep him alive. Take them back to the changing rooms. Lucy doesn't need to see this. Call your men in. They'll need to do some cleaning up.' They looked at the other two men, barely alive and bleeding on the floor.

He tentatively walked over to Lucy, who was now hugging Sophia. Relief flooding his emotions to see she was unhurt. She dropped her arms from around Sophia's shoulders and stepped back. 'Lucy, are you okay?' He wanted so badly to wrap his arms around her, but he could see from the wary look in her eyes that he should keep some distance.

'I just want to get dry and dressed.' She looked at the floor. 'We can talk later.'

His heart broke at the pain he saw on her face. He'd done that to her. He'd put her in danger and broken her heart. 'I'm sorry. Please believe me when I say that I didn't mean for any of this to happen.'

She finally looked up at him and then at Ivan. Her voice was quiet, almost a whisper as she said, 'Don't kill him. However much you want to, don't. I have blood on my hands, and I'll never be able to wash it off. It changes a person. It leaves a black spot on their soul, and I don't want you to go through that.'

He took a small step towards her, his arms itching to wrap around her. 'No.' She shook her head. 'Don't touch me. If you touch me, I'll lose my resolve to stay away. I won't let you, or anyone, hurt me again.'

Sarah gave Tom a nod, wrapped her arm around Lucy, and guided her away.

Tom closed the door, pressing his forehead to the cool, damp wood, trying to regain some composure. He took his time as he strolled over to the viewing window, unbuttoning his cuffs and rolling up his sleeves. His soaked shirt clung to his muscles, his trousers sticking to his thighs as he moved. He drew the curtain closed over the viewing window. This was between him and Ivan.

He made his way over to Ivan, slapping him across the face to bring him round. Ivan groaned, his head lolling as he regained consciousness. Tom lifted his head by the chin, leaning down until their eyes met.

'You're lucky Lucy asked me not to kill you. I intend to take you to the edge, where you'll be begging for the sweet mercy of death.' He took his time walking to the rack of floggers, whips, and paddles. 'I think I'll start by giving you a taste of your own medicine.' Ivan's eyes grew wide as Tom plucked the Cat-o'-nine-tails from the rack. The knotted ends whistled through the air as he tested it out. 'Karma's a bitch.'

As Tom stepped out into the corridor, he saw Andre waiting for him, his hands in his pockets. Three other men that he recognised waited with him. Andre looked him up and down as he walked towards him.

Tom's split knuckles wept blood, mixing with Ivan's. His once white shirt was now a red tie-dye shirt where the bloodstain had seeped into the wet fibres.

'Is there anything left of him for me to take?' Andre's brow rose as he spoke.

'Unfortunately, yes.' He went to walk past but stopped, placing a bloodied hand on Andre's shoulder. 'Make it painful and slow. He doesn't deserve any mercy.'

Andre nodded a silent response, flicked his fingers at the other men, telling them it was time to take him away.

Tom made his way down to the changing rooms, hoping to find Lucy and Sarah still there. He walked in, grabbed a towel and tried to wipe away the drying blood.

It clung to the cracks and crevices of his skin. Lucy was right; blood really does leave a stain.

He looked up as he heard a familiar voice. 'You look like shit.' Katia was fully dressed in jeans and a sweater, standing with Sophia.

'Thanks. I can always count on you for your honesty.' He looked around, his heart sinking.

'They've gone. Lucy wanted me to tell you they're okay. They didn't want to hang around, which is understandable.'

'Are they staying in London tonight, do you know?'

'Yeah, they are. And before you ask, no, I don't know which hotel they're in. She's going to need time.'

He knew what she meant. Leave her alone.

He wasn't sure he could do that.

CHAPTER 44

LUCY

I Am – James Arthur

Lucy and Sarah were sitting on the super king-size bed in their plush hotel suite, wrapped in fluffy white robes, their freshly washed hair wrapped up in towels.

'Are you okay?' Lucy was concerned about Sarah. She'd been uncharacteristically quiet since they got back to the hotel.

Sarah pulled on a thread dangling from her robe. 'I'm good. And that's what's worrying me.'

'What do you mean?'

'I don't feel scared, or shocked, or anything that I think I should be feeling. I was just tied up, flogged by a mad-man and watched a bloody and brutal fight break out involving your ex and the Russian-fucking-mafia. My kitten is purring, Lucy. I'm fucking horny as fuck.'

Lucy's head reared back in shock as she regained her composure. 'Well, that's interesting,' was all she could think to say.

'Interesting? I'm a sicko and you think that's interesting?'

Lucy tried not to giggle as she said, 'You're not a sicko. You like it rough. You probably would like role play, and I'd say you're a sub that would like someone to dominate you, you know, like in BDSM.'

Sarah sat back, hugging a pillow to her lap as she thought. 'That makes sense. In the club that time before, with Ivan, I liked the way he spoke to me. I was turned on and disgusted in equal measure.'

'Imagine it was James using a flogger on you, telling you all the things he was going to do to you. Does that only fill you with lust, or does it make you feel disgust?'

'It turns me on. Can we stop this please, or I'm going to have to take a minute alone with the power shower?'

Lucy went to speak but stopped herself.

'What? What were you going to say?'

'I was going to say we could speak to Tom about it. He knows all about various Dom/sub relationships. I guess that's not an option anymore,' she said with a sigh.

'Why not? Katia is safe. I assume Andre has taken care of Ivan. What's stopping you from going to Tom?'

'He lied to me. He should never have pursued me. Doing so put our lives in danger. And to top it off, I've had to look at photos of him fucking other women.'

Sarah nodded as she listened and then she said, 'That's partially true, but you're forgetting that he was upfront with you, and you wanted to see him. You're a grown woman and you willingly stayed with him.' She threw her hands up in the air. 'I mean, look at you. You've just been through hell again, and you're sitting here worrying about me and giving me advice on my sexual preferences. You're one strong bitch and I think Tom has played a part in that.'

'I appreciate what you're saying. I do, but Tom doesn't get any of the credit for how I am now. I worked hard to come back from what Mark did to me. I stopped being the victim. If I go back to him now, I'm no different from who I was when Andrew was cheating on me and I was blind to it. Now, let's order room service; I'm starving.' That was the end of that conversation.

'Okay. All I'll say is that if Tom comes running, maybe listen to what he has to say. How does cheeseburger and fries sound? And a bottle of tequila?'

'Perfect.'

They woke up the next morning in a carb and alcohol fog. The air was heavy as Sarah opened the curtains and a window. 'Fuck sake, why are hotel rooms either too cold or too fucking hot? We can put a man on the moon but can't develop an air-con system that works.'

Lucy rubbed at her crusted eyes, blinking in the morning sunshine. 'Would you say you're feeling grumpy this morning?'

'Yes, I would. What's the plan?'

'Shower, dressed, breakfast, home.' She pulled the sheets back and made her way to the bathroom, desperate to brush her teeth; a blanket of fur had grown on them overnight.

'What about Tom?'

Lucy stopped in her tracks and turned back to her friend. 'What about him?'

'What if he's called or sent you a message? Are you going to see him?'

Lucy walked over to the table in their small seating area, where she'd left her phone. She'd switched her phone onto do not disturb as soon as she'd left the club. There was only one unread message.

Tom: Lucy. Please let me see you. I need to know you're okay. Come to the club before you

```
leave. If you don't come, I'll
leave you alone, but please
give me one chance to explain.
```

She read the message out to Sarah, who puffed out a breath. 'You need to go see him. Even if it's for closure.'

She threw her phone down on the sofa and strode into the bathroom, muttering, 'I need breakfast.'

'That's what I needed,' said Sarah, balling up her napkin and throwing it down on the table. They'd both consumed every item from the hot buffet in the hotel restaurant.

Lucy sipped at her cup of strong black coffee, wincing as it burned her tongue. She set the cup down and said, 'I've made my mind up.'

'And?'

'We're going to see Tom.'

'Right decision. You need to get this out of your system, if nothing else. Let's go.'

```
Lucy: We're coming over now.
We'll be twenty minutes.
```

She deleted the x she'd automatically typed at the end and hit send. Her phone immediately vibrated.

```
Tom: Thank you x
```

They reached the main entrance to the club, but before they could look for a buzzer, the door swung open and Alex stood there, dressed in jeans and a crewneck sweater.

'Morning. Go straight up. He's left his door open for you.'

They both muttered a thank you as they made their way in. The club was a mess. Empty bottles lay strewn everywhere, the smell of old beer clung to the surfaces. Small cardboard discs from party poppers peppered the floor, their innards abandoned and trodden on the floor.

Sarah let out a whistling sound as she said, 'Wow. You've got your work cut out for you today.'

Alex huffed. 'Tell me about it. I think the cleaners are going to quit when they see this mess, so I'm trying to get through the worst of it. Catch you later, ladies.' He stalked off, black rubbish bag in hand, as they made their way up to see Tom.

The door was open, but Lucy tapped on the frame, calling out a hello. Tom came into view, sat at the kitchen counter as Katia dabbed cotton wool on his knuckles.

'Oh, you're here too.' Lucy didn't understand why she felt a pang of jealously at the sight of Katia tending to his wounds.

'Yeah, I didn't really fancy staying at my place alone after last night.' She nodded her head to Tom. 'And he needed someone to stop him from spiralling.'

His voice was gruff and raspy as he said, 'I told you I was fine. I can look after myself.'

'Bullshit. We both know your idea of looking after yourself is seeing the bottom of a bottle of whiskey.'

'It was a solid plan.'

Lucy grew frustrated at their back-and-forth. 'Do you mind if we have a conversation in private, please?'

Tom stood and walked over to the sofa. She wasn't sure what she expected, but he felt distant and angry when she'd hoped he might have come running. She glanced over at Sarah, shrugged, and followed him through to the seating area.

Sarah called out, 'I'm going to put the kettle on. I reckon we all need a cuppa.'

'I'll help,' said Katia, standing up and busying herself with the mugs and tea bags while Sarah filled the kettle.

Tom had sat down in the corner of the large sofa, his arms spread on either side of him along the back. Lucy opted to sit at the end, feeling the need to keep some distance between them. He looked tired, broken. She wasn't sure what to say, so she sat in silence.

He brought his hands into his lap, clasping them together, his head bowed. 'I hoped you were still there when I'd finished with Ivan.'

Seriously? Was he upset with her for not being there, waiting for him? 'Surely you can understand that I didn't want to hang around? I was cold, soaked through, and had spent the evening being tied up and threatened. Oh, Happy New Year, by the way.' Her voice dripped with sarcasm.

He shifted in his seat. 'Yeah, Happy New Year.' He flexed his hand, grimacing as the wounds on his knuckles wept.

'What did you do to him?'

'Made him question his behaviour. I think it's best we leave it at that.' His voice was lifeless, hollow.

'What will Andre do to him?'

'Is that why you came over? To ask about Ivan?'

Her heart raced as emotions swarmed her. Being so close to Tom made her body come alive like it had a mind of its own, but she was angry. Angry at him for leaving her and angry at the whole sorry mess they were in. 'No. I didn't come here to ask about him. I came because I wanted—no, needed closure.'

He thrust his head up, locking eyes with her. 'Closure? What if I don't want to give you closure? What if I want to convince you to trust me?'

She was standing before she knew what she was doing. 'Trust you? You want me to trust you after I see photos of you balls deep in another woman over Christmas? That's not the behaviour of someone that wants me back.'

'What are you talking about? I've been knee deep in shit, not balls deep in pussy.' He was standing, only the footstool between them.

'You're seriously going to lie to me? After everything I've been through, don't you think I deserve the truth?'

'I'm telling you the truth. How did you see pictures of me fucking someone?'

'It was in the newsletter from K's.'

'Katia, come here,' he roared.

Seconds later, Katia walked in carrying a tray of tea. 'You could've said please.'

'Did you send out a newsletter with photos of me fucking someone?'

Before she could answer, Sarah walked in with biscuits and said, 'Oh, you weren't just fucking her. In one photo you were eating out another woman and she looked very grateful indeed.'

Tom looked at Katia expectantly.

'Come on, Tom. You know we don't take photos in the playrooms, and we certainly don't send out photos of members in the newsletter.'

'Can you check your sent emails on your phone?' said Lucy, desperate to prove they weren't making it up.

She pulled her phone from her back pocket and scrolled through her email. 'Oh, they're right. Here it is. Damn, Tom, you are fucking hot in that one.'

He grabbed the phone and looked at the photos, then passed the phone back to Katia. 'Those photos are old. That night was before I'd met you, Lucy, I swear. Katia, how did this get out?'

'I bet it was Victoria. After you told me last night that she worked for Ivan, I spoke to the owner of the club she used to work at. Sure enough, it was one that Ivan used to frequent. That is, until he put a member in the hospital. She had access to the member database. She easily could have taken photos.'

Tom rubbed at his face. 'Why would she do that? It doesn't make any sense.'

Katia was looking at the email when she said, 'They only sent the newsletter to Sarah and Lucy. You were bait. Ivan must have wanted them to come to the club to get his revenge on you. Sick fuck.'

'So, you haven't been with anyone else since me?' Lucy didn't know how to feel. It changed nothing; she was done with relationships. They only ever ended in tears and bloodshed, but she was holding onto her anger to get her through the heartache.

'I promise. I only want you.'

Lucy looked over at Sarah and motioned for the door. 'I don't want you, Tom. I don't fit into your life, and I never will. You discarded me as soon as things got rough and I can't trust that you won't do it again.'

'Is that what you think happened? That I discarded you? I led the Vory to your door. They knew where you lived. I had to end us to keep you safe. When you piss off the Vory, they don't just come after you, they come after everyone you hold close. So, excuse me for trying to keep you alive.'

411

'It was a waste of time, though, wasn't it? He came after me anyway.'

'Don't give up on us. Take some time to think about it. I don't want anyone else. Lucy, I love you. There is only you. I've spent my whole life giving a piece of myself to others, but when I'm with you, I feel whole again. If you want me to, I'll sell this club without a second thought. I'll move out of London and be whoever you want me to be. Just don't give up on me.'

Sarah and Katia kept their mouths shut and their eyes cast downward as they sipped their tea. The seconds felt like hours to Lucy as she tried to compose her thoughts.

She took a deep breath and said, 'I need to go.' Turning on her heel, she walked out, hoping that Sarah was following closely behind. She heard Tom slumping on to the sofa and Katia consoling him.

As she burst through the door onto the street below, she leaned on the brick wall and gasped for breath. Sarah dashed out seconds later.

Panting, Sarah said, 'I can't believe you walked away from him after that speech. I was about ready to drop my knickers for him.'

Straightening herself out, she said, 'You're welcome to him.'

'Look, I know you're hurting, but don't be so quick to write him off. Take some time to get over all this shit. You need to process all your emotions before you can make any long-term decisions. Let's go home and do some yoga. I reckon we've got some seriously blocked chakras right now.' Arm in arm, they made their way to the station and back home.

'I can't believe you kept all this from us.' Two weeks had passed, and Lucy had gone to every yoga class she could find, but she still felt empty inside. It was Tuesday night book club and Lucy and Sarah had filled the other two in on all the details of what had happened. They figured that with Ivan now gone, it didn't matter if their close friends knew the real reason Lucy was no longer seeing Tom.

'I'm so angry with Tom right now. I can't believe he put you in danger like that. He didn't tell any of this to Cameron, either.' Imogen was sitting, her arms crossed over her chest.

'Can I ask that you say nothing? I don't want to stir up trouble between Tom and his friends. I want to put all this behind me and move on.'

'Has he been in touch since?' said Jess.

Lucy shook her head. 'No. I made it clear that I didn't want to hear from him.'

'Oh. That's a shame. I know, as modern women, we're not supposed to need a man in our lives, but I think he was great for you. I've probably read too many fantasy-romances, but I'd say he was your mate. Would you ever consider going back to him?'

Lucy thought for a few seconds, surprised by her gut reaction to that question. 'I thought time would heal me, but I still feel empty. Tom filled a space in me—'

Sarah laughed as she said, 'Literally. Sorry, couldn't resist. Carry on.'

Lucy rolled her eyes. 'As I was saying. I feel empty without him, and I couldn't do any more yoga or meditation if I tried.'

Imogen had a gleam in her eye as she said, 'Let Operation Tom begin. I might have an idea.'

Lucy had a look of trepidation on her face as she said, 'Oh god, what plan are you hatching?'

'I won't say until I know if it's possible. Watch this space.'

'Lucy, can you come into my office, please?' It was the end of the day and Lucy had been looking forward to getting home. The rest of the week had gone by much the same as every other day in her life. Imogen hadn't announced what her plan was, so they'd assumed it wasn't happening. She grabbed her notebook and walked over to her boss.

'What's up?'

'I've got an exciting new client and you're the perfect person for the job. Come and take a seat.'

James sat down and steepled his hands together, reclining into his chair. 'This new client is a first for Spencer and Black, so no pressure, but I really want you on this project. You'll be the lead designer. I think this is going to be great.' He was so excited he could barely sit still.

For the first time in weeks, she felt something other than the hollow emptiness she had become used to. James' energy was infectious. 'Who is it?'

'Club K's in London.'

'Oh.' Now she felt sick.

'I believe you know Katia Johnson?' He glanced up at her as she nodded. 'Her club took some serious damage when the sprinklers went off, so she's decided it's time for a complete remodel of the entire club and she wants you to work with her.' There was a knock on the door as Sarah walked in.

'You asked to see me? Should I come in or do you want me to wait outside?'

'Thanks for coming, Sarah. Take a seat.' Sarah looked at Lucy and raised her eyebrows.

James continued, 'I was just telling Lucy about a new project that she is going to be in charge of. Katia from club K's wants a remodel and Lucy is going to help. Aren't you?'

Lucy looked between James and Sarah before shrugging and saying, 'Yeah, sure. Why not?'

'Excellent.'

Sarah looked confused as she said, 'Okay. So why am I here?'

'I want you to be Lucy's assistant. This is an extensive project, and the rest of my design team is busy. I've spoken to Cameron, and he's happy to reassign you to Lucy for this project. Do you fancy it?'

Sarah pressed her palm to her chest. 'Do I fancy helping my bestie to redesign a sex club? Does the bear shit in the woods?'

James smiled. 'I'll assume that's a yes.'

Sarah high-five'd Lucy. 'Can I go now, Boss?'

James smiled at her and said, 'Yep, have a good weekend.' She saluted and strolled out.

James turned his attention back to Lucy. 'How are you doing? Are you sure you're okay with this?'

'I'm excited and I feel sick all at once.' She took a moment to think before she said, 'But this feels right. I'm looking forward to doing something new. Have you noticed that my tragic dating history always seems to end with me getting a new project? Tragic, really.'

'The world works in mysterious ways. Katia wants you there as soon as you two can get there on Monday. She's losing revenue while the club is shut, and she

415

strikes me as the type of woman who doesn't sit around and wait.'

'Yeah, she's one hell-of-a woman, that's for sure. I think you'd like her.'

'I think perhaps I would. Right, off you go. Have a good weekend.' As Lucy got to the door, James said, 'Oh and Lucy, I'm proud of you. You've overcome a lot of shit and I have every faith that this is the start of something great for you, and for Spencer and Black.'

'Thanks, James. I feel quite proud of myself too.'

CHAPTER 45

LUCY

Yours – Ella Henderson

'James wasn't kidding when he said the water damage had ruined the club,' said Lucy. It was Monday morning and Lucy and Sarah had taken an early train to get into London.

Katia stopped walking and looked at them. 'Are you two okay after everything? I feel bad that you got mixed up in my shit. It's hard to come to terms with the fact that me simply existing caused so much pain.'

Sarah shook her head. 'You can't help being born, Hun.'

Lucy nodded. 'She's right. No one blames you.' Looking around the room, she said, 'You're the victim.'

They took in the surrounding damage. Katia had cleared out the rooms of all the furniture, as evidenced by the massive skip outside. The sprinkler water had damaged everything it touched, leaving water stains on anything not removable. She'd placed air dryers everywhere they walked, the smell of damp plaster following them.

Lucy got her iPad out ready to take down some notes as she said, 'So what did you have in mind? Do you want it much the same or a complete change?'

'I'd like something similar as the colours were my favourite, but I want the walls knocking down and the space to feel different. The biggest change I want is for the Fishbowl to be opened at both ends and divided from the rest of the space with a glass screen. I don't want it to feel closed in. It was my favourite room before, but now it feels dark and damaged. I want more safety features so people can get out of their restraints if they need to, and I want more alarm buttons. This needs to be the safest club for me, and for my members.'

'Got it.' Lucy was making detailed notes and taking photos as she went round.

Katia stopped walking and turned to face Lucy. 'Forgive me if you think I'm out of line, but I need you to know something.'

'Okay. Go on.'

Sarah busied herself looking around and pretending to take notes.

'Ivan threatened to kill me if Tom didn't go back to my club. I wouldn't allow it. Tom didn't want to do that to you. He knew it would kill any chance of getting you back if he did that.'

Lucy shook her head. 'None of that makes sense. Why would you risk your life, and why would Ivan care about Tom going to your club?'

Katia shrugged. 'I love Tom. He's given so much of himself to protect me, and I wouldn't be able to live with myself if I fucked up his life any more than I already have. Ivan was a power-hungry psycho who wanted to prove to everyone that he could control Tom.'

Lucy stared blankly at Katia. 'I don't know what you want me to say.'

'You don't have to say anything. I just wanted you to have all the information.'

A door slammed, making Lucy jump. 'Are you expecting someone?'

Before Katia could answer, Tom appeared, dressed in his navy-blue suit, white shirt and tan leather shoes. Lucy's heart somersaulted and her core tightened as his aftershave replaced the smell of damp plaster. She could feel her cheeks redden as she wondered if her body would ever stop betraying her around this man.

Sliding his hands into his trouser pockets, he said, 'Hi. Fancy seeing you here.'

Katia took hold of Sarah's hand, leading her away as she said, 'Sarah, I want to show you some of the other rooms. I have some ideas on what I want to provide for people who are new to this, so your opinion would be very helpful.'

'Oh, sure. Lead the way. See you later, Lucy. Tom, nice to see you.'

He nodded at her and waited for them to leave before walking over to Lucy. She stood stock still, her legs unable to move.

He took another furtive step closer. She didn't move, but her skin tingled, goosebumps giving her the shivers.

He took another step closer. His body heat joined hers, replacing the shivers with flushes of heat and desire.

He was so close she could feel his breath on her neck, but his hands remained in his pockets.

And then he stepped back.

'Tell me you felt that.'

She felt breathless as she whispered, 'I felt that.'

'You can't deny this.' He gestured between the two of them. 'I won't let you.'

'I don't want to deny it. I miss you.' It felt good to admit that out loud. She didn't feel weak for still wanting this man. She felt whole again, but she couldn't silence her niggling doubts. She took a step back. 'I can't deny the attraction, but I have to consider that we won't work. We have totally different lives, and I don't want to get in the way of your club. I also don't want to play second fiddle to it.'

He pulled away and said, 'I'm not letting you go again, no matter what.'

'That's easy for you to say, but I deserve more from a relationship than a few hours following you around while you work every weekend.' He stepped towards her again, a smile forming on his lips. 'I'm giving Alex more responsibility and stepping away from actively running the club.'

'Really?'

'Yeah, I want to spend more time with a certain someone. In case there's any doubt, I mean you.'

'You'd do that for me?'

'Of course. I meant it when I said I'd do anything for you.'

'Anything?'

He looked deep into her eyes and repeated, 'Anything.'

A grin spread across her face as an idea came to mind. She'd remind him of that when the time was right.

He brought his hands up to hold her face, his thumbs tracing lines back and forth across her cheekbones. She closed her eyes, waiting for his kiss. He didn't leave her waiting for long.

He pressed his lips to hers and groaned in pleasure. Her iPad dropped to the floor as her arms wrapped around him, her fingers fisting in his hair, pulling him closer. His tongue teased her mouth open, more desperate this time. His hands wandered across her body, one squeezing her arse, pressing her into his groin, the other wrapped around the back of her neck.

'Ah, look at you two. This makes my heart go all funny.' Sarah had walked back in, with Katia close behind.

'I'm so happy to see you've both stopped being stubborn dicks,' said Katia, with a smile on her face.

'Hey, don't call my girlfriend a dick.' Tom draped his arm around Lucy's shoulder and pulled her close to his side.

She couldn't hide the smile on her face at being called his girlfriend again. It felt right. The world was spinning on its axis again.

'Right, I think that's enough for the day. Lucy, I assume you'll arrange for someone to come down and take all the measurements for you to draw up plans?'

It took a second for her to get her brain back into work mode. 'Ugh, yeah, I can do. Or I can get it done now?'

'No. I want to take Sarah out for brunch, we have a lot to discuss. Don't we Sarah?' She wasn't asking.

Sarah caught on quickly. 'Yep, I'm getting lots of info on Katia's new plans so we can talk about that later. Go off and have some brunch with Tom. I'm sure you have plenty to catch up on. I can meet you at the station later.'

'No need to go to the station. I can drive you both as I'm staying at Lucy's tonight.'

That was news to her. 'Oh, you are, are you?'

'Yep. You can come back with me later in the week and carry on sorting out this place.'

Speechless, Lucy raised her eyebrows to Sarah, who giggled and skipped off with Katia.

Tom wasted no time grabbing Lucy's hand and dragging her out to his car.

'You kept the bigger car, then?' The large Aston Martin lit up to welcome them.

'I had to. We didn't have time to fully test it out.'

'What do you mea—' A blush crept up her neck and face. 'Oh.'

He opened the back door. 'Get in.'

'Do I not get to go in the front?'

'You can go in the front after you come in the back. Now get in,' he growled.

As soon as she climbed into the back, Tom pounced. She was on her back, one leg pushed up, her foot resting on the seat while the other leg hung limply off the edge of the seat. 'Once again, I need to catch you up on lost orgasms. This one will be quick. I don't possess the level of self-control required to take it slowly this time. I can't tell you how grateful I am that you wore a dress today. Easy access.'

He didn't waste time by removing her underwear, instead opting to move it to the side before teasing the folds around her entrance with his finger. She gasped at how sensitive she was.

'You've been neglected for too long.'

'And whose fault is that?'

'Mine. And I intend to make up for it. Repeatedly.'

Her reply was lost to a gasp as he dragged his tongue up her entrance in languid strokes. She didn't care that they were in a small car park at the back of the club. The privacy glass kept their exploits hidden.

He dipped his tongue in as far as he could reach, causing her to buck against his mouth. He gripped onto her hips, pinning her in place. 'You taste amazing. I'll never tire of this,' he said through a groan.

She felt her core tighten as heat radiated out from his touch. Her head pressed into the passenger door armrest as her hands searched for something to grasp to.

'You're so close, I can feel it. Come for me, baby.' He pushed two fingers in and stroked against her inner walls as he sucked her clit into his mouth. Her orgasm exploded out of her, ripping through every muscle in her body as she cried out his name.

He sucked and licked away her orgasm as her breathing returned to normal. She watched as he brought his fingers up to his mouth.

'Delicious.' He closed his eyes and groaned again. She blushed and busied herself straightening up and smoothing down her dress. He looked at her, an amused smile on his face. 'Are you blushing?'

She buried her head in her hands, speaking through her fingers. 'A little. Seeing you lick your fingers like that makes me feel hot and squeamish in equal measure.'

'You'd better get used to it. I intend to eat, suck, and lick you as often as humanly possible. Now, be a good girl and get in the front. I want to take you back to mine and fuck you senseless.'

'Morning all. This meeting won't be like our usual Monday morning meeting. Can you all please make your way to the foyer downstairs? Cameron and I have an important announcement for you all.' Murmurs of excitement and some of dread carried through James' team as they made their way out of the office and down the stairs. The rest of the staff were already down there and looking expectantly at Cameron as he stood in the middle of the stairs.

Imogen squeezed Lucy's arm as she went to stand next to her. She whispered in her ear, 'Good luck. I'm so proud of you, I could cry. Fuck it, I know I will.'

'Thanks, Hun. I owe it all to you, really.'

Cameron's deep voice interrupted their conversation. When he spoke, everyone settled and

423

looked up at them. 'Everyone. It wasn't long ago that we were standing here wishing you a merry Christmas and promising a great year to come. Well, we kept our promise. In the next few months, Spencer and Black Associates will open a new company under the name of Steele Interiors. Lucy, would you like to come up here?'

Lucy nervously took the few steps up, stopping just below James and Cameron. Her legs felt like jelly as she looked at all the confused faces below her.

James took over the announcement. 'Lucy is going to be heading up the new sister company, hence the name. Early in the New Year, a new client came on board. Her needs were very specific and highly specialised, and she requested Lucy. We loved what she achieved, and the client couldn't have been happier. In fact, the client was so happy she put a proposal to us we couldn't refuse. Lucy, would you like to explain?'

She nodded and took a deep, steadying breath before saying, 'Some of you will have heard of a club called K's, but for those that are unaware, K's is a club where people can explore their sexuality and kinks in a safe environment full of like-minded people. Thanks to some well-intentioned meddling from Imogen.' Lucy looked to Imogen, who was wiping away a tear. 'James put me on the project and long story short, Katia was so impressed that she wanted to start a new company with us, and Steele interiors was born. With Katia's expert knowledge, we'll be bringing specialist interior design into people's homes. She'll be running an educational side to the business alongside my boyfriend, so all customers can be confident in how to use their new, custom-built playrooms safely.'

The crowd was open-mouthed with shock. Clearing her throat, she said, 'I strongly believe in this new company. Women often talk of empowerment and being strong, independent women, and yet they'll all too often fake an orgasm rather than speak out and ask for what they want. Of course, many don't know what they want as open-minded discussions about sex are still very much taboo. Katia, Tom, and I hope to change that.' She took a moment to gather her thoughts.

'To all the women here, consider yourselves invited to the grand re-opening of K's. I will post official invites in the coming days. You're more than welcome to attend if you're interested. And to the men in the room, my boyfriend will run some exceptionally informative courses in the future.' She blushed as she said, 'I can highly recommend you to enquire. Thank you.'

The room erupted with a round of applause.

'Everyone, everyone,' said James, to get their attention. 'There is more. Lucy will be based out of our new office in London. We'll be posting the new roles up on our website shortly, so if any of you would like to relocate and work in a more specialised field, we are happy for you to apply. Sarah will join Lucy in London temporarily to help her set up, so let's wish Sarah all the best, but worry not, I don't intend to let her go for long.'

Everyone started chatting as the announcement ended. Lucy made her way over to an emotional looking Sarah and Imogen, pausing regularly to accept the well wishes of her colleagues.

'I'm so excited, Lucy,' said Sarah as she wiped the moisture from under her eyes. 'I can't believe that a few months ago you were unsure of yourself and looked up to someone like me, and now you're about to head up your own company designing sex dungeons.'

Lucy laughed as she said, 'They're not sex dungeons, Sarah. They're playrooms for adults. Let's not scare everyone off. And I'll be working alongside Tom and Katia, so it's not just me running the company.'

Imogen said, 'Are your parents excited for you?'

Lucy looked sheepish. 'I haven't worked up the courage to tell them. It's going to be hard enough telling them I'm moving to London. I wonder if they want to adopt Doris? I don't think she'll like city life.'

EPILOGUE

LUCY

Dirtier Thoughts – Nation Haven

'I fancy going to K's tonight. It's time you delivered on a promise.' It was Friday night, and Lucy and Tom were curled up on the sofa in their new home in Wimbledon.

'What promise?' Tom sat up and twisted to face her.

'You promised you'd do anything if I took you back. Well, now I want to collect.'

'Why am I scared?'

'I want to watch you.'

He ran his fingers through his hair and looked at his watch. Puffing out a deep sigh, he said, 'All right. You call K's and get the room booked and I'll get ready. Someone might have already booked it, so we're cutting it fine.'

She grabbed her phone and rolled her eyes. 'Lucky for you I know the owner.'

'Good evening, you two.' The receptionist greeted them as they walked in. 'Good news. We moved some members around and you have the room you requested.'

'That's great. Thank you, Hannah,' said Lucy with a smile on her face.

Tom smiled at Hannah as he placed his hand on the small of Lucy's back and encouraged her in. They were too late for the earlier party, so went straight through to the changing room to get ready.

Lucy was wearing her favourite underwear set tonight, the dark blue lace from her first time at K's. Tom had opted for a simple pair of plain black boxers. They'd both swapped their shoes for flip-flops. Lucy preferred comfort over high heels nowadays.

Tom looked back at his watch. 'We've got an hour before the room is ours. Can I do whatever I want to you in that time?'

Lucy wrapped her arms around his shoulders as she said, 'I think that's only fair.'

'I'm going for a record tonight,' he said as he rubbed his palms together.

'Now I'm the one who's scared.'

'No need to be scared. What's the safe word, Lucy.'

'Do we really need a safe word tonight?'

'You know the rules; when we play, we use the safe word. I might want to use something new on you tonight.'

'Oh, that sounds exciting.'

'You won't find out if you don't tell me the safe word.' He crossed his arms and pursed his lips.

She rolled her eyes as she said, 'The safe word is avocado.'

He leant in and kissed her cheek, murmuring, 'Good girl,' against her soft skin.

They made their way up to one of their favourite rooms. The redesigned Fishbowl was open at both ends and had private viewing bays. At first, Lucy was concerned she'd feel uncomfortable back here, but the design changes had turned it into a different space entirely.

They found an empty viewing area and stepped in. The positioning of the curtains, that acted like walls, meant they had a direct view of the people playing in the Fishbowl, but others couldn't see what they were doing.

The small room was large enough for two. A large leather bench sat in the middle with a chair and cabinet of toys and condoms in the corner. It had everything you'd need for a night of fun.

'I want you to watch while I go to the shop,' commanded Tom.

'What are you getting from the shop?'

'You'll see. No touching while I'm gone. Understand?'

'Yes, Sir.'

'Good girl.'

Ten minutes later, Lucy was flushed and so aroused she could barely restrain herself. The threesome going on in the fishbowl was incredible. The things the woman could do with two cocks were eye-opening. She was relieved to see Tom return.

'What have you got there?' She pointed to the black box under his arm.

'A gift for you.' He stood behind her and lifted the back of the bench, clicking it into place so they could sit back comfortably, their legs outstretched. 'Close your eyes until I tell you otherwise.'

She closed her eyes, hearing him open the box and discard the packaging. The bench dipped next to her. 'Open up.'

She blinked her eyes open and looked around. 'What's the gift?'

'You'll find out soon enough. Let's enjoy the show. Oh, and Lucy.'

'Hmm.'

'I want you to keep count. If you lose count, we go back to one.'

As they watched the action unfold behind the glass wall, Tom traced circles along her collarbone, her breasts and then her mid-section. After what felt like hours of teasing, she was begging him for a release.

He dragged a finger down to her core. 'Fucking hell, you're pulsing with need. I think it's time I give you your gift.' He reached down under the bench and produced a large, black toy that looked a lot like an electric massager.

Lucy stared, wide-eyed and full of anticipation. 'You bought me a wand?'

'It's perfect for multiple orgasms.' He pressed a button, the toy now releasing a low humming noise. He gently pressed it to her thigh and dragged it towards her clit.

'Hmm, that feels nice.' She arched her back, her body desperate to deepen the touch.

'It's about to feel a hell of a lot better than nice.' He brought the wand down onto her clit. She released a moan of pleasure as gentle vibrations spread throughout her core.

'Oh. Oh, *oh*.' She bucked her hips as her climax unexpectantly claimed her. 'Shit, that was quick.'

'Count.'

She panted. 'One.'

'Good.' He moved the wand away but didn't turn it off. Instead, with it slick with her arousal, he moved it across her nipples. Her entrance clenched and pulsed, begging to be filled. She bucked her hips and squeezed her thighs, trying to calm her need.

'Take this and keep running it over your chest.' She did as she was told as Tom's head dipped between her legs. He took hold of her legs and draped them over his shoulders, opening her up completely to him. He wasted no time flicking his hot tongue across her sensitive nub.

She dropped her hand away, forgetting to keep a hold of the wand. Tom stilled.

'What did I tell you to do?'

'Sorry.' She quickly brought the wand back up to her chest, not wanting him to stop. He rewarded her by going down on her clit with his mouth while his fingers dipped inside, stroking her inner wall.

He circled around her clit with the very tip of his tongue and when he plunged his fingers in deeper and sucked on her clit, she exploded once again. Her whole body shook, leaving her sweating and desperate for air.

'Count,' growled Tom.

'T-Two.'

Tom climbed up her body, peppering kisses on her damp skin until he reached her nipples. He sucked each one into his mouth, biting down on the rock-hard peaks. Her arms were lax, flopping lazily to the bench.

He stroked his hand down her arm and took hold of the wand as he kissed her, their tongues dipping into each other's mouths. She could taste her arousal on him, his chin slick.

'Round three.' Once again, he made his way to the bottom of the bench. Lucy had no idea what was going on in the Fishbowl. Her focus was purely on the man between her thighs.

His finger swirled at her entrance before sliding down to her rear. 'Knees up.' His tone left no room for argument. She brought her feet up onto the bench, knees bent.

He continued to swirl his finger over her puckered skin as the wand touched down on her clit once again. She lifted her arms above her head and grasped onto the top edge of the bench, her head rocking from side to side as another climax built.

'Oh, fuck.' She was losing control of her body and mind as she writhed beneath his touch. Animalistic groans escaped her lips as she lost herself to the moment.

'You're taking it so well, baby. You were made for me.' His words of encouragement warmed her heart and her core as he circled the wand over her clit. Her hips rocked in a steady rhythm, bringing her closer to an orgasm she was sure would end her.

Moments before she climaxed, her core was pulsing, desperate to be filled. Her stomach muscles tensed as she lifted off the bench. Tom dipped his finger deeper into her rear, plunged a finger into her sex and increased the pressure with the wand. Her climax rocked through her, her mouth forming a silent 'O,' too spent to vocalise the intense pleasure that made her see stars.

She collapsed, panting and covered in a sheen of perspiration. Her eyes were closed as she felt his warm lips covering her with kisses.

'Count for me, gorgeous.'

She could barely form the word, but said, 'Three.'

'You need a break. Let's head up to our room and grab an energy drink on the way.'

She slowly sat up, swung her legs over the side of the bench, and leaned into the backrest. 'I'm only at three, Tom. I don't think I'll ever be able to reach the levels you normally get to.'

He took hold of her hands and helped her to stand before draping her arms around his hips. He cupped her face in his hands and said, 'You won't achieve twenty orgasms in one session after only a few weeks. You need to build your stamina, but don't worry, I'll get you there.' He pressed his lips to hers, stroking her damp hair away from her face. 'In the meantime, I look forward to training you.'

After grabbing a drink, they made their way to the room they'd booked.

'I'm looking forward to this. I can't wait to see your fine arse clenching while you're fucking.' Lucy giggled at her crassness, shocking herself.

'I think I've created a monster. A sexy monster, but a monster nonetheless.'

The light over the room was green, telling them it was ready for use. The lighting in the room was soft and didn't cast any harsh shadows. Lucy loved how it made her skin glow and look like silk.

'Get yourself comfortable while I set up.' Tom nodded over to the super king-size bed that took centre stage in the middle of the room. It didn't have a headboard, but for people wanting to use restraints, it had posts at each corner with rings attached, giving a clear view of the bed from all angles. A plain black sheet adorned the mattress.

Large screens, set into the centre of each wall and the ceiling, flickered to life as Tom pressed the buttons built into a cabinet set against one wall. Lucy was now met with the image of herself sitting on the bed wherever she looked.

'This is definitely my favourite room,' said Lucy with a look of wonder on her face. 'Katia did such a great job with it. It's genius really.'

Tom had finished setting up the cameras that were in the corners of the room and prowled towards her, his arms cradling toys and props. 'You should take some of the credit. It was your brainchild. It will be great when we get one installed in our playroom at home. We won't have to fight the booking system for this room when we've got our own.'

'That is true, although I worry we won't ever want to leave the house.'

During the redesign of K's, Lucy had confided in Katia how much she wanted to watch Tom, but didn't feel comfortable sharing him, and he didn't want to be shared. Tom had mentioned about using mirrors, but Katia came up with the idea of installing cameras and screens so that you could see every angle from any angle. It was fast becoming their most sought-after room, so much so that they were building more, and Lucy had plans to build them into her designs for home playrooms.

'Flip over.' Tom growled into her ear as he opened the bottle of massage oil. He dribbled the oil across her back, the cool splashes raising goosebumps across her skin. She looked up at the screen in front of her to admire her new tattoo on the base of her spine as Tom's hands skittered across it.

He smiled as he looked down at her. 'Are you admiring your phoenix tattoo again?'

'I am. I love that you finally got to choose a tattoo, and that you chose it for me.'

'Seeing my mark on you when I take you from behind is fucking amazing. I can't believe I get to call you mine.' He pressed kisses across her shoulders as he nudged her thighs apart, nestling between her legs. She gripped the sheets and released a groan of pleasure as she felt him enter her.

'Enjoy the show, Miss Steele. You're in for a long night.'

434

RECAP

LUCY

This is a bonus chapter that takes you back to 'the big fight scene' in Imogen's Story – Book One of the series and is read in Lucy's POV. Do not read this if you intend to read Imogen's Story!

Lucy chewed on her nail as Imogen threw Cameron's car around the tight corners in the office car park, the tyres screaming in protest. As they reached the third floor, Imogen let out an audible sigh as she saw a space and wasted no time in reversing in. They jumped out as soon as the engine was off.

Imogen and Lucy had been at a client meeting with Walter and Holmes, that is until Imogen realised the meeting had been set up by her dangerous ex-boyfriend, who'd stalked her since she'd fled her life in London.

'More haste, less speed, Imogen. Come on, you can do this.' Lucy tried to calm her friend as they collected their things in a hurry to get back to the safety of their office building, and more importantly, Imogen wanted to be near Cameron.

Her pep talk worked as Imogen calmed down enough to lock the car.

'Hello, Imogen. Did you miss me? I bet you hoped you'd seen the last of me? Oh, and here's little Lucy.'

Lucy froze as she came face to face with the man who'd lied to her about his identity and wormed his way into her life and her bed in order to stalk Imogen. She took in his dishevelled look, his eyes darting around maniacally.

She frantically looked around the deserted car park, hoping someone was nearby to call for help, but they were alone. She slid her hand slowly into her bag until she wrapped her hand around her phone.

'Mark, what are you doing here? I'll call the police.' Imogen's voice was shaky as she began to back away.

Lucy pulled her phone out, saying, 'Don't worry, Imogen. I'm already on it.'

'I don't think so, you little bitch.' Mark threw himself at her, knocking her phone to the ground. It smashed on contact. 'I've gone to great lengths to set this up today, and you're not going to get in the way this time.'

As Lucy looked up from her smashed phone, she saw the fist swing at her before she could react. Blinding pain ricocheted through her skull as a black curtain lowered across her vision. She felt the hard concrete as she collapsed to the floor, her final thoughts on her friend.

She blinked, trying to clear the fog from her vision as her surroundings came into focus. The concrete was cold and hard against her now bruised cheek. She winced as daylight flooded her eyes, and she tried to move, but Imogen's scream stilled her. She could see two sets of legs at the front of the car, and immediately knew that Imogen was in trouble. She tried to stand, but her body and mind weren't cooperating, and then the world went dark again.

She came round to the desperate shouts of Cameron. Her relief that he was there was short-lived as her vision returned to the sight of Mark holding Imogen at knife point. She had to think quickly. There must be something she could do to help her friends. She kept her body still as she glanced around her, looking for anything that could be used as a weapon. Her eyes fell on her handbag. She'd dropped it as Mark had grabbed her phone, and from where she lay, she could see the can of pepper spray she kept with her.

She slid her arm across to her bag, never taking her eyes off Mark. She felt the cool metal canister on her palm and wrapped her hands around it, sliding her arm back alongside her. Now she needed to wait for the right opportunity to use it.

She moved her legs, tentatively checking that they'd do as they were told, as the shouting grew louder between Cameron and Mark.

'You don't know what love is, you sick bastard. I won't ask you again. Let Imogen go.' Cameron growled the words through gritted teeth.

Mark threw Imogen to the floor, her hands bound and unable to break her fall. In the commotion that followed, Lucy took the opportunity to jump to her feet.

'Take that, you wanker.' Lucy thrust the can of pepper spray towards his face and emptied the can over him. Mark dropped the knife as he instinctively covered his face with his hands. He wiped frantically at his face before bursting into laughter.

'Oh Lucy, you poor pathetic individual. You can't even spray me properly. You missed most of my face.' His laughter was pure evil and ate away at the last of Lucy's hope that they'd make it out of this alive. 'You were an unfortunate but necessary part of my plan; one I'd rather not be reminded of.' Mark theatrically shuddered. 'Now, do us all a favour and fuck off.'

437

Lucy wanted a black hole to swallow her up. His words ripped away the last of her self-confidence. He was right; she was a loser who couldn't even hit her target with pepper spray at point-blank range. She saw the desperate look on Cameron's face as he inched closer to a distracted madman, and she knew she had to do whatever she could to keep Mark occupied. She dug deep and took a deep breath.

'Our meeting was unfortunate for both of us. I can't believe I carried on seeing you after we slept together that first night. It makes me feel sick.' It wasn't a lie. She'd felt nauseous since she discovered his true identity. She'd never feel truly clean again; his touch was like a stain on her soul.

'Well, it's hardly my fault. You're like a sack of potatoes. Trust me, Lucy, it's all on you.'

She tried to brush his comments off, but they hit hard. She didn't have time to dwell as all hell broke loose as Cameron sent Mark crashing to the floor. Lucy ran to Imogen and untied her, helping her up. As she stood, she saw a glint of metal. Mark grabbed the knife, and as Lucy called out to warn Cameron, Mark thrust the knife into Cameron's abdomen.

Something deep inside Lucy shattered as she watched Cameron fall to his knees. Blood stained his white shirt as the colour drained from his face.

James came running over to them, kicking at Mark to get him away from Imogen. Lucy was frozen in place, unable to think straight. She watched as Mark lay on the floor, and the others ran to help Cameron. Imogen's screams for help echoed through her, but she still couldn't move.

She watched as if in slow motion as Mark rose from the ground and walked towards her friends. She didn't know how the knife ended up in her hand, but before he could threaten her friends any further, she drove the knife into Mark's back. As he dropped to his knees, she whispered, 'I'm sorry. He was going to kill you. I had to do it. I'm sorry. I didn't mean to.' Tears streamed down her face as the realisation that she'd stabbed someone hit her.

THANK YOU

Thank you for taking the time to read Lucy's Story. I hope you loved reading it as much as I enjoyed writing it. I think we can all relate to Lucy on some level, I've certainly had my fair share of 'bad boyfriends.' If you have enjoyed the book, I would be eternally grateful if you could leave a review and spread the word.

After publishing Imogen's Story, I joined TikTok to be part of BookTok, something I hadn't heard of before. It was the best decision I've made in a long time. The community on there is so supportive and I have found some of my best friends on there. Kerri, Keira, Jaquie, Laura and Taysha, to name but a few. You are an amazing group of women and I look forward to our daily WhatsApp chats and video sharing. With your help, support and encouragement I finished Lucy's Story. You are my people.

Special thanks to my Developmental editor, Laura Davies. I enjoyed working with you so much. You understood Lucy and brought out the best in her, and Tom.

Kerri Doyle at Dark Bear Media, thank you for your aggressive proofreading and editing. Your input was invaluable, and I have loved working with you.

Taysha Kunde, thank you for taking time out over Christmas to Alpha read for me. Your messages of support and love for Tom Harper helped me through some tough times when I felt like giving in. You knew when I needed a little nudge, and for that, I will always be thankful.

I must also say thank you to Anna, not only for making me do exercise while on holiday, but for listening to me talk about this book for a full 10k walk. Your help in the plotting process got me through this.

I was a bit more organised with this book, so thank you to all the amazing ARC readers that volunteered. I was blown away by how many wanted an ARC!

And a thank you must go to everyone that read Imogen's Story and gave me the courage to write Lucy's Story. To the mums in the school car park, thank you for nagging me to get Lucy's Story finished.

And finally, thank you to James Hyde for backing me up in the 'should my husband buy me more flowers' argument. I told you I'd mention you in this book, so here it is!

OTHER BOOKS IN THIS SERIES

Sarah's Story and Jess's Story will be out as soon as I can write them!

Printed in Great Britain
by Amazon